THE BLACK
SHAMROCKS

THE BLACK SHAMROCKS

A Novel

Gregory M. Abbruzzese

© 2018 Gregory M. Abbruzzese
All rights reserved.
ISBN: 1530184754
ISBN 13: 9781530184750
Library of Congress Control Number: 2016903129
CreateSpace Independent Publishing Platform
North Charleston, South Carolina

To my sister, Sarah, who left us far too soon. Sarah was a creative soul who enjoyed gardening, painting, and spending time with her dog, Oliver. Sarah was a devoted daughter to her mother and father, a caring sister, and a good friend to all who knew her. Sarah, we miss and love you! May you rest in peace.

November 30, 1973, to August 6, 2015

THE DEBT

LIAM O'HARA AND MIKEY MAGUIRE were best friends, growing up in the tough Irish enclave of South Boston, a paradox of a place filled with crime and decent, God-fearing people.

Liam and Mikey were kept on the straight and narrow by their strict parents.

But eventually time and circumstance put them on different paths. While Liam's father, a Vietnam War hero, died and left him an orphan, a good friend, Father Callahan, and a federal judge took him under their wings, and Liam became a Phillips Exeter Prep School and Harvard graduate as well as a star athlete. He had a lovely Hollywood starlet girlfriend, June. The boys were now twenty and still best friends.

Mikey, on the other hand, whose father "Big Mike" was in prison, fell under the Southie influence of hoods like Connor Quinn and Frankie Hayes, both mobsters. So, although Mikey had a wonderful girlfriend, Sue, he took a different path, a dangerous path, a fateful path.

Liam heard about some trouble Mikey was in, so he went home to Southie to try to talk some sense into his friend.

Later that evening at Flanagan's Bar, Liam found Mikey sitting with his new friends.

Liam walked in and spotted the bartender. "Hey, Eddie," Liam said.

"Liam, I don't see you in what, six or seven years, and now I see you twice in a couple of months. What can I get you? Or are you looking for Mikey again?"

"Nothing, thanks. No, I need to speak to Frankie first and then to Mikey."

"Is Frankie expecting you?"

"No, I don't think so, but he'll see me. We have history."

"I'll let him know that you need to see him."

"Thanks, Eddie."

"No problem."

A couple of minutes later, Liam got the word. "Liam, Frankie will see you now; he's at that back table over there to the left," Eddie said, pointing to the rear table.

"Thanks, Eddie." He put a twenty-dollar bill on the bar.

Walking through the crowded bar, Mikey caught his eye and was looking to see where he was going.

"Frankie," he said as he gave Frankie a hug as a sign of respect.

"Liam, nice to see you again; it's been quite a while. Have a seat," Frankie said, pointing to the seat to his right. "The last time I seen you, you and Mikey boosted that BMW a while back. So how can I help you?"

"Yeah, well, I left that life behind me. I'm here about Mikey."

"Yeah, I figured as much. I read about you at Harvard in the papers."

"Thanks, I have a good thing going over there. Hey, if you don't mind me asking, what's Mikey in to you for?"

"Four hundred large, and the clock is ticking."

"Four hundred grand!" Liam said with an almost audible gasp. "Why did you keep taking his action?"

"He's what, nineteen, twenty years old, Liam? He's a man. He knows what he's doing." When Liam didn't respond he intoned, "Nobody came crying to me when he was up fifty grand."

"How's he paying you back?"

"He does odd jobs for me here and there."

"Odd jobs?"

"You know, boosts—five to ten thousand per car. You know the routine."

"Frankie, you know as well as I do, Big Mike wouldn't like that."

"Liam, he's got no other way to pay me back, except these jobs. His job at the car wash ain't going to cover the vig."

"Can I buy the debt?"

"Sure, if you've got four hundred grand, you can."

"Look, Frankie, Mikey would have to pull between seventy and eighty cars in order for you to make your money back in full. Right?"

"Something like that, yeah, plus the vig—so figure around eighty cars by the time he's done."

"Okay, let's say eighty cars; boosting that many cars means trouble and unwanted attention to you and your operation. What are the odds that he'll get pinched once or twice before he pays you back? Pretty high in my estimation. You know the deal. Then you'll still be out all that money."

"What do you expect me to do? The debt *has* to be paid. This is a business, not a charity. If I make an exception for Mikey, then everyone will want a break; you know that," said Frankie.

"I understand; I really do. Okay, how about this. How about I get you a hundred grand tomorrow and call it even?"

Frankie's voice was steady. "Four hundred grand. I'll forgive the vig, and you have a deal."

"A hundred grand is all I have."

"Sorry, Liam. Twenty-five cents on the dollar is not going to cut it. You're three hundred grand short. If Mikey wants to get out from under this debt quicker, then he has to be part of riskier jobs, not just boosting cars. That's *his* call, though."

Liam shook his head. "Big Mike isn't going to like that."

"Hey, it's not like he's doing these jobs to get ahead; he's doing them to get out of a hole—a hole that he dug, I might add. Big Mike knows the rules."

"Yeah, I know. Just think about my offer, okay?"

"I will, Liam. By the way, a hundred grand cash is a lot of money for a kid your age. Where is someone like you getting that kind of cash?"

"Like I said, Frankie, that's my offer."

Mikey strolled over to Frankie's table. "Frankie," Mikey said and nodded to Frankie, who nodded back.

"Liam, you got a sec?" asked Mikey.

"Sure he does; we're done here anyway. Liam, thanks for stopping by," Frankie said as they shook hands.

"What was that all about?" asked Mikey as they walked back to Mikey's table.

"That was about you and the four hundred grand you owe Frankie!" He leveled his gaze at his friend. "And you were supposed to meet me, June, and Sue for dinner a couple of hours ago."

"Shit, was that tonight?"

"Yeah, it was, and Sue was in tears. She's gonna leave you if you keep this crap up."

"That's none of your business!"

"It *is* my business, Mikey! You're my brother! When are you going to get that through your thick head?"

Mikey was already buzzed, and he looked tense. "Look, Liam, I appreciate what you're trying to do here, but I spoke with Frankie, and he said that all I have to do is five jobs for him, and I'm out," Mikey said.

Liam's words came out between tight teeth. "What are you talking about—five jobs? Who does your fuckin' math? He just told me that you'll have to boost something like eighty cars, and then you're out. And that's how you get pinched!"

"No, these guys Frankie knows take down bread boxes—armored cars—and banks. Next Friday we're looking at the box that's carrying

Carangelo Construction's payroll. It should be about a million heavy in cash! All I have to do is drive, and I get a hundred grand knocked off what I owe Frankie; it's that simple."

Liam rolled his eyes. "Are you fuckin' stupid or what? That's a felony, for Christ's sake! Mikey, you're out of your goddamned mind! You're talking about guns and doing some serious time if you get caught. And if something goes wrong and someone dies or something, even if you are *just* the driver, they'll throw away the fuckin' key!"

"No, that's not how it works."

"Yes, yes, that is exactly how it works! Mikey, don't do this!"

"I have to, Liam. Don't worry about it; nobody will get hurt, not with this crew."

Exasperated, Liam said, "You don't get it, do you? Don't do it! Look, I have to run. I'm supposed to meet up with the judge and June. Let's talk tomorrow."

Off The Job

THE FOLLOWING DAY AND AFTER leaving several messages at the car wash and around town for Mikey, Liam decided to contact Tommy Demps, his ADA friend, about getting a meeting with Mikey's dad, who was still in jail. He eventually hooked up with Tommy later that afternoon.

"Tommy, it's Liam. I hope I'm not disturbing you at work."

"No, no problem at all, Liam. I've been meaning to call you anyway. I've just been swamped at work. How are you feeling after that injury you took in the Yale game? And by the way, what a great game you had! So what's up?"

"Thanks, Tommy. I'm feeling much better now. Tell the boys that I got the card they sent while I was in the hospital. As far as this season, I think I'll probably do track and baseball now that my football career is over. But the reason for my call is Mikey."

"I figured as much. What can I do to help?"

"I need to see Big Mike right away."

"Okay, I'll make the call. It shouldn't be an issue, and I can pick you up tomorrow at noon. Does that work?"

"Perfect. I'll fill you in on the way up there."

"Okay, see you tomorrow."

The following afternoon Tommy picked him up at school in Cambridge Square.

"So, what's going on with Mikey, Liam?" Tommy asked as they headed for the highway and the meeting at the Lawrence jail with Mikey's father, Big Mike.

"He's mixed up with Frankie Hayes and those hoods."

"Big Mike isn't going to like that. What's Mikey thinking?"

"I know. He's in to Frankie for a little over four hundred thousand."

Tommy turned to him, his eyes bulging. "What?"

"Yeah, you heard right—four hundred grand! I had the same reaction."

"Four hundred grand for what?"

"Gambling: puppies, ponies, Pats, Sox, Celts, and the B's."

"Wow! You know Big Mike only has a few months on his bit left. Right?"

"Well, he *has* to know because Mikey is supposed to be the driver on a job in a few days."

"What kind of job?"

"They're dropping a bread box."

"Liam…"

"I know. I told him everything and how the law views his role in such a job even if he is just the driver."

"And?"

"If he does the job, he gets a hundred grand knocked off his debt, so he's still planning on going forward with it."

"Liam, you know the routine. If one goes down, they all go down. And if someone gets hurt, they all get charged as coconspirators. I can't protect Mikey after that."

"I know. Hey, here we are."

Entering the Middlesex Jail, Tommy and Liam went through the previsit process.

"Good morning. ADA Demps to see Captain Muldoon."

"Yes, sir, Captain Muldoon is expecting you. He will be with you momentarily. Please park over there to your right in the visitor's lot and then proceed to the waiting room."

Five minutes later Captain Muldoon entered the waiting room, and Tommy greeted him, "Captain."

"Tommy, and I see you have Liam here with you again as well."

"Nice to see you again, sir," Liam said.

"Tommy said that this was a very important meeting with Big Mike on very short notice. I just want to make sure I won't be expecting trouble from Big Mike. He's been a model inmate so far."

"No, it's nothing like that. He's only got five months left on his sentence, and then he's out, so he won't do anything to jeopardize that; trust me."

"Okay, Tommy, your word is good enough for me."

"Thanks, Captain."

"Yes, thanks, Captain," Liam added.

Out of the corner of his eye, he could see Big Mike Maguire walking into the visiting room, being escorted by two guards. He sat across from them at the table and said, "Okay, boys, so what's up? Everyone okay at home?"

"Yeah, Mike, everyone at home is fine. Liam here just wants to talk to you about something."

"Liam, what's so urgent that you needed to leave school and come up here to see me?"

"It's Mikey."

"I figured as much. What now?"

"He's in the hole."

Big Mike took a deep breath. "How deep?"

"Four hundred thousand."

Mike's eyes popped. "You're shittin' me! Four hundred thousand! Whose action?"

"Frankie Hayes."

"Frankie takes book now, too?"

"Yeah, he's been doin' that for about three years now, and he kicks a piece up to Connor as tribute."

"Mikey owe anybody else?"

"No, not that I know of. Everyone who is in the mix knows that he's in the hole with Frankie so deep that they won't take his action."

"Okay, is that it? I mean no drugs, alcohol?"

"Yes and no," said Tommy.

"What else?"

"Well, a couple of things. Liam spoke with Frankie," said Tommy.

"Yeah, I met up with Frankie to talk about Mikey's debt, and he's not budging from the number. I even offered him twenty-five cents on the dollar. Mikey's boosting cars to pay the vig and down some of the principal."

"Twenty-five cents on the dollar? Where were *you* going to get a hundred grand, Liam?"

"I was going to use what my dad's insurance left me and some of my next semester's tuition. If I needed more, I am eligible for a student loan, too."

Big Mike stifled a groan. "God bless you, Liam, but this is not your problem."

"With all due respect, Mr. Maguire, it is. If something like this happened to you, what would my dad say?"

Big Mike nodded. "Okay, I get it. Thanks, boy. So, is Mikey still working at the car wash?"

"As far as we know, yeah."

"Okay, good; we need to make sure that he is."

"There's one more thing, Mr. Maguire," Liam said.

"What's that?"

"Mikey's trying to get out from under this a little quicker than boosting cars."

"Tell me he's not taking jobs."

"Afraid so, sir."

"Tommy, what do you know about this?"

"This is the first I'm hearing of it, Mike."

"Mikey told me that they're planning to drop a bread box next Friday."

Big Mike dropped his face into both hands. "An armored truck? Is he that stupid? Those things never go right! What's Mikey's part on the job?"

"Just driving."

"Still, anything goes down, he'll be complicit. And if someone dies, they'll throw away the key!"

Big Mike turned to Tommy. "Tommy, you're an officer of the court; you need to excuse yourself."

"No, I'm good."

"Tommy, you have to. It's called plausible deniability," Big Mike said as Tommy got up from the table and waited on the other side of the visiting room.

"Okay then, Liam, proceed."

"They're taking down the Boston Armored truck that's carrying Carangelo Construction's payroll in the Back Bay."

"I know that route. They'll probably try and take them at the Kennedy Boulevard intersection.

"When?"

"Next Friday."

"Tommy, please come back here for a sec." Mike waved him back to the table. "I need you to reach out to Frankie and tell him that Mikey's not working for him anymore and that he's off any future jobs. Got it?"

"Got it, Mike."

"Then tell him the four hundred grand is on me. I'll settle that when I'm out in a few months. Okay?"

"I'll let him know. Anything else?"

"Yeah, one last thing; tell him that he's not allowed to take any more of Mikey's action going forward. And whoever else does take his action will have to deal with me when I get out. Understood?"

"Got it, Mike."

"Liam?"

"Yes, sir."

"Thanks for still being such a good friend. I know that it's hard at times, and Mikey can be stubborn, but he loves you, you know."

"For life, Mr. Maguire."

"Your dad would be proud of you, son."

"Thank you, Mr. Maguire."

"Liam, I'm out in a couple of months. I hope you'll join us for dinner at our apartment, okay?"

"Yes, sir, I look forward to it."

Three days later in Harvard's Yard, Liam was leaving his art-history class with Cam, his friend and teammate, and asked, "How'd you do on the midterm, Cam?"

"B plus—you?"

"I got an A, but to be fair, I mostly wrote about the pieces in the Gardner Museum that I helped set up over the summer."

"So you cheated."

"No! I simply agreed with Professor Catan's interpretation of modern impressionists."

As they turned the corner to grab lunch at the Lamont Library Café, Liam was struck on the left side of the head. He was stunned and took two steps backward before dropping to one knee. Cam reacted quickly and tried to tackle the attacker, who turned out to be Mikey. After realizing what was happening, Liam quickly gained his composure, collected himself, and squared up to defend himself properly.

"Cam, stay away; I got this," Liam said.

"Yeah, Cam," Mikey said, bobbing and weaving, "this has nothing to do with you."

"What the hell, guys? What are you doing? You're best friends for Christ's sake."

"Liam's a rat, Cam; watch your back."

Liam swung at Mikey with a jab and hit him in the nose. He immediately started to bleed out of his left nostril. Blood was everywhere.

"You hit like a girl, Liam; you always have."

"That was a warning, Mikey. I can take you out if you want."

"Show me what you got, tough guy."

"Just remember, you asked for it," he muttered as he struck Mikey in the left temple with a combination of punches. "I hope you brought ice because that's gonna swell up, pal."

Mikey threw a left-right-left combination to Liam's head and body. "Get your own ice, tough guy," he said.

Just then, four Harvard Security officers showed up and surrounded them. "What's going on here?" demanded one officer as he took out his Taser.

"I saw the whole thing, Officer. That guy," a classmate said, pointing to Mikey, "hit the other guy, Liam, without any provocation."

"No, Officer, we're good," Liam insisted. "It was just a misunderstanding."

The cop cocked his head. "If it was just a misunderstanding, then why are you both bleeding?"

Liam said, "Well, I suffer from high-altitude nosebleeds, and I believe my friend over here is just completing his second round of cancer treatments, which causes his condition."

"Yeah, that's it," Mikey said.

The cop looked skeptical. "Let's all of us go to our offices and sort everything out. Okay, guys?"

"Sure...whatever," Liam said.

Back at the Harvard Security office, the university police officer asked for identification. Liam handed him his credentials. Looking at his ID card, the officer said, "So, Liam, you're a student here?"

Another cop said, "Yeah, he's the kid who made that catch to bat Yale this year."

"Yes, sir," Liam said.

"And you, Mr. Maguire? Are you a student here?"

"No, I'm more of a student of life."

"I see. Thank you for that."

"Why don't you guys wait in the tank over here until we get a better idea of what just happened."

"I told you; it was just a misunderstanding. Nobody is hurt, and nobody is pressing charges."

"Nevertheless, I have to fill out an incident report, and I want our medical staff to take a look at you both."

"Great, now I'm going to miss the fucking Saint Patty's Day parade in Southie," Mikey grumbled.

Liam said, "Oh, that is today, isn't it?"

"Yeah, we used to go every year. Remember?"

"Good times! That's the only time it was 'legal' for us to buy booze."

"I know, right."

Sitting on the holding-tank benches, Mikey looked dejected. Liam said to him, "Mikey, what the fuck? What was that all about?"

Mikey contempt showed. "Seriously? Don't play fucking dumb, Liam. You got me kicked off the job. My dad is now on the hook for *my* four-hundred-thousand-dollar debt, and you're asking me what? Why am I pissed? Why did I come down here and beat the shit out of you? I'll tell you why—because you're a rat!"

"First of all, you *didn't* beat the shit out of me. You fucking pulled a Pearl Harbor and hit me when I wasn't looking. Secondly, fuck you, I'm a rat! I saved your goddamned life, and you don't even know it!"

"How's that? My old man is in the can, piling up interest on my debt. Now people think that I'm a deadbeat, and nobody will take my action. Nobody will take any cars that I boost either. How am I supposed to pay down my debt? Thanks a fucking lot, Liam!"

"Okay, on the one hand, I can see where you are coming from, *and* I can also see where you may view this as some sort of betrayal. However, either I did what I had to do, or Tommy was going to have you arrested. If you got arrested, you'd be off the job anyway."

Mikey now bristled. "Bullshit! We're done! We're not friends anymore. When I leave here, I don't want to see you again in the neighborhood, talking to Sue, or anything. You got that?"

"Fine, Mikey, if you want it like that, you got it! Fuck you! You just sit there and keep blaming the world for *your* fucking problems."

"Done! We're done!" said Mike.

They both sat there in the holding tank on opposite sides of the bench. The only thing to read in the holding cell was the *Harvard Crimson*, Harvard's daily student newspaper. That day the headline read, "Happy St. Patrick's Day!" in bright-green lettering on the top of the paper. In the left-hand corner of the paper was an article about Boston's hard-line Catholics protesting against gay Irish Catholics who wanted to march in the Saint Patrick's Day parade in South Boston. The article went on to say how the demonstrators were being supported in their protest by the HGLBTS (Harvard Gay-Lesbian-Bisexual-Transgender Society). On the bottom right-hand corner of the paper was an article about the Isabella Stewart Gardner Museum's latest Monet and Picasso acquisitions.

Mikey's mother, Maggie, arrived forty-five minutes later at the Harvard campus police station to take them home.

"Boys, I'm not sure what is going on, but you are best friends, and best friends don't fight," she said to them.

"It was a misunderstanding, Mrs. Maguire. It was my fault. I apologize," Liam said.

"Ma, it was nothin'. These rent-a-cops blew it way out of proportion."

"Well, you both need ice. Any bones broken?"

"No, Ma."

"You had better check his ribs, Mrs. Maguire; I got him pretty good," Liam said as he smiled toward Mikey.

"Fuck you, Liam. I've been hit harder by Sue for Christ's sake."

"Boys! Stop that. And Mikey, that language!"

Liam said, "Mrs. Maguire, thank you for picking me up. I have class in ten minutes, so I have to go."

"Liam O'Hara, you get back here," she said.

"But, Mrs. Maguire, you don't understand."

"Liam, shake hands," said Mrs. Maguire.

He extended his hand, but Mikey turned and walked away.

"See, this is what I am dealing with," Liam said.

"There is more to this story than you both are telling me. I'll talk to him, Liam." Mrs. Maguire gave him a kiss on the cheek and said good-bye.

Two days later Cam and Liam were in their dorm room, watching Boston College play Connecticut in basketball on the local NBC affiliate when the game was suddenly interrupted.

"I'm Kevin Welks, and we interrupt your normally scheduled programming to give you this breaking-news report. Donna Martin is at the scene of a brazen midday attempted armored-car robbery in South Boston. This botched robbery has left one security guard in critical condition at Beth Israel Hospital and all four assailants dead. Donna, can you please give us an update on just what transpired this afternoon on the streets of South Boston in broad daylight?"

"Absolutely, Kevin. It appears that four armed men were attempting to rob the Boston Armored Car Company in South Boston when they were picking up a local payroll."

"Just how much money was the truck carrying at the time of the attempted robbery, Donna?"

"The officers at the scene said there was a little over one point four million dollars in the transport. The delivery was scheduled payroll for the Carangelo Construction Company here in South Boston."

"And what exactly happened to the assailants?"

"Well, a forty-five-year-old security guard named Anthony Fasani, from Winthrop, foiled an armored-car robbery attempt. Currently, Mr. Fasani is in critical condition at Beth Israel. From what witnesses told us, Mr. Fasani drew his weapon and shot at the assailants as they were drawing their guns and walking toward the armored car. Several shots were exchanged before the assailants were turned back to their getaway car. As the assailants were fleeing, Mr. Fasani fired one last shot at them, hitting the getaway driver in the back of the head. At that point, the getaway car crashed into a Citgo gas station and exploded on impact with one of the gas pumps. All four assailants were declared dead at the scene, and authorities are still trying to determine their identities at this time."

"Remarkable, Donna, thank you for that update. We will now return you to your regularly scheduled programming. Be sure to get a full report on this robbery and other events of the day during our regularly scheduled programming at six and eleven o'clock this evening."

"Did you see that, Liam? Do you think you know anybody mixed up in that?"

Liam shrugged. "Who knows? Probably. Southie is a small community."

"Hey, Liam, do you want to go out and grab a pizza?" Cam asked.

"Are you kidding me? Look outside—it's pouring cats and dogs, and it's supposed to be like that all day."

"Like I said, do you want to *order* a pizza?"

"Perfect! And get some mozzarella sticks and a salad, okay?"

"You got it."

Twenty minutes later there was a ring at their intercom.

"Wow, Cam, that was quick. I thought they told you forty-five minutes."

"They did. It must be express."

"Yeah, come on up. We're on the third floor," Liam said as he pressed the intercom button.

There was a knock on the door. Liam turned to Cam and said, "Cam, you get the cash; I'll get the door."

As he opened the door, he was greeted by a soaking-wet Mikey.

"Mikey? What are you doing here? I thought that you were done with me."

His friend looked miserable. "Can I come in?"

"Sure, come on in. Go to my room and get some sweats and a T-shirt from my closet. The T-shirt may be a little too big for you in the arms, though, but don't worry about it." Liam smiled.

Liam went into the room in a few minutes. Mikey looked more comfortable in dry clothes. "Look, Liam, I wanted to tell you that I was wrong, and I need your help."

"Thanks, Mikey. We're all good." They hugged each other. "Cam, can you give us a minute?"

"Sure. Hey, Mikey."

"Hey, Cam. Look, sorry about the other day." He turned to Liam. "I didn't mean to hit you."

"No worries here. I just have to work on my tackling," Cam said with a smile, on his way out.

"Liam, did you see the news?"

"Yeah, was that your crew?"

"Yeah, that was supposed to be me driving. The other three guys were Danny O'Neil, Peter Haskel, and Ernie Gallow. Joey Adams took my spot driving, and they're dead! All dead!" Mikey began to tear up. "I came here to say that you were right all along. I'm sorry, and I need your help to get out of this mess."

THE PLAN

"HEY, MIKEY, WE'RE ALL GOOD. I'll do whatever it takes to get through this," Liam said.

Mikey's face was wreathed in pain. "I'm so fucked up. I just can't take your money or June's money, and I don't want my dad to pay for my fuckups!"

"I get it. We'll figure something out. You know that."

"I don't know how. I mean, there are only a few options to get the kind of cash that I need, and any way I think about it is dangerous."

Liam's mind was whirling. "Wait. I was thinking while we were in the holding cell together the other day, and I might have an idea. He paused for a while, thinking. "Here, look, did you see this?"

"What? We missed the Saint Paddy's Day parade."

"No, not that, this part." Liam pointed to the article about the Gardner Museum's new exhibits.

"What about it?"

"That's it! We break in, steal a few paintings, and ransom them back to the museum or cash in on the reward."

Mikey gazed at him, querulous. "I don't know, Liam. Is there any money in that?"

"They're worth millions!"

"What about security, schematics, timing?"

"I used to work there, remember! Security is a joke! But wait; before we start anything, and I agree to help, I need five simple things from you if we are going to do this."

"Okay, whatever you need."

"No, it's not that simple."

"Okay, seriously, what are the rules?"

Liam was thinking fast. "First, you have to stay at your job at the car wash."

"That job sucks, but okay."

"Second, no more boosting cars or doing *anything* illegal. This is it!"

"Okay, what about Frankie and what I owe him?"

"Your dad bought you time, so let's take it."

"Third, no more drinking; we're *both* retired."

Mikey winced. "That's gonna be a tough one, but okay," he said.

"Fourth, we need you to get your GED and enroll at Bunker Hill Community College."

Mikey shook his head slowly. "I don't know, Liam; you know that school is not my thing. That's all about you."

"No, you just have to apply yourself, and we need it for the cover," Liam said.

"Okay, if you say so."

"Not that it wouldn't be good for your soul as well."

"Yeah, okay, no problem. My mom, Sue, and Father Callahan will love that."

"Think about what I'm asking you, Mikey. It won't be easy, and it will require a lot of discipline and self-control. You can't take it lightly. You have to make a commitment."

Mikey looked distant. "I know."

"Also, everything that I outlined is part of the plan, so we'll need you to commit to it. We'll have to have everything planned out and timed to a tee before your dad gets out in a few months. Okay?"

"Yeah, now that sounds like a plan."

"And remember, you can't tell anyone, not a soul!"

"I know."

"We can't have Frankie, Connor, or *anyone* know or think that they know what we're doing. That's how you get pinched or end up dead."

"Understood."

Both of them hugged it out.

"Good, now let's have some pizza."

Twenty minutes later, sitting in their lounge, eating pizza, Cam asked Mikey about his eye. "Hey, Mikey."

"Yeah, Cam?"

"That's a nice shiner you got there. I don't see a scratch on my man Liam's face at all."

"Yeah, why is that, Liam? I know I connected at least once or twice."

"One ten alabaster," Liam said.

"One ten alabaster? What the hell is *one ten alabaster* for Christ's sake?" asked Cam.

"It's movie pancake makeup that June sent me after I told her what happened."

"You're shitting me. Right? Makeup?"

"Nope," Liam said with a sheepish grin.

"Then I take that back, Mikey; you *did* get the best of Liam. You must have hit him so hard that he became a metrosexual overnight," Cam said as they all laughed and munched on the pizza.

Three months later, in Liam's dorm room, when Mikey and Liam were on great terms again, Mikey said, "Hey, Cam."

"Mikey, s'up? You working with Liam again? I haven't seen you in months."

"Yeah, just for a few hours."

"What are you guys working on that's so covert?"

"Nothin'—just school. Oh, and we're just planning a robbery," Mikey said as he laughed.

There was a knock at the door.

"Hey," Mikey said as he nodded to Liam.

"Hey." Liam nodded back to Mikey.

"Cam's asking questions," Mikey said.

"Yeah, I heard. He just wants to know if you're okay; that's all. It looks like we're going to have to tell people about the classes you're taking at Bunker Hill Community. If people ask what we're doing all the time, we'll just say that you're trying to get back in school. You're taking a few classes, and I'm just helping you out."

"Okay, but it's embarrassing," said Mikey.

Liam slapped his own forehead. "No, it's not! Actually, it's just the opposite. This helps our cover that much more. Damn it, I should have thought of it sooner! It's brilliant! You're changing your whole life around; that's why we're meeting so much. Perfect!"

"Well, so much for keeping this quiet! You know, we're three months into this, and my dad gets out in two."

"I know, but we've come so far. We'll have to continue this when your dad gets out, you know," Liam said, taking out his encrypted Apple Macintosh disk with the plan. "And you'll have to take a class or two this summer as well."

"I know. You're killing me," said Mikey.

"Hey, it helps build our cover. Also, it's not the worst thing in the world that you build up credits, and then maybe you can transfer to another school. You have a B-plus average in the two classes you took so far. Right?"

"Yeah, with your help."

"So what? You're taking the tests, not me. You can do the work!"

"I guess you're right. Okay, so where do we stand with this?"

"Like I said, I'll outline the options to your dad, and then we can take action, okay?"

"Sounds like a plan. You have the initial list. Right?"
"Yup, here it is."

GARDNER LAUNDRY LIST
I. Supplies

* *Mikey back in school/taking classes at Bunker Hill (CC).*
* *Retain Tommy Demps, attorney.*
* *Buy car wash with letter of credit cosigned by Mr. Daniels (if necessary).*
* *Gardner Museum blueprints.*
* *Faux mustaches.*
* *Maps/exit routes.*
* *Zip ties.*
* *Duct tape.*
* *Gloves.*
* *Sunglasses.*
* *Alarm schematics.*
* *BPD uniforms/body mikes.*
* *Police scanners.*
* *BPD zone schedule on/off duty.*
* *City maps.*
* *WHT BPD sedan, BLK washable paint, with revolving lights.*
* *Fake tattoos.*
* *Shoes—two sizes too small.*
* *St. Patrick's Day parade route/diversion (smoke bomb).*
* *Identify abandoned building on other side of town, smoke bomb—fire/police.*
* *Commercial truck.*
* *Guards schedule—on duty.*
* *Dr./nurse cast.*
* *Parole officer.*
* *Nurse recast (Mikey's mom).*

- *Drop car?*
- *Fake guns on the job (live sniper rifles).*
- *Total crew: two inside, one lookout, one at parade, switch car.*
- *Visit museum in disguise to identify marks and layout.*

"Yeah, that looks like everything we'll need," Liam said. "Now the big question is the car wash. That's critical to the plan, and I'm not sure Tony A. will sell. He's owned it forever." Tony A. was Tony Accorso, owner of the Shamrock Car Wash.

"Word on the street is that he's in to Frankie for some big paper too," said Mikey.

"Okay, let me see what we can do; otherwise we'll have to figure something else out."

THE SHAMROCK CAR WASH

"WHERE DO WE STAND WITH the car wash, Mikey?"

"I know the operation inside and out. It's a money-making machine if it's run properly. If we can expand it, like you said, we can make some legit money here," Mikey stated with confidence.

Liam shared his enthusiasm. "Yeah, if we add two oil-changing bays and a detail shop, we'll really be in business. And Joey and Tommy can do the construction."

"That's perfect!" Mikey exclaimed.

"How much is Tony A. in to Frankie for anyway?" Liam asked.

"I heard he's in for over five hundred grand, and he's about to lose his whole operation because he can't make the vig each week." He paused, thoughtful. "I know the feeling."

"Okay, we need to start phase two. I'll call Tommy Demps today, and you need to study for your sociology test next week."

The following day, after Liam and Mikey analyzed the opportunity with the car wash, Liam reached out to Tommy Demps, the attorney.

"Tommy? Hey, it's Liam. I'm downtown, and I wanted to reach out about something."

"Oh, hi. Okay, what's up?"

"I was wondering if you could help me with some legal documents for a loan I'm looking to get from the First National Bank of Boston."

"Sure. Since you're downtown now, I can meet you for lunch at the Marriott Hotel. How's that?"

"Sure, I'll see you there in twenty minutes."

Thirty minutes later Tommy and Liam sat down to lunch.

"So, Liam, what are you doing this summer?"

"I'll be rehabbing my neck with the hope of participating in track and baseball next year. I'll also be taking some graduate-level classes at the Kennedy School and working in their office as well. Hey, but a few nights, I can still visit with your boys, and we can work on their schoolwork and football drills like we did last year."

"Wow! That sounds like a plan. Yeah, my boys would love that. They really look up to you, Liam. You know, their grades are improving too, ever since we had those tutorials last summer."

"Yeah, no problem, Tommy."

"So, what kind of loan do you need that requires my deep legal expertise?" Tommy asked with a smile.

"I need to secure a loan for roughly two hundred thousand through your connection at First National. You see, I heard that Tony Accorso is in to Frankie for over five hundred grand. He's about to lose his house and his business in a few weeks without any savings he put away. He's leveraged everything to cover the vig and his mortgage. I want you to approach him to buy the Shamrock Car Wash for two hundred thousand. Two fifty is the highest we can go, though, so hold strong."

Tommy chewed his lower lip. "Liam, Liam, Liam, a couple of things. How much cash *do* you have on hand available to you now?"

"I have about a hundred grand in all. I got this from the insurance after my father passed."

"Okay, that's a good start, but what are you going to use as collateral?"

"I called Mr. Daniels and advised him that I might need a cosigner for an investment opportunity that I would like to undertake."

"And?"

"He loved the idea and said no problem."

"I didn't know Tony was looking to sell."

"Like I said, Tony's in to Frankie for five hundred grand. He's got a second mortgage on his house, and he's late on another vig. Either he sells to me and skips town with his family and some cash, or Frankie's just going to take it all, and he'll have nothing."

"Well, that's good inside information I guess. Let me see your proposal." Liam handed Tommy a manila folder with all the paperwork. "So if I am reading this correctly, you want to expand the car wash to cover two additional bays for oil changes and one detailing shop. I had no idea that Tony owned the adjacent lots too."

"Yeah, he does, so there is plenty of room for expansion and more hidden equity."

"I can see that. Who drew up these blueprints?"

"A teammate's father is an architect here in town, and he did me a favor. It's not a complete plan, and they certainly won't pass any zoning boards; however, it will suffice for the bank's inquiry. It's just part of the business plan so that they can see what we're trying to do."

"Looks really good, Liam. I like what you did with the cash-flow statements, the demographic research, and the lack of specialty automotive shops in and around the neighborhood. There is really no other competition for several miles."

"And those are *conservative* numbers, Tommy!"

"The only concern that I can see that the bank will have is that you don't have any collateral."

"I have that letter from Mr. Daniels that states that he will cosign the loan."

"Well, there you have it. That should work then."

"On top of that, my trust kicks in when I turn twenty-one."

"You have a trust?"

"Yeah, my thoughts exactly. But my dad worked out a deal with Mr. Daniels when he was in Nam. I don't even know the exact value of the trust. I find out when I turn twenty-one."

"Okay, that should help as well. I'll see what I can do," said Tommy.

"Regarding the bank, do you have the paperwork to this type of transaction?" Liam asked.

"I do. But we need a private banker and one who will sign a confidentiality agreement. In my opinion, nobody from Southie can know about this deal. I don't want to put anybody in harm's way. I know a guy from First National. Let's use your full name, and we'll do this in downtown Boston. He's a private wealth manager."

"Sounds perfect! But how do you know him?"

"His son was charged with distribution of narcotics a couple of months ago. The DA wanted to hang the kid and even give him time in juvie because his dad was a hotshot banker and friends with the governor. I met up with the dad, and he told me what happened, that the kid only had one joint and gave it to a fellow classmate. That was the extent of it. My boss hates me because I threw it out. This kid is no dealer. Fortunately, the detectives involved in the case agreed with me."

"Good for you, Tommy. That's why we need to be partners," he said with a smile.

"Okay then, meet me at One Hundred Twelve State Street tomorrow at noon, and we'll run it by my guy."

"Okay, see you then."

The following day Tommy and Liam met at the offices of the First National Bank of Boston, on the thirty-fourth floor, to discuss the proposal with Mr. Shaun Fitzgerald.

Mr. Fitzgerald introduced himself and said, "I manage individuals whose net worth ranges anywhere from three to fifteen million, and I provide financial advice for short, intermediate, and long-term investment strategies."

"How's your track record?"

"I win more than I lose," Shaun said with a smile. "Why don't you tell me what it is you need, and I'll see if I can help."

"First, I'll need you to sign a confidentiality agreement if we decide to proceed."

"Okay, young man," Shaun said as he smirked, "but that may be premature. What is it exactly that you need?"

"Well, Mr. Fitzgerald, I need a loan of approximately two hundred thousand dollars. I need to set up a shell corporation here in the States with the global headquarters based in the Cayman Islands. Tommy will be the liaison for the business here in the States."

"I can do all that, but the bank will require some sort of collateral."

"I have a hundred thousand dollars cash and this." He handed Mr. Fitzgerald his paperwork and a letter of credit from H. D. Daniels. Shaun surveyed the paperwork. His eyes went wide. "Have you seen my business plan?"

"I have."

"And?"

"Well, Liam, the first thing that you have to know about me is that I am very candid when it comes to my clients. They don't pay me to tell them what they want to hear; they pay me to give them my unfiltered advice."

"Okay, I respect that. So what do you advise?"

"A car wash is a risky business. I would recommend against it in favor for some more aggressive mutual funds. However, if you still wish to proceed, your out would be the land, which is very valuable. You could build a parking garage or even condos if the car wash/oil-change business does not work out."

"All very good points, and that was exactly what I was thinking, Shaun.

"Then we're good. This could be the start of a lasting relationship, Shaun. I have to run to class. Please let either myself or my attorney," Liam said, pointing to Tommy, "know if there are any issues. Shaun, it was a pleasure." He shook Shaun's hand. "Tommy," he said as he nodded in Tommy's direction, and he nodded back.

Later that evening in his dorm room, the phone rang.

"Liam, it's Tommy."

"Everything okay with the loan?"

"Yeah, I just called to tell you that Shaun was very impressed with you!"

"Really?"

"Yeah, he said that you were mature beyond your years. Okay, we'll get the loan. So now what?"

"I need you to approach Tony A. with this deal as if you are representing a private client. This is his *only* way out with an additional two hundred or two hundred fifty still in his pocket."

"Got it. I'll ask.

"Well, Tony initially rejected the offer, even after I told him why two hundred grand was a better offer for him. For some reason he felt as though he could still get out from underneath Frankie, his mortgage, all of it," Tommy said.

"Gamblers usually think like that. It's always the next bet around the corner. It's a sickness, I'm afraid," Liam said.

"Wait—it gets better. Later in the day, two of Frankie's guys rolled up to the car wash and demanded his weekly vig. Unfortunately, Tony didn't have it, so they broke his hand with a hammer. I got a call from Mass General's ER room a couple of hours after I left, and he decided to accept our terms."

"Too bad for Tony's hand, but otherwise, perfect! Couldn't be better news."

"You are officially an entrepreneur, Liam."

"Yes, I am, and it will reflect on your bonus. Best of all we all have summer jobs, and I can employ Mikey and his father. "This is really good news for the Maguires, believe me."

"Well, hopefully this is a good investment for me as well. I'll send Shaun some Chivas as a thank-you."

"Perfect! So, what are you going to do about management of the site? Tony was very hands-on."

"I'm pretty sure Mikey's dad will be interested."

WELCOME HOME

As LIAM ENTERED HIS OLD housing complex and the Maguires' apartment, it brought back fond memories of his childhood and his dad. All over the modest apartment were signs that said, "Welcome home, Mike!" Father Callahan and a lot of neighborhood friends were there.

"Liam, come here," said Mrs. Maguire. "Let me take a picture of my three boys."

Rolling his eyes, Mikey said, "Ma, enough already."

"Look at you, my college boy, all grown up."

"Ma, it's just two classes."

"No, you got your GED, and you're going back to school. I'm so proud of you, Mikey."

Big Mike added, "Mikey, that's really good. Your mother is right. We're both very proud of you."

"I'm tryin', Dad. And this jerk," he said, pointing to Liam, "won't let me rest. School, school, and school—that's all he's preachin'."

"Good for you, Liam. Stay on top of him!" said Mr. Maguire.

"Yes, Liam, Mikey's even come back to the church thanks to you," said Father Callahan.

"We're working on each other, Father," Liam said. After a pause, he turned to Mr. Maguire and said, "Hey, Mr. Maguire, you got a second?"

"Sure, Liam, come into the other room. What's up? You're not going to fire me before I start, are you?"

"Ha, no! Um, I have this envelope for you from my dad. He told me to give it to you upon your release and to let you read it in private."

Big Mike looked puzzled. "Seriously?"

"Yes, sir. Here. I'll just be with everyone else in the other room."

As he left the room, he heard Big Mike ripping the envelope open.

Mike,

I'm sorry I'm not here to celebrate your release. You've always been a special friend to me and my family ever since Father Callahan called that truce between us when we were kids. I will always be in debt to you for taking care of my family while I was away in the war. I know that it's not going to be an easy adjustment for you on the outside at first, but be strong! I often turned to Father Callahan for personal and spiritual guidance. I hope that you will do the same. Remember, if the feds or our friend from the Triple O come knocking, you know nothing! Steer clear of them both! I also know that you have a family to take care of and provide for. If you can, please check in on Liam from time to time to make sure that he is making the right decisions and following the righteous path. He respects you immensely, and I know that he will listen to whatever you have to say. If he does not, then show him this letter, and he'll know that I gave you permission to steer him in the right direction. The enclosed is a little start-up money to get a car, pay some bills, but more importantly, take your family out to a nice dinner. You're my brother; welcome back!

Always,

Declan

"Honey, are you okay?" asked Maggie Maguire.

"Yeah, Declan gave me a letter for when I got out; that's all. It just brought up some memories." Big Mike cleared a tear from his eye.

"Listen, honey, I know Declan is looking down on us, and he wants you to stay out of prison for good now too. Please tell me that you won't do anything to jeopardize the family. I can't go through another ten or fifteen years without you. Promise me, Mike, promise me."

"Maggie, I don't want to go back. I won't leave you or Mikey again."

Maggie fell into her husband's arms. "I've thought about you every day, Mike. Every day." He kissed her. The front doorbell rang.

It was Tommy. "Hey, there he is. Give me a hug," said Tommy.

"Tommy, my boy!" said Big Mike. "Thanks for everything! I mean it—everything you did for me inside and out."

"Mike, no problem, my friend. Look, I have the boys in the car, waiting for me. We have baseball practice tonight, so I have to get going, but I wanted to make sure I said hello when you got home. Mike, let me know when you and your family can come over for a barbecue. I'll stop by the Shamrock later this week."

"Tommy, I'll walk you out.

Father Callahan said, "Michael, I have to run as well. I must still tend to my flock."

"I understand, Father. Thanks for coming and all your support, while I was away, with Mikey and Maggie."

"It was nothing, Michael. The one you should be proud of is this one over here." Father Callahan put his arm around Mikey. "He left school to help support the family; now he earned his GED; he's taking college classes, working; and he's come back to the church."

Big Mike was beaming. "I am, Father; I'm very proud of Mikey."

Two weeks later while Big Mike was at the car wash, training, there was a knock at the Maguires' door.

"Hello?"

"Is Mike in?"

"No, he's working. May I ask who you are?"

"Look, lady, we're here to pick up a package. Do *you* have the package or not?"

"No, I don't know what you're talking about. What package?"

"He'll know, lady," said Ron.

"Okay, just tell Mike when he gets home that Dickey and Ron, who work with Frankie Hayes, were looking for his weekly package."

"Um, okay, I will, but what is this all about?"

Two minutes later Maggie picked up the phone and called the car wash.

"Hi, Ms. Mulligan, this is Maggie Maguire; is my husband in?"

"Oh, hi, Maggie; yes, he is. One moment, and I'll see if I can get him...Mr. Maguire, Mrs. Maguire on line one."

"Thanks, Ms. Mulligan."

Big Mike went into his office, sat down, and picked up his phone.

"Hey, Maggie, everything okay? What's up?"

"We just had two visitors," Maggie said.

"Visitors? What do you mean—visitors?"

"Two thugs came by and tried to intimidate me. They were looking for you. Something about a weekly package?"

"A *weekly package*? Must be a mistake, honey."

"Mike, don't lie to me; you promised!"

"I know! Hun, it's a mistake—just a mistake is all. Who did they say they were again?"

"Dickey and some guy named Ron—they said that they were with Frankie Hayes."

"Hun, I'll take care of it. It's nothing; don't worry about it."

"We'll talk when you get home, Mike."

"Yes, hun, of course. Like I said, I'll take care of it."

One hour later at Frankie's garage, Big Mike asked for Frankie. "Frankie in?"

"Yeah, one second, and I'll check. Who's askin'?" asked the secretary.

"Don't bother; I know where he is."

"But, sir...sir, you can't go in there."

Big Mike waved her off as he barged into Frankie's office.

Frankie looked up. "Hey, Mike, and to what do I owe this unexpected pleasure?" Frankie asked, his eyes wide.

Looking to his left, Big Mike said, "You must be Dickey." Dickey nodded. "And you must be Ron?"

"Good for you, old man," said Ron with a sarcastic grin.

"So I see you met the boys. What's up, Mike?" asked Frankie.

"You been getting your payments on time, haven't you, Frankie?"

"Yeah, why?"

"These two simpletons came to my house, looking for my installment."

"But, Mike, that's their job," said Frankie.

"Fuck you, Frankie! Have I missed a fucking payment?"

"No, no, you haven't, Mike."

"Well, then, the next time one or both of those two motherfuckers show up at my doorstep with their tough-guy attitude and threatens my wife, I'll bury them in a shallow fucking grave in Quincy and piss over them. Are we clear?"

"Mike, it's *your* debt; they're just carrying out orders. You know the game."

"You know, Frankie, there are three ways for me to get out from under this. First would be to pay you back in installments, like I have been doing. The second would be if I missed some payments, then I'd have to go to work for you. And the third would be to take you out, and everything would just go away."

"That wouldn't do anything, Mike; then you'd owe Dickey here."

"My debt is with you, not Dumbo over there. If he buys your debt, then I'll deal with him."

"Are you threatening me, Mike?"

"My good friend Declan O'Hara had a saying back in the day. He would say, 'I don't make threats; I make promises.' So I promise you this, Frankie. If either of those two pieces of shit show up at my place again, I'll make sure they crawl home, but I'll come looking for you with a shovel and some lye. Are we clear?"

Dickey bristled. "Frankie, you gonna take this shit? He's a fuckin' nobody."

"Relax, boys. Mike here just got out a few weeks ago. Give him time to get the lay of the land." Frankie paused and then turned to Mike and said, "Is that all, Mike?"

"For now, yeah," Mike said as he threw an envelope on Frankie's desk. "Anything else?"

"No, I think we're good," said Frankie.

"You two heard what I said. Right?"

Both Dickey and Ron, grinning broadly, gave Mike the finger as he walked out of the office.

Ron muttered, "Frankie, who the fuck does that guy think he is?"

"He's got six notches on his belt from punks trying to make a move on him on the inside. I would heed his warning if I were you two. He means business, especially when it comes to his family. Got it?"

"Whatever, Frankie," Ron and Dickey said, nodding.

Thirty minutes later, Big Mike arrived back at his home; he knew the *real* interrogation was about to begin.

"Okay, Mike," Maggie said, "what was that all about with those two men? And don't you lie to me!"

"Maggie, I will. Just sit down."

"Oh, Lord."

"Maggie, here it is. You know that sometimes you have to hit rock bottom before you make a change for yourself in life."

"Mike, I think we've already been there, and I can't do it again."

"It's not me, Maggie. Just give me a second."

Mikey could hear his parents arguing, so he walked in from the other room.

"It's me, Ma. It's me," Mikey said.

"What? What do you mean 'it's you,' Mikey?"

"No, Mikey, let me," said Big Mike.

"No, Dad, I got this. You're just trying to protect me. Look, Ma, while Dad was away, I tried to make some fast money gambling. This way I could take care of you and give you things."

"I don't need anything, just my family together—that's it! That's all I ever wanted," said Maggie.

"Well, I got so caught up in some bad—things—and I got behind in my payments. Because I was so far behind, I started to boost cars and take some jobs for Frankie."

"Frankie? Frankie Hayes, the bookie?"

"Yes, that Frankie Hayes."

"Dad made some calls from inside and told Frankie that the debt was his now, and I was out. At this time, I knew that I had to get my act together, so I got my GED, went back to school, and back to the church."

"Mike, what does this all mean?"

"It means that I owe and not Mikey."

"How much?"

"Don't worry about that; it's a lot, but we're paying him back," said Big Mike.

"I said, *how much*?" demanded Maggie.

"Four hundred thousand dollars," said Mikey.

Her hands shot to her throat. "Dear Lord! How in the world are we going to pay that off?"

"We have a plan; don't worry. The problem is that we can't tell you, or you would be complicit."

"But, Mike, how?"

"We're working on it; don't you worry. And Mikey's done with gambling and stealing cars. That's all you need to know for now."

"But why, Mike? Why can't you get on some sort of payment plan with these people?"

"That's not how it works. When you win, everybody expects to get paid right away. When you lose, *they* expect to get paid right away, or you pay the interest. Otherwise, bad things will happen. Those are the rules, and everyone knows that going into these things. Look what happened to Peter Adams: that poor kid owed fifty grand and skipped town because he didn't have the cash and couldn't make the weekly vig. They found him in Connecticut and beat him so badly that he's in a wheelchair for the rest of his life."

"Oh my Lord! What if we go to the police?"

"We can't."

"Why?"

"Then everyone is in danger."

"How did you get yourself into this mess, Mikey?"

Big Mike interrupted. "Maggie, that doesn't matter. There is no need to look back and say how or why. It does nobody any good. We can't change what has already been done. Mikey is a good boy, and he learned from his mistakes; that's all. He got his GED, he's back in school, he has a good job and is straight with the Lord. He's changed. If I was out, none of this would have happened, so it's my fault, and I have to fix it."

"Okay, Mike, okay," said Maggie, and at that she began to cry again.

Neighborhood Insurance

A COUPLE OF WEEKS LATER, at the Shamrock Car Wash, Mike Maguire entered his office.

"Good morning, Ms. Mulligan."

"Good morning, Mr. Maguire."

"Any messages?"

"Yes, a Mr. Peterson, our chemical supplier, would like to speak with you about the expansion plans and our future needs. Then there was a Mr. Oliver who called about waste disposal. The last one is from Lisa Fellows from the *Globe* who called about the ad that you would like to run. Basically, she just needs to know if you want it black and white, color, or a combination. This is the size and cost breakdown of the ad." Ms. Mulligan handed Mike the call slips and her notes.

"Did Lisa confirm the location? I mean, can I put the ad in the sports section?"

"Yes, she mentioned that it was not an issue. Sorry, I forgot that."

"No, no problem at all. Thank you. Please set up a lunch meeting with Mr. Peterson for this Tuesday. I'll call Mr. Oliver back later this morning. And I'll confirm the ad later this afternoon when I speak with Mikey."

"Yes, sir."

Thirty minutes later, after finalizing the paperwork, Big Mike headed out of his office for a cup of coffee.

"Ms. Mulligan, I am going for a cup of coffee in the break room; would you like one?"

"No coffee, thank you, Mr. Maguire, but could you bring me back a tea with a splash of cream and one sugar?"

"You got it."

As Mike left his office and walked toward the break room for the coffee and tea, he saw two men heading toward his new office. The first man was about six feet two, and the second man was about five feet ten. Mike quickly sensed that something was not right about these two, so he turned around and headed back to his office.

"Can I help you, guys?" Mike said.

"No, pal, Mary knows why we are here," said the smaller man.

"Ms. Mulligan?"

"I thought you knew, Mr. Maguire."

"Knew what?"

"Let's just say that we're your neighborhood-insurance company," said the taller man.

"Oh, really? Are you guys from State Farm? Or maybe Northwestern Mutual?"

"We're here for our weekly pickup. Tony knows the deal, so back off before you get hurt," said the smaller man. Ms. Mulligan continued to hand over the envelope.

Big Mike stopped her. "Ms. Mulligan, please do not do that; put the envelope back in your desk. These gentlemen were just leaving. There seems to be a misunderstanding, boys. You see, Tony no longer runs this place. I do. And it's co-owned by Assistant District Attorney Tommy Demps. Are we still going to have an issue?"

"I don't give a fuck who you are or who the new fucking owner is! Neighborhood insurance is two fifty a week, pal," the taller man said, brandishing a gun in his waistband.

Mike didn't think; he just reacted instinctively. He snatched the gun from the taller guy's waistband while simultaneously hitting him square in the throat. He then kicked the smaller guy in the knee so hard that he buckled to the floor and then he hit him with a right cross to his temple. At this point Mike had a gun pointed at the smaller man's head while the taller man was gasping for air on the floor.

"Okay, boys, now that it's settled, I want to see wallets on the table. Now! Ms. Mulligan, you may want to step out of the office for a moment while I have word with these two in private."

"Yes, sir," Mary said and quickly left the office to try to find Mikey, who was working on the wash line.

"Okay, so whom do we have here? Joe Flanagan and Patrick Sullivan III. Patrick Sullivan? Are you any relation to Patty Sullivan from Kennedy Avenue?"

"That's my father."

"Wow! Small world. Well, Joe and Patrick, you're both very fucking lucky that Patrick's father here was nice to me when I was a boy. Otherwise, you'd both be cut up and placed in one of those chemical barrels outside there and dumped in the ocean by Logan Airport. Patrick, does your dad know that you're playing a tough guy now? Forget it; I'll ask him myself. Now, I don't expect to see either of you boys, or whomever else you work with, here again. Are we clear?"

"You don't know who you're fucking with, pal!" said Joe.

"He's right you know," Patrick said. "You fucked up in a *big* way, pal! Things can burn down very easily in this town."

Big Mike looked incredulous. "Are you two that fucking stupid that you would threaten me when I have a gun pointed at your fucking heads? You two fucking morons wouldn't last a day inside, you know that! Now get the fuck out of here before I change my mind!" Mike snarled, kicking them out of his office and slamming the door.

Later in the day, at Patrick Sullivan III's home on Kennedy Avenue, there was a knock on the door.

"Yeah, who is it?"

"Trouble," Big Mike said.

"Huh?" Mr. Sullivan muttered as he opened the front door slowly.

"Patrick Sullivan?"

"Yeah, how can I help you?"

"It's Mike, Mike Maguire here."

Mr. Sullivan smiled. "No shit! Mike Maguire, huh? Come on in! When did you get out?"

"A couple of weeks ago."

"Mike Maguire, how the hell are you? Hey, do you need anything? Some cash? A piece."

"No, nothing like that, but I do need something from you."

"Yeah, what's that? Anything—name it."

"Information."

"Sure, whatever you need, Mike, you know that." Mrs. Sullivan walked in the den. "Connie, bring Mike here a beer and something to eat."

"No, no more drinking for me, and I'm fine. Thank you, Mrs. Sullivan."

"Connie, bring him a water then."

"Here, have a seat, Mike. So how can I help you? It's been a while."

"Yes, yes, it has; you see, I'm working at the Shamrock Car Wash on Washington Street."

"Yeah, I know the place."

"Well, I'm managing it, and two guys came in to pick up the weekly insurance, two hundred fifty bucks."

"Fuckin' animals! They're with Connor. You should have fucking buried them on the spot, Mike."

"Well, that's the problem. One of these guys was your son."

Sullivan went slack jawed. "Patrick? Are you sure?"

"Yup, I'm sure. He said that you were his father."

"Give me a minute. Let me call him. Mike, you didn't hurt him, did you?"

"Out of respect for you, I did not."

"Thank you, Mike. Thank you!"

Ten minutes later there was another knock at the Sullivan's door.

"Ma? Dad? What's so urgent that I had to run over here right away?"

"You! What are you doing here?" Patrick said, glaring at Big Mike sitting in his father's living room.

"So, it *was* you," said Patrick's father between tight teeth. "What are you doing trying to play gangster? And with a gun no less!" Patrick Sr. slapped his son across the back of his head.

"What, Dad!"

"What? Is that all you have to say, you stupid shit? Do you know who this is? His name is Mike Maguire, and you're lucky to be alive right now. That's all I know."

"Yes, sir."

"Now apologize to Mr. Maguire, and thank him for allowing you to walk out of the Shamrock in one piece."

"Dad, come on."

"I said now!"

"Yes, sir."

"That's all right, kid. Forget it. I need to speak to Connor anyway. I'll touch base with him. In the meantime, I'm giving your gun to your father. He can decide what to do with it."

"You pulled a gun on Mike Maguire? Are you crazy! This guy has more bodies on him than you have teeth, and you pulled a gun on him?"

"It's okay, Pat, seriously." Big Mike turned toward the kid. "Just one piece of advice, kid."

"What's that?"

"Cut loose of that Winter Hill Crew, or you'll end up in the can like me."

"I'll keep that in mind."

"So when are Connor's office hours?"

"Tomorrow is Wednesday, so he'll be at the Triple O at around noon. Why?" asked Patrick Jr.

"That's between Connor and me. I'll see him then."

The following day around twelve thirty, Mike arrived at the Triple O tavern.

Eddie the bartender looked up. "Holy shit! As I live and breathe, it's Mike Maguire!"

"Eddie Muldoon, they still lettin' you pour drinks here?"

"It's what keeps me young," said Eddie with a wink.

"You look good, Eddie."

"You too, Mike! What can I get you?"

"Just seltzer. I have to meet my PO in a few hours; you understand."

"Gotcha."

"Is *he* in?"

"Yeah, same spot by the window, as always."

"What kind of mood is he in?"

"Good one. He won a ton of dough at Suffolk last night. It's easy to win when the horse you're betting on is high as a kite," Eddie said, grinning.

"Ha! Good, good to know."

Mike walked over to Connor Quinn's table and leveled his gaze at him. "Connor, Frank," Mike said as he nodded in their direction.

"Well, I'll be, if it isn't Mike Maguire. Look, Frankie, it's Big Mike."

"I can see that, Connor," said Frankie.

"Looks like they fed you well inside. Still built like a bull, I see. I heard you got out a couple of weeks back. Why has it taken so long for you to stop by and say hello to old friends?"

"Busy with work I guess," said Mike.

"I heard something like that."

"Yeah, I manage the Shamrock Car Wash."

"I thought that was Tony A.'s place?"

"No, Tommy Demps bought it."

"You mean the Walpole guard?" asked Connor.

"Yeah, but he's an ADA in Boston now. But you knew that already. Didn't you, Connor?"

"Times are a changing, aren't they, Frankie?"

"Yup. Who would have thought?"

"So what's up, Mike? How can I help you? You looking to make some extra cash, or is this a social call?"

"No, nothing like that. I just had a visit from some friends of yours."

"Oh yeah, who were they? I have a lot of friends."

"Joe Flanagan and Patrick Sullivan, Patty's kid."

"Were they welcoming you back to the neighborhood?"

"Sorta. They wanted to make sure that my fire and theft policies were up-to-date."

"Well, everybody has to pay some sort of insurance, wouldn't you say, Mike?"

Big Mike's grin was nothing short of evil. He stared at Connor and said, "I think my seven years inside cover that. Wouldn't *you* say, Connor?"

Connor paused while looking Mike in the eye. "I'd say you might be right, Mike. If I see them, I'll let them know that you're up-to-date on your policy."

"I appreciate that, Connor."

"Anything else?"

"No, that's about it."

"I'm sure we'll see each other in the near future."

"I look forward to it," he said as he stood up to walk away.

"Connor." Mike nodded in Connor's direction. "Frank." Again, Mike nodded in Frank's direction.

As Mike walked away, Connor whispered in Frank's ear to keep an eye on Mike over the next few weeks. Frank nodded and watched him walk out the door.

THE JOB

"Ms. Mulligan?" Big Mike said.

"Yes, Mr. Maguire."

"There will be no more envelopes that cover neighborhood-insurance policies. Okay?"

"Yes, Mr. Maguire."

"Thank you. I'll be in my office the rest of the day, reviewing the books. No calls please unless it's an emergency."

"Yes, sir."

Twenty minutes later there was a knock on the door.

"Yes, who is it?" asked Big Mike.

"Liam and Mikey," Liam said.

"Come in, boys. Here, have a seat. Wait one second, please"—Big Mike pauses—"Ms. Mulligan?"

"Yes, sir?"

"No calls while I'm here with the boys, okay?"

"Yes, sir."

"So, boys, what can I do for you?"

"We're just checking in. It looks like you already have the hang of things around here."

"I do, thanks to Mikey showing me the ropes: who does what, the books, and where we were losing money."

"That's great! Just figure out that latter part sooner rather than later," Liam said with a smile. "The important thing is that you look happy."

"I am, Liam."

"You know we're having an anniversary Mass for my dad next Sunday. Uncle Tommy and Uncle Joey always come down for it."

"Perfect! Count me in. Anything else? How's school? Work?"

"Good, everything is great. Just winding down the semester. There is something else that we both would like to discuss with you, though."

"Sure, what's that?"

"The debt to Frankie."

"I told you two that's none of your concern! I'm dealing with that."

"Mr. Maguire, with all due respect, we all know that there are only a few ways that you can get that kind of money in such a short time frame. You can either take down a bank, a bread truck, rob drug dealers, or take out Frankie."

"That's about right. And it's on me to figure it out, not you two!"

"What if there was another way?"

"Like what? You two are master thieves all of a sudden? You guys want to play gangster? This is real life, boys, and people do real time."

"No, it's nothing like that! We looked at it like this. If you hit a bank, bread box, or dealers, you're talking about guns, witnesses, and trigger-finger guards trying to play hero. You'll either have to deal with retribution from dealers and the mob or the feds chasing you forever. The risk of something going wrong is far too great. People end up inside because of one of two reasons: they are either betrayed from someone in their crew who flips or they simply have poor planning. When I mean planning, I'm talking about pre-, during-, and post-job execution."

Big Mike couldn't hide his skepticism. "Is that so? How do you account for bad luck? Like there being more guards on a crew? Or a patrol car that is running late on his watch and drives by unexpectedly," said Mike.

"Bad luck is a seven percent variance in a plan if, and only if, it is taken into consideration. That is why we would have contingency plans. With all due respect, Mr. Maguire, look what happened to you and that bank job several years ago. Connor or someone in his crew ratted you out. Connor then took out the rest of your crew because they were going to cooperate with the police. You, on the other hand, did a seven-year stretch because you're a solid guy and were someone who kept his mouth shut. Then look what almost happened to Mikey a few months ago on that armored-car job. If anybody on that job survived that shootout, they'd be doing *life* at Walpole anyway, no questions asked."

"Okay, smart guys, so what's your plan?" Mike asked as he leaned back in his chair with his hands interlocked behind his head.

"It's a low-risk, high-return job. We see it as a five-man crew, and we have three guys already," Liam said.

Mike looked distressed. He looked down, his breathing audible. Then he looked up. "Listen, neither of you can be involved in this whatsoever, so get that out of your heads right now!"

"Okay, we really aren't directly involved anyway, but we do play critical roles in this job, nevertheless."

"For argument's sake, let's hear it."

"Well, while Mikey was visiting me a few months ago, we read about this." He handed Mike the Harvard newspaper.

Mike scanned it and looked up, amazed. "You want to rob the Gardner Museum? You guys have some balls. Didn't you use to work there, Liam?"

"Yeah, a few years ago, I volunteered there, and nothing has changed. I visited them a few weeks ago, and they're so desperate for help that they asked me if I wanted some hours for overnight security. They told me that I could even sleep on a cot."

"What about surveillance?"

"All managed through the control room on the main level."

"Total guards on duty?"

"Two at night—that's it."

"Panic button locations?"

"Just one on the main floor."

"Response time from the precinct?"

"Fifteen to twenty minutes on a normal day, but this response will be longer, if triggered, because they'll mostly be on crowd patrol. We plan on hitting them during the Saint Patty's Day parade."

"Patrols?"

"In sector fifteen they're between ninety and a hundred twenty minutes, depending on the shift changes."

"Escape routes?"

"Easy highway access north and south via Routes Ninety-Three and Ninety-Five and east and west via I-Ninety. Plan B, Storrow Drive through Cambridge or downtown Boston. Or, as a last resort, the subway."

"What's so special about the Gardner?"

"Here is a list of what we're taking, and we can go over where they are located."

Vermeer, The Concert

Rembrandt, A Lady and Gentleman in Black

Rembrandt, The Storm on the Sea of Galilee

Rembrandt, Self-Portrait

Flinck, Landscape with Obelisk

Manet, Chez Tortoni

Degas, La Sortie de Pesage

Degas, Cortege aux Environs de Florence

Degas, Program for an Artistic Soiree (1)

Degas, Program for an Artistic Soiree (2)

Degas, Three Mounted Jockeys

Chinese Beaker or Ku

Bronze Eagle Finial

"In total these artworks are worth, roughly, between three and five hundred million at retail. As soon as we get these pieces, I'll get you your four hundred fifty grand to cover the debt to Frankie and some extra start-up money."

"So why just these pieces?"

"Because they are all part of an ongoing lawsuit against the museum. These pieces were all originally acquired through third parties, most likely thieves. Basically, province of ownership for all these pieces are in question," Liam said.

"If you try and fence the art, you know you're screwed; they'll rat you out," said Mike. "Everybody knows that."

"I don't plan on fencing these pieces. I plan on either selling them back to the museum at a discounted rate or collecting the reward on them from the insurance company."

"How will you gain initial access? Do you have an inside guy?"

"No, we'll use BPD uniforms and claim that we are responding to a silent alarm. That used to happen once or twice a month. Then we'll call out the guy behind the desk, subdue him, and then he'll call his partner for a bathroom break. At that point, you'll disable all the surveillance videos and silent alarms."

"Transportation?"

"We have a drop car. The car wash bought an old black undercover BPD Crown Vic that we got at a police auction a few months ago, complete with spotlight and internal flashers and a siren. It's tuned up with new tires, new brakes, and we run her once a week. We got disposable Crown Vic plates from the junkyard in Revere for the night of the run."

"Uniforms?"

"We have three. They were purchased through a BPD uniform catalog and sent to a post-office box in downtown Boston called 'Boston Costumes that we own.' It was rented by Mr. Joe Carey—the fed who harassed my father a few years ago."

"Nice touch," said Mike. "What else?"

"Diversion number one will be when Mikey starts a disturbance at the Saint Patrick's Day parade. Mikey will lead a group of guys from Southie protesting gays marching in the parade. Mikey will begin throwing rocks, bottles, and pipes at parade goers, starting at around five thirty. From there, hopefully he will get locked up for the night for inciting a riot. You would then go try and bail him out later that evening.

"Diversion number two is when we light smoke bombs in an old abandoned building on the other side of town in Dorchester. This will spread the Boston police and fire even thinner. We won't set fire to the buildings for fear that a firefighter or homeless person who may wander in might get hurt. Instead, we'll use massive smoke bombs, like they had in Vietnam. This type of smoke bomb will give the impression of a four-alarm fire and keep BPD and BFS occupied for hours."

"Okay, what about the team?"

"Like I said, we'll need a total of five guys. I'd like to keep it tight. Here is what we have so far: Mikey would be at the parade. I would start at the parade and be miles away on the other side of town, coordinating the second diversion, then go right back to campus. You will act as one of the police officers visiting the museum. Then we just need two other people that we can trust: one guy to act as your partner and the other to act as a lookout. For your role, two weeks prior to the job, we will need Mrs. Maguire to set you up with a fake broken arm. This will allow you to show up to your parole officer for two consecutive weeks with a cast on your left arm. We'll need you to go to the hospital, have fake x-rays taken, get bills, et cetera, and then cast you up. That'll be part of your alibi. However, after the heist, we'll have to actually break your arm and then recast it. Your partner will coordinate securing the guards and keeping them at bay. The remaining person will be on the roof of the adjacent building acting as a lookout."

Mike did a double take. "Break my arm? You glazed over that."

"A small price to pay for freedom, Mr. M."

Mike thought a bit. "You know, Liam, I have to admit it; this is a pretty good plan, minus breaking my arm. There are some holes that need to be filled in, but it's a good plan, nevertheless. I especially like the number of guards at the museum on the night shift. They won't be armed, and even if we get a couple of pieces, we'll still make out in the end. I'll tell you guys what; I'll case the place over the next couple of weeks and let you know what I think."

"Okay great! What should we do in the interim?"

"Nothing! I need to see what's what, and then I can decide. Go back to school, and, Mikey, get back to work," he said as they walked toward the door. "Boys?"

"Yes, sir?"

"For the record, I think that this is a *really* good idea with low risk of anybody getting hurt!" Big Mike said.

"See, I knew that he would like my idea!" Liam said, turning to Mikey.

"Your idea? I filled in all the blanks; I got the uniforms, the car, plus the second set of plates."

"Okay, I'll give you that. But most importantly, we could be free of all this crap in a couple of months, and then we can get on with our lives!"

"I know. We just need two other guys whom we can trust."

MEMORIAL MASS

ONE WEEK LATER, AND ONE week before his father's memorial Mass, there was a phone call at Judge Mahoney's, Liam's guardian, where Liam lived when school was out.

"Hello, this is Ray Mahoney; who is calling please?"

"Hi, Ray, this is Liam's uncle, Uncle Joey. May I please speak with Liam?"

"Sure, one moment please. Liam, it's your uncle Joey calling."

"Hey, Uncle Joey, what's up?"

"What's up? You tell me?"

"Um, I don't know?"

"Uncle Tommy and I got a call from June, and she said that you and Mikey were in some sort of trouble or something?"

"No, um, I just have a lot going on is all."

"Liam, you have always been a terrible liar."

"No, it's nothing. I'll tell you what; I'll talk to you and Uncle Tommy at the reception after my father's Mass, okay?"

"Okay, but we want the truth."

"I know, I'll tell you everything when we're together."

After his dad's memorial mass, Liam met up with Uncle Tommy and Uncle Joey at the reception, which was being held at the Hibernian Club of South Boston. Everyone who was at mass was invited over for an open bar and food to catch up. Uncle Tommy and Uncle Joey waved Liam over to the corner of the club to have a chat.

"Excuse me, June, Judge, and Ray; I'm being summoned over to the corner by my uncles. I'll just be a minute."

"Nice mass, Liam, your dad would have liked it."

"Thanks, guys."

"Liam, okay, so what's going on that concerns June so much?"

"Nothing, I told you. Don't worry about anything."

"Are you in some sort of trouble?"

"Is it Connor? If so, we still have our envelopes."

"No, it's nothing like that."

"Then what?" asked Uncle Tommy.

"It's me. He's trying to protect me," interjected Mr. Maguire.

"No, don't listen to him."

"Mike, what is it?" asked Uncle Joey.

"My son is on the hook for four hundred grand to a local book and some very bad people. Liam is only trying to help him get out from underneath it. I found out about this just before I got out, so I told the people he owes that it's on me," Mike said.

"But, Mike, if you get caught doing something again, they'll throw away the goddamned key. There is a three-strikes law in Massachusetts for Christ's sake."

"I know, but it's my son; what can I do? I wasn't there for him, so it's either him or me. Don't worry; Liam is not mixed up in this."

"Look, guys, if any of *you* were in trouble, my dad would be there for you. Hell, if any of you were in trouble, I'd be there for you as well! Mikey is my friend, my brother, so I have to help. It's that simple," he said.

"Liam, first of all, your dad wouldn't do anything illegal to get out of trouble unless it was a last resort. Is there some sort of payment plan he can get on? I mean, you can't just throw away everything you have going for you on something that you had no control over," Uncle Joey said.

"This *is* a last resort. The vig alone is hemorrhaging everything Mr. Maguire works for each week. Look, Mikey's changed. He doesn't drink or gamble anymore. He's back in school, and he's back with the church. I can't abandon him."

"So how do you expect to get *that* kind of money so quickly? If you hit a bank or a bread box, the feds will be on you like a fat kid eating a hot dog. If you hit Connor or the Italians, they'll come after you *and* your families. If you hit drug dealers, things will get bloody quickly. So what's the plan?" asked Uncle Tommy.

"Low risk, high reward," said Big Mike.

"That's what everyone says who is still doing time at Walpole. What is it?" asked Uncle Joey.

"I can't tell you guys because you will be considered accomplices for having prior knowledge to a felony and not reporting it to the authorities," said Mike.

"Mike, it's us. And you forget. We were both held in VC POW camps for over a year. I think we can handle a federal interrogation or two."

"I don't question that; it's just not your battle to fight."

"You're right; it's not. And neither is it Liam's. I'm sorry, Mike, but we have to think of Declan's wishes."

"I understand; I get it."

"We have to get going anyway. Mike, best of luck with your situation. Liam, steer clear of this. Understood?"

"Yes, sir," he said as Uncle Tommy and Uncle Joey hugged him good-bye and shook Big Mike's hand.

"I'm serious, Liam," said Uncle Tommy.

"Yes, sir."

One week later, there was a telephone call at the car wash.

"Shamrock Car Wash, can I help you?"

"Mr. Maguire, please."

"Hello, this is Mike."

"Mike, Tommy here."

"Oh, hey, Tommy. What's up? How can I help you?"

"You know that problem that you have with your son?"

"Yeah?"

"Well, we're in."

"You serious?"

"I am, but there are stipulations."

"Okay, like what?"

"The boys can be nowhere in sight of this."

"Understood."

"And this is it—just *one* job. Never again, understood?"

"That's fantastic, but if you don't mind me asking, what changed your minds?"

"Well, we thought about it a lot on the ride back from Boston. We know that Liam will be in either way—regardless of what we say. But more importantly, we asked ourselves, if the roles were reversed, what would *you* do if it were our kids and we needed your help? We both came up with the same answer, so we're in."

Mike was smiling. "That's great, Tommy! And if the situation were reversed, I would do the same for either of you. I can't thank you enough for sticking your necks out like this."

"We need to run this like a military operation, though. There is no room for error. And just in case, we need a plan B if something unexpected comes up. We will meet once a month through December and twice a month thereafter. Got it?"

"Yup, we can use my office here at the car wash."

"We'll alternate meetings between your office in Boston and our Portsmouth office. The first meeting will be in your office next week, okay?"

"Okay, thanks, Tommy!"

"Don't mention it, Mike."

The following week they gathered in Mike's office to go over the strategy once more.

"Okay, boys, what's the plan?" asked Uncle Joey.

"The plan is to rob the Gardner Museum and take a few pieces of art and then either sell them back to the museum, wait for the reward, or hold them for ransom with the insurance company. We figure that we'd be in and out of the museum in twenty to twenty-five minutes, tops. Either way, the goal is to eventually get the museum to buy their pieces back or cash in on the insurance. This is a list of the supplies that we currently have and some items that we still need. We may need your help to secure a few of the remaining items. Over here is a map of the area. As you can see, there are several points of entry and exits to major highway routes north and south of Boston, as well as Storrow Drive east to Route One north and the North Shore suburbs or Storrow Drive west to Cambridge and the suburbs west of Boston, just in case we're hot," said Liam.

"What about BPD patrols?"

"They range between ninety and one hundred twenty minutes—very sporadic rotations."

"Campus security from Northeastern, Simmons, and MA College Pharmacy?"

"All blocked from seeing anything, based on the entrance that we plan to use."

"Transportation?"

"We secured a 'drop' car, it's a retired BPD Crown Victoria that we got at a police auction complete with the pigtail antenna, flashers, a spotlight, and a cage. It's fully tuned up, has a full tank of gas, and is ready to go."

"Secondary plates?"

"We took car plates from a junkyard in Revere a few months ago with the same make, model, and year as our Crown Vic."

"Guards?"

"Two."

"Bullshit! Just two guards overseeing the entire museum? No way!" said Uncle Joey.

"That's it. I confirmed it myself. I've been sitting on it for three weeks now, watching every move. One guard stays in the control booth, and the other one is on a rotating tour around the museum," said Mike.

"Are they armed?"

"No."

"Good news there. How about uniforms and disguises?"

"We have official BPD uniforms including badges and their five-point hats."

"Recon?"

"Well, Northeastern, Simmons, MA College of Pharmacy, Children's Hospital, Dana Farber, and the MFA are in the neighborhood. There are lots of potential cameras, so we may need to disable some of them if possible."

"We can take care of that," said Uncle Tommy.

"Disguises?"

"We have movie-ready moustaches and glasses if necessary. I will have a fake tattoo that will be visible to the guards when we subdue them."

"What else?" asked Uncle Joey.

"The time line is this. Mikey will start a disturbance during the tail end of the Saint Patrick's Day parade around five thirty p.m. This will involve most of BPD on one side of town. On the other side of town at approximately five forty-five, Liam will remotely set off two buckets full of smoke bombs to give the impression that there is a four-alarm fire. He will call it into 911while on-site. Between both incidents, the majority of BPD and BFS will be chasing their tails in two different directions. The night shift starts at six o'clock. We'll make our move at six twenty or six twenty-five," Liam said.

"I can coordinate the smoke bombs with Liam. We'll just need a couple of buckets, two electronic timers, and a transmitter. I'll take care of all the other ingredients. It will be the same stuff that we used in Nam," said Uncle Joey.

"Joey will need to be the eyes of the operation. We'll need access to the rooftop across the street from the museum, and he will have his sniper rifle, just in case," said Uncle Tommy.

Liam blanched. "Will that be necessary?"

"This isn't a game, Liam. If we all want to get out of this alive and without getting caught, then absolutely! Look, Joey will just use the rifle to take out the tires of anyone who is following us—don't worry," said Uncle Joey.

Liam shrugged, but obviously still upset.

Mikey piped in, "There is an apartment complex across the street on the corner of Place Road and Fenway that would give you perfect site lines to the museum and each of the escape routes.

"Okay then, boys, it looks like we'll be rehearsing for the next couple of months. Next month we meet at our offices in Portsmouth. There should only be *one* set of plans. Liam, you keep them. No back-ups in notebooks or on computer disks. Got it?"

"Yes, sir."

"Anything else?"

"Yeah," Liam said. "I need your boot size, Uncle Tommy. We're going to size you and Mr. Maguire two sizes down just in case you leave any footprints as evidence. Don't worry; I'll just take the insoles of the shoes, and this will give you the extra room that you need."

"Good idea, Liam," said Big Mike.

"Oh, and we'll dispose of all the uniforms and the plates at the car wash in one of the chemical containers that will dissolve anything. It will be sealed and picked up the following day to be deposited in a landfill in New Jersey."

"What about IDs?"

"If we get stopped, we'll have BPD auxiliary-police IDs already made up and corresponding driver's licenses."

He scanned the group. "Looks like we're almost there, guys. We'll review the plans just like this over the next couple of months and then do a couple of dry runs in February and the first week of March just before game day. Everybody good?" asked Uncle Tommy.

Everyone nodded.

"Any changes to the plans need to be reviewed by the team. Understood?" said Uncle Joey.

"Yup," said Mikey.

Liam nodded.

"Understood," said Mike.

Over the next couple of months, Cam and Liam finished their freshman year at Harvard very strong academically by both making the dean's list. Liam had never seen Cam so happy. Cam was going to be working this summer at First National Savings Bank as an analyst. The position was secured by Liam's banker, Shaun Fitzgerald. Liam was going to be taking classes at Harvard's Kennedy School and working as a researcher. Mikey was going to be taking two classes at Bunker Hill Community College and working at the car wash with his dad, which was starting to turn a profit now that Mr. Maguire had taken over. Ray was going to be working at the car wash as well, helping out for a few hours a day drying the cars and working in the office.

June was going to be in New York, reading scripts and taking a few classes at Columbia. In addition to helping Cam train for football, Liam had decided to try out for the baseball team next year since the rehab on his neck had been going so well. Next semester he was planning to be a volunteer football coach for the football team a couple of days a week and then train with the baseball team the remainder of the week. Cam and Liam would be suitemates again in Elliot House, along with a couple of other football players.

Throughout the summer, the Gardner crew met at the Shamrock or in Portsmouth to review the plans over and over again.

Today they were in Portsmouth.

"Guys, this plan is starting to come together," Liam said. "I think everyone's role is clearly defined, and they know what they are doing to the minute. Based on the timing, we should be in and out of there within twenty minutes. There shouldn't be any problems with the guards, and nobody should get hurt. I was thinking, though, if something *does* go wrong, or we have to take some sort of action, I think that we need a fall guy or two. My thought is this. Since it is well known that Connor controls this area, we should set up one or two of his guys to take the fall. Everybody knows that Sammy was a sharpshooter in the Korean War; if we could get his prints on something and put them on the roof where Uncle Joey will be stationed, that would be perfect. Then there is Colin Webster, who we can set up as well. Both guys are ruthless sociopaths who won't be missed if they go away, and this will all fall into Connor's lap."

"Okay, good idea, but how do we get their prints?" asked Mikey.

"That's what I was thinking about. They are both chain smokers, so if we can get a few of their cigarette butts, we can plant some on the rooftop and have a separate pile where Mr. Maguire will have the car parked. It will appear as if one was a lookout and the other was waiting in a getaway car for a while. What do you think?" Liam asked.

"I like it. I like it a lot! You know, Liam, if this car-wash thing doesn't work out, you may have a career as a criminal," said Mike Maguire, as everyone laughed.

"Okay then, Mikey, we'll need you to go to the Triple O and sit at the last stool on the left-hand side of the bar. That's where the waitresses dump the trash and clean out Connor's crew's cigarettes. When the waitress empties their table's cigarette butts, you need to pick them out of the trash. You'll have to time it by looking into the bar's mirror and then grab the butts. Just remember, Colin smokes Lucky Strikes, and Sammy only smokes Marlboros."

"Guys, it looks like we have everything except alibis secured for everyone," said Mikey.

"Well, Mikey, hopefully you'll be arrested." Big Mike paused. "Wow! I never thought I'd say those words out loud," he said, and everyone laughed. "You can't get much better than being in the can at the time of the robbery. Mikey, we'll need you to get the crowd going around five thirty because the evening shift starts at six o'clock.

"Liam, you go to class in the morning; then dress in green like you are going to the parade in the afternoon. From there, you'll change and go over to the abandoned warehouse to set off the smoke bombs at exactly quarter to six, just as long as you are in a half-mile radius. After you set them off, you'll call 911 about a fire on the other side of town. Make sure you have that voice modifier we gave you when you make the call! Wear gloves at all times so that there are no prints on the phone booth, and wipe the coins that you use—understood?" said Big Mike.

"Yes," he said.

"Then you go back to school and order takeout dinner with your roommate on your credit card. That way you'll have a timed stamped record of that transaction."

"Joey and Tommy, as we discussed, you guys drive your car to the state border in Seabrook. Leave your car in the transit parking lot and then ride your bikes just over the border to the Amesbury bus depot, where you can put your bikes in the back of the Crown Victoria that we left for you guys the night before. The keys will be under the left front fender. After the job, we have to break my left arm, and then I'll drive you both back to Amesbury, where you can ride your bikes back over the border to Seabrook without any record of you going through any tolls. Remember, we've been having the car-wash expansion meetings in Portsmouth over the past several months now, so if anything comes up with the cops and our relationship, we just tell them about our business opportunity that we have been discussing. Thankfully, we've retained the deputy mayor of Portsmouth, Duncan McDonald, as development counsel for this project months ago.

"I will drive home and watch the taped game of the Bruins. When Maggie comes home, she will recast my now-broken arm, and then we can go pick up Mikey at the police station around ten p.m.," said Big Mike.

"Okay, boys, the next time we meet, game on!" said Uncle Joey.

THE HEIST

Sunday, March 17, 1991, was a rainy, overcast day in South Boston. The recent Supreme Court ruling in *O'Neil v. Irish American Gay, Lesbian and Bisexual Alliance of Boston* had allowed the gay/lesbian/transgender community to participate at the end of the traditional Catholic parade procession, and the city remained staunchly divided. Extra city and state police were on hand with the anticipation of a riot.

At 4:40 p.m., Mikey was leading a group of drunken Irish youths with antigay signs that read, "GOD CREATED ADAM AND EVE, NOT ADAM AND STEVE" and "HOMOSEXUALITY IS A SIN." As the unruly crowd grew, Mikey and his cohorts started to throw bottles, rocks, and pipes at the gay marchers.

Liam met Mikey.

"Liam?"

"Yeah."

"I almost didn't recognize you with your face painted like that. Nice touch with the Harvard football sweatshirt," said Mikey.

"Yeah, well, got to play the role. Let's take a few pictures on this disposable camera, and then I'll go wash my face, change, and do my thing. You good here?" Liam looked around.

"All set. This place looks like a tinder box ready to explode."

"Perfect. Get to it! Remember, you're on by five thirty sharp, and I'm on by five forty-five."

"Good luck, Liam."

"You too. Now do us all proud and get arrested!" Liam said with a grin.

Liam left, and Mikey started to stir the pot with the crowd even further.

"Stand back, kid!" warned a cop.

"Fuck you! Look at those fags; this is a Catholic parade; arrest them!"

"I said stand back, and, kid, don't throw any more shit, or I'm gonna take you in," the cop yelled.

"Take me in for what? I'm expressing my First Amendment right to tell those fags that they're gonna burn in hell for being gay!"

"Don't start, kid!" The police officer called into his shoulder radio, advising that he had identified the group leader of the troublemakers. Eight more Boston police quickly encircled Mikey's group.

Mikey and his group continued to hurl rocks, bottles, and pipes at the marchers. When they got close, Mikey started to spit on them, shouting, "Go home, queer!"

"We're queer. We're here. Deal with it!" was the chant from the other side.

As the procession approached the main stage, a group of local politicians on the dais organized a silent protest by simply turning their backs as the marchers approached the stage, right in front of the local-media feed. Over one million people view the South Boston Saint Patrick's Day Parade each year. They even have a feed going over to Ireland.

It was approaching five thirty, and Mikey needed a sign to make a move. It wasn't until one of the marchers left the procession to blow a kiss directly at him that he saw his opening. He found the nearest cop.

"Did you see that?" Mikey asked the cop.

"Let it go, kid. Let it go! It was just a fake kiss."

"Fuck that!"

Mikey quickly turned to his group and said, "Follow me!" as he threw more bottles and charged the parade to break up the march.

Just as they crossed the parade barricade, a fight broke out with the police right in front of the main stage and cameras. Mikey was struggling with the police as two cops wrestled him down to the ground. One cop had his knee in his back, while the other cop zip-tied his hands. As the police lifted Mikey up off the ground and into the paddy wagon, he was met with a rousing round of applause and cheers from the crowd. The time was 5:40 p.m.

On the other side of town, Liam quickly changed into an entirely new outfit: a black Kangol newsboy cap, a white T-shirt, black jeans, and a black satin Boston Bruins jacket. He looked at his watch and saw that it is 5:44 p.m. He quickly dialed the beeper number that would trigger the smoke bombs. Like clockwork, smoke started pouring out of the two sections that had been staged the night before. Once that was confirmed, he placed the call to 911. With gloves on his hands, he pulled out a quarter and the voice-changing device.

"This is 9-1-1. What is your emergency?"

"Hi...um...I...um, see a lot of smoke coming from that old paper-processing factory on Charles Street, off Merrimac Avenue, in Dorchester."

"Can you see if anyone is in the building, sir?"

"No, it's an abandoned building, but there is a ton of smoke coming from it. You had better get the fire department down here right away."

"They are en route now, sir. May I have your name?"

"Thank you." Liam quickly hung up the phone and could hear the wail of fire-engine sirens off in the distance.

He quickly changed in the T's public bathroom and headed back to campus and his dorm room to order dinner.

At six o'clock, Mike, who no longer had his cast on and was now sporting a fake moustache and lion tattoo on his right forearm, and

Tommy, in his fake glasses and beard, were sitting in the car just a few blocks away from the museum ready to go. Joey, on the rooftop across the street from the museum was the eyes and ears of the operation. Joey had his rifle set up, along with his binoculars, CB radio control, and a pile of Sam Canti's Lucky Strike cigarette butts that Mikey had acquired the week prior.

"Eagle One to Eagle Two, Eagle One to Eagle Two."

"Eagle Two, check; Eagle Two, check."

"The pigeons have left the roost. The pigeons have left the roost. The route is clear. Repeat. The route is clear."

"Affirmative, moving into position."

Mike and Tommy began to drive to the alley next to the museum on Palace Road because the night guards had just completed their shift change.

At 6:10 a.m. Liam arrived back on campus at Harvard and quickly went to Harvard Security and requested a temporary ID because, he claimed, he'd lost his original ID. He then ordered takeout Chinese food for himself and Cam (for an additional credit-card time-and-date record).

At 6:25 a.m. Uncle Tommy said, "Ready, Mike?"

"Yeah."

"Remember, the guard's name is Peter Banks, and he lives at One Hundred Twenty-One Boylston Street, apartment four-B."

"Got it!" He paused. "Hey, Tommy."

"Yeah?"

"If this goes south, I want you and Joe to know that I appreciate everything."

"No need, we're good. Just keep it tight to the plan and on schedule. We're good. Joe sees everything, and he'll make sure that we get out of here okay."

The door buzzer started ringing at the museum, and the night guard on duty got up from his desk to see who was buzzing.

"Yeah, who is it?"

"BPD—we got a call that the silent alarm went off, and we need to check it out," Mike said as he reached over his shoulder for the portable mic. "Yeah, Sarge. It's car fourteen here, and we're ten twenty-three at the museum."

"Affirmative, car fourteen; check all entrances and exits to make sure there were no break-ins," Joey responded on his radio from the rooftop across the street.

"Ten four, Sarge." Tommy now looked up from his shoulder mic and at the guard. "You heard the man; we need to check things out," Joey said, looking at the guard, Peter Banks.

"But I'm not supposed to let anyone in."

"Hey, genius, we're not anyone; we're the police; now open the door so that I can get my sarge off my ass!" said Big Mike.

"Okay, okay, one second." The night guard buzzed both men in.

"So what's the story, kid?" Mike asked the guard who was behind five inches of Plexiglas and a few feet away from the panic button.

"Sorry, guys, those silent alarms go off all the time, but the security agency usually calls us first to see if we're okay."

"Where are your partners? Maybe they triggered it?"

"No, it's only one guy, and he's been here for over twenty years, so I don't think he triggered it."

"Got it." Tommy made it look like he was writing everything down on a small notepad.

"And the security tapes? Did they pick up anything?"

"I don't know. I didn't see anything. I can check if you want. They're down in the basement under the stairwell."

"Okay, thanks, kid. Can I just have your name for our report, and we'll be on our way."

"My name?"

"Yes, your name."

"Peter Banks."

"That's Banks, spelled *b-a-n-k-s*?"

"Yes, that's right."

"Sarge, car fourteen here; all clear on the Two One One. A Peter Banks confirms no break-ins."

"Affirmative, car fourteen." He paused. "Did you say a Peter Banks, *b-a-n-k-s?*"

"Affirmative."

"Does he live on Two Hundred Fourteen Boylston Street, apartment four-B?"

"Hey, kid, do you live at Two Hundred Fourteen Boylston Street, apartment four-B?"

"Yeah, how'd you know?"

"We've got wants and warrants on him for a two seven three D," said Uncle Joey.

"Two seven three D? What's that?"

"Domestic violence, sir. I'll need you to call your partner and tell him that BPD is here responding to a silent alarm and that you need to be relieved until we straighten this whole thing out."

"Yes, sir," Peter said nervously. "Hey, Manny, BPD is here responding to one of the silent alarms, and I need you down here."

"I'm not done with my rounds yet," Manny could be heard saying.

"Hey, man, I said the police are here, so get down here now!"

"Okay, on my way."

"Sir, I'll need you to slowly please come around from that desk so that we can straighten everything out. Please step over to my partner."

Stepping out from behind the security desk and away from the panic button, the guard followed Big Mike's orders.

"Mr. Banks, do you have any weapons or sharp objects in your pockets that I need to be aware of?" Tommy frisked Banks.

"No, sir."

"Hands behind your head, please."

"I thought that we were going to talk this through. It's a misunderstanding; that's all."

Tommy quickly zip-tied Peter's hands behind his back. Just as Banks was subdued, Mike took off his jacket and took out his gun. Vasquez entered the room from the south side.

"Peter, what's this all about silent alarms and stuff?"

As soon as the door closed, Tommy put his gun to Vasquez's head and said, "This is a robbery. Be cool, and nobody will get hurt."

Mike and Tommy quickly blindfolded and cuffed both guards and brought them down to the basement. Both guards were placed on opposite ends of the museum so that they could not talk to each other or compare notes. Then Mike and Tommy rendezvoused at the stairwell.

"How we doing on time, Tommy?"

"Three minutes behind schedule."

"Okay, I'll get the security tapes; you get everything on that list. We'll need you back here in twenty minutes to get back on schedule." He paused and then said into his radio, "Eagle Two, how is the weather?"

"Clear skies, Eagle One, clear skies."

Twenty minutes later, after running around the museum, Mike said, "Did you get everything?"

"All good," Tommy said, carrying several painting canvases.

"Eagle Two, Eagle Two, how is the weather?"

"Still clear sailing, Eagle One. Not a cloud in the sky. All clear to fly the nest."

"Let's go, Mike—in and out just like we said. I need the moustache, jacket uniform, and hats in the bag in the back now!"

"All set, let's move."

"Did you get everything on the list, Tommy?"

"Yup, all thirteen items."

"Excellent!"

"Eagle Two, we've got the eggs. How's the weather?"

"Clear skies, Eagle One, clear skies to fly."

As Mike began to start the car, Eagle Two saw a car turning the corner on to Louis Prang Street, and his heart started to hammer.

"Eagle One, vultures approaching! Repeat: vultures approaching!"

"What's that, Tommy?"

"A patrol car if you can believe it."

"Shit!" said Mike.

Back at his dorm, Liam's mind was going back in time. How the hell had he come to this, he wondered? How? He drifted back in time. He was a kid again.

THE BOSS OF SOUTHIE

MOST PEOPLE IN BOSTON NAÏVELY thought Mayor Kevin White ran the city and Governor Michael Dukakis ran the state, but the truth was that Connor Quinn ran its ruthless underworld, and his brother, Aidan Quinn, the president of the state senate, noted by some as a "smug, pontificating little fraud," *really* called the shots in the state capitol.

Connor Quinn had "won" his heralded position through a specialized form of South Boston politics known as the "Southie Electoral College." This was a unique form of democracy where Connor threatened or maimed his opposition or just made them disappear. Connor's platform was simple: do whatever the hell he said, or you would fuckin' suffer. Everyone in and around the neighborhood knew these rules, but every once in a while, someone had to be reminded of just how things worked. As a result of this system of patronage, there was no major crime in the neighborhoods: no car thefts, no drugs being sold, or no neighborhood break-ins. They all knew the consequences of such actions.

One time, there was a break-in and an assault in the apartment complex right across the street from the Triple O tavern. What complete morons! The day after the break-in and assault on an eighty-year-old woman and lifelong resident, everybody in the neighborhood was looking to Connor for answers—and retribution. Connor eventually found out who'd committed these crimes—two strung-out junkies from neighboring Dorchester, a predominantly black community.

Connor and his crew tortured and interrogated them both until they confessed to the break-in and the assault.

Two weeks later, the Boston Police Department (BPD) found the bodies of two young black men hanging upside down from the Tobin Bridge with their hands cut off. The press called it a "hate crime," and every social activist in the state demanded answers. Even the feds got involved because the Tobin Bridge was part of the federal highway system. They all knew what it was: payback for crossing town lines and breaking "Southie Law." What people did not understand was that Connor wasn't a bigot or a racist; rather, he was an opportunist. But whoever crossed the lines in the neighborhood was roadkill; it was that simple.

Because the incident was being portrayed in the media as a modern-day lynching, heat was coming down from both state and federal law enforcement to solve this crime. All the usual suspects in the city were rounded up to see if they knew anything. Connor quickly reached out to his friends on the payroll at the *Globe* and the *Herald* to point fingers back at the two thieves.

Subsequently, articles were written in both newspapers, painting these two kids as the second coming of Charles Manson. The articles went on to say that they were responsible for over twenty-five recent break-ins in the area, several assaults, and the horrific attack on an eighty-year-old woman, who was still in the ICU at Mass General. Having their hands cut off was Connor's biblical message identifying the two kids as being thieves. Everyone in and around the city got the message one way or another: don't piss in Connor's backyard!

Connor was a Robin Hood of sorts. Some saw it as his warped need for love and appreciation. For whatever reasons, he was the protector of the neighborhood, providing rent money to the needy, shelter to the homeless, and groceries to those who were hungry. On the other hand, he was one of the biggest, most ruthless drug dealers, loan sharks, and murderers in the state. He also provided protection for smugglers and ran the largest gambling ring in the state.

By contrast, Connor's younger brother, Aidan, was a local kid who made good. He graduated from Boston University High School, BU undergrad, and then BU Law—commonly known in local circles as a Triple Terrier. Aidan was a keen negotiator in the Massachusetts Senate and a skilled politician known for taking care of the Irish in Boston. More importantly, he was steadfastly loyal to his family, especially his elder brother, Connor.

That Quinn loyalty ran both ways. One time, as the story goes, when Aidan was running for reelection to the state senate, a reporter was grilling him about his brother's illegal "business dealings." A couple of months before the election, a reporter wrote several unflattering articles (with titles like "Contradictions of the Brothers Quinn") about how bad this relationship was for the city and the state. Connor, sensing that his brother's reelection bid was in jeopardy, quickly found out who the reporter was. He followed this reporter after work one day to his favorite watering hole, O'Neill's Bar, in Dorchester. Connor sat down next to the reporter at the bar, looked over to him, and asked, "Do you know who I am?"

The reporter knew who he was and froze.

Connor Quinn wore his reputation on his battle-scarred face. "It doesn't matter. I'm Connor Quinn, and I kill people for a living. If you write any more shit about me, my brother, or any member of my family, you'll be next. Are we clear?"

Shaking, the reporter nodded.

Connor then looked at the bartender, who was at the other end of the bar, stacking cases of beer; he reached into his pocket and put a crisp one-hundred-dollar bill on the bar. Connor then said to the bartender, "His next round is on me," as he pointed to the reporter and then got up and left.

The reporter got the message loud and clear; he never wrote another negative article about Aidan Quinn or any member of the Quinn family.

A month later, on election Tuesday, Aidan won his reelection bid, and he went on to become one of the most powerful politicians in the history of the state.

Sunday Mass

Sunday, April 6, 6:00 A.M.

Declan O'Hara's voice was harsh like the ex-marine noncom he was. "Get up; take a shower. You're comin' with me. We have to go someplace before Mass."

"Come on, Dad. It's Sunday, and Mass isn't for another *two* hours," Liam whined.

"I said get up! Your uncles will be here in forty-five minutes, and we have some business to get to before Mass."

"Okay, sorry! Christ, I'll get up," he grumbled.

Hands on his hips, Declan O'Hara glowered at his son. "What did you say? Using the Lord's name in vain—on Sunday no less! You're on kitchen detail for a week. Any more lip from you, and I'll make it a month!"

"Okay, I'm going; I'm going."

Being the product of a single-parent household (his mother passed away from cancer while his father was serving in Vietnam) meant that he had extended chores around the house. This included but was not limited to PX, laundry, cooking, cleaning, and shopping. Everyone had his job to do to make the household run smoothly. His dad said it "builds character" and that he'd appreciate it later in life.

Liam whined, under his breath, "Keep your 'character,' and let me sleep!"

No such luck with the ol' man around. There was, however, a period in his life after his mother passed, while his father was still away, that he lived with his neighbors, the Maguires. When he lived there, he didn't have *any* duties at all! Mrs. (Margaret) Maguire was his mother's best friend since they were children in Southie. Like his own family, the Maguires had one child, Michael "Mikey" Jr., who was his age, eight. Mikey and Liam became best friends after Liam got jumped by some local kids when he was five and Mikey came to help him out. They got their asses kicked, but were never harassed again. Mr. Maguire, or "Big Mike," as he was called, was doing a five-to-fifteen-year bit in Walpole Prison for armed robbery. He had been arrested for a failed Brinks heist, but he never ratted out any member of his crew who got away, or the guy who set up the job—Connor Quinn.

"Irish Omerta" is something that the cops or the Italians in the North End never understood. Nowadays, when the Italians got pinched, they would rat out their own mothers just to get a lighter sentence. Not here, not in Southie! The first thing you learned, growing up in the neighborhood, was that you never ever rat out a friend. There was nothing lower than a rat!

"Yes, sir! I'm up!"

Uncle Joey and Uncle Tommy were due any minute. They weren't officially related uncles; they were friends of his dad from his marine unit in Vietnam. Declan never spoke about what he did in the war. All Liam knew was that he was a big deal over there and that everybody else in the neighborhood knew what happened to him except him. People in the neighborhood always looked at his father differently when he got back from the war, as if they were scared or intimidated at times—as opposed to as a hero of sorts, which was what Liam always thought that he was. Whenever he asked his dad about his experiences as a marine, he just said that he did what he had to do, what he was taught to do, and that he wasn't proud of what he did all the time, but he saved lives.

All Liam knew was that "Uncles" Joey and Tommy would come by every so often to pay their respects to his father. His dad usually sent him to bed while they drank all night (although his dad gave up drinking when he got back from the war). When they sent him upstairs, they always thought that he was asleep, but he could still hear them. He never heard grown men cry before, but whenever they talked about Vietnam, they just seemed to wear their hard, grim faces as a kind of respect for the "sarge."

Uncle Joey and Uncle Tommy worked construction in New Hampshire. They were two stocky, hard, and imposing men. When they walked down the street, everybody knew that they meant business, so nobody ever messed with them. Uncle Joey was about six feet tall, 190 pounds, and a stern man with "Semper Fi" tattooed on his right shoulder. He rarely smiled. Uncle Tommy was bigger, about six feet three inches tall, 230 pounds, with the same tattoo. Both had an odd and distant look about them at times. Somebody had said it was the "thousand-yard stare." Whatever that meant.

But to Liam, they were always gentle giants. He used to spend one month each summer with them in New Hampshire just to get away from the city.

"Okay, Dad, all set, I'm up. I have my tie, jacket, and Sunday shoes on and ready for Mass."

"We're not going to Mass right away; we're going to the Triple O before Mass."

"The Triple O? The Triple O tavern?"

"Yes, and we need to get going now."

Okay, he now *got* why Uncle Joey and Uncle Tommy were here. Nothing good could come of this, that much he knew. So he was bringing his camping knife just in case.

The unique thing about the Triple O tavern, or all bars in Boston for that matter, was that they were supposed to be closed on Sundays because of the state's blue laws. The blue laws dated back to the Puritan era and were originally set in place to protect the common workers so that they could rest on the seventh day of the week. But the laws had never been adjusted to reflect today's needs, or more importantly, the drinking desires of the Irish in Southie.

Liam knocked on the Maguires' door, looking for Mikey Jr., his best friend, to join them for Mass. His mother made him come to Mass with them every Sunday, and every weekend Mikey prayed that they would forget to knock on his door.

"You know, Liam, it's okay to forget me once in a while. I'd do it for you."

"No can do, Mikey. If I have to go, so do you. Not to mention, before Mass we have someplace else to go before church today."

"Where to?"

"The Triple O."

"The Triple O? What's there?" asked Mikey, his interest piqued.

"Dunno. Dad said that's where we're going, and you know him on Sundays," he said.

"You think we can cop a beer while we're there?"

"Yeah, only if you don't like your backside. The ol' man will whip us both. And you know the ol' man got the green light from your dad to do whatever it takes to keep you in line while he's away."

Big Mike was Liam's dad's, Declan O'Hara's, best friend, growing up. They initially hated each other and were neighborhood rivals. They fought every day before school, at school, and after school to see who was the toughest kid in the neighborhood. That lasted until they both got temporarily expelled from school. It wasn't until their mothers dragged them to see Father John Callahan ("Father C.") that things changed.

Father C. had a sit-down with them both. As the story goes, he explained to them that they were both Irish Catholic, from "the neighborhood," and they should not fight each other because they were, in essence, fighting themselves. Instead, they should act as each other's protector in and around the neighborhood.

Nobody messed with the wisdom of Father C. Not even Connor Quinn, the neighborhood godfather, could touch him. Father C. was a Golden Gloves champ back in the day, and everybody knew that he could handle himself. After that sit-down, they each shook hands, and that was to be the end of it. Father C. reminded them that if he heard of any more fights between them, he would personally hunt them down and kick their asses! The funny thing was they both knew that Father C. could do it, and more importantly, that he meant it!

It wasn't until Big Mike went away to prison for the first time did Liam realize what a good friend Declan O'Hara was. The Maguires didn't have much money, but Declan always provided them with groceries, rent, or any utility bill money when needed. They never had to ask; Declan was always there, and it was just understood. So while Big Mike was away, he gave Declan oversight of his wife, Maggie, and son, Mikey Jr.—Liam's best friend.

"Yeah, yeah, I know. Your dad and my mom remind me at least once a week. You suck!" said Mikey.

As they all piled into Declan's beat-up blue Chevy Nova, Liam took the front seat, and Mikey was in the back. There was only one side of the seat belt that worked, and Declan always told Mikey that if we ever got in an accident, just hold on to the good side.

"Buckle up, boys," Declan said.

"Hey, Mr. O., how about some tunes?" asked Mikey.

"Hey, Mikey, how about not. We have to make one stop before Mass."

"I know," he said, "The Triple O."

Declan turned and glared at Liam.

"What?" the boy said innocently. "He wanted to know why we were going to Mass so early. Aren't we waiting for Uncle Joey and Uncle Tommy?"

"No, they'll meet us there."

As he parked the car, his father looked over his right shoulder to Mikey Jr. and then to Liam and said, "Listen, you two, when we walk into the bar, Uncle Joey will be sitting at one end of the bar next to the exit, and Uncle Tommy will be sitting at the other end of the bar next to the bathroom. I want you both to sit next to Uncle Joey. If *anything* happens or you see me and Connor get in a heated discussion, I want you both to get behind Uncle Joey and leave the bar. Don't go home. I have a go bag all ready for the both of you in the trunk of my car. Here are the keys. Don't worry, Mikey, your mother knows what I am doing, and so does your father. Understood?"

"Yes, sir!" Liam said.

"Yes, sir," Mikey added.

Liam and Mikey exchanged glances. Mikey looked at him, and he motioned to his shoe. Mikey knew that Liam kept a twelve-inch switch-blade in there just in case of emergencies, so he would be ready if something went down.

Mikey shrugged. "That's great, what about me? Had I known about this shit, I would have brought my dad's nine," said Mikey.

The Triple O Tavern

As THEY WALKED INTO THE Triple O, all eyes in the bar shifted to Liam's dad. The smell of stale beer and cigarette smoke was overwhelming. His dad had stopped drinking when he got back from Vietnam, and everyone in town knew it. So him in the Triple O was a rare sight. Several of the regulars and townies alike nodded and acknowledged who he was as he walked by. It was a sign of neighborhood respect that he'd earned.

Eddie, the bartender, shouted out to him, "Declan, what can I get you?"

"Just water, Eddie, with a lime, please."

"Comin' right up."

Declan got his glass and looked across the room. To his left, at one end of the bar, he saw Uncle Tommy strategically positioned with his back against the far corner wall and right next to the bathroom entrance. To his right was Uncle Joey next to the main entrance and under a vintage sign that read, "Irish Need Not Apply." Mikey and Liam, as they were told, sat at Uncle Joe's table right next to the door.

"Hey, Uncle Joey, how ya doin'?"

"Good, good, kid. Did your father talk to you both?"

"Yup," Mikey and Liam chorused.

"Listen, anything goes down, you two get behind me, and we're out of here. You got that?"

"Yup, we're all good," Mikey said.

Declan then cased the room. He saw Connor's crew, a fearsome bunch of thugs, in the front corner side of the bar, right next to the big bay windows, so they could see who was coming and going to the bar at all times.

As Liam saw his father walking toward Connor's table, two members of Connor's crew leaped up out of their chairs and stepped directly in his pathway.

"Can we help you, friend?" One of the guys extended his right arm and planted his hand on Declan's chest.

Declan paused and studied the hand, then he looked at each of them, sized them up, and said to the one who had his hand on his chest, "No, I'm good. I need a moment with Mr. Quinn."

"Sorry, pal, can't help you. You're not on Mr. Quinn's schedule today." A wicked grin went along with the refusal.

"Look, I just need a minute; we're old friends," Declan said.

"No means no! Mr. Quinn is a busy man and can't be disturbed when he's having his Sunday meetings. So get lost before we kick your ass."

Declan's face grew dark. Through tight teeth he snarled, "Listen, unless you and your boyfriend over there want to learn how to walk again, get the *fuck* out of my way."

"Fuck off, old man!" the thug to his left snarled as he unveiled a gun in his waistband.

Before Liam could blink, Declan snatched the gun out of the thug's waistband and pointed it directly at his forehead and told him not to move. He then hit the other guy in the windpipe, stunning him; followed by a kick in the knee. The thug buckled and dropped to the floor, groaning. Declan grabbed this guy by the back of the head and slammed his face on the table next to where he was standing, splitting his nose wide open, and it began bleeding like an open water faucet.

Uncle Tommy and Uncle Joey jumped up from their seats in their ready position, reaching for their guns. The entire bar fell silent, and everyone stopped to look.

The man who was still standing, but with the gun to his forehead, gave Declan the "Southie stare." It's the type of stare that typically meant that only one man would get up from this fight. They both knew, however, that nothing happened in the neighborhood without Connor's say-so, especially in his own bar, so Declan asked, in an incongruously polite tone to once again see if he could be added to Mr. Quinn's schedule.

With the gun still pointed at his forehead, the guy on Declan's left looked over his right shoulder to Connor's table and asked if it was oaky to let him pass.

Connor reached for his eyeglasses across the table between his coffee and whiskey and put them on. His face was craggy and proudly bore the scars of his life. He squinted to make sure he knew who it was before he gave the nod. Once Connor realized who it was, he went wide eyed and then smiled and quickly motioned to let him pass.

Uncle Tommy and Uncle Joey sat back down with their hands in their pockets and kept staring at the table, as did the rest of the patrons.

"Next time, old man, next time," the offended goon muttered.

Declan just looked at him and grinned as he walked on through.

As he approached, he extended his hand to Connor and then to Sammy Canti, Connor's right-hand man. The others at the table he acknowledged with a nod. They did the same.

Sammy Canti, swarthy and grim, was not a man to be messed with because he lacked fear or any sort of conscience or remorse. Like Declan, Sammy had served in the marines, was a Korean War hero, and winner of the Purple Heart; they shared that bond. The streets said that Sammy had fifteen to twenty bodies to his count since he'd joined the Winter Hill Gang. Later on, the mental-health community would deem him a sociopath who cared little for life, other than his own. That was why Connor liked Sammy so much.

All eyes in the bar were now on Declan and Connor.

Declan was a big guy, about six feet two, 220 pounds, with the frame of a bull. His face too bore life's scars but behind his blue eyes, a twinkle distinguished him from the likes of Connor Quinn. In his youth, he was a Golden Gloves champion, and known to be good with his fists. Growing up, he had a reputation as a street fighter, a tough guy, and a great athlete. Owing to this reputation, he was tested often on the streets. Apparently, he won more than he lost, so he earned his reputation as someone who could handle himself.

"Morning, Connor. I was wondering if I may have permission to sit down and talk to you."

"Declan, my boy, permission? You just went through two of my better guys like a hot knife through butter. You can have all the time you need."

"Thanks! Yeah, good help is still hard to find I see," he said as he turned and grinned at the two thugs, who were sitting just two tables away.

"Declan, you know, if your father was still alive, he would kick both of our asses just because we're talking. I got the sense that he never liked me."

Lapsing serious, Declan said, "No, Connor, you got it all wrong. My father liked you and your family. He would always say to me when mentioning your family, 'Teaghlaigh thar gach.' Do you know what that means?"

"I do. 'Family over all.'" This was meant as a compliment between kindred Irish souls, and even for the ruthless Connor it meant something. "It's been a minute or two since we've been able to catch up, Declan. What have you been up to?" Connor said.

"I'm employed as a custodian at the Cathedral of the Holy Cross and a fill-in custodian throughout the archdiocese, which basically means I'm a traveling janitor. It also allows me the flexibility to confess my sins in different parishes," he said with a smile.

"You're kidding me. Right?" Connor remarked, wide eyed.

"Nope, that's what I do."

"Actually, I'm surprised to see you here, Declan. I heard that you gave up the juice and found God ever since you got back from Nam. You hear that, Sam? Declan found God after what he did over there."

"Yeah, we heard what you did while you were away," Sammy said. "Fuckin' animals, those fuckin' slopes." He took a deep drag on his Marlboro. "Same shit in Korea you know."

"You, of all people, Connor," Declan said, "should know never to believe all that you hear."

"Ain't that the truth! Well, based on what I heard and what your fingers are telling me, some of that shit must be true," Connor said.

"I'll tell you what, Connor, you tell me what you heard, and I'll tell you if you're close."

"Okay, I'll play. I heard that you were a POW for nine months. I also heard that those sons of bitches tortured you like nobody's fuckin' business, trying to get intel. I heard that they plucked out your fingernails, forced you to play Russian roulette, and that you basically told them to go fuck themselves. How's that?"

"So far so good, Connor."

"I also heard that you eventually escaped from those sons of bitches and made it through twenty-five miles of jungle back to your base. Here's the fucked-up part, though. Instead of going home, you went back for the other men in your platoon who were captured."

"Again, all true."

"So let me get this straight. You were fuckin' tortured, left for dead by *this* fucking government, escaped, could have gone home after being a POW, and yet you went *back* for those guys in lock-down?" asked Sammy.

"Yes, that's right. Myself and two other guys in my company went back to get them."

"Semper fi—no marine left behind," said Connor.

"Fuckin' stupidest thing I ever heard of," Sammy murmured, under his breath.

Connor ignored the remark and was now earnest. "So what else I heard was that you not only went back into the camp—I heard you got the son of a bitch who tortured you, and you gutted him like a fuckin' pig in front of the entire camp while the other slopes watched. People said that you chopped off this guy's head and put it on a fuckin' stake right in the middle of the camp. I also heard that your last 'fuck-you' was that you left your dog tags around this fucker's ears so that whoever found him knew that it was you who did it. How did I do, Declan?"

"You know, Connor, my rule of thumb is to take half of what you hear and then take a fraction of that story to think about. The truth usually lies somewhere in between."

"Nevertheless, the government never should have put you in the rubber room at McLean Mental up there in Waltham, after you came home—treating you like a fuckin' psycho up there with the criminally insane and those fuckin' pedophiles. I hope you fuckin' killed some of those fucks while you were up there as well! They should have thrown you a fuckin' parade instead of locking you up!" said Connor.

"War is war, Connor; there are no winners."

"Now you're a philosopher? So what can I do for you, Declan. You need work? Money? What? I know that it's not protection you need. You know, I can always use a guy like you with your skill set on my payroll. If I just mention your name, the fuckin' lowlifes around town who *owe* me will shit their pants and pay on the spot," he said as he and Sam laughed.

"No, it's nothing like that, Connor, but it is something of a personal nature, something that I need to speak to you in private about if you don't mind."

"Okay, everyone, get the fuck out." Connor motioned for everyone to leave. "Go ahead, Declan, sit down. Sammy can stay, though; he knows everything about me."

"With all due respect, Sammy, would you mind if I have a moment with Connor alone. If he wants to tell you afterward what we discussed, I am comfortable with that."

Sammy looked up at him and then at Connor. Connor gave him the nod of approval, and he stepped away from the table. "Thanks, Sammy," Declan said.

"You know, Declan, I think that you just hurt Sammy's feelings."

"Connor, how many one-on-one conversations have we had in the past thirty years? I'm sure that you can indulge me just this once."

"Okay, Declan, the floor is yours. I'll talk to Sammy, and it won't be an issue."

With a matter-of-fact tone, Declan said, "Well, here it is, Connor. I am dying, and I need your help."

Connor's jaw seemed to slacken, and he said, "No shit. Really?"

"Yeah, I have an inoperable tumor in my brain. The doctors think that I got cancer while I was over in Nam."

"Shit! That sucks! Who else knows?" asked Connor.

"Only you, Father C., Big Mike, and my doctors know. I haven't even told my son, Liam, yet. But I will do so shortly."

"So, what, you need money for, your burial or something? Maybe work? What?"

"What I need from you, and from your people for that matter, is to keep your distance from Liam and Mikey Jr. when I'm gone."

Without flinching and as if he didn't even hear what Declan was saying, Connor said, "That's Mikey Jr. Maguire over there next to Liam, isn't it? Big Mike's kid?"

"Yeah, next to Liam."

"You speaking for Big Mike now, even though he's still in the can?"

"Yeah, I went up to see Big Mike last week and told him what I was going to do. I've been watching out for Mikey Jr. and his mother while Big Mike's been away."

With a measure of sincerity, he said, "I heard that. It must be tough to do on a janitor's salary."

"I do what I can."

"It's a shame that Big Mike got pinched. He's a good man, and he never ratted anyone out. Good man, that Big Mike!" Connor said as he raised his glass and took a sip. "But back to your situation, Declan. I'm not sure that I can accommodate your request. Sure, I could say whatever you want to hear now, but the truth of the matter is, if you're gone, what's stopping Liam to come work for me anyway? Or me recruiting him? Half the neighborhood is on my payroll anyway; you know that."

"Yes, I am aware of that, and I know how it affects their judgment. Not only that, but like Big Mike, there are plenty of people who followed your orders and are now on extended vacations at Walpole."

Connor's face darkened. "What does *that* mean, Declan? Remember, you're a guest here, and that can change quickly. You and Liam can end up in body bags for making that kind of noise."

Declan's lips tightened, and then he said, "See, Connor, that's what I'm talking about. Guys like you and me—we get it. We know the game, and we take responsibility for our actions. It's when you bring *family* members in the mix that things start to get complicated." Declan leveled his gaze at Connor, his lips still tight. "Remember, you went there first, Connor. What you don't get is that I'm not *asking* you. I'm *telling* you to stay the fuck away from my family and Mikey!"

"You're *telling* me!" Connor said, his voice rising, incredulous, as he banged his right fist on the table. His glass of whiskey fell off and broke on the floor. "Declan, where the fuck *do* you think you are? And who the fuck *do* you think you're talking to?"

The entire bar looked up and over at them. Just then, Sammy took a step over to Connor's table.

"Everything okay here, boss?"

Connor nodded and waved Sammy back.

Just then, Uncle Tommy and Uncle Joey got up from their table again, their stance firm, and in the ready position.

Mikey and Liam were freaking out, stiff with fear, and too scared to utter a word. Some people sensed the thick tension in the room and started to filter out of the bar.

Revealing a semi-smirk, Connor said, "You have a fucking set of brass balls on you, Declan; I'll give you that."

Declan now appeared resigned. "Connor, I'm way past that. There is nothing that you can do that hasn't already been done to me. I made my peace with what I did over there and with God. This is for my son and Big Mike's son so that they can have a future. I'm sure that you can understand that."

"Declan, I hear that Liam is a really bright kid, and if he's half as tough as you are, we can make a lot of money when you are gone," Connor said with a smirk. "How's that for a future? I—"

Declan interrupted, and in a now pedantic tone said, "Connor, do you know what the difference is between making decisions based on brains versus making decisions based on bravado?"

"No, what? Enlighten me, Declan," he asked.

"It's very simple actually. Making decisions based on brains means that you analyze, assess, and calculate your actions. Making decisions based on bravado is when you react purely based on emotions. When you threaten me, that's fine, Connor, and I get it. But when you threaten my son, you are just making a knee-jerk reaction based on bravado. You're not thinking long term or about *your* family."

"Now you're fucking threatening me? My family? Who? Those fucking humps?" Connor said as he nodded to the table a few feet away. "You think they're my family? I could give a shit if you did anything to them. Declan, you know how things go around here. You either get in line, or we bury you under the line."

Declan kept eye contact. "Connor, I'm going to do you a favor. I'm going to give you something in return for staying away from Liam and Mikey Jr."

"I don't need anything, especially from the likes of a fuckin' janitor." His voice had lapsed; he was now showing his contempt. "I have whatever I need right here. And what I don't have, I take. You can't offer me shit!"

"Connor, you're wrong. I'm going to offer you silence."

"Silence? Declan, my boy, you don't need to give *that* to me. I can just take it from you—forever," Connor said, his grin evil.

"Connor, do you remember when I told you I was a rotating janitor for the archdiocese when needed?"

"Yeah, so?"

"Do you have any friends who live in Weston by chance?" he asked. Weston is an affluent town just outside Boston.

"I know people from all over. Why do you ask?" said Connor, but less cocky, sensing something.

"Let me tell you a story. The crazy thing about being a janitor for the archdiocese is that they make you fill in for your fellow custodial engineers when they go on vacation. For the entire month of March, I was stuck in a parish in Weston. It's a bitch of a drive from Southie, but a beautiful town nevertheless. I worked at Saint Joseph's, right next to the Dunkin' Donuts on Broad Street. Do you know the place?"

"Can't say as I do."

"The funny thing about Saint Joseph's Church is that the confessional booth is directly above the vent in the custodian's office. You wouldn't believe some of the interesting stuff I hear. Most of the time, I leave whatever the parishioner has to say between them and God. However, there was this one guy in particular who caught my ear. This guy felt so guilty about what he had done that he was crying and begging for absolution. As I was listening, it dawned on me that he must have been a cop. Out of respect for the badge, I was going to walk away, and then I heard him say, 'These guys from Southie,' so I decided to stay and listen to what he had to say just in case I had to give some poor guy from the neighborhood a heads-up and let them know they were being watched. It turns out this guy is a fed. Can you believe that?"

"Nope," Connor said like a cat with a canary in its mouth.

"Anyway, apparently, he flipped some guy. Then he allowed this guy to operate his loan-sharking operation, books, drugs, protection, and even murder in return for information. This guy's sin was allowing all this to happen when he knew the consequences of what he was doing. Can you believe that? You know what else?"

"No, what?"

"For all the shit that this guy did, the priest only gave him five 'Hail Marys' and two 'Our Fathers.' That's it! All I'm thinkin' is that the priest must be getting a cut. What do you think?" he said with a grin.

But Connor's demeanor lacked mirth. "Interesting story, Declan, but how does that affect me?"

"I said the same thing, Connor. At first, I thought to myself, who was this guy and, more importantly, who was he talking about from the neighborhood? So after the morning confession, I tailed him home to see who he was. It turns out this guy was a fed named Joe Carey. You wouldn't happen to know him, would you?"

Connor stared at Declan intensely and said, "I don't think I do. Should I?"

"Well, based on these pictures," he said, as he slid Connor an envelope, "it looks like you are fond of Mrs. Carey's coffee cake. Turns out he's from Southie back in the day and lived in the Old Harbor Housing Projects, same as you, when you were a kid."

Connor seemed to regain his bravado. He was into the game now. "You know, Declan, you are treading on thin ice here. You may think you know something when you really know nothing, and that nothing can get you and yours killed."

"Be that as it may, I'm not going to call you a rat; you're a survivor, and you do what you have to do, but if those Italians in the North End or half your crew knew that you're in bed with the feds, well, let's just say that wouldn't be good for you. Especially the way things have been going wrong for them with the feds and all."

"You think some pictures make a difference to me? Bullshit. That doesn't mean shit," Connor said, and he started to fidget.

"No, Connor, I think these pictures *and* this tape will make the difference."

Declan slid him over another envelope.

Connor had replaced his glower with a grin. "Tell you what, Declan. You give me everything—all negatives, copies, everything—or you and yours won't last a week. That's my offer."

"Didn't we just talk about this macho shit, Connor? Why are you threatening me and Liam again? I have the originals. My attorney has a copy, and I have a copy in my safe-deposit box. Just in case you get to all those copies, there are two guys at each end of the bar who have copies as well. No, they're not neighborhood guys; they served with me in Nam, and they'll make sure you keep your distance from Liam and Mikey Jr. when I'm gone. The guy to my right," he said, pointing to Uncle Tommy, "has the longest reported sniper kill ever of a Vietnamese officer; and the other guy," he added, pointing to Uncle Joey, "is an explosives expert. So just know that if *anything* happens to Liam, you and your family will know the consequences. Liam and Big Mike know nothing of this, so this is just between us."

"There you go, threatening my family again. I told you, Declan; those guys don't mean shit to me."

"No, Connor, I'm not talking about those idiots," he said, looking in the direction of Connor's men. "Over the years I know that you only cared for *three* people in your entire life, and one of them recently passed away, your infant son, Peter."

Just then Connor stopped what he was about to say and stared at Declan, his eyes narrow.

It appeared that things had just changed from serious to *real fucking* serious! Connor took his gun out and put it on the table. It was a snub-nosed .38. Nobody outside of a very select few people knew of or dared speak about Connor's son, Peter. Uncle Tommy and Uncle Joey saw what's going on, and they got up from their seats and reached for their guns.

Peter was Connor's illegitimate son from a relationship with his girlfriend at the time, Linda Cross. The child had died of SIDS. Connor didn't want anyone to know about his personal life because he thought it would make him vulnerable to others, and it just did.

Declan's voice kept its conversational tone. "The other two are your mother, Janet, and your brother, Aidan."

Connor's face morphed into stone. "Declan, you just signed your ticket to the hereafter, and your son will be joining you very shortly."

Declan was ready for this reaction. "Well, Connor, it's funny you should say that. In my pocket is some real nasty shit, C-Four that I kept after the war." He took it out of his pocket, with wires all around it and the detonator in his hand. "Let me tell you what this stuff can do. It will make the Triple O into a parking lot, and all in here will be taking their next sip in the afterlife. So we either come to an agreement now, or nobody gets out of here alive, and you and I can finish this discussion in hell. By the way, if nobody gets out of here, the same C-Four is strapped to your mother's boiler in her basement and is set to go off in forty-five minutes. There is also another set of C-Four under your brother's car set to go off in an hour when he and his family get out of Mass at Holy Cross. Don't worry; I'm sure Sammy will know how to disarm these two bombs. They are both off a straight seam line from the timer. All he has to do is disconnect the two wires from the timer. Oh, Connor, and when I'm gone," he said, pointing to Uncle Tommy and Uncle Joey, "those two have full bios on everyone we just discussed should something ever happen to Liam or Mikey."

Connor looked around the room and then stared at Declan, his mind obviously whirling. Connor seemed confused, and for once, he was unsure of himself.

Declan's face remained hard. "Listen, Connor, this is a lot to absorb right now, but the clock is ticking, so what's it gonna be? It's your call, but know this. I'm not fuckin' around."

Connor froze, his eyes shifting as his mind whirled, and he got up. Everyone watching caught a deep breath. The silence was deafening. Connor then gave Declan a hug. With a twisted smile, still in the hug, he said, "Declan, if anything happens to my mother or little brother before we get there, I'll make what those fuckin' slopes did to you over there seem like a walk at fuckin' Disneyland."

His face softened. He assured Declan that nobody would ever go near Liam or Mikey and that he had his word.

He then whispered in Declan's ear, "Teaghlaigh thar gach."

Declan got up and started walking toward the boys, he nodded to Uncle Tommy to his left and then to Uncle Joey to his right. Uncle Tommy nodded back but did not get up and remained in his position until they were all safely out of the bar. Uncle Joey nodded and had Mikey and Liam back out of the bar first, followed by Declan, and then he himself exited. A few minutes later, Uncle Tommy stepped out of the bar when he was sure that nobody would make a move.

As Uncle Tommy exited the bar, Liam saw Connor wave everyone from his crew back to his table.

"Did all of you see that man, Declan O'Hara, and the two kids he left the bar with? He was the guy who made you two idiots look like fuckin' bitches. The kid with the blond hair is his son, Liam, and the other kid is Big Mike's son, Mikey Jr. They live a few blocks away from here. The rule is, nobody is to go near Declan or those two kids unless I say so. It's that simple. If Declan or those kids even want to open up a fucking lemonade stand, you don't go fuckin' near them. This means they don't get taxed, no insurance, no rent, no nothing! If you see this fuckin' guy or those kids walking toward you on the street, you cross to the other side of the fuckin' street. If it's a one-way street, you either turn around or go play in the fuckin' traffic. It's that fuckin' simple. Sammy, if any one of these motherfuckers crosses me on this shit, shoot 'em. You all know that Sammy keeps lime and a shovel in his trunk, so you know I'm not fuckin' around here. Pass the word. Are we all clear?"

"What's so special about that fuckin' guy, Connor?" said the guy with the broken nose.

"First, he broke your fuckin' nose, and now you're asking what's so special about him? Yeah, you go ahead and get in his way again; this time I'll let him fuckin' kill you. Let me tell you a little bit about that guy. When he was away in Nam, he carved up a gook's body like a sushi chef carves up a fresh piece of tuna, and you think you can do what? Believe me, I'm doing you a favor. You know what? I *should* do everyone a fuckin' favor and just shoot you now for your pure stupidity! And when I want *your* fuckin' opinion, I'll be dead first. So shut the fuck up, fuckin' moron! Don't ask fucking why. Just do as I fucking say. That means *all* of you! Are we all clear? I don't want to repeat myself because if I do, I'll fucking kill you myself!"

None of the hoods present were sensitive enough to see the masked admiration in their boss's voice. Not enough to change anything, but yet it was there.

Looking at the guy with the broken nose, Sammy asked, "Should I shoot him, Connor?"

"If he asks another stupid fuckin' question, then yes, shoot him! Anybody else have any stupid fuckin' questions?"

Nobody said a word, and most of them just looked down at their feet or shook their heads.

"Good, now go. I have to speak to Sammy alone."

"What's up, Connor? What the fuck did Declan want that's so important?"

"I'll tell you on the way. Get your jacket; we have to go."

In Connor's car, Connor said to Sammy, "He's got some pictures and some tapes that could put us all out of business."

"Want me to take care of him?"

"No, he's dying with some cancer or some shit like that. All he wants us to do is stay clear of his fuckin' kid and Big Mike's kid too. Look, I'll tell you about it on the way."

"On the way where? Where we goin'?"

"Two stops. One to my mother's house and the other to Holy Cross to see my brother, Aidan."

"What's there?"

"Fuckin' Declan put some C-Four next to my mother's boiler and then some under Aidan's car. Declan said that you would know what to do."

"Yeah, no problem, C-Four is some crazy shit, but it's easy to fix. That guy has some fuckin' balls, Connor; I'll give him that. That's something *we* would do."

"I know. I said the same thing."

"Too bad he can't work for us, eh, Connor?"

"Funny you say that, I asked him, and he told me to fuck off," Connor said with a smile.

"So what happens after this?"

"Don't know. I have to think it through. First, we have to find out who those other two fuckin' shooters were at the bar. They served with Declan's unit in Nam. We also need a sit-down with Father C. to see what he knows. Then we need to find out which bank Declan has a safety-deposit box at and then who Declan's attorney is."

"Okay, Connor, on it."

"We may need Big Brother to help us out with some of this. I'll give him a call."

ON TO MASS

WHEN THEY LEFT THE TRIPLE O, Liam said good-bye to Uncle Tommy and Uncle Joey. Declan wanted a word with them in private before they took off for Mass.

"Tommy, Joey, thanks for that."

"Are we good, Sarge?" asked Uncle Tommy.

"Yes, it went off just as we planned. We'll see what happens, but all good for now. I really appreciate it."

"Come on, Sarge, that was nothing. You know that if you ever need anything, just call."

"Always, my friends, always—and the same to you. Now you both have those packages. Right?"

"Yep," said Tommy.

"Got it, Sarge," said Uncle Joey.

"Remember, if anything happens to me or Liam or Mikey, I need you guys to take care of this."

"Okay, Sarge, understood, whatever you need. Are you sure that there isn't anything that we can do now?" Joey said.

"No, guys, all good. I'm meeting with the doctors regularly. This means a lot to me, especially looking after Liam."

"Sarge, we'll treat him as our own, whatever he needs." Uncle Joey and Uncle Tommy nodded.

"Thanks, guys; it's very comforting, especially since his mother is gone and he will have nobody."

"All good, Sarge!" said Joey.

"Thanks, guys, we'll talk in a week or so."

Declan hugged them both good-bye. Unlike most parents, especially fathers in Southie, Liam's father was not afraid to show his emotions. He often hugged him and Mikey and frequently told them how proud he was of them and how much he loved them. Behind that tough exterior was a man with a giant heart. Mikey and Liam never talked about it, but it just felt good that someone cared.

"Dad?"

"Yes, son?"

"What was that all about in there with Mr. Quinn? He looked kinda mad. I didn't even know that you knew him."

"No, we were just talking; that's all. We're old friends. It was a minor difference of opinion about the future. Did you see us hug afterward?"

"Yeah."

"Well, there you have it; we're all good. Now let's go to Mass."

"Okay, Dad, if you say so."

Going into church Mikey sidled up to his friend. "You don't believe that shit, do you?" Mikey whispered to him.

"No, I wanted to, but I didn't." I was sure I would find out soon enough, though.

SPECIAL AGENT JOE CAREY

"JOE, IT'S CONNOR."

"Connor, what the hell are you doing calling me at home? This had better be important. You know the rules!" said Carey.

Joe Carey, one of Boston's most decorated FBI agents and over his twenty-five-year career had been credited with bringing down the Boston Mafia.

"We need a sit-down. We have a problem," Connor said.

"Problem? What kind of problem?"

"The kind that puts *us* either on the run or in the can."

"Okay, my place tonight, after Elizabeth and the kids go to bed," Joe said.

"No, can't do that. Let's meet where we first met when we started this. Ten p.m. tonight," Connor said.

"Okay, see you there, but this better be important!"

"It is, so just fuckin' be there!" Connor said as he hung up the pay phone abruptly.

The meeting was set to take place in Charlestown, in the glass-littered shadows under the Tobin Bridge at the fourth pillar. Sammy and Connor got there early to case the area and make sure they were not being followed. At about five after ten, Joe Carey arrived.

He got out of his government car and approached. "Okay, Connor, what's so almighty important?" Carey asked.

"What's so important is that there is a fucking problem. The fucking problem is that you're a fuckin' moron! We had an agreement, and you opened your fuckin' mouth!"

"What are you talking about? Only the bureau knows about us, and *that* is only half of what you *really* do."

"Really? Think about it, Einstein. Who else did you tell about what we've been doing, you fucking idiot!"

Carey blanched. "Nobody! I swear, nobody!" Regaining his composure, "Enough of these fucking games, Connor—what are you talking about?" he said.

"You feel so fucking guilty about what we do that you have to go and speak to your fuckin' priest about this shit!"

"What?" Joe said, his jaw slack, his voice shaky.

"Yeah, you heard me. Your fuckin' priest! You confessed to your fucking priest!"

"How the hell did you know that? There is no way Father Taylor spoke to anyone; he's bound by Canon law! He's been a priest for over twenty-five years, and I've known him for fifteen years in my parish. Not to mention, I never named names!"

"Fuck your Father Taylor, and fuck your fuckin' Canon law! You should have kept your fucking mouth shut! Next time you want to unburden yourself, do everyone a fuckin' favor and put your gun in your mouth and eat a fucking bullet."

"How did you hear about this, Connor?"

"Here's how, genius. There's a fucking vent in the confessional of your church, and a fucking janitor overheard you during your confession. Not only did he hear you but he also had a neighborhood guy who followed you home. He knows who you are, where you live, and he even took these photos." Connor threw the eight-and-half-by-eleven-inch manila envelope at Carey.

As Carey opened the envelope, he shook his head and said, "Connor, this is a problem, a real problem! This isn't good for either of us—me, you, or Sammy. This guy has to go. He'll ruin everything we've got going on."

"Like I said, a real genius."

"What is he looking for? Money? What?"

"He's looking for me and Sammy to stay away from him, his kid, and another neighborhood kid—that's it. Not to mention, Anthony Pesini and his crew would have no problem clipping a dirty fed."

"No way, that can't be it. He's got too much invested in this to have it just be that: surveillance photos, tapes—no way!" said Carey.

"Look, this is what he said to me. This guy, Declan O'Hara, is a neighborhood guy who recently got God in his life. I'm sure that you can appreciate the irony here, Joe, since you're the fuckin' pussy that got us in this fuckin' mess at confessional! He's one of those reborn Christians who is looking for redemption after some of the shit he did over there in Nam. He said that there are only three other people who have this information. The two shooters who were with him yesterday at the Triple O as backup—I need you to get the information on them. They were in his unit and aren't from around here. One was a sniper, and the other was an explosives expert or some shit like that. His attorney/priest, Father Callahan—I'll handle that. And the final set is in his safety-deposit box, which you may have to get access to and clean out."

"Connor, extortion is not part of any path to redemption that I am aware of! Are you sure that he's not working with any of the Patriarcas?" (The Patriarcas were the family out of Rhode Island who controlled the Boston mob.) "Also, Connor, stay away from all members of the cloth! They're not in this, and you're not taking any out. That's that!" Carey stated emphatically.

"As far as I know, none of the Italians are involved in any of this shit. Otherwise, we'd be dead by now. I just need to know if you hear anything on your end too. Okay, Joe?"

"Yeah, I get it. I'll look into this guy, Declan O'Hara, his friends, and the safety-deposit box. You get to his attorney. In the meantime, until we straighten this out, you stay away from him, his family, and that kid. Get it?"

"Sammy and I know what we're doing; just do your fuckin' job."

"Anything else, Connor?"

Connor's eyes took on their secretive squint. "Yeah, there is a shipment of guns coming in two days that you might be interested in. They are being transferred in international waters from a British trawler, called *King George III*, to a fishing boat out of Gloucester, called *Lucky*."

"Thanks, Connor, whom do these guns belong to?"

"Tony Pesini and his group of guineas out of Nahant."

"When is this happening?"

"The boat should arrive in two days, before dawn. Make sure that you fucking feds hide somewhere, or they'll dump the fuckin' guns in the ocean."

"What are we talking about here? I need to get the Coast Guard and the ATF involved too. And do you have a piece of it?"

"Yes and no. I can protect my end. And I don't give a shit whom you call. But there will be several cases of semiautomatic rifles and nine millimeters on this ship; and the load is heavy!"

"Thanks, Connor! I'd better get moving on this. And I'll take care of the other thing later this week."

"Hey, when they give you another commendation for all the shit I give you, don't forget to thank Sammy and me at your press conference," Connor said with a smirk.

"Thanks, Connor; thanks, Sammy. I'll let you know how things turn out—on all fronts."

Connor and Sammy both nodded and turned back to their car and drove away.

Shipment Of Guns

Two days after Connor, Sammy, and Joe Carey spoke, every major news agency was notified of the largest gun seizure in the history of Massachusetts. The FBI agent in charge, Joe Carey, was front and center, sticking his chest out for all the cameras to see. This was followed by a perp walk of what the press dubbed the "Firearm Fishermen." Joe was surrounded by the local Gloucester PD, the FBI, ATF, and the Coast Guard while he explained the seizure. In the background were cases upon cases of guns on display. And then came the news conference.

"My name is Joe Carey, and I am the agent of record for this seizure. Working in collaboration with GPD, the ATF, and the Coast Guard, this was a multiagency sting that took months of planning to execute."

"Months of fucking planning—did you hear that, Connor? We told the fucking guy this information just the other day! Man, he lies better than Nixon did in Watergate," said Sammy.

"Shut the fuck up; I want to hear this!" said Connor sternly.

"GPD, the AFT, and Coast Guard were critical partners in this seizure that netted over three hundred semiautomatic handguns and over one hundred fifty assault rifles. These guns originated in different parts of Europe and were transferred over international waters before they came into US territory, ultimately landing in the port of Gloucester. Are there any questions?"

"Agent Carey, can you please tell us how you came about this information?" the WBZ reporter, Jane DiReeno, asked.

"The information spawned off a yearlong investigation whereby we were working with informants who are currently incarcerated and/or in federal custody."

"Do you know where these guns were supposed to be delivered? And to whom?"

"Yes, we had a location. However, we did not want to take the chance of losing the shipment in any way. It was our decision to keep these guns off the streets of Massachusetts at all costs, and that is why all four agencies collectively decided to react now. We are currently interrogating the captain of the *Lucky Seven*, Mr. Alex Williamson, fifty-seven, of Gloucester, for further information. To date, however, he has invoked his right to counsel and is not making any statements at this time. We hope to provide additional information as our investigation progresses. I would once again like to thank Chief Thomas Madigan of the Gloucester Police Department, Major Joseph Serino of the Boston ATF, and Captain Peter Geaney of the US Coast Guard, for all their cooperation and assistance with the apprehension of these fire arms."

ANTHONY PESINI

In Francesco's Restaurant in the North End, the local news was on in the background of the bar. The place smelled of tomatoes sauce and oregano. "Anthony, did you see that shit?" said Carlo "the Knife" Napoli.

Carlo was a captain for the Patriarca family and the second-highest-ranking member of the Boston mob. The Patriarca family was considered the New England branch of "La Cosa Nostra," headed by Raymond Patriarca, Sr., and his underboss, Anthony Pesini. Carlo Napoli was a skilled businessman who was in charge of bookmaking, loan-sharking, and racketeering in the Boston area. He was second-in-command only to Anthony Pesini.

"They just got our shipment of fuckin' guns. It's on the news now! They even have a fucking helicopter over our boat! More fucking bad luck. Man, we are catching it all lately. Makes me wonder. I—"

"Shut the fuck up! I'm trying to listen here," whined Anthony.

He was seething mad. "If that fuckin' mick or any of his crew said one word about this fuckin' shipment, clip them all! I don't fuckin' care! Forget about Rhode Island; I'll deal with that. If any of those fucks opened their mouths, bury them all—and make it public! Find out what the fuck happened! Also, why didn't our guy in the Gloucester PD give us the heads-up? What the fuck are we paying him for?"

"I already checked on that, and he said that they all came out of nowhere yesterday morning. By that time, the boat already entered

US waters, and he didn't have time to warn the captain to dump the shipment."

"Well, someone ratted us out to the feds. Find out who, and bring the person to me. We're out over a half mil here, Carlo!"

"I know, Anthony. I'll see what Connor has to say. If I think he's the rat, I'll clip him myself on the spot. Tony?"

"Yeah, just get it done. I've had just about enough of those Irish fucks! We seem to be getting all the bad luck. Carlo, set it up a sit-down with Connor."

Carlo dialed Connor's number.

Connor picked up the phone at the Triple O. "Yeah, who's this?"

"Carlo."

"Yeah, what's up?"

"Did you hear about that thing?"

"Yeah, fuckin' shame."

"Yeah. Well, my guy wants to know what happened?"

"Me too. Let me know when you find out because I had interest there as well, you know. Sounds like someone is a *rat*."

"Yeah, I know; that's what it sounds like. Someone had a conversation with the man," said Carlo.

"Yup, I was thinking the same thing," Connor said.

"Yeah, my guy and I were thinking the same thing too. Can you meet me at Francesco's?" Carlo asked.

"Is *he* going to be there?"

"No, just me and the pigeons. How does noon look?"

"See you then," Connor said.

Connor hung up the phone and turned to Sammy. "Sammy, Carlo wants to see me about that thing."

"I'm comin', right, Connor?" Sammy asked.

"Shit yeah! We need to go in heavy. I think the fuckin' guineas think that I dropped a dime on them."

"Well, they're pretty fuckin' smart then. Let's be prepared just in case things go south. You know, I like Declan's style; maybe we should bring a grenade or two?"

"Not a bad idea. Get a few just in case."

"We got to leave in fifteen minutes to get over to the North End," Carlo said.

"Francesco's?"

"Yep."

"Okay then, we're off, Connor."

Sammy and Connor parked the car on Franklin Street. They walked up Broad Street and crossed over to Prince Street. Francesco's is halfway up the block on the right-hand side—Ninety-Eight Prince Street.

As they walked into Francesco's, they were greeted by the aroma of fine Italian cooking and by a burly six-foot-two, 280-pound Italian named Dominic. Connor knew that Dominic was not a made man, but an associate of the Patriarcas who was looking to make his bones. More importantly, Dominic knew both Connor's and Sammy's reputations.

Dominic had eyes that seemed too small for his fat face. He said, "Mr. Quinn, Mr. Canti, how are you? Mr. Napoli is expecting you in the back." As they started toward the back of the restaurant, Dominic stood in their way.

"Mr. Quinn, I'm sorry about this, but I have to frisk you and Mr. Canti before meeting Mr. Napoli."

Connor eyed the man, steel in his eyes. "Dominic, I understand you gotta do what you gotta do, but if you put your fuckin' hands on either me or Sammy, I'll fuckin' cut them off." He leveled a squinty stare at the big man. "It's your call," said Connor.

Dominic just grinned and motioned his arm in the direction of Carlo in the back room.

Just then Carlo stepped out from the back and waved them in. "All good, Dominick," Carlo said.

Dominic let them pass, and Sammy and Connor noticed that there were a few extra shooters in the room along with the regulars who they expected sitting around the bar.

Sammy waited just outside the main room while Connor and Carlo sat down. Sammy ordered an espresso and cannoli.

Carlo motioned for Connor to sit down. "Connor, this is a big fuckin' mess up there. There were people who that shipment was promised to."

"Yeah, I know. Remember, half of that load was mine!"

"Connor, Tony and I want to know, who in your crew knew about the shipment?"

"Just me and Sammy knew about it, and that's it. You need to look at leaks in your own crew." Carlo rolled his eyes and stared at Connor. "Wait a fuckin' minute. You think *we* dropped a fuckin' dime? I came here expecting *you* to pay me the two hundred fifty thousand we're out!"

"Pay you? Are you fucking kidding me? The load got jacked by the feds. Did you miss that fuckin' part, you Irish prick?"

"Fuck that! I gave you two hundred fifty K for half the load of those fuckin' guns. So, I either get the guns or my money back. Part of that two fifty was for guaranteed transport. Remember?"

"Connor, you know the game. Those are the risks," Carlo said.

"Look, Carlo, if I find out anybody in your crew dropped a dime, you're on the hook here. And in the future, don't do me any favors; I'll get my own guns."

Carlo's eyes narrowed. He let a grin escape. "You got a mouth on you, don't you, mick?"

"Whatever. Are we done here? Anything else, Carlo?" Connor asked.

"No, that's it for now, Connor. But know this. If we find out anybody from your crew had anything to do with this, we won't want our money back; you'll just need body bags."

"You know, Carlo, a friend of mine recently told me something. Do you know the difference between making decisions based on brains versus making decisions based on bravado?"

"No, I have no idea what the fuck you're talkin' about, Connor."

Taking a scholarly tone, Connor said, "Making decisions based on brains means that you analyze the situation and think things through. Making decisions based on bravado is when you react based on emotions and without forethought. You see, Carlo, when you threaten me or any of my crew for this shit, you're just making a knee-jerk reaction based on bravado. Think about what I lost here too."

"You know, Connor, I'll have to remember that piece of mick philosophy," Carlo said. "Let *me* tell *you* something, Connor. Brains, bravado, I don't give a fuck. You see these?" He reached in his pocket for his gun and pulled out some ammunition. "These are fuckin' bullets. Each one has a name on it. And those names belong to each member of your crew if we find out you had anything to do with this shit. Are we clear?"

"Crystal. Now I got to go, or is there anything else, Carlo?"

"No, that's it, Connor. But if you hear anything, you make sure you let us know."

"Will do, and you do the same. Always a pleasure, Carlo."

Connor stood and reached out his hand to Carlo to shake it. This was a sign of friendship directed at Sammy; things were basically under control, at least for now. Connor then nodded to Sammy to get up and head for the door.

As they walked through the restaurant, all eyes were on Connor and Sammy. They got to the entrance; Dominic was still standing there. Connor said to Dominic, "Hey, Dominic, next time you want to feel me up, bring me flowers first. I want to be wooed before I get felt up."

Dominic smiled and said, "Cannolis make good silencers, Quinn. Remember that next time because if I'm bringing you cannoli, that'll be the last thing that you see." Connor and Sammy kept walking toward their car.

Carlo told Dominic to get Anthony on the phone.

"Tony."

"Yeah, who's this? Carlo?"

"Yeah, how'd it go?"

"That fuckin' guy thought I was going to give him back his cut of the money for the guns that got picked up."

"No fuckin' way! The balls on that mick. What did you say to him?" Tony asked.

"I told him to fuck off and that those are the risks! I also said that if we find out that anyone from his crew had anything to do with it, they'd all go."

"You think he dimed us out, Carlo?"

"No, not by the way he was talking. He lost a pile too. We'll find out, though. I'll keep my eyes and ears open."

"Okay, work on our guy out there on Gloucester PD to see what he can find out."

"Will do, Anthony."

THE FALLOUT

A FEW WEEKS AFTER DECLAN met with Connor, people started looking at Liam and Mikey differently. He didn't understand it at first. Neither did Mikey. It wasn't until they ran into Kevin Riley, their neighbor, who was a senior in Southie High School, that they heard what happened.

As they were getting into the elevator going off to school, Kevin was already in the elevator, and he was holding it for Mikey. As he was holding it, Kevin tried to get off.

"Where are you going, Kev? You'll be late."

"No, I'll just get the next one; go ahead."

"Get the next one? The other elevator has been out of order for a month. You'll be waiting another half hour if you wait."

"Naw, I'm good. I...I...forgot my lunch money."

"No worries—here's a buck. Pay me back later."

"Shit, Liam, give me a buck too," Mikey said.

"No way! I know you're a deadbeat, and I won't get the money back," he replied with a smile.

The door closed.

"So what's up, Kevin?" Liam asked.

"S'up, Kev," Mikey said.

Kevin just nodded and stared at the floor.

"Hey, Kevin," he said. "What's up?"

"I heard you; I just don't want any trouble with you or Connor's guys."

"Kev, what are you talking about?" Mikey asked.

"You know what's up," Kevin said.

"No, we don't! What's going on?"

"Seriously, you guys *don't know?*"

"Know what!" Mikey asked.

"Word is out that you, your dad, and Mikey are like Switzerland, neutral, and not to be messed with—by anyone! That's directly from the man, himself."

"What? What are you talking about?" Liam said. "Mikey, you know anything about this?"

"Nope. Wait a minute. That's what must have gone down with your dad's meeting with Connor at the Triple O the other day."

"No shit, you're right," he said.

"Yep, that's it," Kevin said. "Way I heard it was that your dad told Connor to go fuck himself, and Connor backed down."

"No, that's not like my dad," he said.

"Man, way I heard it was that there's a shitload more to your dad than pushing that broom at the cathedral—more than any of us know, except maybe Connor."

"No shit, wow!" Mikey said. "That's what must be going on, Liam. Hey, if your dad's such a badass, Liam, why are you such a pussy?"

"Yeah, it makes more sense now, especially what's going on around here. Oh, and screw you, Mikey!"

"Look, guys, I don't want any trouble, so I didn't say shit to you. Got it?"

They all stepped off the elevator.

"Yeah, yeah, no worries. Thanks, Kev, for telling us, though," he said.

Kevin went left toward South Boston High School, and Mikey and Liam went right to the Cathedral Catholic School.

"Holy crap, Liam, what's your dad got on Connor that makes him so scared?"

"I dunno. You ask him."

"I'm not asking him. You think my dad knows? I can ask him," Mikey said.

"Good idea, write him and see what he says. I might ask my dad too; we'll see."

As they started walking to school, they saw Declan outside, raking the grounds of the church and picking up trash. Their school was attached to the church, so they saw Declan a lot.

"Hey, Dad."

"Mornin', Mr. O'Hara, the place looks spotless."

"Thanks, Mikey; need to keep at it. You kids need to pick up after yourselves better—not you guys, but the other kids."

"I'll make sure nobody litters here, Mr. O.," Mikey said.

"Thanks, Mikey. You guys ready for your algebra test?"

"Well, I hope Liam is ready so that I can copy off him," Mikey said with a smirk. "Not to worry, Mr. O., I'll go to confession afterward, so all will be good."

"That's not how it works, Mikey."

"I know, we studied last night. I'm good," Mikey said.

"Good luck, guys! Remember, Liam, you have guitar and piano lessons after school, followed by language lessons with Dr. Cheung after that. I'll be home around six thirty or seven. Supper is in the fridge; just heat it up."

"Okay, Dad, got it."

This was his routine every Monday and Wednesday after school. His dad valued an education and demanded that he be the first O'Hara to go to college. Mikey, on the other hand, had the life. He got to play in the neighborhood and hang out after school. Although Declan was constantly on Mikey, he would always find an excuse to sneak out of his apartment to play.

THE FBI

A FEW MONTHS AFTER DECLAN'S meeting with Connor, he was walking the boys to school; they were crossing Charles Street on to Bay Street, about a hundred yards from the entrance to the Cathedral School. Mikey and Liam were in the middle of a heated debate about the Red Sox; Fred Lynn versus Jim Rice versus Dwight Evans in the outfield. Just as Mikey was breaking into his imitation of Louis Tiant's delivery, three black Crown Victorias appeared out of nowhere with lights flashing and sirens wailing. The first car jumped the curb and cut them off in front of their pathway. The other two cars angled against any possible retreat to their left and right. Declan, Liam, and Mikey had no idea what was going on? Then, suddenly, several men, dressed in black suits, poured out of their cars and took up defensive positions surrounding them. The first man said, "Declan O'Hara?"

"Yes, what can I do for you?" Declan said as he nodded to the man. Turning to the boys he said, "You boys go over there to the curb and sit down."

"Stay right where you are, boys!" demanded the suit, as he drew his gun from his holster, and the other agents did the same. "My name is Agent Jones with the FBI, and you need to come with me."

"Really, is that necessary? Listen, pal, if you want to speak to me, fine. The boys are just going to school," Declan said.

"Agent Jones, check their backpacks," said Agent Carey from a distance.

Just then, Father C. came out from the rectory to see what all the commotion was about. "What's going on here? Is everyone okay?" asked Father C.

"Relax, Father, I'm Joseph Carey with the FBI," he said as he flashed his badge, "and we would just like to speak with Mr. O'Hara."

"Speak to him about what? Are you arresting him?"

"Father, this doesn't concern you."

"Well, I am acting as Mr. O'Hara's attorney in this instance, so I'm afraid I will need to know immediately."

"Nothing in the bags, Agent Carey," Agent Jones said.

"Okay, let them go on their way. Mr. O'Hara, I will need you to kneel on the ground with your hands interlocked behind your head."

As Declan knelt, he said to the boys, "Don't worry. It's either a mistake, or they just want to talk about something from the war—that's all. If I don't make it home tonight, stay with Mikey tonight, okay?"

"Okay, Dad."

"Don't tell them shit," Mikey said.

"Thanks for the support, Mikey. Your dad would be proud!" Declan said as he winked at him.

"Declan, I'll meet you downtown, and we can sort this all out," Father C. said. "Agent Carey, where are you processing him?"

"One Federal Plaza, Father."

Declan uttered, "Thanks, Father, but it's really not necessary; I'll be home this afternoon."

"Nevertheless, I'm coming. And *you*, Agent Carey, should be ashamed of yourself, pulling guns on two young boys."

"Listen, Father, the kids in *this* neighborhood see me sooner or later. These two just got a chance to see me sooner—that's all." He put his gun back in his holster and put the cuffs on Declan.

"Fuck you!" Mikey said.

"See, Father, sooner or later."

"So where are we going, boys?" Declan asked the agents.

"No place that you'll like, pal," Agent Jones said.

"Will there at least be cable where we're going? I don't want to miss *Days of Our Lives.* Rebecca is supposed to come back from the dead today, and I didn't set my VCR to record it, since you boys didn't give me advance notice."

"A character—most of you Southie scumbags are," said Agent Jones.

"Southie scumbags—now that's no way to talk, Agent Jones. What would your mother say about that potty mouth? So you're a tough guy with a badge, huh, Agent Jones?" Declan said.

"Tough enough—especially tougher than a janitor, yes."

"If you read my file, you'd sing a different tune, my friend."

"I did read your file, and you're nothing special. You were a cook in the Corps who was dishonorably discharged. Big fucking deal. You couldn't hack it in the marines."

"Is *that* what it says now? Interesting. Well, my name will be flagged in the system now that you brought me in, so I suspect you'll be getting a call shortly from Virginia when we land at Federal Plaza."

"Whatever, pal, you're just a name on a list of assholes that I'm picking up today."

"Hey, do I get a phone call where I'm going? I forgot to call my psychic today. She's supposed to give me the Pick Six lottery numbers. Not to mention, she should have given me the heads-up on you guys coming today. I still get that call. Right?"

Agent Jones's partner, Agent DaSilva, started laughing.

"You'll think it's funny when you end up in Walpole and a lifer makes you his punk!" Jones said.

"Sounds like you have experience, Agent Jones. Whose boyfriend were you?"

As the agents drove Declan into One Hundred Federal Street Plaza, Agent Jones flashed his badge and proceeded through the initial security gate, past another security checkpoint, and then down to the main underground garage, marked "For Prisoners Only." Underneath the garage they took Declan out, led him upstairs, searched him, and left him in an interrogation room chained to a table for about twenty minutes by himself. Just then, Agent Carey walked in with a manila file and threw it on the table.

"Mr. O'Hara, do you know who I am?"

"'Mr. O'Hara' is so formal; please call me Declan."

"Okay, Declan, do you know who I am?"

"Yes, you're Connor's friend, Joe Carey; how can I help you?"

"I know Connor Quinn, yes, but we're not friends. You see, Mr. O'Hara we have a problem."

"A problem? What kind of problem, Agent Carey?"

"It seems that you are in possession of some information, some pictures, and a tape that you think might give you some type of leverage."

"Leverage? What are you talking about? Leverage of what? Have I asked you for anything, Agent Carey? Have I demanded any money, favors, anything?"

Carey got defensive. "No, but that's not the point. I have an ongoing and active investigation that involves Mr. Quinn, and you are jeopardizing it by potentially bringing this information to light." Agent Carey pointed to the manila envelope.

"How so?" Declan asked.

"That, Mr. O'Hara, is none of your business. My concern, however, is that the four years that the FBI has vested in this investigation will be all for naught because of you."

"I don't know what to tell you, Agent Carey. I had a discussion with Mr. Quinn, and we came to a mutual agreement. As far as I am concerned, that's the end of it, unless, of course, he violates our agreement."

Carey got up and leaned into the table with both hands on top. "Well, I'm afraid that I can't take that chance, Mr. O'Hara. I will need all originals, negatives, and all the tapes that you have. Mr. Quinn tells me that he will still abide by the agreement you both struck."

"This is *Connor Quinn* we're talking about. He's a drug dealer, a gun runner, a loan shark, and a murderer—and you want me to just *trust* him?"

Just then Agent Jones peeked his head in the interrogation room and motioned toward Agent Carey to come to the door. "Sir, there is a Father Callahan out here looking for his client, this guy Declan. He's making a lot of noise up there. He's threatening to sue," Agent Jones said.

"Relax, just tell him that his client is in the system, that he's being processed, and that he's in our Mattapan office."

"You want me to lie to a priest? Over *this* guy?"

"Just do as you are told, Agent Jones."

"Yes, sir."

Declan laughed. "You're a funny guy, Agent Carey. Don't mess with Father C., though; he's got a long mean streak."

"Let's get back on track here, Declan. If you don't trust Connor, then trust me; I'm a federal agent. Trust the fact that I will advise Mr. Quinn to keep his end of the bargain."

Declan locked eyes with the FBI man. "Yes, Agent Carey, you *are* a federal agent, and yet you receive envelopes full of cash from Connor Quinn."

Carey looked away. "O'Hara, that sounds like a threat," Agent Carey said.

"No, that was an observation."

"You know, Declan, I looked up your service record in the marines. On the one hand, from my interviews with people who knew you, you're not all that different than Connor. In fact, you may have a bigger body count than him. The funny thing is that people say one thing, yet your service records indicate something else. It says here that you were a cook. Look at this," he said as he threw his file on the table. "Most of this file is blacked out. How many cooks were dishonorably discharged and have blacked-out files? I can't find a thing out about you or your unit. Interestingly enough, I'm pretty good at investigating stuff like this, and I can't get anywhere with this file or with finding anything out about the two friends who were in town with you the other day. The *only* time I ever saw a file like this was when I was looking at a group of Black Bag guys? Are you and your unit a Black Bag group, Declan?"

"As you can see, Agent Carey, I was just a cook."

"And the dishonorable discharge?"

"Too much cayenne pepper in the bouillabaisse, so they put me in the brig. But that should have been reversed on appeal, and the most recent records should state 'honorably discharged.'"

"Don't worry, Declan; I'll get to the bottom of this, and then we'll chat again."

"Knock yourself out, Agent Carey. Be aware, though, that you may be stepping on some big toes if you dig too deep."

Agent Jones peeked his head in again and motioned toward Agent Carey. "Jesus Christ, Jones, can't you handle one goddamn priest?"

"No, sir, it's not that. You have a call."

"A call? I'm in the middle of an interview here, Jones; just take a message for Christ's sakes."

"Can't do that, sir; it's the Director, and he wants to speak with you—immediately."

Carey's face dropped. "The Director? You're telling me that Director Kelley, Clarence M. Kelley, Director of the FBI, is on the phone?"

"Yes, sir."

"Jones, you watch him. I'll be back in a minute."

"Hey, Agent Jones, it's been a long time. Where is your boyfriend, Agent DaSilva?" Declan said, grinning.

In another room down the hall, Agent Carey took the call.

"Sir, Director Kelley? This is Agent Carey. You requested to speak with me, sir?"

"Yes, Agent Carey, do you have a Declan O'Hara in custody?"

"Yes, sir, I do."

"Is he under arrest?"

"No, sir, he's just in here for questioning."

"For what?"

"Sir, it's in relation to a RICO investigation involving the Patriarca family."

"If it's just questioning, then release him immediately," Director Kelley said.

"Respectfully, sir, my interrogation is not complete yet."

"I'm sorry, Agent Carey; maybe I wasn't clear. I said either release him or your next post will be in Alaska, checking border crossings for endangered polar bears. I do not want to get another phone call from Archbishop Matthews about you arresting one of his employees unless you have something on them that will stick. Are we clear?"

Archbishop Marcus Matthews was the archbishop of Boston and had been Father Callahan's roommate for two years while they were in the seminary together.

"Yes, yes, sir, crystal clear, I understand. He will be released immediately. My apologies."

"Just get it done!" he snarled and abruptly hung up the phone.

Agent Carey called Agent Jones out of the interrogation room.

"Go locate Father Callahan and bring him here immediately! Go, go!" he said and waved Agent Jones away.

"Yes, sir."

Agent Carey reentered the interrogation room. "Sorry about that, Declan. I had to take the call. You know—bosses. Listen, Declan, if something were to happen to you, what would happen to your son, Liam? You have no living relatives. Your wife's family is gone. You have no options. Foster care in Boston is a bitch. It's a one-way ticket to Walpole. You know that. On the other hand, if you give me everything that you have, there would be no concern for such unpleasant happenings in the near future."

Now he had Declan's ire. "Agent Carey, that sounds like a threat. Are you threatening me and my son? Your friend tried to do the same thing you know. Now he's got you doing his dirty work. Is that how it works?"

"No, Declan, that's me putting the entire weight of this office against you and your boy. I'll put you away and watch your kid grow up in foster care, and then he can be someone's punk in prison. If you don't want any of that, then just get me those negatives, all the pictures, and all the tapes."

"Agent Carey, do you know what the difference between you and Connor is?"

"No, enlighten me, Declan," Agent Carey said.

"A badge—that's it. You both are parasites on this earth. As I told Connor a few weeks back, if you threaten me, then fine—I get it. But when you threaten my boy, who has *nothing* to do with this, then it's you who needs to worry."

"Now are you threatening me, Declan? A federal agent?"

"Let me make *one* thing perfectly clear, Agent Carey. I don't make threats; I carry out promises. And I promise you this. If you come at my boy again, I promise you that your wife, Barbara, will be living off the shitty pension of a dead fuckin' agent. Your kids, Bobby and William—their only memory of you will be of the GI Joe action figures you got them last Christmas. We can play this any way you want. But before you do so, Connor has a vested stake in this as well. So you may want to check with him first."

Just then there was a knock at the door. Agent DaSilva was outside with another prisoner.

Agent Carey said, "Okay, good, bring him in."

In through the door walked Big Mike Maguire, Mikey's father and Walpole inmate 2012871871. Mike was dressed in a bright-orange jumpsuit with state-issued slippers and both his hands and feet in shackles. Agent DaSilva sat Big Mike across from Declan at the table and then left the room.

"Do you know this guy, Declan?" Agent Carey said.

"Yes. Big Mike, how you doin'?"

"Declan? What the hell? What's going on? They picked me up and sent me down here. Are Mikey and Maggie okay?"

"Yes, everyone is just fine—don't worry! My new friend here, Agent Carey, is just showing me how big his dick is and that he can get close to me if need be."

"Smart guy, Declan, even if you didn't finish high school. I don't think you understand what can go wrong with your friend Big Mike over there. I can have him transferred out to the Super Max at Pelican Bay in California if I want. He'll be on lock-down for twenty-three hours for the remainder of his three-year sentence. He'll come out of that place not knowing his own name and drooling like a newborn baby. That much I can *promise* you."

"Fuck you, fed!" Mike said. "I can do time anywhere—Walpole, the Bay, wherever. Don't listen to him, Declan, and don't give him what he fuckin' wants."

"Thanks, Mike. Agent Carey, I don't think you are playing by the rules here. Mikey has nothing to do with this, and yet you're making him part of it."

"Declan, my friend, rule number one is that there are no rules."

"Okay, then I will offer you what I offered Connor."

"Connor? Connor who? Quinn! What the fuck, Declan? You're messing with Connor too? Declan, what the fuck are you in to?" Big Mike asked.

"It's better that you don't know, Mike."

"I'm listening," Agent Carey said.

"I'll offer you silence. Not a word about what I have ever has to see the light of day just as long as Connor and you stay away from me, Mikey Jr., Big Mike, and my family. And one last thing, Agent Carey, since no rules apply here, I will need something from you."

"What's that, Declan?" Agent Carey said, his inquisitive smirk.

"I want Big Mike here transferred from Walpole to Middleton regional. If you do that, then we are like two passing ships in the dark that never have to see port. Keep in mind that I have several copies of that out there should anything untimely happen to any of us," Declan said, as he pointed to the manila envelope on the table.

"Is that all, Declan?"

"No, when Mike's parole hearing comes up in the next six months, I don't want any interference. In fact, a nice letter of cooperation from you would go a long way—don't you think, Agent Carey?"

Another knock at the door and Agent Jones stepped in with Father Callahan.

"Hey, it's Father C.," said Big Mike. "It's a Southie reunion!"

"Mike? What are you doing here?"

"I'm a guest of that asshole fed over there," he said, pointing to Agent Carey.

"Ah, now it's starting to make sense," Father C. said.

"Well, Father, you found us. You can take Declan home now. We just needed to chat—that's all," said Agent Carey.

"I'll be filing a complaint with your supervisor; that's for sure, Agent Carey," Father C. said.

"Having the archbishop call the Director in Washington wasn't enough, Father?"

"That was just to get your attention. If you go near my client again, without proper cause, I'll have your badge!" said Father C.

Agent Carey motioned to Declan. "Declan, you can go, but I think that we'll be in touch real soon. Not to worry, Father C., I'll call first."

As Declan left, he whispered in Agent Carey's ear, "Think about what I said, Carey. You had better make that transfer and parole happen, or when you go home tonight, check behind your son's dresser drawers. I left you a message."

"We'll be in touch, Declan," Agent Carey said.

"Look forward to it, Agent Carey."

As Big Mike was escorted out of the interrogation room by Agent Jones, Father C. shouted, "Mike, keep going to Mass up there. Father Gregory says that you've been a regular and that you have been participating in his workshops. Keep it up!"

"Will do, Father."

"Mike, see you this Saturday," Declan said.

"Look forward to it, Declan, and some answers," Mike said.

Walking out of the interrogation room, Declan saw Agent Jones and Agent DaSilva. "Not to worry, boys; I'm sure that we'll be seeing each other again real soon." And as Declan was walking toward the main elevator, he shouted, "Hey, Jones, just do yourself a favor and come *out* already. I'm sure Agent DaSilva will be cool with that."

Agent Jones was about to walk toward Declan, but Agent Carey motioned for him to stay put.

THE EXPLANATION

"Declan, what the hell was that?" Father C. asked.

"Look, Father, I told you that there was nothing to it, and as you saw, they let me go. They just had some questions for me—that's all."

"Questions? What did the federal government want from you, Declan? What questions? And why did it involve Big Mike? I thought that you weren't in the life, Declan? You've done everything right ever since you got back from the war and out of McLean. And remember, I vouched for you!"

Declan shrugged. "It's better and safer that you don't know, Father."

"First of all, I'm your attorney of record, and nothing you tell me can ever go anywhere. Secondly, and most importantly, I am your priest!"

"Father, I told you. There is nothing to it—nothing at all."

"Nothing to it, huh? Nothing to it when three carloads full of agents pick you up on the street in broad daylight and pull guns on you, Mikey, and your son? Does this have anything to do with the incident at the Triple O and Connor a few weeks back?"

"Man, how do you know about these things, Father? You were supposed to be preparing for your sermon that morning."

"It's a small parish, Declan; you know that. I'm still part of the community, and I hear things."

"Can't get into it, Father, because I don't want to put you in jeopardy. You've done a lot for me, Mikey, and the neighborhood. I can't have you in harm's way. I can take care of myself."

"Declan, I will need to know, because if anything happens to you, we need to think of Liam."

"I have, and I've been meaning to talk to you about that. Let's get out of here, and let me take you to lunch."

"Okay, let's go grab a slice and a Pepsi at Sal's."

"Good idea. Did you drive or take the T?"

"Are you kidding? Parking over this side of town is too expensive. I took the T," said Father C.

"Okay, good, pizza is on me."

As they walked toward the Green Line subway station, Declan asked, "So what's this about the archbishop and the director of the FBI?"

"Well, let's just say that Archbishop Matthews owes me a couple of favors," said Father C.

"Well, sorry you had to reach into that bag, Father C."

"That's what it's there for, Declan, no worries."

Fifteen minutes later they reached their stop, Park Street Station, only a couple of blocks from Sal's.

"Hey, Sal," said Father C.

"S'up, Father C.? Hey, Declan. The usual for you, Father C.? And you, Declan, what can I getcha?"

"Two number ones with Pepsi please," said Father C.

"You got it, Father."

They got their food and sat in a corner booth next to the entrance window. Father C. said, "Okay, Declan, what's going on here? And please pass the pepper flakes and garlic salt."

"Well, first of all, Father, I haven't told really anyone, so don't feel bad. Remember when I had those headaches a few months back? You advised me to go to the VA to see what was going on."

"Yeah, but you said that it was nothing, as I recall."

"Well, during my last visit, they received the results of all my tests. I was diagnosed with pituitary tumors. The doctors at the VA told me I have twelve to twenty-four months at most. I haven't even told Liam yet."

The priest's face dropped. "Oh, Declan, no, you've overcome so much. I'm so sorry."

"Thanks, Father, but I've made my peace with it. My only regret is that I won't be there for Liam, especially since Eileen passed away. Father, the thing at the Triple O with Connor and this bullshit with that fed Carey—it's all because I have some information on them both. Please, Father, don't ask me what it is because I don't want to lie to you, nor do I want you to get messed up in this bullshit."

"Listen, Declan, without asking, I can only imagine what it is. I get it, but do you know what you're getting into? Connor is one thing, and I can handle him, but the feds? Talk about being in both ends of the dung pile here."

"Father, seriously, all I asked from Connor was to stay away from Mikey and Liam when I am gone and not allow them to get mixed up in his bullshit, especially with his crew."

"And how would you do that if you are gone?"

"Two guys in my old unit have the exact info I shared with Connor, and if anything happens to me or the kids, they'll take care of it."

"And Connor agreed to this?"

"He didn't have a choice. Not to mention, I gave him some incentive to know that I meant business."

"And Agent Carey?"

"I offered him the same deal, and I left something for him in his house so that he knows I'm serious."

"And is that going to work?"

"We'll know in a few days. If not, well, let's just say that this has implications outside of Boston."

"How bad is what we're talking about here?"

"It's bad, Father, like Moses parting the Red Sea bad."

"Declan, what do you have that can keep the devil and his keeper at bay?"

"Silence, Father, silence. And if what I have on them sees the light of day, the North End and Providence will start a war in Boston against our guys on the Hill. The feds in D.C. will be running for cover, and Connor will either be dead or on the lam for the rest of his miserable life."

"Interesting, Declan, very interesting. So Liam knows nothing of this?"

"Nope, neither does Maggie, Mikey, or Big Mike, although I will tell him as much as I have told you this weekend when I visit him."

"Got it, Declan; just let me know what I can do to help you."

"Well, Father, I have been advised by my physician at the VA to start to get my affairs in order. He is going to begin an aggressive protocol of chemotherapy at Mass General next week, and we'll see what happens. I just need to figure out what to do with Liam. He's only eight years only, with no living relatives. Maggie and Mikey are barely hanging on. Big Mike, who I love like a brother, is a question mark when he gets out. That may leave foster care as the only option, and I can't have that."

"What about the guys in your unit who are part of this thing?"

"Maybe, Father, maybe. They have families of their own, and the construction business has been tough. They are barely scraping by. No room at the rectory?" Declan said with a smile.

Father C. laughed. "I wish there were, Declan; I really wish there were. He's a great boy, that Liam, compassionate, respectful, loyal, and he is a fantastic student. You know what? When the time is right, let's see what Archbishop Matthews can do for us if need be. Maybe we can work things out with one of the Catholic boys' homes or something along those lines? But about this diagnosis. I think we should get a second opinion. One of our parishioners, Dr. Suldan, is a cancer specialist at Dana Farber."

"Father, my guy, Dr. O'Neil, is a good guy, and based on the background that I've done on him, I'm okay with his diagnosis. Let's just enjoy Sal's mastery of pizza for now."

SOUTH BOSTON LITTLE LEAGUE

PRIOR TO THE START OF the 1980 Little League season, Father C. was contacted by a longtime parishioner, Judge Michael Mahoney, about a family matter that needed his attention. Judge Mahoney was a federal judge appointed to the bench by President Carter in 1978. Judge Mahoney and his family had been parishioners at Holy Cross for over forty-five years, even though he lived on Beacon Hill and there were several other Catholic parishes closer to his residence. Judge Mahoney was a local kid who'd made good and stuck to his roots by continuing to donate time and money to Holy Cross parish.

The problem that the judge needed to discuss with Father C. was his son, Raymond "Ray" Mahoney. Ray was a special-needs child who had Down syndrome. Ray had what is known as "functional Down," which means that he attended a mainstreaming school, could ride on a bus or subway independently, could hold an entry-level job, and could eventually live on his own with minimal assistance. One of Ray's passions was baseball. He was an avid Red Sox fan and had been playing organized baseball with Beacon Hill Little League since he was five years old.

As a twelve-year-old, this was to be Ray's final year of Little League and most likely his last year of playing organized baseball. But four weeks prior to the season starting, the board of the Beacon Hill Little League (BHLL) advised Judge Mahoney, by registered mail, that his son would not be asked back to participate in Little League this year due to liability of the league because of Ray's disability. The letter that was sent simply stated that Ray could not play, "for the safety and well-being of his son and the rest of the athletes."

The judge was appalled by this action, especially since his friends and neighbors who were on the BHLL board had blindsided him. Furthermore, the judge was not given the opportunity to counter this and explain why his son should be allowed to participate. On top of that, the Little League season was supposed to start in just a few weeks.

As soon as the judge was notified of the board's decision, he immediately filed an injunction against the Beacon Hill Little League and District Nine. In addition, the judge filed a federal discrimination lawsuit against the National Little League organization because he felt that they were not in compliance with the Americans with Disabilities Act. The judge then contacted the editors of the *New York Times* and *Washington Post* about this story in an attempt to evoke a response from the president of the National Little League, Andy Foils. The judge then went on to make local news by pointing out this discriminatory practice through op-ed pieces that he wrote in the *Boston Globe* and in the *Boston Herald* regarding his son, his disability, and his plight with the BHLL.

Within a week of both op-ed pieces hitting newsstands, along with the inquiries from both the *Times* and the *Washington Post*, and the federal lawsuit reaching the Little League headquarters, Andy Foils flew up to Boston to meet with the judge and the BHLL board. The goal was to see if they could come up with a better understanding of the situation and resolve this matter amicably and before the season started.

The judge won his point. A lot of sour faces marched out of that boardroom. Father C. was grinning.

THE SOUTH BOSTON INDIANS

"OKAY, FATHER, NOW THAT RAYMOND'S playing this summer is out of the way, I have to break the news to Ray that he can't play his final year of Little League baseball with the kids he grew up with."

"Mike, Raymond is a zealous Sox fan, right?" asked Father C.

"Yeah, why?"

"Well, let's tell him that he was traded to the Southie Little League just like Fred Lynn was a few years ago when he left the Sox for the Angels."

"Okay, but why do I tell him he was traded? Lynn left for bigger money than the Sox were offering and the chance to play back in Southern California, where he grew up."

"Let's tell him that he was traded because his new team, the Indians, needed a right fielder with his fielding ability and that he was heavily recruited."

"Okay, let's go with that. So you want him to play on the Indians?"

"Yes, the team is run by a man named Declan O'Hara, who works at our parish. You may have seen him around. He's the custodian at our church, and he collects offerings during Mass."

"I think I have. He's a big guy. Right? Well built? Occasionally walks around in the fall and winter with an olive military jacket?"

"Exactly, that's him. He was a war hero of sorts over in Vietnam. He earned a couple of Purple Hearts, a Silver Star, and a few other commendations. He doesn't talk about it much; other people have advised me of his service awards. At any rate, he will be Ray's coach. Also, his son, Liam, is the team captain and a wonderful young man. Liam is a talented musician and takes Chinese language lessons, if you can believe that."

"Chinese? You're kidding me."

"No, it's the darndest thing watching him have a conversation with tourists who are lost in Boston and giving them directions."

"Wow! That's impressive! I'd like to meet both of them if that's okay, Father. I just want to tell them a little bit about Ray, the circumstances, and hopefully the boys on the team will be understanding."

"Declan is fully aware of the situation, and he actually requested to meet with you privately first and then be introduced to Ray with Liam."

"Perfect! That is even a better plan. Thanks, Father! Maybe you and the O'Haras would like to come over to our house for lunch this Saturday? What do you think?" asked the judge.

"Sure, we'll be there," said Father C.

"Wonderful news, Father, wonderful news! I'll talk to Ray tonight, and hopefully we can meet this weekend."

On Saturday morning, just before going to Judge Mahoney's house, Declan said, "Come on, Liam, we're going to be late. We have to pick up Father C. and then go to Newman's Bakery to pick up some coffee cake and fig squares."

"Okay, I'm ready. You know Father C. is *never* on time, though, so what's the rush?"

"He promised me that he would be on time this time," said Declan.

They waited fifteen minutes outside of the Holy Cross rectory, and then out walked Father C. "Sorry, guys, confession ran about ten minutes over. Have you been waiting long?"

"See, Dad, I told you he would be late," Liam said with a smile.

"Ha, ha, Liam. Another word from you, and I'll put you on the late-night acolyte schedule," said Father C.

"Hey, I was just kidding, Father, and I have seniority there!"

"And I trump your seniority."

"I know; I know. Jeez, I was just kidding, Father."

"No, Father, we weren't waiting long. No big deal. Although I did have to tell Liam to stay away from the fig squares we picked up."

"You're bringing fig squares? Nice touch! What do I owe you?"

"Please, Father, we're good. So do you have the address?"

"Kind of. I have the address, but he said that it was the biggest brownstone on the Hill and we couldn't miss it."

"You mean that big brick brownstone on Washington Street?"

"I guess; it sounds about right. Yup, One Hundred Twenty-One Washington Street is the address that I have."

After navigating Boston's notoriously bad traffic and maze of one-way streets for thirty minutes, Declan said, "Okay, I think that's the place. Boy, it's big—I mean really big! How many people in his family live there?"

"Well, there *were* five of them; however, his wife, Eleanor, and two daughters, Charlotte and Savannah, were hit by a drunk driver and killed," said Father C.

"Sorry to hear that. I think I remember that accident. It was on I-Ninety-Five south a few years ago. Right?"

"Yes, that was the one. It took the judge a while to get over it and move on. It still remains a struggle for him from time to time to understand why things happen the way they do, but he has to move on for Raymond's sake. Raymond is his life now."

"Understood, Father, understood. Thanks for letting us know. Liam, you get that?"

"Yes, Dad, understood."

"Take a right up here after Mass General and then another right on Winthrop Street. It should be at the top of the hill. Yes, there it is, One Hundred Twenty-One Washington Street."

"No friggin' way! Just two people live here? This might be bigger than our school, Father."

"Well, actually four people live here. The judge, his son, and they have a live-in nanny, Ms. Chow, and her husband. She's been with the Mahoneys for over twenty years now. She has her own living quarters on the first floor with a separate entrance as well."

"Look at that—they have a private driveway and a garage in downtown Boston, no friggin' way!" Liam said.

"Liam, language!"

"Yeah, Dad, got it."

"Yes, the judge said to just park in the driveway, and there shouldn't be an issue," said Father C.

"Will do."

As we walked up the steep front stairs to the entrance, they saw Ray peeking through the third-floor window.

"Good afternoon, Ms. Chow."

"Good afternoon, Father," she said in a deep Chinese accent.

"Please allow me to introduce you to two friends of mine, Declan O'Hara and his son, Liam."

"It's a pleasure, Ms. Chow, a pleasure. And this is my son, Liam."

"Greetings," Liam said in Chinese with an American accent.

"Oh my, your son speaks Chinese quite well!"

"Thank you, he's still learning, but he's getting there."

"Thank you, Ms. Chow," Liam said in Chinese.

"Gentlemen, please come in. The judge and Raymond are expecting you. May I take those and put them out," she said, reaching for the bakery box.

"Yes, by all means, please."

"Judge, this is the gentleman whom I was speaking of, Declan O'Hara. Declan is the manager of the SBLL Indians; and this is his son, Liam," Father C. said.

"Judge, nice to meet you. I've heard a great deal about you."

"And I of you, Declan."

"This is my son, Liam."

"Nice to meet you, sir," he said with a firm handshake and looking the judge directly in the eye.

"Nice to meet you too, Liam. I'd like to introduce you to my son, Raymond; he likes to be called Ray," he said as he whispered in Liam's ear.

"Ray, this is Liam and Coach O'Hara. Can you say hello?"

"Hello," said Ray sheepishly.

"Raymond loves baseball, and he's looking forward to being part of your team, Liam. Ray, why don't you go show Liam your room while we grown-ups chat for a little bit."

"Okay, Dad. Come on, Liam. Do you like the Red Sox? I've been to seven games this season already."

"Yeah, I'm a Sox fan, and I've been to a few games this year too. Who are your favorite players?"

"I like Jim Rice and Butch Hobson."

"Yeah, they're good, but I like Dewy and Yaz."

"Oh, me too."

They walked up the first flight of stairs. There were two bedrooms on the second floor, along with a laundry room and a full bath. Liam had never seen laundry being done on a floor other than the basement, but it made sense when he thought about it. Why carry the laundry up and down several flights of stairs if you don't have to? As they walked up to the third floor, Liam saw the master bedroom, which was arguably bigger than their entire apartment, and then two empty rooms, another full bath, followed by Ray's room.

"Wow, Ray, you have a really nice house."

"Well, it's my dad's house, but this is my room."

"So, what do you do if you're tired after baseball and don't want to walk all the way up here?"

"Oh, we have an elevator."

"I was kidding! Seriously, you have an elevator? You're kidding me. Right?"

"Nope, at the end of the hall is an elevator. I never use it, but my dad and Ms. Chow use it on occasion. It was in the house before my dad bought it. I had two sisters and a mom you know."

"Yes, I heard. I'm sorry, Ray."

"That's okay. They're in heaven with God now, waiting to see me and Dad someday. That's what Father Callahan says, and priests don't lie, you know."

"Yes, I know priests don't lie. Is that a picture of them?"

"Yes, that's Charlotte to the left. Savannah is to her right, and my mom's in the middle."

"Wow! They're beautiful. You're a lucky kid. My mom is in heaven too. She passed away from cancer a few years ago."

"Maybe your mom knows my mom and my sisters in heaven? My dad really misses them. I hear him cry sometimes, especially on the date that God took them to heaven. I know I'll see them some day because Father C. says so. We visit them every week at our family cemetery, and I bring flowers sometimes."

"That's great, Ray. I visit my mom at the cemetery too. Hey, I like your room. Those are really nice posters of the Sox. I see you're a Celts and Bruins fan too."

"Yeah, the Sox and the Celts. Larry Bird is my favorite Celtic."

"What's in here?"

"That's just a closet with my clothes."

"No frigging' way—that's a lot of clothes, Ray."

"My dad takes me shopping a lot for school clothes."

"Where do you go to school, Ray?"

"It's a private school called the Fessenden School just a few miles from here. I'm on the student council."

"Cool. Hey, you have a TV in your room too, huh?"

"Yeah, but my dad only allows me to watch it if my homework is done before eight thirty p.m. on week nights and nine thirty p.m. on weekends."

"You're lucky!"

"How's the team going to be this year? I played for the Tigers on my Beacon Hill team. I played right field," said Raymond.

"We're good. We're young, lots of ten- and eleven-year-olds, but good. You'll play a lot."

"My old team would sometimes only let me get one at bat and play a half inning on the field."

"You're kidding me. Right?"

"No, it was awesome!" Ray said with a smile as he motioned like he was taking a swing with a bat in his room.

"Well, we'll let you play a lot more than that on our team; we'll need you to—"

"Really? I'll have to talk to my dad about that."

Downstairs they were conversing about South Boston back in the day and how things had changed over the years.

"Thank you, Ms. Chow, for setting out the pastry. And thank you, Declan and Father, for bringing the coffee cake and fig squares. Is this from Newman's Bakery by chance?"

"Of course, the best in the city!" said Declan.

"Excellent! They *are* the best in the city! So, Declan, tell me about yourself? The good Father here tells me that you work at the parish and that you were in the service."

"Yes, I've been working at the parish for the past couple of years. I started a little while after I got out of the corps."

"Father Callahan tells me that you were awarded several commendations for your service."

"They were mostly unit citations, Judge."

"And your rank was marine gunnery sergeant?"

"Correct, at the height of my rank, but some things changed at the end of my second tour, though."

"I was over there as well, you know," he said, pointing to a picture of himself and four other senior officers at the Saigon HQ on his mantle, "a lieutenant colonel, First Air Cavalry. I was in Theatre Operations Headquarters, strategy, in Saigon in the late sixties, early seventies."

"So I heard."

"Forgive me, Declan, but I am very protective of my son, Raymond; he is all that I have left in this world. In your service file, it says that you were discharged as a cook?"

"Service file? Michael, was that really necessary? I've known Declan since he was a boy. I vouched for him, and he is a good man!" said Father C.

"No, that's quite all right, Father. I would do the same due diligence myself, especially if it pertained to Liam."

"Still, this is a bit invasive, Michael; he's a friend of mine," said Father C.

"Father, ninety percent of his service file is dedicated. That can only mean one of a few things: Black Ops, CIA, or he was off the grid in places that he shouldn't have been."

"That's fine, Father, really. Okay, the reason why I got busted in rank, Judge, is because I was part of an unsanctioned rescue operation that crossed a few unauthorized borders. You see, I was a POW in the province of Quango Nam for about seven months, but I escaped. After making it back to a US outpost in Phi Yen, I was transferred to a hospital in Saigon for debriefing. While I was recuperating in Saigon, I received a call from my lieutenant's father, Hunter Daniels Sr."

"*The* H. D. Daniels, the oil magnate? You know that he is one of the richest men in America?"

"Yes, that's correct, but I was unaware of who he was at the time, not that that would have made a difference. He was asking me about his son, H. D. Jr., who led our platoon that was captured in an ambush just south of Dong Ha. Mr. Daniels informed me that the military advised him that they would *not* attempt a rescue of his son and the remaining members of his unit because the POW camp was too far north of the seventeenth parallel. Even though I was at the end of my second tour, and I was scheduled to be on my way home, as soon as I heard what he was planning to do, I offered to go back in the jungle after them and see if I could help. I knew the location of the camp, and I was familiar with the terrain since my escape, so I had to do something. After a few weeks of planning and recon, I and a few other marines were dropped in north of the camp by some contracted helicopter pilots, and we were fortunate enough to free five out of the six remaining prisoners. Unfortunately, one member of our unit died in captivity from malaria."

"Just a couple of things, Declan. How did you, with your lower rank, secure an air drop *and* an airstrike north of the thirty-eighth parallel?"

"That's a funny story, Judge. From what I understand, Mr. Daniels called in some major favors with the Texas Air National Guard and the State Department. He had them blanket napalm on a good chunk of real estate a couple of clicks north the POW camp after we got out."

"I vaguely remember hearing something like that. But if you got the guys from your unit back safely, they usually pin medals on guys like that. What happened?"

"Well, we had a long way to go after we found the guys from our unit, and nobody wanted to pick us up that far north of the thirty-eighth parallel, so I had to slow the North Vietnamese down. In order to slow them down, I had to do some things that would make them think twice about following us. That, combined with the fact that we crossed through Laos, resulted in my court-martial and that of the other participants. I made peace with what I had to do to get the guys out of there, but the State Department thought otherwise, and we were made examples of."

"How did you get away without doing time in the brig then?"

"Well, Mr. Daniels stood up for me at my court-martial hearing. His son was still recuperating months after his rescue, but he sent a note that was read in open court by Senator Kennedy. In addition, his father had half of the US Senate write letters in support of my actions. In the end, I was put in McLean Psychiatric Hospital for six months as a compromise with the military court. So, look, Judge, that's everything you need to know about me and even some things Father C. did not know; if you want Ray to play on another team, I'll more than understand."

"Declan, I'm proud to have Raymond play on your team. I truly appreciate your honesty, integrity, loyalty, and service to our country. Father, he even has more character than you claimed. I will be proud if you will allow me to call you a friend as well." The judge reached out to shake Declan's hand.

"Friend it is, Judge. And since we are new friends, can you please pass me a fig square before they are all gone?"

"Ha! By all means. Father, what's your poison, coffee cake or fig square?"

"I'll have a slice of coffee cake and some tea, please."

"Ms. Chow, some tea for the good father, coffee for the rest of us, and milk for the boys, please. Thank you."

At that moment, Ray and Liam came running down the stairs.

"Dad, Dad, guess what, guess what?" Ray said.

"Raymond Mahoney, what did I tell you about interrupting adults while they are in the middle of a conversation?" the judge said with a smile.

"Right, right, excuse me; excuse me. Dad, guess what?"

"What, Ray? What's so important?"

"Liam is a Red Sox, Bruins, and Celtics fan too!"

"That's fantastic! See, I told you that you would have a lot of things in common."

"That's not the *big* news, Dad."

"Okay, Raymond, what is the big news?"

"Liam's birthday is next week, and he invited me to his birthday party! Most of the team will be there and a few of his other friends as well. Can I go, Dad? Please, please, Dad, can I go?"

"Yes, yes, of course."

Raymond turned to Liam. "Liam, I'm coming! I'm coming!"

"That's *great*, Ray, but remember, the only rule of the party is no gifts. It's just a party with some cake and ice cream, okay?"

"Okay, boys, go grab something to eat," the judge said. "I just want to talk with Father Callahan and your dad for a minute more, and then we can all eat together."

"Declan, Father, do you realize what just happened there?"

"No, what?" asked Declan.

"This is the first birthday party that Ray has *ever* been invited to—outside of his immediate family of course. You see, the kids on his Beacon Hill team over the years never asked him to do anything socially. And when Ray invited them to his party, they would either be conveniently out of town, just sent presents in the mail, or never showed up at all. I can't thank you enough."

"To be honest, Judge, I didn't have anything to do with this. You, Father?"

"No, I forgot it was Liam's birthday next week, but thanks for reminding me."

"Well, then, you have a wonderful boy, Declan."

"Thank you, Judge."

"Declan, what can we bring? What does Liam like?"

"Thank you, Judge, but that is completely unnecessary. The reason why Liam doesn't want or need any presents is because he realizes the financial hardship most of his friends and their families are under. He just doesn't want to embarrass the friends who can't afford anything; that's all. What will truly make him happy is that you share his cake and song."

"What a nice young man! Okay, we'll be there, sans presents, but our voices will be heard throughout South Boston!"

THE CHAMPIONSHIP GAME

As the final year of the Little League season concluded, the last game of the year was against the league-leading Oakland A's (Mikey's team) and Liam's team, the second-place Indians.

Mikey was on the mound pitching for the A's, and he was arguably the best pitcher in the league. His fastball topped off in the mid-seventies; that's why he was 8–0 this year. Liam was pitching for the Indians, and they were down 0–2 after five innings. So far, Mikey had struck Liam out three times already, and he knew he was going to hear it from him throughout the summer. It was the last inning, and Liam's team was down to their final three at bats. Unfortunately, Mikey was showing no sign of fatigue. No matter how much trash Liam yelled at him from the dugout, it only seemed to fuel him. As Liam was about to get his helmet for his final at bat, Declan approached him with his clipboard.

"It seems like Mikey's got your number today."

"I think I have him this time, Dad."

"What do you say we give Ray a shot?"

"Ray? But, Dad, there's a guy on first, and I *know* I can hit him."

"Look, Liam, you've had a great year. You'll be playing again next year. This is Ray's final year of baseball. They won't let him play organized baseball beyond this year. What do you say? The decision is yours."

As he put his helmet on and approached the plate, all he could hear was Ray yelling and cheering me on. "Come on, Liam, you can hit him! You're the *best*, Liam; come on."

"Yeah, Liam, come on, what do you say we make it oh for four and four strikeouts?" said Mikey from the mound with an arrogant grin.

As Liam approached the batter's box, he looked at Ray and then at Mikey on the mound and then back at Ray.

"Hey, ump, time out. Ray, our first-base coach is going to pinch hit for me."

"You're kidding, right, Liam?" said Mikey from the mound.

"Come on, Ray, we're switching places; you're up!"

Liam gave Ray his bat and helmet and instructed him to *only* swing at good pitches. Declan called a time-out and came to the plate to give Ray additional instructions about how to swing.

"Remember, Ray, keep your head down and your eye on the ball, just like we practiced."

As Declan left the batter's box, he stared at Mikey on the mound. Mikey looked back at him and simply nodded. Mikey's fastball averages in the low to mid-seventies. When Ray stepped to the plate, everybody in the stands was cheering for him. As Mikey was about to pitch the ball, he looked at Liam coaching at first base and winked. Mikey then wound up and lobbed the first pitch over the plate like a softball pitch. Ray swung and missed, but not by much. The next pitch Mikey put in the dirt, and Ray was grinning from ear to ear. The third pitch was over Ray's head. The count was now two balls and one strike. The fourth pitch was right over the plate again, and Ray fouled it off. Judge Mahoney was screaming and cheering and smiling from ear to ear. Everybody was cheering for Ray, even the bench of the A's. Just then, a chant began from the stands: "Ray-mond, Ray-mond, Ray-mond!" The fifth pitch was right over the middle part of the plate, and Ray didn't swing.

There was a long pause and silence throughout the park. Ray looked down at the plate and then turned back at the umpire. The silence in the stands was deafening. The umpire looked at Ray and then over to his right at Father C. and then to his left at Declan and said, "Ball three!" Father C. nodded and smiled back at the umpire. The shouts for Ray got even louder from the stands. Liam was just telling him to keep his eye on the ball. For the final pitch, Mikey wound up, threw another lob over the plate, and Raymond made contact! It was a slow ground ball directly to the pitcher's mound. Everyone yelled, "Run, Ray, run!" Mikey fielded the ball cleanly, and he could have run the ball to first base to get Ray out if he wanted. Instead, Mikey got the ball, looked at Ray, and then launched the ball over the first baseman's head into the outfield. Ray was safely on first base, and the crowd was standing. Mikey went to first base after retrieving the ball from the outfield and handed it to Ray. Mikey smiled at Ray and said, "Next time, I'm going to put the pitch right between your eyes," as he walked back toward the mound. Ray was waving to everyone in the stands, especially his father.

As things settled down, the umpire called, "Play ball!"

The next two batters went down in a total of six pitches from Mikey. Liam's team eventually lost the game and the league title. But in the end, it was all worth it.

ALL-STAR TEAM SELECTIONS

LAST YEAR, MIKEY AND LIAM were the only eleven-year-olds fortunate enough to make the South Boston all-star team. The rest of the team was comprised of twelve-year-olds.

Declan was explaining some new rules to the judge, "After Father C. and I reviewed all the eligible players who were not going away to camp, traveling, or moving away, we both decided that we would like to extend the last slot to Raymond. Now, I know that you and Ray had plans to go to Europe this summer, so just think about it, and let me know by tomorrow if you can. Is that enough time, Judge?"

"Declan, are you serious about this? Really? We can go to Europe later this summer or even next year. Do you have any idea what this will mean to Raymond? He will be ecstatic! You know, just between us, Ray begged me to ask you and Father C. if he could work out with the all-star team. No need to have the discussion with Ray about our trip to Europe—we're in!"

"That's great, Judge; glad to hear that! We're happy to have him on the team. May I please speak with Raymond and let him know the good news?"

"Sure, one moment please. Ray-mond! Ray-mond! Telephone."

"Telephone?" said Ray.

"Yes, please pick up the phone; it is for you."

"Really? Who is it?"

"It's Coach O'Hara."

"What does he want?"

"Raymond, please, the phone is for you. You can ask him what he wants yourself."

"Hi, Coach. Did you find my SpongeBob watch?"

"No, Raymond, sorry about that; we couldn't find your SpongeBob watch. We looked everywhere, though."

"Oh, that's okay, Coach. Thanks for looking. So what's up?"

"Well, Ray, we would like to extend an invitation to you to be part of the all-star team this year."

"Really, Coach, really? On the team? Are you serious?"

"Yes, we begin practice in a couple of days. We start this Saturday at two p.m., and the first game is in two weeks. So do you want to be on the team?"

"Yes, yes, yes! Thanks, Coach. I can't wait to tell my dad! Good-bye, Coach, and I'll see you and the guys this Saturday at two p.m."

Raymond hung up the phone and ran downstairs. "Dad, Dad! Guess what? Guess what!"

"Raymond, what did I tell you about running and yelling in the house?"

"I know, but I made the all-star team! I'm an all-star!"

"See, Raymond, I *told* you that if you worked hard and stay focused with your tasks, good things will happen for you."

"You were right, Dad; you were right!" said Ray, hugging his dad.

"Ms. Chow, Ms. Chow, I made the all-star team! I made the team!"

"Good, Raymond—good for you! We're so proud of you!" Ms. Chow gleamed with a smile and hugged Ray.

"Dad, can I call Liam and see if he made the team too?"

"It's a bit late now, Ray; how about we call him in the morning? It's time to go to bed now."

"Okay, Dad, okay. I'm an all-star! I'm an all-star!" Raymond chanted, walking back upstairs to his room and off to bed with a huge smile on his face.

The Birth Of The "Seamrog Dubh"

AFTER THE FIRST WEEK OF all-star practice, the team really looked like they were making progress, especially with Mikey on the mound and Liam behind the plate. They found out that the district brackets were selected last night and that the matchups would look like this. In the north bracket, the winner of the Charlestown–South Boston game would play the winner of the Chelsea-Dorchester game. In the south bracket, the winner of the Roxbury–East Boston game would play the winner of the Beacon Hill–Hyde Park game. The district final would be between the winners of the north and the winners of the south. The district finals would be played at Beacon Hill on their new turf field.

Two weeks into all-star practice, they hit a major hurdle. During a routine examination of their playing field by the US Environmental Protection Agency (EPA), the city of Boston suddenly condemned their practice field because of suspected contamination in the soil. The city immediately closed the field until further studies could be conducted. Basically, they were screwed for a practice field, and their first game was less than a week away!

Now they were forced to use the asphalt area of the church's parking lot to practice. They were only allowed to hit balls into the fence (to work on our hitting and timing), and fielding ground balls and fly balls was just a question of dodging the parked cars and potholes.

"This sucks!" Liam whined. "We get screwed at every turn, Mikey. No field, our equipment is broken, and we can't even hit ground balls because Johnny keeps tripping over those friggin' potholes in the parking lot."

"No shit, I wonder what other teams doing, while they wait for practice in the parking lot to begin," said Mikey. "Hey, I know what we can do to kill some time. Let's see if you can hit my new fastball."

"Your *new* fastball?"

"Yeah, Liam, I have a new grip; it's a two-seamer just like LT. Just get up in the batter's box."

"Mikey, Father C. said that we're not supposed to hit balls here because there are too many windows in the neighborhood that could be broken."

"Seriously, Liam, what makes you think you can hit me anyway?" Mikey said with a grin.

"Fine! Just shut up and pitch!"

"Liam, just do me a favor; promise me that you won't cry when you *can't* hit what I'm throwin', okay?"

"Funny guy! Just be prepared to get the ball when I hit it in the Charles River."

"Remember, Liam, you can't hit what you can't see," Mikey intoned with a grin.

As Liam lined up against the chain-link fence, there was a square taped off, outlining the strike zone. To his left was Father C.'s beat-up 1976 Honda Accord. To his right was the monsignor's brand-new Ford Taurus. One step outside the batter's box, and he'd be smashing the side-view mirrors of those cars.

Mikey was five feet eight and using a milk carton as a mound. He was about to start his windup.

The first pitch went by Liam, and he barely saw it as it was dead center against the fence.

"Should I throw it underhand, Liam? Maybe then you can hit it that way?"

"Screw you! Just pitch the damn ball!"

"Watch out, Liam, here it comes."

Mikey gave his famously elongated Louis Tiant imitation windup and delivery.

"Strike two!" shouted Mikey. "This isn't even fair! Who's next? I'm wasting my time with you. Are you sure you made this all-star team, young man? Maybe Sister Michelle can swing for you."

"Screw you, Mikey—I'm not out yet."

"I'm not positive, but didn't I say that you'd be out in three pitches? Wait; let me check my notes." Mikey flipped through a fake notebook. "Yep, here it is on line number four. He said, 'Three pitches'! Here comes number three!"

He swung at that pitch with every ounce of muscle that he had.

Smack!

As they looked at the ball leaving the parking lot, Mikey and Liam chorused, "Holy shit!" The ball was heading out of the yard directly at a brand-new Volkswagen Jetta parked right across the street from the church.

Bang!

It hit dead center in the windshield of the Jetta, and the car alarm sounded. Everyone on the team scattered except Mikey and Liam. As they walked toward the car, Liam dropped the bat (evidence), and a guy in a blue Red Sox ball cap came running out of one of the new assisted-living buildings across the street. It turned out that this guy was Doug Chase, who used to live in the neighborhood.

"Shit! I was praying it wasn't my car! I just got the thing! Hey, did you kids see who did this? What happened?" he said as he clicked off the alarm.

"I kind of know," Liam said.

"What do you mean you 'kind of know'?"

"Well, it's like this." Pointing to Mikey, Liam said, "He kind of pitched the ball, and I kind of hit it over the fence onto your car."

"Seriously?"

"Yeah, that's what happened," Liam said. "To be honest, mister, it's kind of your fault."

"My fault? Okay, this ought to be good. Just how is that my fault?"

"Well, first of all, you are parked illegally; you're double-parked on a street that does not allow double-parking. And you're parked in a loading zone for class-two trucks. And that doesn't look like a truck to me," Liam said, pointing to his Volkswagen Jetta. "Lastly, you don't have a Southie sticker on your car."

"What does that have to do with anything?"

"It just means that you're not from the neighborhood. People with that sticker are left alone. Non-Southie residents will get their cars jammed up."

"Truth be told, I grew up here. I was just visiting my mother, who's in this new senior care facility." He pointed to the building behind him. "I just ran up to her room with some of her belongings."

"Hey, rules are rules," said Mikey.

"Funny, kid. So who is going to pay for this?"

"Tell you what," Mikey said. "I'll send you to Frankie's shop up the street, and he'll cut you a deal. That should cover any deductible you have, and you split the balance of the claim with him."

"Frankie still runs that chop shop? Are you kidding me?"

"Who said chop shop? Not us," said Mikey. "What are you—a cop or somethin'?"

"Please! Do I look like a cop? And what if I was a cop?"

"Yeah, right, we would have made you walking out of your car. Not to mention, you're wearing New Balance 1600s. Those puppies are two hundred bucks apiece. No cop would be wearing two-hundred-dollar sneakers."

"What if I got them at the outlet?"

"Nope, they're not seconds. I can tell because there is no dot on the heel above the number. Those are first-run shoes."

"What are you—a future cop?"

"Hardly, if you grew up around here, you know then what to look out for, even basic shoes," said Mikey.

"Hey, what are you guys doing playing ball here anyway?"

"Doug, is that you?" Father C. interrupted.

"Father Callahan?"

"My boy! How are you? Liam, Mikey, do you see this young man? Do you know who he is? He's a local kid who made good. He is a Pulitzer Prize–winning writer! As a cub reporter, he wrote about the plight of inner-city bussing in South Boston in the midseventies. So what brings you back in the neighborhood, Douglas? Are you writing another piece?"

"No, nothing like that, Father. My mother just moved into this assisted-living facility across from the parish, and I was just dropping off some of her stuff. As it turns out, I am returning one of your baseballs."

"My baseball? How so? What do you mean?"

"Yeah, it says 'SBLL' on it," he said as he rotated the ball in front of the boys, "and you're still running things over there, aren't you?"

"Yes, but what are *you* doing with it?"

"Well, it apparently fell out of the sky into my windshield."

"Boys! We discussed this! You were explicitly told *not* to take batting practice in the parking lot! Did I not explain this to you? You both will need to pay for this."

"But, Father," they protested.

"But Father nothing!" the priest mimicked. "Now you will learn your lesson! Liam, I'll be advising your father about this incident later this afternoon. And, Mikey, I'll tell your father when I see him this weekend."

"It's okay, Father, really. Not to mention, this one over here," Doug said, pointing to Liam.

"Liam," said Father C.

"Yes, Liam—he explained to me that it was really my own fault that my windshield is broken."

"Really, how's that?" said Father C. Liam started to shrink.

"Well, Liam eloquently pointed out that I was illegally double-parked *and* that I was parked in a loading zone when I did not own a truck. He then went on to point out the two signs that state this fact as well."

Doug pointed to the signs to his left.

"Then this one over here," he said, pointing to Mikey.

"Mikey," said Father.

"Yes, Mikey—he advised me that *any* car without a Southie sticker was fair game and that I should be aware of neighborhood rules."

"Really, how nice of the boys to enlighten you; nevertheless, they will pay!"

"No, seriously, Father, I'll take care of it. Look, they didn't run. They owned up to it right away. Consider it a donation to the Little League. But tell me, Father, why are you practicing here when I thought that I read somewhere that you have your own field now?"

Liam interrupted, "Because the field was condemned late last month."

"Condemned? What do you mean—condemned? Did they find some of Connor's bodies there or something?"

Mikey and Liam looked at each and then directly down at the ground. Everyone in the neighborhood knew never to joke about Connor and *anything* that he might or might not be associated with.

"Liam is referring to some soil contamination. You see, Doug, carcinogens were found in the soil by the EPA when they were conducting their annual tests on landfills. The levels were very low, but the city and state wanted to be cautious. Actually, I can't blame them because they are looking out for the health of the kids, but the timing is terrible. Since we lost our field, and all the other parks were reserved months in advance, we can only practice in the church's parking lot before our game this weekend. It's tough, but we manage."

"I can see that you guys are tough and resilient. Speaking of which, when did they allow twelve-year-olds to get tattoos?" asked Doug as he pointed to the ink just above Mikey's bicep.

"What do you mean?" asked Liam.

"It's nothing," Mikey said, lifting up his left sleeve and showing him a drawing of a black shamrock inside a circle with the term "Seamrog Dubh" written around it. "Liam has one too; show him, Liam." Liam lifted up his sleeve.

"What does that mean?" asked Doug.

"It's Gaelic for 'Black Shamrock,'" Liam replied.

"Is that your gang or something?"

Liam laughed. "No, nothing like that. Are you kidding me? We read about it in our history class. It's about when the Irish immigrated to Boston around the 1820s. It represents the struggle of the Irish here in Southie, that nothing will keep us down. We may not have a lot, but we have each other. We take care of our own, that's what *seamrog dubh* means."

"You're kidding me, right? Father, is that *really* what it means?"

"Yes, that's exactly what it means. It seems to unite the boys. It teaches them valuable lessons about looking out for your fellow man, faith, and community," said Father C.

"And these kids are what—eleven, twelve years old?"

"Yes, that's about right," said Father C.

"This is unbelievable. Father, would you mind if I speak some to the boys individually and then with the rest of the team? I'd like to write a piece about them. I promise that it will be a complimentary piece. I would like to focus on their plight, the obstacles that they've overcome, and how they've bonded together against all these odds to become a successful team."

"Not a bad idea, Father; we could use the positive press. Maybe we'll get some donations for the league and even the church," said Mikey.

"Okay, why not? I'll make some of the boys available for you to meet with after I call their parents for permission first. Doug, why don't you come by our practice tomorrow, but just remember to park your car around the corner this time so that there are no more mishaps. Remember, our first game is this Saturday in Charlestown against the Charlestown American team. The game starts at one p.m., so you had better get cracking on that article."

"You got it, Father! I'll be here tomorrow, the next day, and the day after that to make sure I get everything. I may have to take the bus to the game because my car might still be in the shop," he said with a wink to both boys, "but I'll see you at one p.m. Good luck this weekend, Father, and you too, boys!"

"Thanks, Mr. Chase!" Mikey and Liam chorused.

"Boys, please, just call me Doug."

"Boys, what on earth were you thinking? Didn't we have this conversation about hitting practice in the yard?"

"Yes, Father," both said together.

"Okay then, you guys will be picking up and transporting all the equipment to and from these games from now on. Are we clear?"

"Yes, Father," both said in chorus again.

"Well, then, we'll just keep this matter between ourselves for now. No need to trouble your parents. But if this happens again, I will be forced to speak with them. Now go. Go collect all the equipment."

"Yes, Father!" said Mikey.

"Yes, Father!" Liam said.

"Boy, we really dodged a bullet there, Mikey, didn't we?"

"I'll say! Although I'm not sure what I am more shocked about? Father C. giving us a pass like that or the fact that you actually hit my pitch? It's a coin toss," said Mikey with a smile.

"Screw you, Mikey! If Doug's car wasn't in the way, that ball would be still going!"

"Whatever makes you sleep at night, Liam, whatever."

Southie's Black Shamrocks

Three days later, an article came out on the front page of the sports section of the *Boston Globe*. There was a picture of Mikey and Liam showing their faux tattoo that read, "Seamrog Dubh," while flexing their muscles through a chain-link fence in the church parking. They were all wearing their SBLL all-star hats while Ray was jumping on top of them both, smiling and goofing around.

I was first introduced to the South Boston Little League all-star team when I discovered a baseball that belonged to them found its way dead center on the windshield of my brand-new car; seriously, the car was just three days old. On the mound was a stocky young man named Mikey Maguire, who was using a discarded milk carton as the mound. Mikey stands five feet eight inches tall and has a gregarious personality for a twelve-year-old kid. By all measure, he is the best player on the South Boston Little League (SBLL) team. His best friend, Liam O'Hara, is a very strong but wiry young man. Liam stands five feet seven inches tall, and he was at the plate. Liam grew up with Mikey in the same Southie housing projects along with most of their teammates. Liam is more reserved and cautious when meeting strangers. After getting to know the boys a bit, it turns out that Liam is an accomplished pianist who also enjoys reading and math. Mikey, on the other hand, enjoys drawing, and he is currently on scholarship taking art classes at the Fine Arts Museum. Mikey hopes to someday become an architect.

It turns out that the boys were taking batting and fielding practice on the asphalt of Holy Cross Church's parking lot because their practice field was condemned by the EPA. The boys were afforded the opportunity to practice here because the South Boston Little League's president, Father John Callahan (Father C.), who has been running the league for over twenty-five years, is the senior priest at Holy Cross. Several years ago, Father C. started the league with the hopes of offering the boys of South Boston an alternative to the streets. The sixteen boys from the SBLL all-star team lost the use of their home field because carcinogens were found in the soil of their home field. The EPA was performing their annual soil tests on area landfills (where the SBLL field is currently built over), and they found high levels of benzo, pyrene, polychlorinated biphenyls, and mercury. The city and the state immediately closed the field until further tests could be conducted. The result was that the boys had to find a new location to practice. All the other area fields were reserved, and the only other option was the church's parking lot.

Back to my car. Usually, when kids hear the crack of a pane of glass, in this case my windshield, they scatter like scared mice and run for the hills. However, this was not the case with Mikey or Liam. These two young men did not run, nor did they deny their act. Rather, they stood their ground and took responsibility for their actions—and even offered restitution for the cost to repair my windshield. Liam advised me that all this really could have been avoided if I wasn't illegally double-parked in a loading zone, as he pointed to two signs that clearly stated, "Commercial Vehicles Only" and the other sign adjacent to it that stated, "No Double-Parking." Liam went on to say that, to some extent, the cracked windshield could be construed as my fault because I wasn't paying attention to the street signs. I ask, how do you argue with a twelve-year-old who espouses such sound logic?

As I got to know the boys and the rest of the team a bit more, I discovered that these are all remarkable young men. Eighty percent of the team members are from single-parent households. Several of their parents are either in jail or have died on the streets of South

Boston. *Two of the players and their families are homeless, and three others are in group foster homes for boys. The team uses dated equipment with cracked helmets and bats. Their all-star uniforms are basically T-shirts that were printed at the local hardware store. This is in sharp contrast to the shiny new equipment and uniforms that all the other leagues have at their disposal. In fact, most of the kids on the SBLL are using aged baseball gloves that they either received from Goodwill or were hand-me-downs from family members. To repair the gaping holes in some of their gloves, the team has been using the services of a local shoe-repair shop owner who knows how to work magic with leather materials.*

I was especially impressed with the team's center fielder, Rick Perryman (the only black player on the team), and his makeshift glove. Ricky is legally deaf in one ear and uses a cochlear implant in the other. In addition, Ricky is fluent in ASL (American Sign Language) to assist him with his day-to-day communication. Most of the team knows rudimentary sign language so that they can communicate with Rick as well. Basically, Rick's glove is constructed from bits and pieces of three different glove manufacturers. The frame of his glove is from a Wilson-A2000 model. The remaining pieces of webbing are leftover pieces from a Mizuno catcher's mitt and a Rawlings outfielder's glove. Ricky hasn't made an error in over two years.

The last player on the team that I would like to tell you about is Ray Mahoney. Ray is the team's reserve right fielder and a special-needs child who has Down syndrome. Ray came to be part of this team after he was unceremoniously kicked out of the Beacon Hill Little League (BHLL) two weeks before the season was to start because of his disability. Ray's father, Federal Judge Michael Mahoney, subsequently filed several lawsuits against the BHLL and the National Little League Association on behalf of Ray. The final terms and conditions of the lawsuit were not disclosed. However, as a result of his action, Ray was allowed to play as part of the South Boston Little League this year, and the Beacon Hill Little League was subsequently fined several thousands of dollars as a penalty. Unfortunately, trying to interview Ray proved to be very challenging even for this veteran reporter. It was not a difficult discussion due to Ray's disability; rather, it was because all he wanted to talk about was a hit against Mikey Maguire in the championship game a few weeks prior. Ray was going on and on about how he broke up Mike's no-hitter (as Mikey Maguire was fielding ground balls nearby and overheard what Ray was saying).

Mikey started to walk toward us during the interview.

Ray quickly looked up at me and said, "Shhh. Please don't say anything about my hit. Mikey gets really upset when I talk about it."

Mikey politely interrupted the interview to tell Ray, "Hey, I heard you're talking trash again, Ray. Just remember, even a blind squirrel finds a nut once in a while," he said as he smiled, hugged Ray, and walked away.

What was remarkable to me as I was researching this story was that, with all the obstacles that these kids encounter and hardships that they endure, I never heard a single complaint from any of the boys. They never focused on all the things that they didn't have; rather, they chose to focus on what they did have, and that was each other. The team's mantra is "Seamrog Dubh," which is Gaelic for "Black Shamrock." Loosely translated, it means that even though things may seem dark and bleak at times, they can always count on one another for support. If one of their own needs a roof over his head, food, money, or whatever, they can go to each other for assistance without judgment. Several of the players have makeshift tattoos (a circled clover insignia) drawn on their left shoulders just above their bicep.

The real lesson to learn here is that through the eyes of these disadvantaged eleven- and twelve-year-olds from South Boston, we can still find faith, humility, and compassion among ourselves.

The South Boston Little League's first game is tomorrow afternoon at one p.m. against Charlestown American, in Charlestown. Please come out and join me to support the team. I'll be the guy driving the car with the cracked windshield.

If you wish to support the team financially on their quest for a state title or donate equipment to the South Boston Little League, please send your tax-deductible donations to the Cathedral Church, Attn.: Father Callahan.

At five thirty a.m. Saturday morning, the phone was ringing at Doug Chase's apartment.

"Doug?"

"Yeah, who is this?"

"It's Jake, your editor!"

"Jake? What are you doing calling me before the sun's up?"

"I'm your boss, and I can call whenever I want."

"Okay, what's up?"

"I'm getting calls."

"Calls?"

"Yeah, about your article already."

Shuffling through the notes next to his bedside table, Doug struggled to get his bearings. "Listen, Jake, I checked those facts against the housing authority's own records. Their outside bid practices were a joke—"

"No, not the piece about the bid rigging. That puff piece on those kids from Southie."

"The Little League kids?"

"Yeah, that one."

"Okay, what about it?"

"I'm getting calls from the mayor's office, city councilmen, everyone. Hell, even Jean Yawkey called me."

"They called you already?"

"Yeah, they must have read the early edition."

"Wow, I never thought those people woke up that early."

"Yeah, well, they do."

"Okay, so what do you want me to do?"

"You're following these kids until they lose."

"Yeah, I was going to the game today anyway."

"No, you don't get it—until they lose. Look, based on what you wrote, it looks like it will just be a couple of weeks, no big deal."

"No big deal? I was going on vacation next week."

"Consider it canceled. Just go after they lose, but you get a quarter of a page for each game they play and then a follow-up article when they lose. Got it?"

"Okay, got it. Hey, Jake, since this could be considered research and I'm stuck on this story, what do you say to the *Globe* covering the deductible on my cracked windshield?"

"Whatever, okay, fine. Just follow these kids and get some more in-depth stories. People are eating this stuff up!"

CHARLESTOWN AMERICAN
LITTLE LEAGUE

IT WAS GAME DAY AT the O'Hara and Maguire households. Excitement was in the air.

"Liam, here's ten bucks; go see if Mikey is up; then go to Perry's Grocery Store around the corner and get the paper, some eggs, milk, juice, pancake mix, and I'll make you guys some pancakes for breakfast. Also, see if Maggie wants some too."

"Okay, Dad, on it. I'll be back in ten minutes. Thanks!"

He knocked on Mikey's door.

"Good morning, Mrs. Maguire, is Mikey up?"

"Sure, come on in. Mikey's in his room getting dressed; go ahead in. Hey, Liam, big game today, huh? Good luck!"

"Thanks! We'll be ready."

"I know Mikey is looking forward to it; he couldn't sleep."

Liam walked down the hallway to Mike's room and went in. "Mikey, let's go! My dad gave me money for supplies. He's making us pancakes in twenty minutes."

"Pancakes? I'm in! Let's go."

"Mrs. Maguire, my dad says that you're invited too."

"Thanks, Liam. Please tell your dad that I appreciate the offer, but I have to go to work. Mikey, my shift ends in the afternoon, and I'll to make it to the end of your game."

"No problem, Mom. I understand; thanks!"

Mrs. Maguire gave Mikey and Liam each a kiss on the forehead and said, "Boys, be good, play hard, and bring home a win!"

"Will do, Mom!"

"Sure thing Mrs. M."

As Mikey and Liam walked to Perry's, they saw a piece of cardboard with a circle shamrock that read, "SEAMROG DUBH," in his window.

"Hey, Mikey, look. That's our mark!" said Liam.

"Hey, Mr. Perry, what's up with jacking our mark?" asked Mikey.

"Your mark? Well, it's out there now, guys."

"What do you mean?"

"Didn't you read the *Globe* yet?"

"No, why?" asked Mikey.

"There is an article in there about you boys."

"You're kidding. Right?" he said.

"No, here it is."

"Holy shit! Look, Liam, it's a huge picture of me, you, and Ray. The article is all about us and the team."

"Hurry—hurry; get a couple of papers and the other stuff my dad wants, and let's get out of here."

The excitement was spreading. Even at the store. "Here you go, Mr. Perry. What do I owe you for the eggs, milk, juice, pancake mix, and papers?"

"Nothing boys, this one's on me; now go beat those kids from Charlestown!"

"You serious, Mr. Perry?" Liam said.

"Go ahead, boys, and keep it up. Represent the neighborhood proudly!"

"You got it, Mr. P., and thanks!" said Mikey.

"Hey, Liam, if I knew we were going to get that stuff for *free*, I would have thrown in some bacon and donuts."

"Be thankful for what we got, Mikey."

"Okay, but we can keep the ten bucks. Right? I mean, since this stuff was free?"

"You never give up, do you, Mikey? It's my dad's money, and no, I'll have to give it back."

"Hey, just askin'."

Mikey ran into his apartment to show his mother the article before she left for work.

"Mom, Mom, take a look at this. I'm on the cover of the sports page!"

"What? What's this? What a great picture of you boys! Let me read what it says," she said and paused as she read the article. "What's this about a windshield?"

"Nothing, Mom; read further. Why are you focusing on the negative?"

"Okay, okay. Oh, this is so nice, Mikey. I can't wait to show your father."

"Yeah, me too."

At his apartment, Liam said, "Dad, here's your change," as he handed him the same ten-dollar bill that his dad gave him twenty minutes ago. "And take a look at this." He showed him the *Globe* article.

"Change? I gave you ten bucks, didn't I? What's this?"

"Yep, and Mr. Perry *gave* everything to us for free!"

"You and Mikey didn't steal this stuff, did you?"

"Dad, come on, no! We know better than that! Not to mention, we know never to steal inside the neighborhood," Liam said with a smirk.

"Not funny, Liam. Why would he give this stuff to you for free?"

"Because of the article."

"Article? What article?"

"Here, look," Liam said as he handed his father the *Globe*. "And there is a picture of me, Mikey, and Ray on the *cover* of the sports page."

"Wow, there certainly is, and you guys look great! Hold on one second."

Declan picked up the phone and dialed a number.

"Dad, who ya' callin'? It's pretty early," Liam said.

"I know; just wait a minute; this is important."

"Hello, Tommy; it's me, Declan."

"Hey, Declan, what can I do for you? Everything okay? Mikey and Mags okay?"

"Yeah, yeah, everything is fine, nothing like that. I need a favor."

"Sure, what can I do for you?" said Tommy.

"Can you pick up a *Globe* and give the sports section to Big Mike when you make your rounds this morning? Liam and Mikey are on the cover, and there is a nice story about the boys in there. I know that he would like to see it as soon as he could."

"One second, I have the paper right here in front of me. Let me see what you're talking about. Yep, there it is. Sure, Declan, no problem."

"Hey, Tommy, I really appreciate it."

"No problem, Declan. Tell the boys good luck today against Charlestown."

"Will do, Tommy, and thanks again," Declan said as he hung up the phone.

"Good idea, Dad!"

"Yeah, I thought that Big Mike would like to see the article. I know he's looking forward to hearing about the game as well," Declan said and read on. "Now what's this about a broken windshield?"

"Dad, Mikey and I offered to pay, but Doug, the reporter, said no and that his paper would cover the deductible because he was doing research on a story."

"Okay, but you know you should tell me about these things."

"Yes, sir."

"Now go get Mikey; pancakes in fifteen minutes."

"Hey, Mr. O, did you see the article? That picture makes my guns look huge!" Mikey said as he pointed to his photo on the cover of the sports page.

"Yeah, well your father may not like the ink you put on there."

"It's not permanent, just like Liam's."

"Liam and I are having a conversation about that shortly, Mikey."

Liam winced. "Thanks, Mikey, just what I need, another lecture!"

"And that's what you'll get, Liam. No tattoos! This comes off when you guys lose, okay?"

"Agreed, thanks, Dad!"

"Now you both go wash up for breakfast. The game is in a few hours."

Later that day at the Charlestown American field, they began to take infield practice. This was our first practice on grass in over a week. Mikey was all warmed up on the mound, and they were ready to go. As Declan and Father C. approached home plate to hand over the lineup cards to the umpire, Paul Richards, the manager and president of the Charlestown American team, shook their hands and exchanged his lineup card.

"Hey, Declan, Father C.," he said and nodded toward each of them. "I read the article in the paper about your boys. It was a nice piece."

"Thanks, hopefully they'll stay focused for the game today," said Declan.

"Look, if your boys win today, why don't you use our field to practice on for the remainder of the tournament. I'm sure the parish wants their parking lot back."

"That's very generous of you, Paul. We may take you up on that if we're lucky enough to win today. And yes, the parish doesn't want any more broken windows," Father C. said with a smile.

"Well, if that Maguire kid is pitching today, then it's us who will need the luck."

Mikey went the distance, and they beat Charlestown 6–2 in the opening round of the tournament. Next up was Dorchester, who'd beaten Chelsea by one run in extra innings. On the other side of the bracket, Beacon Hill soundly beat Hyde Park by eight runs, and Roxbury beat East Boston by four runs.

After the *Boston Globe* article hit the newsstands, the team became celebrities of sorts around town. At the Charlestown game, for example, the crowd was three times the size of our normal games, and people were carrying homemade signs and towels that read, "Seamrog Dubh" with their circled shamrock logo.

After the Charlestown game, everywhere in South Boston they saw their mark in windows of houses, apartments, and area stores. The team was now doing interviews with local papers; people were sending donations to the South Boston Little League, and neighborhood kids were even copying their logos on their arms with pens and markers as a sign of support. Just before the Dorchester game, while practicing on the Charlestown American field, they received brand-new uniforms that rivaled what the Major League Red Sox were wearing. They were a donation from the Triple O tavern, which meant that they were from Connor Quinn. Everyone in and around town was rooting for them. What was unique about these uniforms was that a patch of our mark was on the right shoulder of these uniforms.

The next game against Dorchester was a pitching duel in which Liam edged out a tight 2–1 win. They were actually losing 0–1 in the top of the sixth inning because Liam gave up a solo home run. In the bottom of the sixth, their last at bats, Rick Perryman walked on four pitches, and then Mikey got up and blasted a two-run walk-off home run over the right-center-field fence. The paper's headline read, "The Luck of the Irish Prevails: Southie Kids Win Again!" In the other bracket, Beacon Hill beat Roxbury 5–1. The district championship game would feature South Boston versus Beacon Hill. This was the furthest that a South Boston Little League team had ever gone within the district tournament, and now they could provide a little payback to the kids who shunned Ray.

As the Beacon Hill game approached, Ray was giving them the breakdown of each player and their strengths and weaknesses. Ray advised them that Beacon Hill's best player was Mike Desimone (their first baseman), but he couldn't hit a curveball to save his life. He also went on to tell them that their catcher, Bob Wasserman, had a wild arm and couldn't throw down to second base accurately at all. On their side of the field, Mikey would be on the mound for them, so they felt pretty good about their chances. Ray's father, Judge Mahoney, was at each practice this week, cheering them on and telling them to stay focused. They all wanted to win; Judge Mahoney wanted revenge! Father C., on the other hand, wanted to win because a South Boston team had never gone this far in the tournament. The team wanted to win because they just wanted to stick it to those rich kids on the Hill. And stick it to them they did! They were up 9–0 by the end of the fifth inning, and then they started to empty their bench so that more kids could play; even Ray had an opportunity to play right field for an inning. Liam had never heard the judge scream louder at a game. Beyond their win, the crowds kept getting bigger and bigger for their games. They were finally District Nine champions! This was the first championship in South Boston Little League history. The next game would be the bi-district eliminations, followed by a regional elimination game, and then to the Massachusetts state finals, which represented the top four teams in the state.

After beating Tewksbury in the bi-district game by a score of 6–4, the team fell behind in the regional finals game against Canton by three runs. They were never that far behind in any of their games. The "long ball" strategy (hitting home runs by the key players) was clearly not working as Mikey and Liam each struck out twice. Father C. and Declan decided to play "small ball," which consisted of bunts, stealing more bases, and just trying to hit singles, to chip away at the lead one run at a time. Unfortunately, they were running out of innings. Eventually, the strategy worked as the Canton team kept throwing the ball all over the field when the boys bunted and stole bases. They finally tied the game in the bottom of fifth inning with three consecutive bunts, five stolen bases, and four throwing errors by Canton. The score was now 4–4 going into the fifth inning. They eventually took the lead when Josh Fillmore hit a solo home run over the left-field fence. This was Josh's first home run of the tournament, and the team escaped with a 5–4 win. Southie was now regional champs and headed to the state finals!

State Finals: Worcester

EACH YEAR AT THE STATE finals, there is a master of ceremony selected by the Massachusetts Little League Board of Trustees. This individual throws out the ceremonial first pitch, gives a speech at the team banquet on the Friday night before the games, and awards the championship trophy to the winning team that will represent Massachusetts in the eastern regionals. This year's master of ceremony was former Major League baseball player Mark "the Bird" Fydrich. Mark was a local baseball legend who grew up in a town just a few miles from Worcester called Northborough. Mark was the perfect selection by the committee because he often remarked throughout his career that his fondest memories in baseball were while he was playing Little League ball.

After practicing on the new fields, the boys saw their competition for the first time, Hyannis. They were a cocky bunch of kids who paraded around the practice field as if they owned it. To be honest, they ran their infield like a military regiment. They were very precise and skilled. Just by watching their warm-ups, Mikey immediately pointed out their top player, a kid named Nick Hirou. Just then, the East Lynn team pulled up to the field to practice after Hyannis. Their captain, a kid named Cameron Pedro, came over to introduce himself.

"Hey, what's up?" Cam said, with an upward nod of his head in a friendly tone.

"Not much, you?" said Mikey.

"You guys from Southie?"

"Yup, I'm Mikey, and this is Liam." They reached out to shake Cameron's hand.

"And you're from Lynn."

"What gave it away?" he asked as he pointed to his sweatshirt emblazoned with "Lynn Pop Warner Football."

"You're their pitcher, aren't you?" said Cam.

"One of them, anyway," said Mikey.

"No, but you're the one everyone is talking about. Right?"

"Well, it's either me or Liam."

"No, it's you."

Liam frowned at his friend. "Why are you feeding into his ego, man? He's already got a big head!"

"Ha! No more, I promise," said Cam. "You see that kid over there?" he asked, pointing to the big first baseman. "His name is Hirou; he's a total prick!"

"You know him?"

"Nope, just the type. Arrogant piece of shit. Thinks he owns the world. I hope that you kick the shit out of those guys. I look forward to playing you guys on Sunday."

"What makes you think you'll be in the finals?" Liam asked.

"That's easy: I'll be on the mound," Cam said with a smile as he started to walk back toward his teammates. "Oh, and by the way, guys, *seamrog dubh*," Cam said with a wink.

"He's a pretty funny kid. Huh, Mikey?"

"Yeah. He seems cool enough."

"We'll see what he's got tomorrow against Springfield."

"Sure will. But let's get going. We have to get back to the hotel and wash up before the banquet."

At the banquet dinner, the team captains were seated at the dais table next to Mark Fydrich and the Little League board members. Mike and Liam were sitting next to the Hyannis captains, Nick Hirou and Pete Garrett. The entire Hyannis team was each dressed in blue blazers, white oxford shirts, yellow ties, khaki pants, and penny loafers. They all looked like they came straight out of a Brooks Brothers catalog. Mikey and Liam were just dressed in polo shirts, their gray church pants, and dress shoes. The rest of the team wore a mixture of jeans and dress pants. The Springfield team all had on white polo shirts with khaki pants and dress shoes. They looked like they were dressed for a Mormon mission. The guys from Lynn were in jeans and polo shirts.

While at dinner, they quickly found out how arrogant, intolerant, and bigoted the Hyannis team was. In front of the dais table were the Southie team tables. Ray kept waving to Liam and Mikey and trying to talk to them throughout the meal. He would get up and call to them, asking them if they needed anything or if they could get Mark Fydrich's autograph for him. The team noted that Rick Perryman was signing when dinner was being served. Basically, Ricky was asking the serving staff for more drinks. While all this was going on, Liam overhead Nick Hirou (Hyannis's captain) speaking to his co-captain, Pete Garrett.

"Hey, Pete, look at those kids from Southie," he said, pointing to the table in front of them. "Look at the black kid; he's using gang signs," Hirou said with a smile and a laugh.

"Yeah, and I can't understand that other kid either. He keeps yelling up here, but I can't figure out what the hell he's saying. I don't speak retard, do you, Nick?" said Pete, as they both started to chuckle louder.

Liam leaned over to Mikey and told him what each of them said. Mikey was fuming! Mikey and Liam waited for Father C. to finish the dinner blessing; then they got up and walked over to Hirou and Garrett just as the appetizers were being served.

"Hey, if either of you two open your fuckin' mouths again or I hear you talk shit about any of my teammates again, I'll take that shrimp cocktail and shove it up your ass," Mikey said.

Hirou quickly jumped up from his seat and stuck his chest out. "You kids from Southie think your tough shit. I'll say whatever the fuck I want to whomever I want. So go mind your own fuckin' business!"

"You guys are really fucking tough making fun of a deaf kid and a kid with Down syndrome," Mikey said.

Just then, the Hyannis head coach, who was also Hirou's father, jumped in the middle of this heated exchange as blows were about to be thrown.

"Boys, boys, what's going on here?"

The Hyannis guys acted innocent. "I don't know, Dad; we were just eating our dinner, and these two came over and threatened us. Isn't that right, Pete?"

"Yup, that's right, Coach. We didn't say a thing."

After the blessing, Father C. saw the group getting heated and headed over toward the boys. "Coach, what's going on here?" asked Father C.

"I'm not sure, Father, but it appears that your boys threatened my kids. Your boys need to learn some manners."

"Fuck you!" Mikey said.

"Mikey!" Father said with a stern voice.

"See what I mean, Father?" said Coach Hirou.

"No way, Father! They said that they couldn't understand Ray because 'they didn't speak retard.' And that other piece of shit," Mikey said, pointing to Hirou, "said that Ricky was using gang signals when he was just signing for more drinks."

"Is that true, boys?" asked Coach Hirou.

"No, sir," chorused both boys.

"Well, Father, apparently they are liars as well. What are you going to do about it?"

"Boys, let's just go back to the hotel," said Father C.

"But, Father," Liam said, "we didn't do anything, and Mikey is telling the truth, me too."

"I know; let's just go for now," Father C. said and grabbed both of them by the sleeve and walked them toward the exit.

As Mikey and Liam were walking toward the exit, Mikey heard something. "Don't worry, boys; what do you expect from white trash like that," said Coach Hirou.

All Liam saw was a blur. Mikey broke away from Father C.'s grip and ran toward Coach Hirou and his son. Mikey wound up and cold-cocked Coach Hirou, hitting him in his right temple. Coach Hirou buckled to one knee, and then Mikey went after his son. Before Mikey got to the son, Declan tackled Mikey and carried him outside.

As Father C. and Declan were screaming at both and reading them the riot act about the way they were acting, Cameron Pedro, the captain from the Lynn team, came outside with his coach, Bill Cannon.

"Excuse me, Father."

"Yes, Coach, how can I help you?"

"Well, Cameron here wanted you to know something."

"You see, Father, I was sitting on the other side of the dinner table next to the Hyannis kids, and I overheard their entire conversation. I just wanted you to know that every word that your boys said was true. The Hyannis kids lied."

"Thanks, Coach Cannon, and thank you, Cameron, but this is still no way to act."

"Be that as it may, Father, if it were my kids they were talking about, I would have done the same thing," said Coach Cannon as they returned to the banquet.

Mikey and Liam headed toward Declan's car, and they headed back to the hotel. After Declan heard what the guys from Lynn had to say, he whispered in their ears that he was proud of them for sticking up for their friends.

Father C. went back inside the banquet hall to be with the rest of the team and calm them down. Just as Father C. was sitting down and assuring the rest of the team that everything was fine, Coach Hirou from Hyannis got in front of Father C.

"Father, I assume that you will be suspending that boy for accosting me and my son."

"I will take that into consideration and review what action we take, if any, with my other coach."

"What is there to review? You saw that kid hit me."

"Well, you called him 'white trash.' And your son and the other young man made racial and bigoted remarks toward his teammates. Is that not correct?"

"No, my boys said they never said those things; your kids lied."

"Actually, Coach Hirou, we heard from a third party that your boys did indeed make those disparaging remarks about our players, so you might want to speak with them about what the 'truth' really means. In addition, you may want to sit with them and teach them to be more tolerant and understanding of people with special needs."

"You know, Father, if you weren't wearing that collar, we would be having a completely different conversation. And who is this mysterious third party you're talking about?"

"I am not at liberty to say who this individual is, but this person corroborated everything my boys said. Furthermore, he came forward on his own volition, so I believe him. This does not by any means excuse my boys' behavior. For those actions I apologize, but I understand why they did what they did. Oh, and by the way, if I chose to drop this collar, rest assured, I would drop you as well," said Father C. while staring Coach Hirou directly in the eye.

The team at the table was completely silent and stunned with Father C.'s firm and supportive manner.

"And you believe them?" asked Coach Hirou. "Is this what they taught you at the seminary? To vouch for hooligans? Just so you know, Father, I have friends who know the cardinal very well, and I don't think that he would like how you are reacting to all this."

"Really? Well, Cardinal Flanagan was my roommate at the seminary, and I'll advise him to expect your call."

"I'm bringing this matter up to the Little League board before the game tomorrow, just so that you are aware."

"As will I, Coach Hirou, as will I."

The following day South Boston played Hyannis.

THE LUCK OF THE IRISH
COMES TO AN END

SOUTHIE LITTLE LEAGUE GETS SCREWED!

THE LUCK OF THE IRISH finally came to an end in Worcester, Massachusetts, as the boys from South Boston Little League lost to Hyannis Little League 2–1 on a controversial call in the bottom half of the last inning. I've seen a lot of things in my life as a reporter, but this one takes the cake. Not since the 1972 Olympics, when the Russians controversially "beat" the US basketball team, have I seen such a travesty and injustice in sports. The only difference between the two incidents is that the United States was playing Russia, and South Boston was playing Hyannis. Simply put, like the United States in 1972, the kids from Southie got screwed!

Against all odds, this group of overachieving youths could not overcome a gross case of incompetence by the Little League umpires overseeing the game. How the Hyannis base runner could have possibly been called "safe" when he was stopped several inches before he reached home plate is incomprehensible. The players knew it; the fans knew it; even the rookie first-base umpire who had the best angle of the play knew it.

These Southie kids overcame a great many obstacles to get here: secondhand equipment, a lack of practice facilities, and even homelessness. But the one thing they couldn't overcome was the incompetence of the umpiring staff at this year's Little League state finals yesterday.

I even asked the master of ceremony, Mark Fydrich, his thoughts on what just transpired, since he witnessed everything firsthand from the press box. His response was telling: "I haven't seen a team get screwed like that since the Red Sox sold Babe Ruth's contract to the Yankees in 1919."

After several protests were lodged, the MLL committee still refused to overrule the umpire's decision. They stated that "human error" was part of the game. After hearing that excuse, I blinked, and it was the 1972 Olympics all over again.

As a footnote to the championship game, I asked the East Lynn team captain, Cameron Pedro, how he felt about playing Hyannis in the final game.

"I feel happy for my teammates, our supporters, and the city of Lynn to be in this position; however, we feel cheated in a way. We all felt as though we didn't beat the best competition in the tournament. South Boston deserved to play us in the finals. I was at the Hyannis game. I saw that it was a bad call by the home-plate umpire, and I would have liked to have seen how a game between our teams would have turned out. I'm sure that we'll meet up with those guys down the road, but for now, this feels a bit shallow. We can't help but feel cheated for them as well; I know I do. Seamrog dubh!"

East Lynn eventually beat Hyannis by a score of 6–2 and went on to win several games thereafter representing Massachusetts in the national tournament. East Lynn eventually lost to Maryland in the eastern regional finals.

THE PASSING OF DECLAN O'HARA

DECLAN LIAM O'HARA, FORTY-ONE, OF South Boston, passed away June 4, 1981, after an eight-year bout with cancer. Born in Dublin, Ireland, Declan moved to South Boston with his parents, Connie (Rourke) and Daniel O'Hara, in early 1941. The family settled in South Boston, where they remained until both parents passed away in a car accident in 1957. Declan attended South Boston High School, where he starred in football, baseball, and basketball. Declan was the first three-sport all-state athlete in the school's history. Declan married his high-school sweetheart, Eileen (Mott) O'Hara, and was a loving husband until her passing from breast cancer in 1974. Declan worked at General Electric for several years as an engine-parts supervisor prior to joining the marines during the Vietnam War. While in the marines, Declan was twice awarded the Purple Heart for wounds that he received during combat, along with a Silver Star for bravery and courage above and beyond the line of duty. Declan was also nominated for the prestigious Medal of Honor when he was credited with saving the lives of several of his platoon members who were captured by the North Vietnamese. Declan and two other platoon members brazenly went behind enemy lines to rescue his comrades from a POW camp and eventually led them to freedom. Declan lived every day with a simple code of loyalty, honor, integrity, generosity, forgiveness, and love. He shared these principles with his family, friends, and even strangers every day of his life. Declan is survived by his devoted son, Liam, thirteen. In lieu of flowers, the family requested to make a charitable contribution in Declan's honor to the Holy Cross Church or the Dana-Farber Cancer Institute.

WHAT TO DO NOW

THANKFULLY, DECLAN HAD FATHER CALLAHAN act as the O'Hara family attorney and as his priest.

Personally, Liam was devastated: a feeling of aloneness overwhelmed him. Thank God for Father Callahan; otherwise, Liam did not know what he would have done without him. How many thirteen-year-olds are supposed to know what to do when their whole world is turned upside down like this? Liam had no living relatives to turn to for support or guidance. And the only family that he ever really knew was gone. There are no instructions on who to contact or what to do when a loved one passes. What preparations need to be made? What happens after the funeral? What does Liam do at the wake? Where will he go? Who will he live with? Where will he sleep? Can he still go to his school? What does he do for money, clothes, and food? What does he do if he gets sick? Does he have insurance? How does he pay the rent? Does he need a checking account? Credit cards? What does he do with his dad's car? Fortunately, his father had the foresight to arrange 90 percent of this prior to his passing. He guessed that in some ways he was lucky, but he missed him terribly!

Father Callahan handed Liam a safety-deposit box. In it was his father's "Last Will and Testament" and some other miscellaneous items. In his will he gave all his "worldly possessions" to Liam, including his 1978 Chevy Nova. With his military benefits, his stocks, and US savings bonds, the total his dad left him was approximately $200,000, which was to be used toward his education. Per Father Callahan, this money was to be used for tuition until he graduated from the Cathedral School. The rent in their apartment was paid through the end of next month, so he could stay there until his room in the basement of the church, an old janitor's residence, was settled. The funeral, wake, and burial arrangements were handled by O'Malley's Funeral Home, something that his father had arranged for prior to his death and paid in full. Declan would be laid to rest at St. Mary's Cemetery next to his mother and his grandparents. Thankfully, there were no outstanding credit cards, medical, or other debt that had to be resolved. The last two items that were in the safety-deposit box were two brand-new Irish passports. Declan must have renewed his passport since he was born in Dublin, and the surprise was his dual citizenship. Liam would have automatically been granted citizenship as his son. That was a trip they often talked about taking together. Someday he'd make that trip to Dublin in his honor.

Dallas, Texas: June 4, 1981

AT THE GLOBAL HEADQUARTERS OF the Daniels Funds, H. D. Daniels, the chairman and CEO, was in attendance for their annual board meeting.

"Excuse me, Mr. Daniels, you have a call," said his secretary, Ms. Moffitt.

"HD, we're in the middle of our meeting here," said Frank Cerano, the head of the Daniels European Fund. "Can't it wait? This is important."

"Thanks for the heads-up, Frank; I'm aware of that since I called the damn meeting in the first place! This isn't Ms. Moffitt's first rodeo. She's been with me for over forty years and knows what is important enough to pull me from this type of meeting."

He paused, as he looked around the room. "Junior, you take over. Remember, just steer the discussion to what we reviewed last night."

"Yes, sir."

HD left the boardroom with Ms. Moffitt. "Ms. Moffitt, this better be important," he said as they walked briskly to his office.

"I believe that it is, sir."

"Okay, what is it?"

"There is a Father Callahan from Boston on the phone for you."

"Father Callahan? I don't know any father Callahan. What does he want?"

"He said that it was a private matter."

"Ms. Moffitt, you know better than that."

"Sir, I think this is different; he knew things about you and your son, sir."

"Okay, I'll handle it. What line is he on, Ms. Moffitt?"

"Line number two, sir."

"Father Callahan?"

"Yes, is this H. D. Daniels?"

"It is. Father, I am a very busy man—how can I help you?"

"As am I, sir, so allow me to get right to the point. Does the name Declan O'Hara mean anything to you?"

There was a pause. "Father, I do know that name very well. My family and I owe that man a great debt, more than you can possibly imagine. If he is in some sort of trouble or needs anything, please let me know immediately."

"Sir, I regret to inform you that Declan O'Hara passed away last night after a long bout with cancer. He passed peacefully at his home here in South Boston with myself, his son, Liam, and his close friends by his side."

"Cancer, you say? I had no idea that he was ill. Father, if you don't mind, how did you know that we were connected?"

"Declan and I were close friends. I am the executor of his will, and he left a note for his son, Liam, to give to you in the event of his passing. I thought that you should know about it."

"Yes, of course, of course. You did the right thing. Thank you, Father. When is the funeral?"

"It is scheduled two days from now on Saturday, the sixth of June, at the Holy Cross Church here in South Boston."

"Father, I am going to transfer you over to my assistant, Ms. Moffitt, in a minute; she will take down all this information. Please tell me, Father, how is his son, Liam, doing?"

"He is doing as well as can be expected under these circumstances."

"Yes, yes, of course. I will be there in two days. I would like to meet with you both privately if I may."

"I look forward to it, as will Liam."

"Father, I'm going to transfer you now, and thank you for the call."

HD transferred the call back to Ms. Moffitt, dropped his face into his outstretched hands, and sat there at his desk for a minute as he reflected on the memory of Declan O'Hara. Ms. Moffitt rang his office shortly thereafter.

"Mr. Daniels, is everything oaky? I have all the information from Father Callahan. Should I have not told you about the call?"

"No, by all means you did the right thing. Please give me a minute."

Several minutes later HD left his office and went back to the board meeting. HD sat down at the head of the boardroom table.

"Everything okay, Dad?" asked Junior.

"No, it was a call about Declan, Declan O'Hara."

"Declan? How is he? It's been over ten years. You know, Dad, I send him his shareholder's statement every quarter. Has he finally responded?"

"No, it's not that." HD whispered in his son's ear. "He passed away last night."

H. D. Jr. abruptly stood up and said, "Gentlemen, please excuse me; I have to leave immediately. I just found out that a dear friend of the family recently passed away, and I must go pay my respects. I will not be back for the remainder of this meeting. Anything pressing that will require a vote will have to be done through a proxy. Ms. Moffitt can address this."

HD followed his son out the door and said, "Gentlemen, we'll have to reschedule this meeting. We are leaving for Boston in the morning. Oh, and Frank, when last I checked, my name is still on the door, so I had better not hear another word from you. Are we clear?"

"Of course, HD, our sincere condolences," said Frank.

As HD exited the boardroom, he waved for his head of security, Mike Colt, a Columbia University–educated former Navy SEAL who'd done two tours in Vietnam and earned several commendations, to come to him.

"Mike, I need you to call Senator Tower's office and tell him that we will need an honor guard in Boston this Saturday. Ms. Moffitt has all the particulars. I'll need you and the team there as well. Wheels up tomorrow at ten a.m. I want confirmation on this matter before we're wheels up. I don't want to call that SOB Kennedy or Tsongas and then owe them a favor."

"Yes, sir. Senator Tower, and wheels up at ten a.m. The team and I will be there, sir."

The following morning HD and Junior were in their office, getting ready to fly to Boston.

"Sir, the team is here, and we're all set to go. I relayed the information to Senator Tower's office but have received no response, sir."

"And he knew that it was me who was calling?"

"Affirmative, sir."

"Give me that damn phone!" HD demanded and started dialing.

"Mary Anne?" said HD. "Is that you?"

"Mr. Daniels?"

"Yes, it is, ma'am. How are you?"

"Fine, fine, sir."

"Good to hear! Is your boss around by chance?"

"No, I'm afraid not. He's in Pebble Beach, playing golf with the secretary of the navy."

"Do you happen to know if he received the message that Mr. Colt provided yesterday?"

"Yes, sir, I took the message myself, and I have been instructed that any message from Mr. Colt is to be considered as if the message came directly from you. That is my understanding."

"Excellent, perfect! That is correct. Please see if you can locate John, would you? I have thirty minutes before we take off. If I do not hear from him within that time frame, it will cause me great concern."

"Absolutely, sir! Is there anything that I can do?"

"No, but thank you, Mary Anne. You have my number?"

"Yes, I do, sir."

Ten minutes later John was on the phone. "HD, how are you? John Towers here."

"Johnny, my boy, how are you? At Pebble Beach I hear. Enjoying the sunny California weather and some golf with Commander Edwards, I hear? Did you by chance get my message from yesterday?"

"Yes, yes, I did, but I'm out here with the DOD reviewing budgets. How are we looking for that fund raiser in Dallas in two weeks?"

"All set in Dallas. We have over a thousand people coming to hear you speak at five hundred dollars a head. Your coffers for the Senate race will be filled. Now, about my matter—"

"Great, great news! About that other thing—I did get your message, and we're running into a bit of a problem there, HD."

"Problem? What kind of a problem?"

"Yes, you see, you are requesting an honor guard for a vet who was dishonorably discharged. And I can't do anything with that."

"That's a mistake! He was honorably discharged on appeal several years ago. Hell, he earned two Purple Hearts and a Silver Star for Christ's sake! Need I remind you what this vet did for me and H. D. Jr.?"

"No, I understand that; nevertheless, HD, his current records show 'dishonorably discharged,' and my hands are tied on this one."

"Listen, I want you to fix this and fix it now! You're the chair of the goddamned Armed Services Committee. Get this done! I land in Boston in three hours, and I want answers. Are we clear?"

"HD, I can give you the answers now. But, like I said, this one's out of my hands."

"Listen, Johnny, you can either get this thing done or enjoy your last days in office. Mark my words."

"HD, I'm a sitting US senator, there is no need to make threats like that."

"Johnny, you know by now that I don't make threats. I simply carry out promises. And I promise you this: if that guard is not set by the time I land in three hours, there will be repercussions."

"HD, I'll see what I can do."

"You had better!" HD angrily hung up the phone.

"Sir, should I make alternative arrangements in Boston?" asked Mike Colt.

"No, this is a simple enough matter for that idiot Towers to clear up. He had better make it happen."

"Yes, sir."

"Thanks anyway, Mike."

"No problem, sir."

"All set to go, guys?" asked HD.

"Dad, I brought Tripp with us too," Junior said, referring to H. D. Daniels III, or "Tripp," for "triple." "He thought that he should meet Liam and know about Declan."

"Great idea, son! I should have thought about it myself. Tripp, you sit next to me. I can tell you where we are going and who this man was whom we are honoring."

"Sure, Grandpa."

"Well, Tripp, no, you never met this man. Nevertheless, we are going to pay our respects and honor him. He is someone who this family owes a great debt."

"How so, Grandpa?"

"Well, this man, Declan, Uncle Mike over there too," HD said as he pointed to Mike Colt, "went in and rescued your father when he was captured by the North Vietnamese during the Vietnam War. You see, this man escaped the POW camp where your father was being held. He was supposed to be discharged after his stay in the hospital, yet he did me a very big favor and helped get your dad out of harm's way."

"Wow! Is that true, Dad, Uncle Mike?"

"Yes, that's the truth."

"Declan was a special man," said Uncle Mike. "I can tell you some stories on the flight."

"Did he get a reward or something for bringing my dad home?"

"No, just like Uncle Mike here, they would not accept any money. They both did it out of respect for your father. What I did do, though, is offer them both jobs and stock in my company. Uncle Mike doesn't have to work now; he just doesn't know what he would do with himself if he wasn't working," HD said with a smile.

"As far as Declan goes, he has amassed quite a sum of money with our company over the past twenty years, but he has refused to claim it. Instead, he told me that if I insisted on doing something for him, I put it away for his son, Liam. Upon his passing, I was to give the money to Liam when he turns twenty. Begrudgingly, I relented and agreed to his terms. So we are going to pay homage to this man and meet his son, Liam. He's about your age, maybe a year or so younger."

Three hours later as they landed in Boston's Logan Airport, HD said, "I see that I have three missed calls from Senator Towers. He had better have good news!

"Johnny, this is HD. I assume that we are all set here?"

"HD, I tried everything, but this is out of my hands. Like I—"

HD hung up the phone.

"Mike, Junior, I want you two to follow up on a couple of things. First, go get in touch with this Father Callahan, and see if there is anything that he or the funeral home needs for Declan's burial. Let me know if he needs money, flowers, whatever. Just take care of it. Then ask Father Callahan if he has any local connections with the military reserves or state or local police—we need that honor guard and flag given to his son. Finally, call Ms. Moffitt and cancel the fund raiser for Senator Towers. Refund all the money through my personal account, and this will now become a dinner for homeless vets in the Dallas area. I want Ms. Moffitt to call Rich Samuelsson, head of the GOP, first and then the top people who were supposed to be flying in from D.C. Tell them this fund raiser is off—and all because Senator Towers is incompetent! Let's see how those sons of bitches like that!"

"Yes, sir."

"On it, Dad."

"Thanks, boys. I'll take Tripp with me back to the hotel. We'll all be at the Ritz Carlton on Avery Street. I would like an update within the next couple of hours. Okay, boys?"

"Will do, sir," said Mike.

Thirty minutes after H. D. Daniels landed in Boston and settled into his hotel room, HD received a call from Rich Samuelsson, head of the GOP.

"HD, Rich Samuelsson here."

"Rich, how are you?"

"I'm fine, but apparently you are not. What's going on?"

"I helped put that son of a bitch Towers in that goddamned office, and all I needed was a bullshit favor, a simple goddamned favor that even a blind monkey could do, I might add. Do you think Lloyd Benson would have this problem? Towers failed me, and now he's out! I don't give a shit what you say or do; that son of a bitch is out. Your best bet would be to distance yourself from him if you ever want my support again."

"Okay, okay. Listen, HD, I get it; you're upset. My job is to fix things. What can I do to fix this misunderstanding?"

"No, no! Don't you dare oversimplify what he did as a *misunderstanding*. A misunderstanding is when you ask your waitress for coffee and milk and she comes back with a tea. What *that* bastard did was step on the memory of a war hero!"

"Okay, poor choice of words, I get it. This is all over an honor guard for a vet? That's it?"

"No, not just any vet, the soldier who risked everything to save my son—that's who."

"Okay, I get it! Hell, if that's what you need, I'll get seven guys with rifles up there by this afternoon."

"Too late. I have sought out alternative arrangements."

"HD, please, what can I do to make this right?"

"Nothing! I never ask twice on matters that are of this grave importance to me, especially as it pertains to my family."

"Well, what about this fund-raising dinner in two weeks? We have over one thousand people planning on attending for Senator Towers."

"It's off! My people will refund all the tickets sold, and the venue will now host an event for homeless vets in the Dallas area. Towers is dead to me."

"HD, please, we have people coming in from all over the country to attend this event."

"That's not my problem. You guys should have thought of that before treating me so callously."

"HD, I'm leaving Colorado in an hour. Can I meet you in Boston?"

"I'll be here through Sunday. I'm staying at the Ritz. I do not want that SOB Towers or any of his cronies to contact me. Understood?"

"Yes, of course. I'll be there in a few hours."

H. D. Jr. and Mike Colt walked into HD's suite.

"Who was that, Dad?"

"Nobody. Just Rich Samuelsson from the GOP."

"What did he want?"

"To apologize, fix it, and keep that damn fund raiser on for Towers."

"And?"

"Nothing has changed! Screw him and the GOP! What have you two found out?"

Mike Colt opened up a small notebook and flipped through his notes. "Well, Father Callahan is as advertised, really nice guy and revered in his community. He is friendly with a federal judge here in Boston by the name of Mahoney, Michael Mahoney. Judge Mahoney was a lieutenant colonel in the war and a Carter appointee. This judge and Declan were good friends as well. Judge Mahoney has a son, Raymond. Raymond has Down syndrome and is friendly with Declan's son, Liam, as well. They played Little League baseball together. It turns out that Raymond's godfather is Colonel Bob Ferry, the superintendent of the state police. Colonel Ferry has agreed to have an honor guard at the cemetery for Declan on Father Callahan's say-so. All this will be off the books for the troopers."

"What is this costing us? Mike, make sure all these troopers are compensated for their time."

"Nothing, Dad. We spoke with the judge and the colonel, explained the situation, and they were fine with it. It turns out that this colonel was an ex-marine, and he would not accept any contributions."

"I would like to meet with this colonel and the judge after the funeral."

"Already confirmed, sir."

"Good job, boys. Really good job!"

FUNERAL MASS

AT MASS LIAM WAS SITTING next to Mrs. Maguire and Mikey. They couldn't believe the number of people who walked into the church. Liam had no idea that his father knew so many people. I mean, he knew the Cheungs and Uncle Joey and Uncle Tommy would show up. Then Ray and Judge Mahoney arrived.

"Judge, Ray, this is very kind of you to show up like this. But, Ray, why are you crying?"

"Because I feel bad for you, Liam. Your father isn't here anymore."

"No, he's not. He's with my mother, and I'm sure that he's introduced himself to your mother and sisters by now too."

"I have a very nice mom. Right, Dad? And my sisters are good people too."

"Yes, of course, Raymond," said the judge. "Now let Liam go back to his pew."

"I'm sure they are, Ray. Thanks again for coming; it means a lot to me, and I'm sure to my father as well. He had great respect for you, Judge," Liam said.

"Liam," Judge Mahoney said and grabbed my arm, "I want to meet with you sometime next week so that we can discuss a few things. Your father and I spoke about certain circumstances and what to do should they come to light. Okay?"

"Yes, thank you, Judge. I'll call you."

"No, nonsense! Please just stop by the house next Saturday evening for dinner, and we can chat. Okay? Bring Father Callahan if he's free, or I'll just send a car for you."

"Will do, Judge, thanks."

As Liam began to walk back to his seat, he nodded to more strangers paying their respects. He also saw Doug Chase in the back of the church. He waved and smiled at him, to thank him for coming.

Back in his pew, Mikey said in disbelief, "Holy shit, Liam, look how many people are here!"

"Mikey, we're in church; watch your language," Liam said.

"Okay, okay. Oh, shit, Liam, look how many people are here!"

Liam looked at Mikey and just rolled his eyes.

Just before Mass began, a friend of Declan from church, Javier Crowe, agreed to sing one of Declan's favorite songs, "End of My Journey" by Harry Stewart. All present in the church were silent as they embraced his beautiful voice. As soon as the song was finished, the Mass began. Several minutes later, Father Callahan delivered the eulogy.

FATHER CALLAHAN ON DECLAN

"FOR THOSE OF YOU WHO do not know me, my name is Father John Callahan. I have been the parish priest here at Holy Cross for over fifty years. I had the pleasure of knowing Declan, his wife, Eileen, and his son, Liam, for over thirty years. Declan was a loving husband, an adoring father, a dedicated parishioner, and a good friend.

"As I look out over this church today, I do not see an empty pew. This is a true testament to how many lives Declan has touched. After reading all the personal notes posted, the cards written to Declan and his son, and listening to all the compliments and accolades that were given to Declan at the wake last night, I am humbled to stand here in front of you today and tell you about a man whose legacy will not soon be forgotten.

"There was the story of the homeless man who frequents our church by the name of Jack Johnson. Jack was a military veteran whose shoes were stolen at a local shelter the night before. As we opened up our kitchen for breakfast, Declan noticed that Jack had no shoes. Jack explained what happened the night before when he went to take a shower. Someone stole his shoes. Without hesitation, Declan immediately took off his own shoes, gave them to Jack, and Declan walked around the rest of the day in socks. When I asked him why he did such a thing, he simply said, 'Because it was the right thing to do.'

"Declan was a humble man who never spoke of his athletic or heroic accomplishments during high school or the war. There is the story of a young man who was a two-time Massachusetts Golden Gloves champion and three-sport all-state athlete who had several scholarships offers from area schools. There is the story of how Declan, along with other marines, helped save the lives of several of his platoon members who were captured by the North Vietnamese during the war. Declan and the other marines selflessly went back into harm's way to free them from their captors. Declan always seemed to put the needs of others before his own. Declan would pick me up weekly so that I could deliver the Holy Eucharist to Mr. Robertson, a neighbor who is homebound and could not make it to Mass regularly. Or helping his new neighbors, Dr. Cheung and his family, settle into their new country. The Cheungs spoke little English, yet Declan would help them by doing odd jobs in their apartment, registering their son for school, and helping Dr. Cheung find a job in town. Even if it meant sacrificing something for himself, you could always count on Declan.

"Declan never had an opportunity to go to college because he needed to contribute to his family's circumstances, and he was just starting a family of his own. Yet he was one of the brightest, most well-read, and intellectually gifted men I knew. Declan was a voracious reader. We would sit for hours discussing Homer, Nietzsche, Heidegger, and Kant. For the life of me, I couldn't understand half of what he was telling me about the differences between these philosophers, yet he tried his best to simplify it for me. He was also very fond of chess and had a keen ability to grasp complicated strategies within the game. You could often find Declan in the local park during his lunch break, playing speed chess with master-level players. Declan often had two or three games going on at once; he was that good.

"I always tell my parishioners here in South Boston that, throughout life, you're lucky if you have one or two people whom you can call a true friend. The test of a true friend is someone with whom you can share any thought you have, enjoy their company, be separated for a period of time, yet when you come back together again, you pick up right where you left off. A friend is someone who will always forgive your faults and affirm your virtues at the same time. Declan O'Hara was one of those people for me, and I believe that he was for many others who were blessed to know him as well.

"His son, Liam, asked me the other day, why would God do this to us? His father was a good and honorable man. Even as a man of the cloth, it is difficult at times to come to grips with God's plan. We ask ourselves, why would he take someone so young, so gifted, and someone who touched so many lives in a positive way? Someone who had so much more to give. I told him that God has a plan. Declan's time on this earth helped shape many lives. For this we are all richer. What is important for today, for tomorrow, and for the next day is that we honor Declan's life by living it the way he would have lived it: with honor, virtue, courage, and faith.

"So please, let us all stand.

"To our friend Declan.

"May the Lord bless you and the angels guide you to our Savior's side. We say farewell for now, until we meet again.

"May you rest in peace, our dear friend.

"Amen."

Father Callahan turned, bowed to the cross, and all proceeded to exit the church. As they began the procession out of the church, Javier started to sing "In the Arms of an Angel," by Sarah McLachlan, the final song that Liam's father requested for his funeral Mass.

At the funeral parlor, Liam stood transfixed in his best suit, staring at his father. He wore his grief on his face like a mask. Eventually he had to pay attention to other mourners, offering their condolences.

Laying Dad To Rest

After the funeral mass, Mikey, Father C., Mrs. Maguire, and Liam all piled into O'Malley's limousine and drove from the Holy Cross Church to Saint Mary's Cemetery in Dorchester, where they were to lay his father to rest alongside his mother and his grandparents. As they drove up to the cemetery, he noticed a number of state-police cars near his father's tombstone. There were seven state troopers dressed in marine dress blue uniforms armed with rifles alongside his grave. Just behind them was a colonel from the state police. In addition, Liam saw three black SUVs next to the troopers' cars as well. As their limousine approached the cemetery, he noticed three men exit from the first SUV, the driver, followed by two men dressed in back. They stood still as if they were standing guard. As soon as they exited, the third vehicle started to empty. The same thing happened, and they were just standing there in a ready position. Finally, the center vehicle's passengers' doors opened. Two men and a young boy exited from the back door. The first was an older man in his late sixties or early seventies. The second was a younger man about Declan's age. The third was a boy around Liam's age. The younger man carried a cane and walked with a noticeable limp.

When they sat down in front of Declan's grave to say good-bye for the last time, Liam felt a calming peace, as if his dad were watching over him.

Father Callahan said the following prayer as they were laying him to rest.

"God, our Father, your power brings us to birth, your providence guides our lives, and by your command we return to dust. Lord, those who die still live in your presence, their lives change but do not end. I pray in hope for my family, relatives, and friends, and for all the dead known to you alone. In company with Christ, who died and now lives, may they rejoice in your kingdom, where all our tears are wiped away. Unite us together again in one family, to sing your praise forever and ever. Amen."

As Father Callahan finished the prayer, and they began to lower the casket into the ground, the colonel of the state troopers nodded to the honor guard. At that point he commanded, "Atten..." and then the seven troopers aimed in the air and fired one shot. Again, the colonel commanded, "Atten..." and all seven members of the guard aimed and fired another round in the air. One last time the colonel commanded, "Atten..." and a final set of shots rang out. When they were finished, the colonel approached Liam with a precisely folded triangular flag.

"Liam, please accept this flag in honor of your father for his patriotic service to this country."

"Thank you, sir," he said as he stepped back to his men.

Liam was very proud of his father for many things: the example that he set for him, the faith by which he used to guide his life, and now for his honor and bravery in defense of our country.

Before they left, he promised his father that he would be back in a couple of days to lay some plants down next to his family's grave.

From here they were driven to Sullivan's bar for a postfuneral gathering in honor of Declan, an old Irish tradition to eat, drink, and tell stories in remembrance of the person soon not to be forgotten.

H. D. Daniels walked over to Colonel Ferry and Judge Mahoney. "Colonel Ferry? And you must be Judge Mahoney?"

"Yes, can we help you?"

"Please allow me to introduce myself. I'm Hunter Daniels; this is my son, H. D. Jr., my grandson, Tripp, and my head of security, Mike Colt."

"Gentlemen," the colonel said and nodded to each of them.

"I just wanted to thank you and your men for extending this service to a fellow vet."

"Judge Mahoney and Father Callahan explained everything to me and my men, and it is the least that we could do for a fellow marine."

"Yes, yes, of course, thank you! But I want to compensate you and your men for your services, especially taking time from their families over the weekend."

"Sir, like I said, he was a fellow marine; he received a double Purple Heart and Silver Star; it is the least we could do for all his service to our country. That is completely unnecessary."

"You Bay Staters amaze me! Declan was the same way. You never pronounce your *r*'s, and you guys never accept any type of gratuity," he said with a smile. "I'll tell you what, Colonel. I would like to make a fifty-thousand-dollar donation to the honor guard in memory of Declan."

"Mr. Daniels, I guess what they say about you is true."

"What's that, Colonel?"

"That you're a ruthless son of a bitch when it comes to business, but you have the heart of gold when it comes to friends and family. The men will be very grateful, sir."

"I'll take that as a compliment, Colonel. But only if we're friends," HD said with a smile and extended his hand.

"And you, Judge, I heard that Carter put you in office. Is that correct?"

"Yes, that is correct."

"Never cared much for the man after he screwed up that whole hostage thing in Iran, but he moved up one rung on my ladder if he selected you to the bench."

"I'll take that as a compliment, HD."

"And this must be your son, Raymond. Pleasure to meet you, young man."

"Nice to meet you too, sir."

"I'm sorry for the loss of your coach, Raymond."

"He was my friend too."

"Yes, I can see that. My apologies—a coach *and* a friend."

"Shall we all go to Sullivan's now? I believe that is where we can meet up with Liam and this father Callahan."

"Yes, that is where everyone is headed; however, my team will be going on their way, sir. Again, thank you for your generosity, Mr. Daniels," said Colonel Ferry.

"Please, Colonel, it's HD to my friends."

"Okay, thanks, HD, and I'll let the boys know of your generosity."

"You and your men are more than welcome, Colonel." HD handed the colonel his personal card. "If there is anything that I can ever do for you, please do not hesitate to contact me. The top number is my home line, and the second number is to my executive assistant, who knows how to get in touch with me twenty-four hours a day. In the interim, my associate Mike will be sending you over the check for the guard. If there are any issues, please do not hesitate to contact me. Again, Colonel, it has been a pleasure, and thank you for everything!"

"Judge, would you and Raymond like to ride with me?"

"Sure, that would great since we left our car at Sullivan's."

"Great, let's get going."

"Mike, tell the team that we're heading to Sullivan's Tavern, Three Hundred Twenty-Two West Broadway, off Dorchester Street."

"Do you always travel with an entourage, HD?"

"Regretfully, it is a necessity these days. But I'm in good hands with my son and Mike here."

"Raymond, you will have to excuse me while I talk some business with your father, is that okay? My grandson, Tripp, has some baseball cards in the back, if you want to play."

"Sure, no problem, sir."

"Judge, we don't have much time, so forgive my candor. Where do we stand with Liam?"

"In what regard?"

"What I mean is, what is next for him? Where will he be staying? Does he have any relatives that will take him in? We would like to make sure that he is properly taken care of. If he would like, we can take him to live with us if he would like. My son and I have discussed this, and it's the least that we could do for both him and Declan."

"That's very generous of you, HD, however, arrangements have been made in accordance with Declan's wishes. Liam will continue to live in the apartment where he is currently staying for the next couple of weeks while he collects his things. Neighbors will be checking in on him regularly. From there, he will move into the basement of the church, where he will be under the guidance of Father Callahan. Declan thought that it would be in Liam's best interest to be around people he knew and stay close to his friends. Let's run it by Father Callahan and see what he says. Father Callahan has been the executor of Declan's estate."

"Fair enough, Judge. We only want what's best for Liam."

"Agreed. Maybe we can break away for a few seconds and have a discussion at Sullivan's."

LETTER TO LIAM

"Wow, FATHER, I STILL CAN'T believe how many people came to my dad's funeral. I had no idea he knew so many people. Hey, who were those guys in the black SUVs?" he said.

"I'm not sure, but I have an idea."

"Now what?"

Father Callahan handed Liam a letter while they were en route to Sullivan's bar.

"What's this?" Liam asked.

"It's a letter from your father. This may answer some of your questions, and I am sure that you have a few as well."

He took the envelope and ripped it open.

Liam,

There is so much I have to say to you, my dear son. First, I would like to tell you just how proud your mother and I are of how you turned out. You are a warm, generous, caring, and compassionate young man, well beyond your years. The way you embraced our new friend, Raymond; how devoted you are to your best friend, Mikey; and your dedication in faith truly show your character and how selfless and giving of a person you really are. You proved to excel as a student, an athlete, and as a role model for others. For that, we are so very proud of you! I am sorry that I will not be there to see you graduate from high school, college, or grad school. I regret that I will miss your wedding, the birth of your children (remember, "Declan" is an excellent name for my grandchild, if it's a boy, and "Eileen" if it's a girl!), and sharing these experiences with you. Please know that your mother and I will always be looking over you and guiding you. We taught you what is right from what is wrong, and we know that you will live your life as an example for others to follow. I want to thank you for making my life richer with the time we had together.

I have put your immediate care under the supervision of Father Callahan. Father Callahan and I discussed what we thought would be in the best interest of your health and well-being. We both felt that you would be best served to live with him in the basement of the church and stay close to where you grew up for the next couple of years before you go off on your own. We have great expectations for you, my son, and we know that you can achieve those goals in the right environment. I know that Maggie, Mikey, and Uncle Mike wanted you to live with them; however, we knew that the state would have issues with the crammed living arrangements, as well as Uncle Mike's circumstances. Please know that they all love you dearly and that you can approach them for anything that you ever need. In addition, Dr. Cheung has agreed to keep up with your Chinese lessons without any additional costs. I worked out those arrangements well in advance, and he is more than willing to continue with your lessons. Remember, be respectful of their time; I know that you will. Do not be late for your lessons, keep practicing, and listen to what they have to say.

Lastly, Uncle Tommy and Uncle Joey will be there for you whenever you need them as well. They both requested to take you in, but times are tough in the construction industry, and I did not want to burden either of them. They emphasized that it would be no burden, but Father Callahan and I wanted to maintain a sense of normalcy for you as best we could. We felt that keeping you in school here and around the friends you grew up with would be best.

I left Father Callahan in charge of the money that your mother and I had set aside for your college education since you were a baby.

You should be fine with tuition at the Cathedral School through the remainder of high school. I want you to focus on school and your education first and not have to work just yet. One of my only regrets was not attending college myself, and now you will have that opportunity. You can work in the summer to pay extra bills if you want, but not during the school year. If, however, you ever find yourself in a major financial or personal bind, I want you to visit a friend of mine from the service, Lieutenant Hunter Daniels Jr., who lives in Dallas, Texas, or his father, H. D. Daniels Sr. These are a couple of pictures of us together during the war. I have enclosed a separate note for you to give them that will explain everything. Please allow them to open it in private.

The last letter here is for Connor Quinn. Liam, a week or so after my funeral, you may get summoned to speak with Connor. If you do, call Uncle Tommy and Uncle Joey immediately and tell them the time and location of the meeting; then tell Father Callahan about Connor's request. I assume that the meeting will take place at the Triple O, so plan on going to the meeting with Father Callahan. Uncle Joey and Uncle Tommy will know what to do, and they won't be far away. Hand this note to Connor. Look him in the eye, and answer all his questions truthfully. That should be the end of it. Shake his hand firmly, and then go on your way. Before you leave, tell him that you have one last thing to say: "Teaghlaigh thar gach." It means "Family over all." You shouldn't be bothered by him or his crew now or in the future. Remember, Liam, stay true to the path of righteousness (Ps. 23:3b).

One last thing, my son: an old Irish saying that should guide you, "Life is like a storm; one minute you will glow in the bright sunlight; the next, you may crash among the rocks and breakers. What makes you the man who you are is how you react when the storm comes your way. You must look into the eye of that storm and fear it not, for your honor and faith will guide you back to the sunlight."

"Wow! That's a lot to take in, Father; did you read this?"

"No, it was addressed to you."

"Would you like to? There's a lot in there about you too."

Liam handed the letter to Father Callahan and waited until he read it. Father looked up after he finished the letter and handed it back to Liam.

"Now what?" said Liam.

"Well, you have two weeks to pack up your apartment, and then you can move into the custodial apartment in the basement here in the church. It has a separate entrance, so you can come and go as you please, but there are rules, Liam. In the interim, I want you to meet one of your father's friends, Mr. Hunter Daniels and his son, H. D. Daniels Jr., and their grandson, Tripp. We can talk about this Connor thing later."

Twenty minutes later, the driver announced that they had arrived at Sullivan's tavern.

"You ready, Liam? Lots of people want to pay their respects to you. This may be hard, but remember, look them in the eye, give them a firm handshake, and thank them for coming."

"Okay, Father, I'm ready."

As they walked into Sullivan's tavern, a large table in the rear was reserved for them. They sat down with Father Callahan to his right and several empty seats in front of him. There was a buffet line full of food and an open bar. An open bar in an Irish neighborhood is never a good thing, but Liam was sure that everyone would behave out of respect for Declan.

Uncle Tommy and Uncle Joey came over first to pay their respects before their long drive back to New Hampshire.

Looking stricken, both men held it in. Then Uncle Tommy said, "Liam, you know that we are only an hour away; anything you need, just call."

Liam got up from his seat to give each of them a hug. He thanked them for their friendship and loyalty to his dad.

"Father, you call us if he steps out of line," Uncle Joey said with a smile.

"Will do!" said Father C.

After Uncle Tommy and Uncle Joey left, an enormous Tommy Demps stopped by to pay his respects.

"Father," he said and nodded in his direction. "Liam, sorry for your loss. Declan was a great guy and someone who I looked up to and admired."

"Thanks, Tommy! That means a lot coming from you. My dad always said that you were a great guy and a hell of a football player! How are you and your kids doing?"

"Fine, thanks for asking. Everyone is fine. Hey, one more thing. Since Big Mike got transferred to Middlesex, I haven't seen him as much, but word got back to me that he wants to speak with you. If you want, I can take you and Mikey."

"I'll go. Big Mike doesn't want Mikey to visit any jails—ever."

"Understood. I'm going up there on Tuesday. Can I pick you up at seven thirty?"

"Perfect, I'll be ready. Thanks again for everything, Tommy," Liam said as he walked away.

Just then, Judge Mahoney, Ray, and the men from the black SUVs who were at Saint Mary's Cemetery walked in. As they approached the table, the elder man, HD, whispered in the ear of the man to his right, Mike Colt. They created a half-circle barrier around Liam's table and asked if they could sit down.

"You must be Liam? My goodness, you look just like your father."

"Thank you, sir."

"Son, my name is Hunter Daniels, and this is my son H. D. Daniels Jr. He served in the war with your father."

"Pleased to meet you, son," H. D. Jr. said and extended his hand to Liam. "Your father spoke of you often, and he showed us your baby picture every day when we were together. He was a great man, Liam; you should know that."

"Thank you; thank you both for coming," Liam said and extended his hand.

"This other man's name is Michael Colt. He was on your father's last mission. Although he only knew your father for a few months, Declan impressed him greatly," said HD.

"Declan was a true warrior, Liam, someone who was brave and honorable. It is my pleasure to meet you," said Mike.

"Thank you, sir."

Mike had a firm and powerful grip, just like his father, Uncle Tommy's, and Uncle Joey's.

Liam just then realized something. "Mr. Daniels, I actually have a letter that my father requested I give to you and your son in the event of his passing. Since I'm not sure when I would be visiting Dallas any time soon, I'd like to give it to you now if you don't mind," Liam said.

"Yes, yes, of course, thank you, son. We will read that in a minute. Liam, if you don't mind, I would like a word with the judge and Father Callahan here for a minute."

"Absolutely. Sure, no problem. I'll just go get something to eat. Would anybody like me to bring something back for him?"

"No, thanks anyway, Liam. Just go get yourself something to eat," said Father Callahan.

As Liam approached the buffet, Mikey was there filling his plate.

"Hey, Liam, who the hell are the men in black?"

"Dunno? Just some guys my dad knew from the war, I think."

"Well, I do," said Mikey.

"Okay, who is it then?"

"That's H. D. Daniels; he's one of the richest guys in this country."

"No way. You don't know shit," Liam said.

"You're right. I don't, but Doug Chase does, and he told me who that was."

"No shit!" Liam said.

"I'm serious! That's what he said. Wow! I wonder what he wants."

"I dunno. My dad left him and his son a letter or something. I'll let you know, though."

Back at the reserved table where Father Callahan, the judge, HD, and his son discussed Liam's future, HD waved over Mike Colt, his head of security. "Mike, please find the owner here, and let's pick up the tab for this gathering."

"Will do, sir."

"That Liam is really a nice and polite young man. Declan did a great job with him."

"Yes, he did indeed," said Father Callahan.

"It is my understanding that you are the guardian of Liam. Is that correct?"

"Yes, I am," said Father C.

"Father, I want you to consider allowing us to take Liam back to Dallas with us. He can live with us instead of the basement of a church. We can offer him the best schools, living arrangements, and a new life. No offense, Father, it's just that his new accommodations don't sound that conducive for a growing teenager. Furthermore, my son and I would like to pay for Liam's schooling and college, either way."

"That's very generous, HD, but his father's wishes were that he stays in the area if at all possible. In fact, two of his platoon members made the same offer, and they only live in New Hampshire. We decided that it would be best if we don't disrupt his life, his school, or his friendships. His father also set aside his tuition at the Cathedral School for the remainder of his high-school years."

"Father, I'm not questioning that. Listen, our offer still stands either now or in the future. We only want what's best for Liam."

"As do we, HD. We'll keep your offer in mind should circumstances change," said Father C.

"Father, you are the executor of Declan's will; is that correct?"

"Yes."

"Judge, we may need your expertise here."

"Okay, how can I help?"

"Well, after Declan's escape from the POW camp during the war, he was laid up in a Saigon hospital just before he was to go home from his second tour of duty. I flew to Vietnam to meet with him and ask how my son was holding up in the camp. During that time, I learned that the government would not try and rescue my son because he was too far north of the seventeenth parallel in North Vietnamese territory. I explained the situation to Declan, and I offered him a million dollars to go back and see if he, along with my head of security, Mike Colt," he said, pointing to Mike behind him, "would consider an off-the-books rescue mission."

"Yes, Declan told us about the mission and some of the details, but not everything, especially the million-dollar offer," said Judge Mahoney.

"Well, Declan agreed to go because he thought that it was the right thing to do. He adamantly refused my money, but he said that if he did not return, he requested that whatever I was going to give him should go to his son when he turns twenty-one. Well, as you can see, he helped save my son, and my grandson still has his father. For that we are forever grateful. Even though he refused my money, I decided to invest the money I set aside for him in my fund. H. D. Jr. sent him quarterly statements, but they were always returned unopened. Today the value of his stock is just north of—what, Junior?"

"Just north of twenty-two million, Dad."

"Thanks, son."

"And Dad, if the fund does what it is supposed to do, it may be worth a bit more depending on how we end this year."

"See, Judge, so Liam should be comfortable for some time."

"So you're telling me that Liam will inherit twenty-two million when he turns twenty-one?" said Father Callahan.

"How should we handle this?"

"Twenty-two million. Are you serious?"

"Father, when it comes to family and money, I am always serious."

"Okay, then, now I know who to go to in a few years when I need a loan," said Father C. with a smile.

"Father, I'll have my son send the statements to your attention from now on. My personal opinion would be not to say anything to Liam until he has a firmer grasp of money, finances, and how the world works."

"Agreed, HD, we will keep that to ourselves. We want him to stay focused on school."

"Gentlemen, I have to run back to Dallas on some business. This is not good-bye, rather, only so long for now. We will be in touch. Father, that was a beautiful sermon," he said as he extended his hand to Father Callahan first and then to the judge. "Thank you again for all that you and Colonel Ferry did at the cemetery. Mike here will make sure that everyone has our personal contact information. I just want to go say good-bye to Liam before we leave."

HD, his son, and his entourage got up from the table and headed toward the buffet line, where Liam was standing with Mikey.

"Heads up, Liam. Men in black coming our way," Mikey said as Liam turned toward them.

"Liam, I must be off for now. I spoke with your guardian, Father Callahan, and I would like us to become friends if you are okay with that."

"Yes, I'd like that, sir. Any opportunity I have to learn more about my father and his friends would mean a great deal to me."

H. D. Jr. gave Liam a hug and said, "You're a fine young man, Liam, just like your father. If you ever need anything, we are just a phone call away. Please know, Liam, that this is not an empty offer. I cherish two things in life: family and friendships. I consider you a friend, so please do the same. I would also like it if you can keep in touch with me if you don't mind. I'd like to see how you are doing while you're growing up; is that okay?"

"Yes, sir, I will keep you updated on my happenings if you would like."

"Yes, Liam, I would like that very much. Thank you, son."

HD, Junior, Mike Colt, and his security force all left the bar. As they sat in the car, Junior asked, "What did the letter say, Dad?"

"Oh, I almost forgot. It's addressed to us both; why don't you read it."

Dear HD and Lieutenant Daniels,

If you are reading this note, I believe the cancer got the best of me before I could reach out to you both and thank you in person. I wanted to thank you for sending me those quarterly reports over the years. Unfortunately, I didn't have the heart to open them. I felt very uncomfortable taking money that way, especially since it was to be set aside for my family if I did not return from that last mission. I believe that if the roles were reversed, your son would have done the same for me or any of the men under his command. HD, I want you to know that your son was an exceptional officer and a natural-born leader! He was honest, courageous, and the men had great respect for how he led the platoon. He saved our necks on more than one occasion in the jungle, and for that we are forever grateful. I thought that you might like the enclosed picture that shows us carrying out LT just before we hit the Laotian border and the one of us just before our weekend pass in Saigon. (The remainder of that night's mission will remain classified!*)*

HD, although your son is a skilled tactician on the battlefield and a great leader of men, he had yet to grasp the complexities of the "Queen's Gambit" or the "Tarrasch's Rule" in the art of chess. During our time in captivity, we passed the long hours playing chess. The enclosed IOUs are an accumulation of nine months' worth of "lessons" I gave your son. Actually, you're lucky that I escaped when I did because, at the rate that he was losing, I would have owned half of your holdings by now. The enclosed IOUs (signed on the attached banana leaves) give me ownership of your farm in Dallas, your vacation house in Aspen, several of your classic cars, your Civil War gun collection, your oil rights in West Texas, and breeding rights from your 1974 Kentucky Derby–winning horse, Cannondale. Because I consider myself a fair man, I will not call in these IOUs. Rather, I will humbly accept the money that you invested on my behalf (for my son), if that offer still stands. If that is not an option, I completely understand, and it was indeed a pleasure serving under you, Lieutenant, and meeting you as well, HD. I wish you both long and healthy lives.

Lieutenant, we were both blessed with a second chance in life. Make sure you hug your son, Tripp, and tell him that you love him every day. Life is too short and precious and should never be taken for granted.

Semper Fi,

Declan

PS: If you are still in contact with Lieutenant Mike Colt, please tell him I owe him one for that shot he took back on the trail and saved my life. He's a good man, and I look forward to continuing our chess rematch on the other side.

"What's this about these IOUs, son?"

"I was under duress, malnourished, and had early-onset malaria—plus I was wounded."

"But what about all those lessons we paid for when you were a child?"

"Obviously, those were the worst investment ever!" said Junior with a smile.

"You lost all that in nine months?"

"Well, to be honest, I lost most of that in two months? The other seven months I was still losing to Declan but just at a lot slower rate."

"In just two months!"

"Dad, like I say, I was wounded and sick," Junior said with a smile.

"Understood, but I want my money back from that Dr. Simon, your chess tutor."

"Even in death that man brings a smile to my face. He had quite a sense of humor. Didn't he?"

"Indeed, sir, indeed," said Mike Colt.

Sit-Down With Connor—Part 2

About one week after Declan was laid to rest, Liam was still trying to come to grips with what was going on around him. As he was cleaning up the apartment and getting ready to move to his new residence in the basement of the rectory, he noticed that a note was slipped under his door. It simply read, "Triple O, 2:00 p.m., Saturday." He immediately knew what that meant, and his father was right, a sit-down with Connor Quinn.

Suddenly, there was a knock at the door—it was Mikey and his mother to see if they could help out with the cleanup. As Liam quickly hid the note, he said, "Thank you both, but I'm okay. Mrs. Maguire, is it okay if Mikey stays for a bit?"

"Sure, Liam, no problem. Remember, dinner is in twenty minutes."

"Yes, Mrs. Maguire." She was soon out of sight. "Hey, Mikey, guess what?"

"What's up? Did your dad leave you a pot of gold or something?"

"No, nothin' like that, I wish. I got summoned by Connor."

"Quinn? What does he want?"

"Not sure, but look what my dad wrote me before he passed away."

Liam handed Mikey his dad's note from the table. He read it and said, "Holy shit! That's scary! How did he know?"

"Not sure, but in three days I have to go meet the man."

"You going in strapped?"

"Are you out of your mind? Connor's guys will pat me down. If they find anything, I'll be shot dead on the spot."

"You goin' in alone? I'll come if you want."

"No, I'm good. My dad's note says to call my uncles and to just bring Father C."

"Good, because I was only shittin' you. I don't want any part of that guy," Mikey said with a grin.

"Really good friend you are, Mikey!"

"Hey, I'm just being honest; that's all," Mikey said with a smirk.

Per Liam's father's request, he immediately called Uncle Joey and told him what his dad's note said to do if Connor reached out to him. Uncle Joey said not to worry about it, and they knew exactly what to do. He went on to say that he and Uncle Tommy would both be there, whether he saw them or not.

As Saturday approached, he talked to Father C. about his dad's note and part of his final request. Against his better judgment, he relented and agreed to take him to the Triple O. The one thing that Father C. would not waver from was that he would be in the bar with Liam throughout the meeting just in case something happened.

When you had a meeting with Connor Quinn, you really never know the outcome, other than the fact that you were guaranteed one thing—that he's going to screw you over one way or another. On the one hand, Liam was thinking that it could be his last few moments on earth and that he'd be seeing my parents sooner rather than later. On the other hand, he might just be paying his respects to his father and he just wanted to convey those sentiments in person. Who was he kidding? He was screwed! He just didn't know how badly yet.

Saturday afternoon, he was outside the Holy Cross rectory, waiting for Father C.

"Good afternoon, Father."

"Good afternoon, Liam, you ready to go? You know, Liam, you *don't* have to go to this meeting."

"Yes, I do, Father. My dad said that I should, and he even knew that I would be getting this call."

"Okay, that's your decision. Don't you worry about today, though. I'm not sure what your dad had in mind or what Connor's involvement is in all this, but I'll be with you every step of the way to ensure that nothing will go wrong. Just respect your father's wishes. On a lighter note, Mr. D'Amico will be finished painting your last two rooms in the basement by early next week, and you can move in the week after that, okay?"

"That's great, Father. I should be all packed up by the end of next week anyway and ready to go. If everything goes okay after today, that is," he said with a smile.

As Father C. and Liam drove up to the Triple O, Father C. told him to always look Mr. Quinn in the eye. "If you look away or down, he sees that as a sign of weakness. If anything goes wrong, I'll be in the bar, so don't worry."

"Thanks, Father. You know, this is a worse feeling than going to confession for the first time."

"Why is that, Liam?"

"Well, in confession, if your sins are bad, you still know that you're getting out of church with just a couple of 'Our Fathers' and a few 'Hail Mary's.' In a meeting with Connor, you never know if you're walking out the front door or if they're carrying you out the back."

"Point taken, Liam, but we have God on our side today."

"I know that, Father, but Connor's got Mr. Smith and Mr. Wesson on his side."

As they walked up the stairs to the Triple O, Liam saw Connor in his regular booth, watching them as they walked in. Out of the corner of his eye, he saw someone riding a bike toward them. It was Mikey! Liam waved, and he waved back. Before he went in, Mikey lifted his shirt, revealing his dad's nine-millimeter in his waistband. Liam smiled and nodded.

In the Triple O, Mr. Quinn sat across the room with his lieutenant, Sam Canti. He saw Liam and Father C. and waved them over to his table.

"Are you Liam?" asked Connor.

"Yes, sir."

"I believe my note said to come alone. What's with the backup?"

"My apologies, sir; Father Callahan insisted."

"He can be like that. Can't he?"

"Yes, sir."

"You look flush; anything wrong?"

"No, sir."

"No, you're not scared?"

"No, sir, I am not."

"Why is that?"

"Because my dad told me that you would be reaching out to me, so I was prepared for this meeting."

"No shit? Was this in a vision? What did he say?"

"No, sir, it was in the form of a letter. He said that you may want to speak with me after his passing and to let Father Callahan know."

"Interesting. Well, then, do you know *why* I called you here today, Liam?"

"No, sir."

"Your dad didn't tell you?"

"No, sir."

"Well, your father was holding on to some things that are very important to me. In the event of his passing, those items were to come back to me. Are you aware of these items?"

"No, sir, I don't know of any such arrangement, and I have no such information."

"He didn't give you anything? No safety-deposit keys? No lock-box keys, nothing?"

"No, sir, nothing like that. He did, however, give me this letter for you." Liam handed Connor the letter.

Connor,

Thanks for the beautiful Irish lilies that I am sure you sent to the wake on my behalf. I suspected that you would call Liam in for a sit-down a few weeks after my passing. You are, if nothing else, shamelessly predictable. How you've stayed out of prison this long escapes me. At any rate, regarding our deal and the information that remains in my possession, Liam still knows nothing of our arrangement, and I want to keep it that way. However, as I had mentioned from the onset, three other people still have the copies of these records and understand our deal. The bottom line is that our agreement still stands even in my passing. I expect you to keep your distance from my son and Mikey so that none of this information will ever see the light of day. Remember, whether you stay or you're on the run, I can still get to you and the ones you love if something happens to Liam. My friends know where your mother, brothers, and your nephews live. Like Liam, they are civilians in this, and they need to be spared. I'm sure that you can appreciate that. Remember, Connor, I don't make threats; I carry out promises. To remind you of this, look under your table.

Connor paused from reading the letter and looked under the table to see a block of C-4 explosives and some wires hanging from it to a remote trigger.

The device you are looking at is triggered by a remote control, which is in the hands of the man at the bar to your left. Should you or your men take him out, the man at the bar to your right has you in his sights. Nothing will happen as long as our agreement stays intact. Now please reach out to my son, shake his hand, and tell him that you still think that I am a son of a bitch but that our agreement still stands.

Connor, I look forward to finishing this discussion on the other side.

Best,
Declan

"Liam, did you read this letter?"

"No, sir."

"Are you sure?"

"Yes, sir, not a word."

"Your dad is one crafty son of a bitch; I'll give him that."

"I'm not sure what that means, sir."

"It means that even in his death he is a pain in my ass, but you were very lucky to have had him as your father, Liam."

"Thank you, sir."

"You may go now, Liam. Nobody here will ever bother you."

"Thank you, sir. One last thing, Mr. Quinn."

"Yes, kid?"

"My father said to tell you something before I leave."

"What's that?"

"Teaghlaigh thar gach."

Connor smiled. "Do you know what that means, Liam?" asked Connor.

"Yes, sir, I do."

"Then, teaghlaigh thar gach it is."

Father Callahan, Uncle Joey, Uncle Tommy, and Liam left the bar.

"Are we good, Liam?" asked Uncle Joey.

"Yes, I believe so. But what exactly did my dad have on Connor?"

"Don't worry about that. We'll tell you another time," said Uncle Tommy.

Mikey rolled up on his bike. "Everything okay here?"

"Mikey, what are you doing here?" asked Father Callahan.

"Backup," said Mikey.

"Liam!" Father C. shouted in disbelief.

"What? He was there when the note was slipped under the door. What could I do?" Liam said to Father Callahan.

"Okay, Mikey, go home, and we'll catch up later."

"See you at your crib, Liam."

"Yup. And thanks, Mikey!"

"No problem; that's what brothers are for. Later…"

"Gentlemen, thanks for coming. I'm sorry that you still have to deal with this matter."

"Understood, Father. Thanks for coming," said Uncle Joey. "Liam, be good, and if you need anything, just call."

Back in the Triple O tavern, Connor yelled for Sammy, "Get over here, now!"

"Yeah, Connor, what's up? Want me take care of that kid?"

"No! Our arrangement still stands! Just take care of this shit under the table, will you?"

"Son of a bitch! That fuckin' Declan did it again—this time from the grave. Fuckin' balls on that guy," said Sammy, shaking his head.

"Just disarm the damn thing and keep the C-Four in case we have to deal with those guineas from the North End in the future; then I want you to reach out to our *friend* for a meet to see what this kid really knows. Maybe Joe can sweat it out of him. He's on the line here too."

"Okay, got it, Connor."

A couple of hours later, Sammy said, "I got in touch with our friend; we're on for tonight, same place as usual, seven p.m."

"Good, seven it is; thanks, Sammy."

The meeting was set to take place at their usual location in Charlestown underneath the Tobin Bridge at the fourth pillar. As always, Sammy and Connor got there early to case the place and make sure they were not being followed or watched. At about quarter past seven, Joe Carey arrived and got out of his car.

"Sammy, Connor," Joe said as he nodded in the direction of them both. "Sorry I'm late, guys, damn MBTA construction around the Garden!"

"Yeah, that fuckin' thing will never be completed, especially with those guineas getting a piece of every inch of construction in that tunnel," said Sammy.

"So what's up, Connor?"

"Declan's dead, and he's still holding on to that information."

"Well, does his kid have it?"

"Don't know. I had him in at the Triple O to sweat him, and it seemed like he didn't know anything about the pictures or the tapes. Unfortunately, we can't take that chance. We need you to pick him up and see what he has to say."

"Pick him up? You can't just pick people up for no reason, Connor. Pick him up on what charges?"

"I don't give a fuck what charges; figure it out! Say he's a fucking terrorist or a fucking person of interest in a murder. I don't know; just get him in the box and ask him! Do something for Christ's sake! We're all on the line here."

"Fine, I'll figure something out."

"Whatever you do, do it quickly. We need answers!"

"Okay, okay. Is that it?"

"Yeah, that's fucking it! And that *it* could put us in prison for the rest of our fuckin' lives. Either that or the guineas will put us in the fucking Brockton landfill."

"Okay, Connor, relax. I'll take care of it."

"You'd better fuckin' take care of it because we are in this mess because of you!"

"Understood. I'll see if I can get some answers by the end of next week."

As the school year ended and the transition to Liam's new home in the basement of the church became more of a reality, he finally settled into his new lifestyle. Surprisingly, not that much changed. He maintained his Chinese lessons, Mikey still came over to Liam's new apartment to hang out most of the time (but no visitors past nine o'clock, per Father C.), and he had a schedule by which Father Callahan would check his homework every night.

Life in the basement wasn't bad at all. He had a separate entrance from the rectory, so it felt like his own apartment. There was no cable TV, but that just forced him to read more. He had a small stove, a microwave, a small shower, and a rack to hang his clothes. There was no door in front of the rack, so he didn't think that you could actually call it a closet. His goal was to put up a tarp within the next week, just to give it the impression of a closet. He had an ironing board and iron, and he could do laundry in the basement of the rectory without quarters! Mrs. Maguire would cook for him, or he would eat over at their apartment three nights a week after his language lessons. The rest of the time, he ate a lot of peanut butter and jelly sandwiches, canned tuna, or rice and beans. Someday, he'd learn to cook. Father Callahan was always checking on him, so he was never really alone.

Father Callahan gave him an allowance so that he could buy food and clothes whenever he needed. He started looking for a job when school let out, and he would do chores in and around the parish to help Father C. out on occasion. That was his routine for the next couple of months. Father C. made sure they ate Sunday meals together in the apartment, and they would just talk about things going on in school and life in general.

During one Sunday dinner, Father C. said, "Liam, I understand that these may not seem like the best accommodations for a young man of your age, but we're doing the best that we can under these circumstances."

"No, Father, no complaints here. I'm fine! It's better than being homeless."

"Well, you would never be homeless, and I appreciate the fact that you think this is a step up from that," Father C. said with a smile, "but your father and I only want the best for you."

"I know, Father, thank you for everything."

"Liam, if you don't like it here or want to move somewhere else, I'll understand; that's all I'm saying."

"No, Father. Mikey's here, you're here, my walk to school is shorter; what else could I ask for?" Liam says with a smile.

"Just let me know if you need anything else. Okay, Liam?"

"Sure, Father, and thanks for everything—really! Just a heads-up that Tommy Demps will be picking me up tomorrow morning at around nine a.m. to go see Mr. Maguire at the Middlesex Jail up in Lawrence."

"What's up there?"

"I'm not sure. Tommy said that Big Mike reached out to him and that he wanted to see me. I assume that he wants to pay his condolences since he couldn't attend the funeral."

"Would you like me to come?"

"No, that's okay. I know that you have a lot going on here, Father."

"Okay, let me know how that turns out, and give Big Mike my best."

"Will do, Father."

"Hey, are you bringing Mikey too?"

"No, Mr. Maguire still doesn't want Mikey to see him like that in jail."

"Understood. Just let me know if he needs anything."

"Sure will, Father."

At quarter to nine the next morning, Tommy Demps's truck pulled up. "Hey, Liam, you ready?"

"Hey, Tommy. Yup, all good."

"You ever been up here?"

"Where? To Lawrence or to Middlesex Jail?"

"To the jail," said Tommy.

"No, but my dad has, a couple of times since Big Mike got transferred out of Walpole a few months ago. What's it like?"

"Yeah, it's nothing like Walpole; that's for sure! Mike is fine up there. Nobody will give him any shit. Even if they do, Mike knows what to do."

"Hey, Tommy, how are your kids?" Liam asked.

"Everybody is okay, but school is a problem. The boys don't do well in school. I know that they're trying, so I can't kick their ass or anything like that, but they just don't seem to get it."

"Sorry to hear that. What subjects?"

"Math and writing. They're not dumb like their old man. Trust me, they're not lazy, and they don't cause any trouble in school. I just don't get it? Me and my wife are spending hundreds of dollars on testing, tutors, and even therapists, but nothing seems to work."

"You know, Tommy, I was just like them when I was their age, and now I'm number one or two in my class."

"Really? What happened, because your dad told me that you're an all-A student."

"To be honest, Tommy, I found out that each kid learns at a different pace when it comes to schoolwork. Or at least that was the case with me. The problem is that if you struggle on a concept early on in a lesson, and the teacher doesn't identify the issue from the beginning, some kids just get left behind and won't want to learn. The key is to understand the concept from the beginning. This applies to math, reading comprehension, and writing. I'll tell you what, why don't I visit with your boys this summer and see what I can do? How about every Tuesday and Thursday for just an hour a night (at first); what do you say?"

"Seriously, Liam, you'd do that for me? The boys look up to you, so that might be a good idea."

"Sure, no problem!"

"Hey look, I have to pay you, though."

"Tommy, come on, don't insult me! After all that you've done for Mr. Maguire. Are you kidding me?"

"That's different, Liam. That's between me, your father, and Big Mike."

"No, my dad would kick my ass if I took a penny from you."

"Your dad was good to me, growing up. You're just like him you know. You have a heart of gold. I'm not going to argue with you, Liam, but thank you!"

"No problem! See you on Thursday at seven o'clock. Hey, I just have to tell Father C. that I'll be home late those nights. I have a nine-o'clock curfew."

"Perfect, I'll let the boys know, and I'll call Father C. to square things for you."

"Excellent, thanks!"

THE ARCHDIOCESE

Two months after Declan's passing, FBI Agent Joe Carey needed to find out if Liam had any of the incriminating evidence that Declan showed Connor. He knew that it was time to rattle Liam's cage. He called for his secretary, Sharron, to get the wheels in motion.

"Sharon, please call Agent DaSilva in here immediately."

"Yes, sir, one moment please."

"Sir, you called for me?" asked Agent DaSilva.

"Yes, do you still have your connections with the archdiocese?"

"Yes, sir, my uncle is the monsignor in charge of the archdiocese's business affairs; why?" asked Agent DaSilva.

"Well, I think we can rattle the Liam O'Hara and the good father Callahan's cages now."

"How so, sir?"

"It was brought to my attention that Liam O'Hara is living in the basement of the rectory of Holy Cross Church. I bet His Eminence, Archbishop Matthews, doesn't know about this arrangement; especially in lieu of all these abusive lawsuits against the church, I'm sure that they would like to get ahead of this potential inflammatory situation. I also want you to contact Social Services to start an investigation on this as well."

"Yes, sir, I'm on it."

One week later, Father Callahan received a call from the archdiocese.

"Father, are you in?"

"Yes, who is it, Diana?"

"There is a call from His Eminence's office."

"Thanks, Diana; send it through."

"This is Father Callahan—"

"Father, this is Monsignor Carroll, and I am calling on behalf of His Eminence. He would like to meet with you later today to discuss a matter that involves the archdiocese. How does four p.m. look?"

"Yes, that's fine, I can make it. May I ask what the nature of this meeting is?"

"My apologies, Father; I am not at liberty to discuss the context of what His Eminence wishes to discuss with you. We will expect you this afternoon at four p.m.," he said and abruptly hung up the phone.

"Father, is everything okay?"

"Well, Diana, I'm not sure. I guess I'll find out soon enough, though. I'll be at the archbishop's residence in Brighton this afternoon at around four p.m. Please do not expect me back for dinner. Please let know Liam know as well so that he doesn't wait for me to eat dinner tonight."

"Sure, Father, will do. Do you need me to prepare any documents for your meeting with His Eminence?"

"No, Diana, they requested nothing of the sort. Thank you, though."

At quarter to four, Father Callahan arrived for his appointment with His Eminence at the archbishop's residence in Brighton. The archbishop's residence was modeled after an Italian palazzo and full of beautiful Italian marble and mahogany. This residence represented the embodiment of the church's stature in the heavily Roman Catholic city of Boston.

"Father Callahan to see Archbishop Matthews, please."

"Do you have an appointment, Father?"

"Yes, a four-o'clock appointment with His Eminence."

"Ah, yes, here it is: four-o'clock with His Eminence and Monsignor Carroll. Please take a seat, Father, and I will call you when he is ready."

"Thank you. Excuse me, but you look familiar, do I know you?"

"Yes, Father, I am a parishioner at Holy Cross Church. My name is Mary O'Malley."

"Of course, I thought that you looked familiar. You and your family sit in the first pews on the right side of the church, don't you?"

"Yes, that's us, every Sunday."

"Well, nice to see you again," Father Callahan said with a smile.

Ten minutes later, Monsignor Carroll arrived. "Father Callahan," he said, extending his hand.

"Yes, and you must be Monsignor Carroll."

"I am. Let me take you into the archbishop's office. We're just waiting on another person to arrive and join us."

"Join us? What exactly will they be joining us for?"

"His Eminence will explain everything shortly." Father Callahan and Monsignor Carroll entered His Eminence's office.

"John, it's been a while," said the archbishop as he extended his hand.

"Your Eminence, so nice to see you again," Father Callahan said as he kissed His Eminence's ring. "To what do I owe this honor?"

Just then Ms. Sarah Wile, from the Massachusetts Department of Social Services, arrived. Ms. Wile was a leading case specialist for the Boston area Social Services.

"Good afternoon, Sarah. This is Father Callahan, and this Monsignor Carroll," His Eminence said as he gestured to each of them to sit down.

"Thank you all for coming in on such short notice. I have called you all here to address an anonymous inquiry that has been brought to this office's attention to which I am *obligated* to investigate. Ms. Wile is here to act as the liaison from the state, and she will offer her recommendation on how we proceed."

"I'm not sure what this has to do with me," Father Callahan said.

"Well, John, unfortunately, it has everything to do with you."

"How is that, Your Eminence?"

"Well, is there a young man by the name of Liam O'Hara living with you in the basement of the rectory of the Holy Cross Church?"

"No, he is *not* living with *me*. He is living in the basement in the former custodial quarters. His father, Declan, was a parishioner at Holy Cross for over thirty years. Declan passed away a few months ago from cancer, and he requested that I become Liam's legal guardian since there he had no other living relatives."

"John, where is this young man living?" asked Monsignor Carroll.

"As I just told you, in the former custodial quarters. His room is separate from the priests living quarters."

"And where is that exactly located, Father?" asked Ms. Wile.

"On the church grounds," Father Callahan replied.

"John, John, we are not set up for this; you know that," said the archbishop. "And the boy is a minor. He's only thirteen years old."

"I'm not sure what the problem is here. We allowed a custodian to stay there without any issue."

"Yes, but our records indicate that the former custodian was a staff member as well. Is that correct?" asked Monsignor Carroll. "Furthermore, the previous custodian was an adult, and this boy is a thirteen-year-old minor. Is Mr. O'Hara employed by the archdiocese, like the former custodian?"

"No, but he helps out around the rectory and church grounds."

"Does he pay rent?"

"No."

"Then, Father, we have a real problem here," said the monsignor.

"Problem? What problem? The church is saving a boy from becoming a ward of the state while maintaining his ecclesiastical studies. Isn't that what we're here for, to save souls? And if it is a question of paying rent, then his father provided for that along with his education."

"John, John, we're giving you the benefit of the doubt here." The archbishop paused for a moment and said, "Ms. Wile, can you excuse us while the monsignor and I speak with Father Callahan in private for a moment?"

"Yes, Your Eminence, by all means," Ms. Wile said as she got up from her seat and left the room.

"Thank you. We'll be just a minute."

"John, do you see that stack of papers over there on my desk?"

"Yes. And?"

"Well, that stack represents two hundred fifty allegations of sexual abuse by priests against *this* archdiocese alone."

"Those cases have *no standing* with this situation! I can assure you that my name is not associated with any of those cases, and this situation is completely above board."

"John, it is the sense of impropriety that is at issue here. With all this going on in the news today," he said, pointing to the stack of cases again, "we simply can't have it, especially on church grounds."

"Who submitted this grievance?" Father C. asked.

"We are not at liberty to say."

"This is a witch hunt; you should know better!"

"Father! Remember whom you are talking to!" said Monsignor Carroll sternly.

"My apologies, Your Eminence, but I have been nothing but a faithful and loyal servant to this archdiocese for over thirty-five years."

"John, that is the reason why we are having this meeting in the first place, as a courtesy to you. We have taken all your years of service into consideration. However, with everything that is going on surrounding the church, we are left with few options here. Regardless of the findings, which I am sure will identify no abuse by you, we need to discuss where we go from here. As the monsignor and I have discussed, one option would be for you to leave the rectory and find a private residence for you and the boy while maintaining your pastoral duties. Another option would be for you to relinquish your guardianship of the boy and have him become a ward of the state. The last option, which is something that neither of us wants, would be for you to leave the priesthood. Either way, we cannot have the boy living in any residence associated with the parish, especially at this time. After Ms. Wile officially cites her findings, you will have forty-eight hours to advise us of your decision," said His Eminence.

"I'm not sure that any of these options are fair to me or to the boy," Father Callahan said.

"Father, I have to look at what is best for the entire archdiocese, a flock of tens of thousands, not just two wayward sheep. Father, I will need your answer within a week."

"I understand Your Eminence; I understand..."

ANOTHER MOVE FOR LIAM

BY THE TIME FATHER CALLAHAN got back to Holy Cross, he had a message from the His Eminence's secretary, Ms. O'Malley.

"Ms. O'Malley, this is Father Callahan, I received a message that you called me. Did I forget something after my meeting with His Eminence?"

"No, Father, it is nothing like that. I wanted to tell you something in confidence."

"By all means, Ms. O'Malley, what is it?"

"As you know, the walls in this office are very thin, and I know that you asked His Eminence who brought this matter to his attention."

"Yes, I would love to know who it is because I was completely caught off guard regarding this matter."

"I know, Father, I know. You are a good man, and I have been a parishioner at Holy Cross for over twenty years, and I have seen all the work that you have done over the years. The man who made the inquiry was a gentleman by the name of Joe Carey. I believe that he is with the FBI."

"Thank you so much, Ms. O'Malley; it all makes sense now."

"I hope so, Father. Let me know if I can be of any further assistance." Father Callahan handed up the phone.

"Diana, are you still here?" Father Callahan asked loudly from his office.

"Yes, Father, what do you need? I'm about to head home in about fifteen minutes, but I can stay if you need me to."

"No, no need to stay. Before you leave, can you please get Judge Mahoney on the phone and call Liam up to my office."

"He's already on his way up here, Father. He wanted me to tell him when you got back from His Eminence's office."

"Great—I'll see you tomorrow, Diana; thank you."

Liam knocked as he entered Father Callahan's office. "Father, may I come in?"

"Liam, sorry I missed dinner tonight but was called to His Eminence's office unexpectedly."

"So I heard; is everything okay?" asked Liam.

"Well, that's what I want to talk to you about, Liam; have a seat." Father Callahan motioned for Liam to sit in the seat next to his desk.

"This sounds serious, Father."

"It is; we just have to review our options and make some grown-up decision."

"Okay, Father, tell me everything," Liam said with a long-drawn face.

"Here it is Liam. Someone called the archdiocese and told them that you were living in the basement of Holy Cross."

"So what's the big deal?"

"Well, as it turns out, the archdiocese received a complaint of an unaccompanied minor living in the basement of the church. And with all these allegations against priests these days, it is causing a major issue."

"Who lodged the complaint? And what can we do?"

"The 'who' doesn't matter now. His Eminence gave us three options to resolve this matter on our own, and we need to let him know our decision by the end of the week one way or another."

"Okay, Father, what are the options?"

"Here it is, Liam, with no filter. Option number one is for us to move to an apartment outside of the church while I still maintain my pastoral duties within the parish. Option number two would be for me to separate myself from the church completely, and we would have to move to an apartment in the area. Option number three would be for me to relinquish my guardianship of you and put you into the care of the state."

"Father, let me cut you off right there." Liam stood up. "I can't let you do that. I can't let you leave the church, or any part of it. I'll take option number three and just go into foster care. Don't worry about me; it will only be until I'm eighteen. I'm sure that I'll be close, and I'll see you and Mikey every week."

"Liam, I knew that you would say something like that, but I can't let you fall into the system; I promised your father."

"Father, I get it, but the parish needs you more than I need you. Look at all the good that you do for these people. I can't be the cause of that loss."

"Thank you, Liam, but before you came up here, I called Judge Mahoney to ask his legal advice on what my options might be? Without hesitation, he asked me if he could take you in. I said that I would ask you. I mean, it's up to you."

"Are you sure that he wants me and that you're not just saying that?" Liam asked as he cleared a tear from his left eye.

"Liam, I'm a priest; I don't lie—with the exception of telling Diana that her pound cake is delicious," Father C. said with a smile.

"Okay, Father, then that's what we'll do if you are okay with it."

"I am, and I think that it is a great option for you. I know that the judge is very fond of you, and Ray already thinks of you as a brother." They both got up from their seats and hugged.

Three hours later Liam was all packed up and ready to move in with Judge Mahoney and Ray.

Phillips Exeter Academy

After completing his freshman and sophomore years at the Cathedral School, Judge Mahoney thought that it would be in Liam's best interest to transfer to a school with a more challenging academic environment. He recommended visiting a prep school, Phillips Exeter Academy, in Exeter, New Hampshire. Exeter was Judge Mahoney's high school alma mater. The judge often remarked how Exeter was the foundation of his success. Actually, Exeter was also the school where both of his two daughters were attending prior to their car accident. The judge had established two scholarships at the school in honor of his children who passed away. After visiting Exeter and seeing what the school was like, Liam realized that it simply was an opportunity that he couldn't pass up if he was accepted. Not to mention, Uncle Tommy and Uncle Joey were only twenty minutes away, working in the Portsmouth area.

Liam agreed to submit an application. As it turned out, his application was a mere formality since the judge was a former trustee of the school. To be honest, his biggest concern if he was accepted was what he was going to tell Mikey. The Maguires and Father C. were really the only family that he had left.

The next day, Liam went back to Southie to see the Maguires.

"Hey, Mrs. Maguire, how are you?"

"Fine, Liam, just fine. How are you doing living on the Hill?"

"Everything is good; no issues here. Is Mikey in? What's he up to these days?"

"Summer school if he wants to move up a grade."

"Seriously? I thought our tutorials were going well."

"They helped a lot, but he started too far in the hole. They're about to kick him out of the Cathedral School. He may have to transfer to Southie High. You'll be on your own there."

"Well, that's kinda why I'm here."

Mikey arrived home. "Hey, Liam, what's up?" asked Mikey.

"Hey, Mikey, you got a minute? Excuse me, Mrs. Maguire—I need to talk with Mikey."

"Sure, Liam, no problem."

"So what's up? You're still coming to the Sox game tonight, aren't you? And you need to bring a date because me and Susan hate having you as a third wheel," Mikey said with a grin. "Why don't you bring Kim Madigan; she's easy."

"Shut up, Mikey! I'll bring a date, fine. I'll see if Melissa Marlo is busy."

"Nope, you can't ask her out. She's seeing Jimmy Peterson now; you know that."

"Since when? She wasn't dating anyone as of last week."

"Jimmy asked her out on Monday, so you can't do anything for a minimum of three months from their last date—'Guy Code.'"

"Guy Code?"

"Yeah, Guy Code—you know the rules. You can't ask her out unless it's been three months."

"Guy Code—are you kidding me? Remember how I was going to ask out Sue a week before you did? And what did you do? You swooped in and asked her out behind my back. Remember that? Where was the code then?"

"I did not violate the code!"

"You sure as hell did!"

"I sure as hell did not! Look, we're best friends. Right?"

"Yeah, so."

"Part of Guy Code is that best friends can never date exes or girls that they previously hooked up with. Since Sue represents neither of those conditions, I stayed true to the code."

"Mikey, who feeds you this crap? I told you that I was going to ask her out on a Saturday, and you went behind my back and asked her out that Friday."

"Then I call the 'Gay Exception.'"

"Gay Exception? What the hell is that?"

"To be fair, she thought that you were cute, but gay."

"*Gay, really*? Why would she think that?"

"Yeah, well, I told her that you liked Jordan from New Kids on the Block."

"Isn't that a violation of the code as well? Lying about a friend's sexuality to get a girl?"

"Technically, yes. However, Sue is too much woman for you anyway. So I did you a favor."

"You suck, Mikey!"

"I know; I know, but I'm gettin' some, and you're not."

"On a separate matter, I have some good news and some bad news. Which do you want first?"

"I'm going to mix it up this time and say, bad news first."

"Well, I'm probably going away to prep school for the next couple of years."

"You mean you're leaving the Cathedral School? And Southie?"

"Afraid so."

"When?"

"In a few weeks."

"You're shittin' me. Right! We have so much to do before you leave. I can't believe that I have to run solo now! Okay, what's the good news then?"

"Well, I want to know if you would like my dad's car."

"The Nova? You're kidding me. Right? What's the catch?"

"No catch. You and your mother could use a car. As you know, my dad took great care of it. It's like new, so it's in great shape. I won't need it, and you can visit me up at school—it's only an hour away."

"No, how about I just borrow the car while you're away."

"Nope! It's all yours. Just promise me that you won't sell it after you get the papers."

"Wow, Liam, I don't know what to say. What was the bad news again because I'll be livin' large in this whip!"

"Funny guy!"

"Hey, Mom, guess what? I own a car now. No more busses for you! That is, of course, as long as you treat me nicely."

"What's this you're talking about?" said Mrs. Maguire.

"Liam just signed over his dad's Chevy Nova to me because he's going to some stupid prep school or something next year?"

"Liam, that was your dad's car; are you sure about this?"

"Well, I can't use it, and you can, so I thought that it would help everyone out. Not to mention, now Mikey can visit me when I'm at school in New Hampshire. I'm sure that I'll have to pay for his gas, but it'll be worth it to see him."

"Well, if you're okay with it, Liam, then thank you! It will help out a lot, and it will allow me more flexibility to visit Mike's father now that he transferred to Lawrence."

"Yeah, that too. Ma, you can only use my car when I'm not out with Susan, okay?" Mikey said with a smile.

"Then enjoy being homeless, Mikey," said Mrs. Maguire.

"Fine, then we're settled. Mrs. Maguire, here is the title, and I'll just sign it over to you."

"Thanks so much, Liam. You're a good boy! Now keep that one out of trouble," she said, pointing to Mikey.

"Will do. Mikey, let's go."

"Okay, okay. Ma, can I have ten bucks? I want to get some drinks at the game."

"What?" said Sue. "Wait a minute; back up. What was that last thing you said?"

"That I didn't pay for the tickets to tonight's game?"

"No, the other thing."

"You mean the Liam-not-being-gay thing?"

"Yeah, that's what I thought you said."

"You lied to me about Liam being gay? You lied to me about your best friend being gay? Why in the world would you do that?"

"Well, because there was a slight chance that Liam was kinda going to ask you out before I got up the nerve to, and I didn't want the competition. Don't worry; I didn't violate any Guy Code or anything like that."

"How about violating the code of human dignity?"

"If I knew what you meant by that, I think I would be offended," said Mikey.

"She's saying that you're a selfish ass!"

"Thank you, Liam. Come here, Liam; I want to tell you something." Sue pulled Liam in from across the table and planted a long, passionate, deep kiss on him.

"What the hell was that?" said Mikey.

"Payback!" said Sue.

"Dude, do you realize how many Guy Codes you just violated?"

"What? Me? She kissed me!"

"Okay, are we even now?" said Mikey.

"We'll be even after I sleep with him," sue said with a smile.

"No, we're good now!" exclaimed Mikey.

"Okay, we're even," Liam said.

"Good! So does anyone want anything else? I'm going to get another soda."

"I'll have lemonade," said Sue.

"Liam, anything?"

"No, I'm good."

Mikey left the table. Liam said, "Thanks for that, Sue."

"No problem! I knew you weren't gay all along."

"You're kidding. Right?"

"Nope, I just wanted to teach Mikey a lesson, and I've seen you checking me out on more than one occasion. Not to mention, now I won't be wondering anymore."

"Wondering what?"

"What it would feel like to kiss you."

Liam's knees buckled, and Mikey returned. "What? What's that look, Liam? You look like the cat that just swallowed the canary."

"No, nothing, I'm ready."

"Okay, then, let's go, or we'll be late."

"Mikey, I have to go meet Ray and the judge at the will-call window in fifteen minutes."

"Let's get going then."

"Wait—is Ray your date?" said Mikey.

"Hey, I didn't have time to ask anybody, and Ray wanted to go. What's your issue with Ray?"

"I have no issue with Ray. In fact, I haven't seen Ray in a while, and I like Ray. I just have issues with your lack of game. I bet Ray has more game than you."

At the will-call booth, Liam greeted Ray and the judge.

"Hey, Judge," Mikey said.

"Hi, Mikey, how've you been?"

"Great, thanks, Judge! This is my girlfriend, Sue. Sue, this is a friend of mine, Judge Mahoney."

"Nice to meet you, Judge."

"My pleasure, Sue."

"Sue, you remember Ray."

"Hey, Ray, nice to see you again."

"Hi, Sue. You comin' to the game with us?"

"Yeah."

"Liam, do you have enough money for snacks and a ride home?" asked the judge.

"Yes, Judge, we'll be back right after the game, if not sooner."

"Okay, see you boys after the game. Mikey, take care. Sue, try and keep these boys out of trouble." The judge winked at Sue.

"Will do, sir."

At the Sox game, they were sitting on the first-base side right in the front row.

"Wow, Liam, your security friend really came through with these seats!" said Sue.

"Bro, you need to keep this hookup going. Get him whatever he needs."

"I know. I'll figure out something."

"Hey, Sue, I was trying to explain to my man Liam over here that I have more game than him. Can I have an 'amen' to that."

"By 'amen' do you mean like you when you were stuttering when you first asking me out?"

"What's this? Stuttering Mikey?" Liam asked.

"No, I just ate an ice-cream cone too fast when I was about to ask her out, and I had a brain freeze; that's all."

"Are you kidding me? This is priceless info. Keep going!"

"Yeah, Liam, tell them about all the girls that you asked out that said no," said Ray.

"Hold on, what's going on here? Ray, I want all the details; don't leave anything out, and I want them now!" said Mikey.

"Yeah, me too," said Sue.

"Ray, shut up! That was in confidence! Hey, Ray, look—Jim Rice is up."

"No, forget about Jimmy Rice. I want to know about Romeo over here," said Mikey.

"Fine. Forget it; I'll tell you what happened. I asked out Mary Ryan, Linda Hollis, and Rebecca McNeil."

"Okay, well?"

"They all said no!" Ray screamed. "Come on, Jim; we need a hit!"

"This is priceless!" said Mikey. "I can go home now and be totally fulfilled."

"Wait a second; what happened when you asked those girls out? What did *you* say, and what did *they* say after you asked them out?" asked Sue.

"This is embarrassing. Do we have to talk about this now?"

"Yes! And spare no details," said Mikey.

"Aw, I think it's cute," said Sue. "Liam, I could have gotten several of my girlfriends to go out with you; they think you're cute."

"Thanks, Sue. I may need that help after all. Okay, this is what happened. Mary said that her father wouldn't let her date until she was seventeen."

"Sorry, Liam, that just means she wasn't interested. I saw her out with my brother last week."

"What? Ugh!" Liam said with a long-drawn face.

"Linda said that she was interested in some guy from Dorchester."

"Well, that's true; I know the guy. And Rebecca? She's a nice girl; what happened with her?" said Sue.

"Well, she originally said yes, but she heard a rumor that I was gay and so then said no, thanks to Mikey!"

"No shit!" said Mikey.

"Yeah, true story."

"Awesome!" said Mikey.

"Do you want me to talk to her?" asked Sue.

"No, just tell her I'm not gay. It would be awkward to ask her out again. Just set the record straight—no pun intended. I'd appreciate that, Sue."

"No problem, Liam. I'll even spread the rumor that you're great in bed if you want," Sue said with a smile.

"Hold on; hold on here. I think you did enough already," said Mikey.

"No, this will give me great street cred."

"Okay, it's settled. I'll do it!" said Sue.

"Bro, the things I do for you."

"For me? Are you kidding? You're the one who did this to me in the first place!"

"Liam, Liam," Ray said.

"What, Ray?"

"Jim Rice just struck out."

"See, Liam, both you and Jimmy Rice struck out!" said Mikey. They all started laughing together.

Three weeks later, Judge Mahoney, Ray, Father Callahan, and Liam packed up the judge's Range Rover with most of my belongings so that he could get set up in my new dorm room at Exeter.

"Liam, remember, these kids aren't like the kids from Southie. These kids are focused on school first and then athletics. You just need to be focused and stay on top of your homework," said Father C.

"Yes, Father."

"Don't worry, Liam; my dad says that to me every year when I start school too, and I do fine," said Ray with a smile.

"And remember, Liam, you can't hide in class when you are at the Harkness table." This was an oval-shaped classroom table used at the school to foster peer engagement and dialog. "You *have* to do your homework, and be prepared at all times," said the judge.

"Yes, sir."

"School is a priority, so stay away from the girls too. There will be plenty of time for that after you graduate high school," said Father C.

"Oh, that's okay, Father; Liam's terrible with girls. They think he's gay. That's what Mikey says anyway." Ray smiled.

The judge started laughing.

"No, Judge, it's not true. Look, Father, Mikey started that *rumor* so that I wouldn't ask out Sue Dunbar," Liam said with his most serious face.

"Okay, Liam, whatever you say, but it's still funny!"

"Yes, Judge, I will be prepared. And, Ray, you heard Mikey; he said that he was lying!" he said with a grin.

They arrived at Exeter, which is about an hour and twenty minutes outside of Boston. They walked around campus for a bit and then headed over to the George H. Love Gymnasium in search of Head Coach Ed Long's office.

"Boys, you wait right here. Father Callahan and I have to speak with the coach," Judge Mahoney said to them.

Ray and Liam waited by the car while the judge and Father C. looked for Coach Long.

"Coach Long? Coach, are you in?"

"Yes, who is there, please?"

"Judge Mahoney and a friend."

"Judge, come on in! The door is always open to you. Is Ray with you?"

"Thanks, Coach. Yeah, Ray is waiting outside. You remember my friend father Callahan, don't you?"

"Yes, of course, we met a couple of times at your home in Boston, if I remember correctly."

"Yes, a few times there and once or twice after the Andover games that he drags me to."

"Yes, of course, Father. Nice to see you again."

"Well, Coach, we just wanted to say hello. So are you ready for the season?"

"We have a good group of kids coming back this year and several key PGs (postgraduate students) who should give us a few wins."

"And Andover?"

"Judge, they got a lot of PGs this year, and my quarterback decommitted to us for Andover at the last minute."

"Yeah, I heard about that, but I have some good news for you."

"What's that? Do you have a six-feet-four, two-hundred-sixty-pound defensive lineman in your back pocket?"

"No, but close, we have a six-three, two-hundred-twenty-pound all-state quarterback with two years of eligibility in your waiting room."

"Judge, Father, don't kid with me here."

"Liam, Ray, come on in."

"Hey, Ray, how've you been?"

"Fine, Coach, thank you."

"And you must be Liam."

"Yes, sir."

"Liam, we have an opening on the team for you, but you have to earn the spot. The judge told me about you last year as a possible PG. However, now it's fantastic that you're coming in early! Practice starts tomorrow, and you can meet the rest of the guys. Welcome aboard!"

"Yes, sir. Thank you, Coach."

"Boys, give us a minute; Father C. and I will be right with you," said the judge.

"Listen, Ed, I want you to look out for this boy. He's tough, but he's been through a lot. Both parents passed away when he was young. Father Callahan here has done a great job with the boy up to this point. Here are our emergency contact numbers if he needs *anything*." The judge handed Coach Long a sheet of paper with all my emergency contact info.

"Judge, Father, I'll look after him as if her were my own son, okay?"

"Thanks, Coach," said Father Callahan.

"Appreciate it, Ed," said the judge.

Back in the coach's waiting room, the judge said, "Okay, Coach, we'll get out of your hair."

"Father, I'll see you later. Judge, I'll call you sometime this week when things get settled with an update. Liam, we start practice tomorrow morning at eight o'clock in the gym right here. Your dorm room is right across the street there in Wentworth Hall."

"Yes, Coach, eight a.m. sharp. See you tomorrow."

The judge, Father C., Ray, and Liam moved his suitcases and boxes up the staircases to his room on the second floor of Wentworth Hall. As they reached the top of the stairs, the judge remarked, "Liam, I lived in the dormitory next to this one called Cilley Hall. It's basically the same type of dormitory but with fewer kids." He paused to catch his breath. "Okay, here is your room. It looks like you're the first one here, so you can choose which side of the room you want."

"How many kids will be living here?" he asked.

"I think just two other students. Since you were a relatively late admit, I didn't get their names. I only see three beds, so I assume just three of you. You're lucky; this is a huge room."

"Where is the bathroom and shower?"

"Right down at the end of the hall to your left. You're lucky; it's close by. Thankfully, we're here early so that you can choose where you want your stuff, your desk, and your bed. Let's get settled first, and then you'll have time to acclimate yourself to the school. If you need something, downtown is walking distance, and the grocery store is only a mile outside of campus. Are you okay with all this, Liam?"

"Yes, Judge. Thank you."

"Liam, be a good boy. I know that your father is looking down on you and is proud of you."

"Thanks, Father."

"Liam, can I come for overnight visits?"

"You sure can, Ray."

"Now listen, Liam, if you need anything, just call either Father Callahan or me. Your uncles, Tommy and Joey, are really close by too, so they can be an emergency contact as well. I have advised the school as much, and their names are on your visitors list."

"I should be fine, guys. I'm all set, thanks!"

"Do you need any money, Liam?" said Father Callahan.

"No, Father, I'm fine. I put some of my dad's money in the bank here in town, Portsmouth Savings and Trust Bank, and the scholarship I have covers tuition and books. So I'm good."

"Okay, if you need anything—"

"I know. I'll call. Just try and look out for Mikey. Okay, Father?"

"I'll do my best. And remember, go to Mass every Sunday."

"I will, Father. Ray, give me a hug, and I want you to study in school too."

"I will, Liam. I love you!" said Ray.

August 28, 1986

Hey Mikey,

I hope all is well with you. I've been up here at school just a few days now, and it's been an eye-opening experience to say the least. All here are really nice and extremely focused in whatever they do. Whether it's football, school, music, or the arts, they all want to succeed at everything that they set their minds to. It's very competitive from that point of view, but I'll be fine. I'm not intimidated by them in the classroom or especially on the football field. It's all about time management and completing all your homework before class. The good news is that there aren't many, if any, distractions. We're not allowed to watch TV, except in what is called a "common area," and even then, it has to be a consensus of what to watch. Let's just say that there are not a lot of Red Sox fans at this school, at least that I've found yet.

Football is going well. The football team consists of mostly underclassmen, a handful of seniors, and several of what they call "PGs." PGs are postgraduate students who are taking an extra year of high school to refine their academics and are trying to get into better colleges. The good news is that last year's quarterback graduated. The backup quarterback quit the team to play soccer this year, and the quarterback that they did recruit opted for another school. So basically, I have a shot to start this year.

As far as the girls go here, this is a whole new ballgame. I'm afraid that my swagger will not work here. It's a totally different approach to

*these girls. They don't like games; nor do they like cocky and arrogant
kids. More on that to follow.*

*The food here is good, but not as good as your mother's cooking or
Ray's Pizzeria.*

*Be well, Mikey, and stay out of trouble! Don't wreck the car either!
Please give your mom a hug for me, and tell Sue that I may need her
help up here!*

Seamrog dubh,

Liam

*PS: You have my old computer and printer, so there is no excuse
for not writing me back!*

Back at Wentworth Hall, Liam's new roommates arrived. And they introduced themselves to him.

"Hi, I'm Liam."

"I see you already moved in," said Tom Humphrey.

"Well, I had to put my stuff somewhere."

"I'm Tom, Tom Humphrey."

"So, Tom, where are you from?"

"New York City. And you?"

"Boston."

"This is Brett Welch."

"Hey, Brett."

"Hey." Brett nodded.

"We've been roommates since freshman year."

"So, Liam, what's your story?" said Tommy.

"My story?"

"Yeah, everyone here has a story. For example, Brett over there is from San Francisco, and his dad is the provost at Stanford. He was a senior advisor to President Reagan."

"Yeah, and Tom is a Broadway triple threat: actor/dancer/singer. He won a Tony Award for *La Cage aux Folles* a couple of years ago. So what's your story?"

"Wow, both very impressive! I'm not sure I have a story that can compete with that I'm afraid."

"Are you a PG?"

"No, but I'm trying out for the football team."

"Were you recruited?"

"No, I was a late admit."

"Where are you from again?"

"Boston."

"Yeah, but where in Boston?"

"Well, I'm actually from South Boston, but I live on Beacon Hill."

"Ah, Mayflower money," said Tom.

"Yup, that must be it," said Brett.

"Mayflower money? What does that mean?"

"Well, you live on Beacon Hill. Duh, that's where there all the old Boston money lives. There is no reason to be ashamed of having money."

"I'm not ashamed. The truth is, I'm here on scholarship. Both of my parents passed away, and an alum is sponsoring me to come here."

"Okay, so you're a scholarship kid. But there must be something else? Do you have any skills? For example, the kid next to us, Maxwell Smith, is a scholarship kid, but he won the national spelling bee two years ago. Or there is another scholarship kid here, named Melissa Wright, who earned a perfect score on her SATs—when she was in eighth grade! They're both freaks of nature if you ask me."

"Wow! No, sorry, I don't think I have a unique skill set, old money, or influential parents."

"No, there is something about you. I'll figure it out. Well, plenty of time for that. Let's grab lunch, and I can give you the lay of the land here. Liam, beware, lunch is a form of social hierarchy here."

"Social hierarchy?"

"Yeah, you'll see; all the jocks sit together. Then you have the different ethnic societies, like the Asian American Society, African American Society, followed by the math geeks, science nerds, and the artsy people. The artsy kids don't care about anything except getting high and playing guitar. Most of those kids don't have a care in the world because they come from a lot of money. Basically, their parents sent them here so that they wouldn't have to deal with them at home."

"Okay, so where do you two fit in?"

"Excellent question, Liam. We consider ourselves a hybrid group—who live on the social fringe, if you will," said Tom.

"I would say that is fairly accurate," said Brett.

"I'm not sure what that means."

"To be honest, Liam, neither are we, but it sounds really cool," Tom said with a smile.

"Got it. What do you say we discuss this over lunch?"

"Good idea; let's go."

Walking to the dining hall, they saw a group of girls from the dorm heading over for lunch as well.

"Okay, Tom, Brett, what's the story with the girls here?"

"Liam, that's a whole other story."

As they entered the dining hall, they saw a bunch of the guys on the football team sitting together, and Liam nodded in their direction. Tom, Brett, and Liam sat down at a table across from Liam's teammates. Just then, John Caru, the nose guard on the team, walked over. "Dude, what are you doing with these geeks?"

"Geeks? They're my roommates. They're cool—relax, John."

"Cool? These two? Are you out of your mind? Tom and Brett play Dungeons and Dragons for Christ's sake. Come over and sit with us. Would you?"

"No, I'm all set unless they can come over too."

"Dude, you are committing social suicide by sitting here!"

"Go ahead, Liam; we can catch up later," said Brett.

"No, we're good."

"Go away, John, you Neanderthal," said Tom.

"Fuck you, Tom."

"Okay, John, we'll all go over there and eat," Liam said.

They all got up and left for the jock table.

"Guys, how's it going? You guys know my roommates? This is Tom and this is Brett."

The guys nodded. "Guys, watch out for this one; he wears tights," John said, pointing to Tom.

"John, I don't know why you insist on constantly insulting me? Are you that insecure about yourself that you have to pick on me?" said Tom.

"Shut up, you little shit, before I lock you in that closet over there," he said, pointing to the janitor's closet. "The only reason I will tolerate you in the first place is because of Liam." He motioned toward him across the table. "For some reason he likes to save lost puppies."

"Brilliant analysis, John, just brilliant," said Tom.

"You know, John, you should find some common ground with Tommy, and you'll see how much you two would get along," said Liam.

"That geek and I have nothing in common! He's a ballet dancer for Christ's sake."

"See, John, that's where you're wrong; we actually have a great deal in common. For example, when I go back to New York, I can go on Broadway where people will pay to see me dance. When you go back to New York, you can go see your mother dance. The only difference is that she uses a pole," he said and got up and sprinted out of the lunchroom with his books falling from the table to the exit door.

Liam spit his milk out in hysterical laughter.

John got up and screamed, "You're dead, Humphries! When I catch you, you're freakin' dead!"

Both Dave Easterly and Joe Jaxx, who were also on the football team, were sitting straddling John and holding him down in his seat.

"That was some of the funniest stuff I have ever heard," said Joe.

"That was priceless! Freakin' priceless!" said Dave.

"Screw you both! If—no, when—I catch him, I'll take care of it. And you need to stay out of this, Liam. It's between him and me."

"Come on, John; seriously, that was pretty funny," Liam said.

"Yeah, I have to admit it was pretty funny. That friggin' little shit."

"What are you laughing about, Brett? I can still stick you in that closet."

"Never mind him, Brett; his bark is worse than his bite," said Liam.

Lunch was finished, and Brett and Liam walked back to our dorm room.

"Well, that was entertaining; thanks, Liam," Brett said.

"For what?" he asked.

"Sticking up for us and not succumbing to those guys."

"Hey, no big deal. You know, if you give them a chance, they're really nice guys."

"Nevertheless, thanks. Hey, Liam, can I ask you for a favor?"

"Sure, Brett, what's up?"

"You know that kid we were talking about earlier today, Maxwell Smith?"

"The spelling-bee kid who lives next to us?"

"Yeah, him."

"What's up?"

"Well, he's a friend of mine and Tommy's, and he's having a little bit of trouble with some upperclassmen. You see, he sleeps with a nightlight, and they make fun of him and pick on him."

"How so?"

"Well, last night, for example, they taped him to his bed."

"That's what all that noise was about?"

"Afraid so."

"What did he do to them that they would tape him to a bed?"

"Nothing. They pick on him because he's smart."

"Who is leading these guys?"

"A lacrosse player by the name of Billy Nottingham."

"Okay. What room is he in?"

"He's two floors above us."

"Okay, go back to the dorm, and tell Max that I'm on my way to talk to him."

Brett and Liam parted ways as Liam headed over to Abbot Hall, where John, Dave, and Joe lived.

"Where are Dave and Joe?" Liam asked John.

"Down in Dave's room, why?"

"I need some help with something."

"With what?"

"Some kid named Billy Nottingham is giving a neighbor of mine a hard time."

"Who's your neighbor?"

"Max Smith."

"The spelling-bee kid?"

"Yup."

"So who gives a shit? How is that any of our business?"

"Look, I need a favor. I just need backup in case this goes sideways."

"You're telling me you can't handle those lightweights? Nottingham is a pussy."

"I don't want to get kicked out after the first week, so I'm open to suggestions."

"Go get Joe and Dave."

He left for ten minutes and came back with Joe and Dave.

"Okay, guys, that prick Nottingham is giving one of Liam's 'projects' some shit. He's asking us to help him handle this with him. You guys in?"

"Sure, I hate that Nottingham kid anyway!"

"Okay, I'm in too. Who is he giving shit to?"

"Max Smith."

"You mean that little spelling-bee kid?"

"Yeah, him."

"Okay, how do you want to handle this?"

"Just wait in the hallway and follow my lead."

John, Joe, Dave, and I walked into the Wentworth dorm and knocked on Max's door. "Hello?" said Max with the door closed.

"Max, it's me, Brett. Open up."

Max started to open the door a crack, saying, "Hey, Brett—"

Then he quickly slammed the door shut when he saw me and the other guys behind him.

"No, Max, they're here to help."

"Do they have tape with them?"

"No, of course not! Seriously, just open the door."

"Look, kid, either open the door or I'll break it down!" said John.

Max sheepishly opened the door.

"Okay, kid, let's go," said John.

"Where are we going?" said Max.

"To the fourth floor," Liam said.

There was a knock on Billy Nottingham's door. "Hey, are you Billy? Billy Nottingham?"

"Yeah, and you are?"

"I'm Liam O'Hara. I'm new here in school, but I just wanted to introduce myself to you."

"Okay, I guess. And this is my roommate, Dexter Raddle."

"Nice to meet you both."

"Is that it?" asked Billy as he turned to Dexter, shrugging.

"Well, there is one other thing."

"Yeah, what's that?"

"I need you guys to lay off my cousin."

"Oh yeah, who is your cousin?"

"Max Smith."

"You know, Liam, for a new kid, you're in no position to be giving orders. You have to earn that respect here."

"You know, Billy, I thought that you might say as much, so I want to introduce you to Max's other cousins, who've been here a couple of years already: Cousin John, Cousin Dave, and Cousin Joe. Get the picture?"

"Screw this, Liam! Look, Nottingham, leave this kid alone, or I'll tape you up and stick you in the quad in your underwear," said John.

"You do that, and you'll get kicked out of school," said Billy.

"Listen, tough guy, we could report you for what you already did to little Max. So if you or any of your lacrosse fag friends go near him again, one of us will deal with you! You got that!" John said.

"Whatever, he's not worth my time anyway."

"Yeah, I thought so," said John. They all started walking downstairs.

Meanwhile, in Max's room he was contemplating leaving school.

"Max, why are you crying?" Liam asked.

"I'm not crying."

"Guys, give me a minute with Brett and Max. I'll meet up with you guys at the gym." Liam waved off John, Joe, and Dave. "Help me out here, Brett; what's up?"

"I don't know. Max?"

"It's just that..." he said between sniffs. "It's just that nobody has ever stood up for me before."

"Hey, Max, guys like Nottingham are assholes! Just ask Brett and Tom."

"Thank you, Liam."

"Hey, no need to thank me. You should be thanking Tommy and Brett here. They're the ones looking out for you. And another thing, I want you to sit with me and the guys at lunch if you want. You should get to know them. They're really nice guys.

"Hey, I have to run to the gym. We'll catch up later. And remember, I want you to tell me if any of those guys bother you again! Got it?"

"Yes, will do, and please thank the guys again for me too."

"Okay, will do, Max."

CLASSES BEGIN

September 14, 1986

Mikey,

I'm a couple of weeks into school, and things are going really well. I'm taking Chinese, calculus, American history, music theory, and creative writing. That's going to keep me busy for the first half of the year. I do, however, miss you, the guys, and Sue. I tried calling you the other night, but your mother said that you were out. Sorry to hear about you getting kicked out of the Cathedral School. Southie High shouldn't be that bad. You know everyone there anyway, so you'll be fine. Now Sue can keep an eye on you 24-7. Ha!

My roommates are cool, different than what we're used to in Southie, but cool nevertheless. Tommy (Humphrey) is from NYC and won a prestigious Tony Award a couple of years ago for one of his Broadway performances. My other roommate is a kid named Brett Welch. Brett is from San Francisco, and his father is the provost at Stanford. And then we have me: the orphaned scholarship kid from Southie. These guys are nice because they don't judge me for what I have (or, in this case, do not have), and they take me at face value. Other kids at this school tend to be more superficial and are very status conscious.

Good news on the football front: it looks like I'll get the nod at QB. I'll send you the schedule, and maybe you can come catch a game if it doesn't conflict with any Southie football games. If not, maybe you can make it up for a weekend visit? Our season starts next week against a team called Choate Rosemary Hall in Wallingford, CT. They supposedly have a hotshot running back, but we should do well against them anyway.

I hope that you're getting my letters. I know that you must be busy, but try and write when you get a chance. Give my best to your mother and Sue.

Seamrog dubh,
Liam

"HEY, LIAM, I JUST GOT back from the PO, and you have a letter. Here it is," said Brett.

September 22, 1986
Liam,
My bad for not getting back to you sooner, but a lot has been going on since you left for prep school. I got your letters and your messages from my mom, thanks! School is going okay (your computer actually helps a lot, thanks), but it's not the same without you. For example, Sue won't let me copy her homework like you did, my new tutor knows less than me, and the administration stuck me in remedial classes because they heard that I flunked out of the Cathedral School. That doesn't bother me because this makes me the smartest kid in idiot classes. Now I know how you felt all these years. On the flip side, there is no dress code at Southie High, I know everyone here, and nobody is chasing after me when I cut school, except Sue.

Regarding football, it turns out that I am academically ineligible to play this season due to some Mass Interscholastic Athletic Association (MIAA) transfer rule. Apparently, some of my credits from Cathedral didn't transfer because I flunked a few classes last semester. I hope to have everything in order by baseball season. The Southie High administration has me as a second-semester sophomore, so I have a little bit of catching up to do if I want to graduate on time.

Great news on the football front for you! I knew that you would do equally well up there as you were doing down here. The good news is that Sue and I should be able to catch a couple of your games this year since I won't be playing ball at Southie. Naturally, you'll have to reimburse me for gas and additional expenses. Send me your schedule.

Hey, Sue and I were very concerned about your social life after reading your last letter. First of all, what makes you think that you have any *game with the ladies whatsoever? Who are you kidding? And what the hell is this about your* swagger? *I'm embarrassed for you that you actually wrote that. You have a better shot with someone on the men's water polo team (kidding!). Sue is here with me, and she said that she'll help you out.*

Talk later kid.

Seamrog dubh!

Mikey

"Liam, you have a phone call. Hurry up, though, because there are a few guys here waiting to make some calls," someone yelled from the basement, where the phone is located.

"Sure, thanks."

Liam ran down the hallway and stairs and grabbed the phone.

"Hi, this is Liam."

"Hey, Liam, it's Ray."

"Hey, Ray! How's it going? How's school goin'? And the judge? How's he doing?"

"Great! School is great. I have the same teacher as last year, and I asked a girl out."

"What? You asked someone out? Who?"

"Mary Holly."

"I don't know her. What did she say?"

"She said no because she said that her dad wouldn't let her date yet."

"You know what that means, right, Ray?"

"Yup, just like what happened to you, it's code for 'I don't like you.'"

"You're too funny, Ray."

"Well, it happens, just like you, right, Liam? But I'll keep trying."

"Yes, Ray, just like me. I haven't given up either."

"My dad and Father Callahan are here, and they want to speak with you."

Ray handed his father the phone. "Liam?"

"Yes, Judge."

"How are you doing, young man? Staying out of trouble I hope."

"Yes, sir."

"Headmaster Johnson says that you are doing well in your classes, and Coach Long tells me that you are resetting the record books up there."

"Yeah, school is going well, really well, in fact. You and Father C. were right, though. You have to study each night and be prepared for every class. This place has no room for slackers."

"Yes, but try and enjoy yourself too."

"Yes, sir."

"Liam, are you okay for money?"

"Yes, sir, I kept a record of all my expenses for you."

"No, there is no need for that. Just make sure you budget for your books, clothing, and if you want to go to the movies or something. Father Callahan is here and wants to speak with you."

"Okay, sure."

"Liam?"

"Hey, Father."

"Liam, my son, how are you?"

"Great, Father. How are you feeling?"

"Well, this new diet is challenging to say the least. I sneak in a slice of Ray's pizza once in a while, but don't say anything to Ms. Spina—she'll kill me! Other than that, it's mostly salads. But enough about me. I'm glad to hear that you are keeping up with your grades and that football is going so well. Your dad would be very proud of you."

"Thanks, Father! I really appreciate all that you and the judge have done for me. Hey, did you guys get the sweatshirts that I sent?" Liam asked.

"Yes, yes, we did, and that's the other reason for our call, to thank you for your generosity. We are all wearing them now with great pride. Keep up the good work, Liam!" Father C. said.

"I'm glad, Father. Will you and the judge be coming up for parents weekend this week? We play Deerfield, and they're supposed to be the best team in the league," Liam asked hopefully.

"Yes, Liam, we're all coming up to the game, and we look forward to catching up with you and your new friends."

"See you then, Father. Tell everyone good-bye. There's a line here to use the phone, and I don't want to be rude to everyone who is waiting," Liam said.

"Okay, son, one last thing: you're going to Mass, aren't you?"

"Yes, of course, Father."

"Good boy. See you this weekend."

"Bye."

Parents Weekend

Judge Mahoney pulled him aside as he was exiting the football locker room. "Well, that was quite a game, Liam! You passed for over three hundred yards, ran for ninety, and threw two touchdowns."

"Thanks, Judge, but this really was a team effort. Hey, these are some of my friends and guys on the team. This is John Caru, the offensive tackle and nose guard; Joe Jaxx, the tight end; and Dave Easterly, the defensive tackle."

"Congratulations, boys. So you are the guys making our Liam look good?"

"Finally, someone gets it," John said, and everyone laughed.

Coach Long exited the locker room.

"Coach, another great win! You have quite a team here."

"Thanks, Judge, but we still have a few kinks to work out. Don't we, boys? How many off sides are you going to get called, Mr. Jaxx?"

"Yes, Coach," said Joe with his head down.

"Nevertheless, all that is behind us; it was a great win, and you all played exceptionally well. Please excuse me. I have to see some other parents. Enjoy this evening, boys, and we'll see you Monday for film review."

"Ed, we'll talk later," said the judge. "So, boys, are all of your families here?"

"Yeah, mine are over there," said Joe. "They're waiting to go grab a bite, so I gotta go. Nice to meet you, sir. Guys, I'll catch you later."

"Later, Joe," said Liam.

"Yeah, see you guys back at the dorm later," Joe said as he ran to catch up to his parents.

"Well, it looks like it's just us. John, David, are your parents here this weekend, or would you like to join us?"

"Well, sir, my parents couldn't make it up this weekend because they are traveling. However, I do not want to be intrusive," said John.

"Same with me, sir," said Dave.

"Nonsense, you both will join us. This is our good friend father Callahan. That means no swearing, boys," the judge said with a wink and a smile, "and this is my son, Ray."

"Father," John said as he nodded in his direction. "And, Ray, how are you? You are all that Liam talks about, and he has the picture of you both from Little League on his desk."

"Really, Liam? Me too," Ray said as he gave me a hug.

"Okay, boys, let's go. How about some Italian food?"

Later that evening Liam said, "Judge, Father, Ray, thanks so much for coming today and for taking my friends to dinner."

"No problem, Liam, we're all very proud of you."

"Thanks! Hey, Father, how's Mikey doing? I've only received one letter from him since I've been here."

"Not good I'm afraid, Liam. He's starting to hang out with the wrong crowd and skipping school far too much."

"Well, after winter break, I'll speak with him, and I'll see what's up."

"I went up to visit Big Mike the other day, and we had a chat about Mikey. I think things will change when Tommy speaks to him. I'll let you know otherwise. Don't worry about Mikey; we'll look after him. Just stay focused in school and stay out of trouble," Father C. said with a smile.

"Will do. I'll see you guys in a few weeks, or sooner if you can make one of the next few games."

Liam walked back upstairs and into his dorm room.

"Hey, Liam, how was your visit?" asked Brett.

"Fine. And yours? I wish the judge could have met your parents. I told them all about you."

"Me too. My parents had some business at Harvard and MIT that they had to attend to, something to do with a joint degree program that my dad is trying to put together."

"Sounds interesting."

"Whatever, at least they stopped by. By the way, Tom and I went to your game. Nice job out there."

"You guys don't even like football, though."

"I know, but my dad does, and he's happy that you're my roommate."

"Well, thanks."

"Hey, one more thing, the PO accidentally put your letter in my PO box. Here it is."

"Thanks! Hey, it's from my friend Mikey from home."

"Just tell your 'friend' that there is only one *t* in *Exeter*."

"Oops, will do, and thanks."

October 14, 1986

Liam,

I know that you have a lot going on with school, ball, and everything, but I really need to talk to you. Things aren't going so good here at home. School is not working out too well because the administration wants to put me back a full year, as opposed to just one semester behind. My mother lost her job because of downsizing at the hospital, and I have to get a job to help pay rent.

I tried calling your dorm again the other night, but it seems like they never give you my messages. Next time I call, I'll try not to threaten them if they don't give you the messages. On second thought, Sue and I will be up there next week to see you. We can talk then. Father C. said that he had a good visit with you last week. Thanks for the sweatshirt for me and the T-shirt for Sue. She really likes it, and I can cut up the sweatshirt and use it for rags when I wash my car! Ha! See you this weekend.

Talk later, kid.

Seamrog dubh!

Mike

Liam immediately decided to call Mikey.

"Hi, Mrs. Maguire, it's Liam. How are you?"

"Fine, thanks. How are you, Liam?"

"Great, thanks. Busy, but great. Is Mikey around? I just received his letter."

"Sorry, Liam, you just missed him. He's on a job interview. He's been trying to help out more after all the layoffs at the hospital."

"Yeah, I heard. I'm sorry to hear about that. Where is he lookin'?"

"The car wash down on Kennedy Boulevard was looking for some help. They said that they would offer him plenty of hours."

"You mean the Shamrock Car Wash?"

"Yeah, that's the one. Father Callahan knows the owner and set it up. I don't know what we would do without that man."

"I hope it works out. Yeah, Father C. is a savior; that's for sure."

"Thanks, Liam, we'll pull through this; we always do."

"Well, tell Mikey that I'm looking forward to seeing him and Sue this weekend if they can make it."

"I know that he can't wait to see you too; stay well."

THE DEERFIELD GAME

OUT OF THE CORNER OF his eye, he could see Mikey and Sue in the top left section of the home team stands. It was the first time that he'd seen Mikey in over three months.

He looked up and waved at them with a huge smile just before the game started. Mikey nodded, and Sue stood up and screamed, "Go, number one!"

The game was going back and forth, and Exeter really couldn't put Deerfield away. It was late in the fourth quarter; they were only up by three points (20–17) when Deerfield took a punt fifty-six yards all the way back and scored a touchdown. They were now in the unfamiliar position of being behind in the fourth quarter. They were losing 24–20 with just under two minutes left in the game. A field goal would do no good, so they had to score a touchdown to win the game. Their perfect season was in jeopardy, along with the league championship. Deerfield kicked the ball off to them, and they were pinned down on their own twelve-yard line. Seven passes and one penalty later, they made it all the way to the Deerfield fifteen-yard line with twenty-three seconds left on the clock.

At this point, Mikey and Sue made it down to the sidelines from the stands where they were sitting. Both sides of the fans were screaming at their respective teams. Coach Long decided to call his final time-out.

"Okay guys, we only have twenty-three seconds left, so we're going to have to score quickly. We don't have any time-outs so here it is— Liam, I want you to do a fake bootleg left and see if you can find Joe dragging across the end zone. If's he's covered, just run for your life!"

Liam faked the bootleg left and was looking for Joe as they planned. Unfortunately, Joe was covered by the middle linebacker as he was crossing the back of the end zone, so Liam was forced to run. Liam tucked the ball under his arm and he made two Deerfield players miss him. Just as Liam was about to cross the goal line, he was hit by two defensive linemen two yards short of the end zone. Exeter lost the game 20–24, but Liam had his coming out party as one of the premiere players in the league.

THE ANDOVER GAME

EXETER WAS LEADING 8–0 INTO the last game of the year against Phillips Andover. Andover had a record of 7–1; their only loss was to Deerfield Academy, and that was only by one point, 21–20. Liam had no idea that the rivalry was as big as it was. This would be the 104th meeting between the two teams since its inception in 1878. Only three times during the eighteen hundreds was the rivalry put on hold and no games were played. As one of the captains of the team this year, he attended a banquet at Phillips Academy a couple of nights before the game. After meeting the other players and taking pictures, there was the usual Q&A by the media. In most cases, it involved both school newspapers and the local area press. But after these particular sets of questions were over, a man came up to him and asked some additional questions.

"Excuse me, are you Liam? Liam O'Hara?"

"Yes?"

"You have a unique name. By chance, are you from South Boston?"

"Yes, I am; how did you know?"

"You mean you don't remember me?"

"I'm sorry, no. Should I?"

"How about this. *Seamrog dubh.*"

"No way! Doug? Doug Chase, *Boston Globe* reporter, is that you?"

"Jeez, finally!"

"No freakin' way! What the hell are you doing here?"

"I'm doing my boss a favor. You see, I graduated from Phillips Andover many, many moons ago. Actually, this is the place that taught me how to write. Anyway, the local sports guy is sick, so he asked me to cover the banquet and the game. Okay, that's my story. What about you?"

"Well, you know about my dad's passing because you were at the funeral."

"Tragic. Again, my condolences."

"Thanks, and it meant a lot to me that you showed up."

"It was the least that I could do after all the time we spent together during that glorious Little League run."

"Anyway, after my dad's passing, I was supposed to live with Father Callahan, per my father's will. Father C. was cool with it, and things were going well. Unfortunately, about three months into the arrangement, the archdiocese decided that a thirteen-year-old orphaned boy living in the rectory with adult priests was not a good idea; especially with everything going on in the media. The state was about to intervene, which would have meant Foster Care, but Judge Mahoney came in at the eleventh hour and agreed to take me in. The judge then set me up at Exeter, his alma mater."

"Wow! that is an incredible story! So what position are you playing here at Exeter?"

"I'm the quarterback."

"No way! I spoke with Coach Gray, the Andover coach, earlier, and he told me that the Exeter QB was the best that he's ever seen in thirty years of watching film. He said that you've already passed for over three thousand yards this season. Is that true?"

"Yeah, something like that. It's really not that hard when you have a pair of six-five wide receivers who can run like deer and a tight end who is a beast."

"Once again, very modest. Your problem this weekend will be the fact that Coach Gray has one DB going to Michigan, the other going to Boston College, and the free safety signed with Notre Dame."

"Yeah, I heard all that. No big deal. We have some players too."

"I hope so because this is for a share of the prep-school title as well."

"No worries. *Seamrog dubh*," Liam said with a smile.

"Hey, I have to run. Good luck and see you Saturday. Make sure you say hello to Mikey, the judge, Ray, and Father C. for me, okay?"

"Will do. Thanks, Doug. Great to see you again! We'll talk after the game."

SUNDAY, NOVEMBER 10, *BOSTON GLOBE* HIGH SCHOOL SPORTS SECTION

SOUTH BOSTON'S O'HARA LEADS EXETER OVER

ANDOVER IN CHAMPIONSHIP SHOWDOWN

—DOUG CHASE

EXETER, NEW HAMPSHIRE: PHILLIPS EXETER quarterback Liam O'Hara, a Cathedral High School transfer from South Boston, threw for a league record 460 yards and four touchdowns as host Phillips Exeter Academy beat Phillips Andover Academy 31–24 in the 104th meeting between the two storied schools.

What I witnessed today was quarterback perfection as Liam O'Hara picked apart the Phillips Academy defense as if they were standing still. O'Hara, who is only a junior, threw for over four hundred yards for the third time this season, giving him over three thousand passing yards for the year and earned him game MVP. The Phillips Academy defense was not without merit going into this game. Phillips Academy had two All-American defensive backs, Chatham's Nick Burns and Natick's Paul Garner, who will be attending Michigan and Boston College, respectively, on full scholarships. The free safety, Mike Morgan, from Fort Wayne, Indiana, just signed with Notre Dame as well.

"These Andover kids are tier-one athletes and this O'Hara kid made them look like they were playing for the JV team," said the Syracuse scout who was at the game, looking at Andover's defensive lineman Sean Enos, from Framingham.

I saw that Phillips Academy was in for a long day after the first set of downs. O'Hara, who was pinned down on his own fifteen-yard line, rolled out to his left in a play-action fake and then threw a forty-five-yard strike across the field hitting his six-feet-five-inch wide receiver, Brian Leonard, a Duke commit, right in stride for an eighty-five-yard touchdown on the third play of the game. Later in the game, it was fourth down and three yards to go on Andover's forty-five-yard line. O'Hara took the ball in shotgun formation and threw a perfect fade in the far-right corner of the end zone for his second score just before the half.

The Stanford scout, who was recruiting Enos as well, said that he "hadn't seen an arm like that since John Elway." The scout went on to say that the way O'Hara threw the ball, he "could start at Boston College, Northwestern, and a few other D-I schools right now. I'm sure we'll offer him after Coach Walsh sees this film."

The game went back and forth from that point on with an aggressive running attack by Phillips Academy. They were led on the ground by junior Rob Chen, a hulking six-foot-one-inch 215-pound running back from San Diego, California, who rushed for over 100 yards, and in the air by postgraduate Jason Werth, who decommitted from Exeter late in the fall to attend Phillips Andover Academy. Werth, who threw for a respectable 175 yards and one touchdown, was injured late in the third quarter, and Andover never found their momentum again.

After the game, O'Hara, who shuns the spotlight, gave the entire credit for the win to his offensive linemen: John Caru (Lynnfield, Massachusetts), Dave Easterly (Liverpool, New York), Joe Jaxx (Portland, Maine), and Peter Callahan (Lexington, Massachusetts). "Without their excellent play on both sides of the ball, we clearly would not have won today." After his record-breaking performance, O'Hara reflected on what he accomplished and then said that he had to excuse himself because he had a Chinese language final exam to prepare for. This is what high-school sports are all about: true *scholar athletes.*

WINTER BREAK

AFTER THE ANDOVER GAME AND the very flattering article by Doug Chase, Liam's dorm phone had been ringing nonstop. Finally, he had to put up a sign next to the phone saying that if a call was for him and it wasn't a family member, then whoever answered should take the name/number and he would call them back. Football recruiters all over the country wanted to talk to him about their summer camps; media outlets wanted to talk to me about doing in-depth articles on him, and for some reason, he had been invited to three local high-school proms.

The prom invitations seemed most interesting of all since none of the girls here would give him the time of day. Even his six-foot-two, 260-pound offensive lineman John Caru had a girlfriend! That's how bad his dry spell had been at Exeter. He thought maybe Sue could set him up with one of her friends Southie High when he came home for break.

After meeting with Coach Long, they reviewed his options for summer football camps. They decided that Liam would attend the Stanford, Notre Dame, and Boston College camps, provided that it was okay with the judge. The judge had no issue with the idea just as long as Liam agreed to work between breaks and camps. The judge secured Liam an internship at the Isabella Stewart Gardner Museum in downtown Boston. The museum allowed Liam flexible hours with his schedule. Even though he had five weeks off before school started, his internship began on the second week of his break.

While at home over the next few weeks, Liam really didn't get a chance to spend much time with Mikey and Sue. They went out for pizza a few times, but he was learning his new job as greeter at the Museum. Mikey was working at the car wash most of the time since his mother was still out of work, and Sue was still in school. It seemed like they were all going in different directions.

The weekend before he was supposed to go back to Exeter for the winter semester, Liam decided that he would surprise Mikey and Sue with a blowout weekend that they wouldn't soon forget. The gang would start with surf-and-turf dinner at Legal Seafood, followed by concert tickets at the Boston Garden to see Aerosmith, and then dessert at Faneuil Hall.

At Mikey's house he rang the intercom, "Mikey, it's Liam. You ready?"

"Yeah, come on up, though; my mother wants to say hello."

Liam bounded up the stairs. "Hey, Mrs. Maguire, how are you?"

"Come here, Liam; give me a hug. How are you?"

"Fine, school is great, and I'm working at the Gardner Museum during break."

"I heard that. What are you doing exactly at the museum?"

"Well, my title sounds good, it's 'Assistant to the Curator.' But it's about as entry level as it gets. Basically, I prepare the museum for rotating exhibits—which means clearing out exhibit space and boxing up paintings and sculptures. In addition, I assist artists in residence with their needs—paint, carving materials, and anything else they require while they create their art. Oh, and I also pick up all the trash in and around the museum. I've become especially adept at that," Liam said with a smile.

"Your mother and father would be so proud of you, especially about that article in the *Globe* a few weeks back," she said as she opened her family photo album and pulled it out.

"Thank you. That's very nice of you to say, Mrs. Maguire. Mr. Maguire was also kind enough to send me a note as well."

"Well, I won't keep you, young people, any longer. You kids have fun tonight. Mikey, do you need some money?"

"No, Ma, we're fine."

"Okay, Sue, keep them out of trouble."

"Yes, ma'am."

Over dinner at Legal Seafood, they discussed their next five-to-ten-year plans about going into business together, since playing for the Red Sox didn't look like it was going to pan out. They talked about how they were going to live, raise their kids, and grow old together in South Boston.

"So, Sue, how many kids should we have?" asked Mikey.

"What makes you think I'm marrying you?"

"You're kiddin' me. Right? I'm the total freakin' package!"

"What makes you the total package?" Liam asked, choking on his water.

"What do you mean? It's pretty evident I'd say," Mikey said as he looked at both Liam and Sue in disbelief. "What? I'm good looking, in shape, smart—maybe not as smart as Liam, but smart, nevertheless—loyal, honest, and trustworthy."

"Well, I kinda have to give him that. Those are admirable traits for a spouse. Based on that criteria alone, I guess he does qualify. He's got a lot going on, Sue," Liam said, stifling a giggle.

"The question is, how can he support someone other than himself? And even that is difficult," said Sue.

"Wait a minute, I make four hundred fifty dollars a week at the car wash."

"Okay, after rent, gas, insurance, and food, what's left over?"

"Whatever *you* make," Mikey said with a grin. "Not to mention, Ms. know-it-all, Liam and I have a plan. Whoever makes it big will employ the other, so I just doubled my odds."

"Liam, is that true?"

"Yup! That's what we agreed to do since we were little kids."

"Well, then maybe you have a shot, Mikey," said Sue. "We'll see after college."

"Whatever, let's get going to the concert, or we'll be late."

After the Aerosmith concert, they went to the Four Clover Bar in Faneuil Hall.

"Hey, look, there are three seats over there in the corner. Let's grab 'em quick before someone else does," Mikey said.

"On it," Liam said.

"Sweet! Nice job, Liam!"

"See, Sue, I told you he was good for something," Mikey said with a smirk.

"You know, there is no way the waitress will find us over here."

"No problem. I have to go powder my nose. I'll pick up a pitcher. Mikey, give me twenty bucks."

"Here you go," he said as Sue walked away. "So, Liam, what's this— a preppy bar or somethin'?"

"I dunno? Why?"

"I'm seein' lots of preppy shit here; that's all. Like stuff up at your school—Lacoste, Brooks Brothers, and that J. Press crap that your roommate was telling me about."

"Who, Tom?"

"Yeah, the kid from New York."

"Figures, but he's really nice, though."

"Hey, Liam, heads-up. Is that guy at the bar giving Sue a hard time?"

"No, she's just trying to get by him; that's all. Mikey, relax. Sue is a beautiful girl, and she's going to get hit on outside of Southie. That's just a reality."

"Yeah, I know, but I think that guy put his hands on her."

"No way. Let me go over there and show you that you're wrong."

Liam walked up to the bar and joined Sue. "Hey, Sue, you need a hand?"

"Thanks, Liam, take these glasses."

The guy in question interrupted. "Sorry, pal, looks like she's going to stay here awhile. Why don't you go back over there and sit with your boyfriend?"

"Sue, step on through while I talk to this guy," Liam whispered in her ear. "Tell Mikey to keep his distance."

Mikey quickly stepped up because he could read Liam face as Sue approached with their pitcher of beer. Sue begged Mikey to sit down.

"Mikey, if you love me, you'll just stay here and let Liam deal with that jerk!"

"I can't. I do love you, but it's Liam."

"He told me to tell you to sit tight; he's got this."

"Okay, Sue, but if he swings at Liam, I can't stay."

"Yes, I know."

A pushing match ensued, and then Liam returned to their table.

"Well?" asked Mikey.

"You were right; he was hitting on Sue. In fact, he called us fags for sitting together like we were waiting for Sue."

"What? Sure, I can see him calling you a fag, but me?" Mikey said with a grin. "So what happened?"

"Nothing happened, it was bullshit bravado. He pushed me. I pushed him. He pushed me back, and I lifted his wallet and car keys!"

"Shut up!" said Mikey.

"Nope!" Liam said, flashing a BMW key chain and wallet loaded with cash. "Drinks are on that douchebag tonight! There must be a few hundred bucks in here. Mikey, you take the cash, and I'll put his wallet, keys, and credit cards in the mail tomorrow."

"No argument here," said Mikey.

"You guys are unbelievable!" said Sue.

"Hey, we could chop that car and make a few grand," said Mikey.

"No, we're just going to teach this asshole a lesson," Liam said.

"Seriously?" said Sue.

Later that morning, Liam said good-bye to Mikey and Sue and thanked them for another memorable night. He told Sue to please keep Mikey out of trouble while he was away and that if either of them needed anything, to give him a call. The judge and Ray drove him back to Exeter later in the day, just before head count.

Winter Semester 1985

As the judge and Ray drove him up to Wentworth Hall, he saw his roommates, Tom Humphreys and Brett Welch, walking into the dorm.

"Thanks, Judge; thanks, Ray! See you in a few weeks."

"Liam?"

"Yes, sir."

"You have a very good start here. Let's keep the momentum going, okay? That means no fighting with the locals and being a role model on campus."

"Yes, sir. Understood."

"Good boy! Give us a call when you get settled in tonight."

"Will do, sir."

"Ray, we'll work on a weekend that you can visit, okay?"

"Awesome, Liam, thanks! Awesome!"

"Give me a hug, Ray." They embraced good-bye.

Back on the Exeter campus, Liam walked into my dorm room. "Boys, how were your vacations? Tom, how were the Virgin Islands? Brett, how was Saint Petersburg?"

"Well, we went down to the islands for our annual family Thanksgiving, but as usual, by the end of the trip, it was just myself and Consuela, my nanny, sharing drumsticks again. It's the same old story every year, so no big deal. My dad had to run off to close another deal in China, and my mom decided to go to Europe to visit her sister. It's a completely dysfunctional family. I mean, I could have gone to Europe too, but that would have meant spending a couple of extra days on a plane. I decided to swim with the dolphins and the sting rays. Consuela didn't care either. It was a paid vacation for her, and we ate out most nights anyway. You guys should come next year."

"Okay, well, that's a lot to digest. How about you, Brett? How was Russia?"

"Well, funny you say that; I spent six hours each way studying for the SATs. And when we got to Saint Petersburg, I was in intensive Russian classes for the next two weeks."

"No shit?"

"Yeah, it was horrible! We had chicken for Thanksgiving dinner too. My sister cried the entire meal. Actually, she's three years younger than me and ten years wiser. She refused to go to Russian immersion class. Yeah, if I don't get into Stanford or Harvard, they're holding a slot for me at Saint Pete's University. I'll take the Caribbean over that any day!"

"What about you, Southie's finest?"

"Well, I interned at a local museum as an assistant to the curator—which basically meant setting up and taking down exhibits, getting painting and sculpting supplies at local art stores for resident artists, and, oh yeah, picking up trash in and around the museum."

"Is that it? I thought I had it bad," said Brett.

"Hey, Liam, enough reminiscing about our vacations, we have something for you, and we need to ask you a question."

"Yeah, what is it?"

"Well, we wanted to give you something for your birthday, but it arrived after we left for break, so here it is. Then we'll ask you our question."

"Sure, what is it?"

"Well, this is first," Brett said as he handed me a small box.

Liam opened up the box and started grinning from ear to ear.

"You guys...you really shouldn't have. Seriously, that's so nice of you both."

"Nah, it was nothing," said Brett.

"Do you like it?" asked Tom.

"Yes, of course! I was so jealous of how cool *your* cards were. Thanks so much, guys! You really shouldn't have."

The card was a pure white business card with Liam's name on it in the middle, the school logo on the lower left side, and "Since 1968" on the bottom right. The back had Liam's school post-office address and his dorm phone number.

"Nah, it was nothing," said Tom.

"Hey, guys, one small problem. Don't get me wrong; I love the cards; it's just that they have the wrong house and dorm address."

"Well, that's the second part of our discussion that we wanted to have with you, Liam," said Tom.

"What's that?"

"We just found out that Tom and I have really low numbers on the senior residence list. We were wondering if you would like to live with us again next year as well. Regardless of what your number will be, we can pool our numbers to get rooms together. We know that you have your jock friends, so we won't be upset if you say no. Just give it some thought," said Brett.

"Well, I thought that you guys would like to live with Paul, Aaron, or one of your debating friends or something?"

"You know, Liam, we thought about it, but we think our three different personalities work well together. Don't you think?" said Brett.

"Yeah? Well then, I'm in. Don't worry about the guys on the team. I get more school work done with you guys around anyway."

"Where do you think that we can we live next year?"

"Tom and I have our eye on Kirkland House. They have three two-person rooms, one on the first floor and two on the second floor, followed by three single rooms on the top floor. That's our target!"

"That sounds perfect! What are the odds?"

"Seventy-thirty depending on what number you get in the draw, and then I'll speak with Mr. Johnson to see if we can seal the deal."

"Brett, every time you mention housing with Mr. Johnson, he shuts you down," said Tom.

"My trump card this year is Liam."

"You have no shame, do you, Brett?"

"Oh, and I'm going to apologize for trying to get our final year in comfort? Maybe *you* like using dorm bathrooms where fifty guys use the same shower and lavatory? I think not! All guns must come out!"

"Dude, go ahead, but you've lost it. I'm in either way," Liam said.

"Great! It's settled then! On to dinner."

January 21, 1985

Dear Judge,

Thanks again for a great winter break! I really enjoyed relaxing at home and spending time with you, Ray, Father C., and the Lee family. I also enjoyed my job at the museum, and it provided me with a greater appreciation and understanding for art.

Looking back over the past year, I find it hard to believe I am where I am today versus where I could have ended up in the foster-care system. I can't thank you, Father C., and the Daniels family enough for everything that you've done for me. I won't take this opportunity for granted. I know that my father would be equally grateful.

For the winter semester, I decided to run track and lift to stay in shape for the baseball season in the spring. As far as my academics, I am sticking with intermediate and conversational Chinese, calculus-II, critical writing, art history, and chemistry. I think that will keep me busy and out of trouble—kidding!

Please tell Ray that we'll work out a weekend that he can visit before the end of the semester.

Always,

Liam

THE BUSINESS OF NCAA FOOTBALL

AROUND THIS TIME OF YEAR, most of the guys on the football team were participating in track for the winter semester to get stronger and faster for next year. Also at this time, college scouts started to come visit Exeter, looking at seniors who were being recruited to play football. The most sought-after recruit on this year's team was Dan Morris. Dan was a six-foot-five, 280-pound lineman who was heavily sought after by Yale, Princeton, BC, Penn State, Syracuse, Michigan, and Northwestern. Dan was a scholarship kid like Liam, who was also a great student. Dan was a day student who lived in Portsmouth, New Hampshire, just fifteen miles from campus. In the winter semester, Dan wrestled, which all the recruiting schools really liked because that meant that Dan had great balance with his feet, strong hands, and he was disciplined. Liam ran into Dan in the waiting room of Coach Long's office shortly before he was to have follow-up visits with some college recruiters.

"Hey, Dan, what's up? Welcome back," Liam said as they shook hands.

"Hey, Liam, how's it going?"

"Good, thanks. How was your break?"

"I was on a plane each week, checking out schools."

"Oh yeah? Sounds like fun."

"How was your break?"

"Uneventful I'm afraid. I worked at a museum mostly. But it was good to sleep in a few days a week."

"Yeah, well you'll be doing all this stuff next year, so be prepared," said Dan.

"We'll see; I hope so," Liam said with a smile.

"Every coach I meet with asks where you are leaning, if that's any comfort," Dan said as he shrugged.

"That's good to hear. So what have you narrowed your choices down to, Dan?"

"Syracuse, Penn State, Michigan, and BC. I haven't made up my mind, though."

"What about Yale and Princeton!" Liam exclaimed.

"I don't want my parents to go into a ton of debt because of me. They're already stretched as it is to pay for this place," Dan said as he looked down at the ground.

"Wait a minute—aren't you on scholarship here? I mean, I am, too, so no big deal," he said.

"No worries, Liam; I'm not offended, but what's your point?"

"I assume that Princeton and Yale could match what those other schools are offering in scholarship," Liam said.

"I suppose, but these schools include books, summer classes, and if I redshirt, a possible master's degree. Also, if I do well, they keep telling me that I have a shot to go pro."

"Yeah, all good points, Dan, and I don't disagree with any of that, but if you're good enough, pro teams will find you wherever you go play anyway. And what if you get hurt, then what? Your scholarship will be in jeopardy, they won't want to keep you around for a fifth year, and you can forget the pros. Hey, it's your call, but I don't want you to think short term. What schools are you meeting with today?"

"Penn State, Michigan, BC, and Syracuse are my four finalists, and they'll all be here at one p.m., two, thee, and four. National signing day is at the end of the next week."

"Okay then, do me a favor," he said as he put his hand on Dan's shoulder.

"Sure, Liam, what do you need?"

"Just ask any coach what their top ten graduating seniors are doing today and how many received fifth-year master's degrees."

"What do you mean?"

"Look, statistics in last month's *Sports Illustrated* showed that less than one percent of Division I football players ever go pro. I mean, there are only twenty-eight NFL teams, right? You want to play offensive line, so that means that there are fifty-six tackles that start and maybe another fifty-six that are backups, totaling one hundred and twelve spots in the NFL for your position. Based on those numbers, you have to be one of the best one hundred and twelve players in all of college football, and that doesn't include players who already have guaranteed contracts with current teams. I'm just saying that the statistics are overwhelmingly against you going pro. So, to me, that argument is moot. Furthermore, probably two or three of the best players from each team are in the pros. Where does that leave the rest of their top ten players? I imagine that they are in coaching, teaching, or working blue-collar jobs. I'm not trying to sound elitist because those are all honest and honorable jobs. Hell, my dad was a custodian, and he was the most respected man I know. All I'm saying is that you have to ask the question. Then ask Princeton and Yale what their top-ten graduating senior players are doing after graduation? I'm sure that you'll hear that they are either going to get their master's, law school, medical school, or they're on Wall Street. In my humble opinion, you just need to compare the short-term and long-term opportunities for yourself and your family."

"You know, Liam, I never looked at it like that. My dad paints houses, and my mother works in the Portsmouth High School cafeteria. There is no shame in that. They are simple and hard-working people. And when I say simple, I mean that they don't require much to live a happy life. When the recruiters came by the house, they were amazed at how much each of these schools was willing to give me, including the food stipend. My mom was amazed at that the most." They both laughed. "I'll ask the questions, make some calls, and let you know what happens."

"I'm just looking out for your best interest, Dan. Look, I have to run and get a lift in before track practice, and it looks like Coach Long is running late. Please tell Coach that I will be able to show some of the recruits around campus later today. I'll be back from track practice around five p.m. By the way, if you decide to reconnect with Yale and Princeton, and they say that they still have a slot for you, then you need them to fax over a document called a 'Letter of Likelihood.' Basically, this letter tells you that you are provisionally admitted to their school, and they should also give you a range of the financial aid that you can expect. Then you can make an educated decision about your future."

"Okay, I'll let Coach know, and thanks for the advice, Liam."

"No worries, Dan!"

"Hey, Liam."

"Yeah?"

"Seriously, thanks for your help."

"Hey, no problem, Dan. Let me know what you decide, okay?"

"Will do. See you later."

At five p.m. Liam walked back into the gym and Coach Long's office.

"Hey, Dan, wasn't that Coach Jack Bicknell from Boston College leaving Coach Long's office?"

"Yup."

"What's he like?"

"He is a nice guy I guess."

"Well, how'd it go?"

"It was fine. He said that they'd probably redshirt me for my first season, and I should play by my junior year if I work hard."

"Junior year, huh? Well, at least he's honest."

"Too honest I'm afraid, but he did say that of all the schools re-cruiting me, BC was the closest to my home, and my parents could see me play each week that we were at home. If I attended any of the other schools, it would cause a greater financial burden on my parents to see me play."

"Well, that's a plus."

"I guess."

"How did the rest of the meetings go?"

"Let's just say that Michigan, Penn State, and Syracuse were more enthusiastic about my playing time, but BC is a better school."

"Look at it like this. You have choices, whereas some kids don't have any choices at all."

"Yeah, I hear ya."

As Dan was leaving the office, Liam turned to him and asked, "Hey, Dan, how did my question go over about their top ten graduat-ing players and what they are doing now?"

"Funny you ask. *Nobody* had a good answer for me. Yeah, a few were in the pros, some were in grad school, and most were either working for the state in some capacity, or they just didn't know."

"Did it help?"

"Well, let's just say that I have a new list. Hey, I have to run to wrestling practice. Just tell Coach Long that everything went well. I have to make some calls, but I'll let him know what I decide by Friday morning."

"You got it, Dan. Good luck."

"Thanks, bro."

The following week, Friday morning at 5:00 a.m., there was a knock at Liam's dorm-room door.

"Hello, who is it?" said Brett.

"It's Dan, Dan Morris, looking for Liam."

"Liam, it's your idiot friend, Dan, who is banging at the door at five a.m. in the morning. Please tell him to shut up."

He opened the door.

"What's up, Dan? Everything okay?"

"Brett, you little shit, if you ever talk to me like that again, I will hang you upside down in your underwear off the flagpole next to the post office."

"Dan, it's five a.m.!"

"I don't care. If you open your mouth again, up you go!"

"All right, all right, just relax. If I don't get my eight hours of sleep, I'm cranky, and I'm at hour seven."

"Here, this is for you," Dan said as he handed Liam a Yale football T-shirt.

"You're kidding."

"Nope," Dan said, grinning from ear to ear.

"What happened?"

"I did exactly what you said. I called the Yale and Princeton coaches, told them that I had a change of heart, and that if he had a slot for me, I'll take it."

"Wait, why Yale over Princeton?"

"I gave both coaches the same speech. I said that I needed that Letter of Likelihood that you were telling me about to show that they were committed to me and a projected financial-aid package by the end of the week. Yale had everything ready to go by Wednesday afternoon, but they weren't going to send anything until I answered a couple of their questions."

"What questions?"

"First, they wanted to know if any of my scholarships got pulled? And if so, why? I said no. In fact, Syracuse and Michigan promised me playing time during my freshman year. The second was, why the change of heart? I had to answer those questions prior to them sending me anything in writing."

"That's fair," Liam said.

"So, I explained to them that there were two primary reasons for the late change of heart. First, I didn't want to put a major financial burden on my parents. If they could come close in aide, then that was half the battle. The other reason, and what really swayed my decision, was a question I asked each of the Division I coaches recruiting me: What were the top graduating seniors doing after they graduated from school versus what were the seniors at Yale and Princeton doing?"

"And what did they say?"

"I guess it worked because Yale got back to me right away. Here is the Letter of Likelihood and the financial aid came in at twenty thousand dollars in loans."

"Wow! Just eighty grand for four years—that's nothing!"

"No, you don't get it. Twenty thousand dollars *total* for all four years!"

"No way!"

"Yeah, and I have *you* to thank for it."

"Then, thanks for the T-shirt, but I prefer cash," Liam said with a grin.

"Okay, great! You're going to Yale. Now can I go back to sleep?" asked Brett.

"Wait—what happened to Princeton?"

"Well, they said that they could match Yale's financial aid, but they couldn't get me the Letter of Likelihood right away. So screw Princeton and New Jersey!"

"Awesome!"

"Thanks again, Liam."

"Hey, no problem, Dan, and congrats again! Let's go grab some breakfast and let these guys sleep."

MS. JUNE BELLE

As the winter semester concluded, school was going great, and Liam was earning high honors. Track kept him occupied and ready for baseball season. So life was good! The weekend before he was to go home for spring break, he invited Mikey, Sue, and Ray up for the weekend. They would stay Friday and Saturday nights and drive him home Sunday. Ray was the most excited out of everyone. Ray would stay with Liam in his dorm, and Mikey and Sue would stay at the local Marriott in Portsmouth.

His roommate Brett and he were leaving chemistry class and discussing this weekend's social events before break.

"What are your plans for the weekend, Liam?"

"My brother and friends are coming up. We're going to the movies in town, then to the dance, and finally to hang out at the Grill. You wanna come with us?"

"Tom and I may join you for one or two events; however, we have a debate function to attend, and I'm not sure how late that will run."

"Okay, great, you guys can join us whenever. What are you doing the rest of today?"

"Are you kidding? I'm going back to the dorm and going to sleep! Chemistry kills me on Saturday mornings!"

As they were walking by the admissions office to their dorm room, they saw Mr. Lowe, their dorm headmaster.

"Dude, there is Mr. Lowe—duck! He's going to ask us to do a bullshit campus tour; I know it! Quick, come up with an excuse, or you're screwed!"

"Gentlemen…"

"Hi, Mr. Lowe," they said in unison.

"Have you boys finished your Saturday classes?"

"No, not yet Mr. Lowe, I have to run to my piano lesson."

"Okay, on to it then, Mr. Welch. I don't want you to be late for your lesson."

"And you, Mr. O'Hara? What does the remainder of your day consist of?"

"Um…I have to lift with Coach Long, and then my brother is coming in for a couple nights' visit."

"Well, I need some assistance giving a tour or two of the campus for prospective students if you don't mind, Liam. Some of my regular tour guides are out with the flu."

"Well, sir, what about Coach Long?"

"I'll call him and leave a message with his secretary."

"But, um…"

"Liam, do you realize how many times you have been late for curfew this past semester and I haven't put you on restrictions?"

"Yes, sir, I am available for however long you need me," Liam said with a smile.

"And Mr. Welch…"

"Yes, sir."

"I look forward to hearing your progress on the piano."

"Ah, yes, sir."

"Liam, you can go back to the dorm and change if you wish. Our next candidate will be here in thirty minutes."

"Yes, sir, no problem," he said as they walked back toward our dorm.

"Brett, you are unbelievable!"

"Hey, I told you to come up with something."

"Yeah, it's no big deal. Look, if my brother and friends come up early, please tell them that I'll just be a few minutes late because of this tour. Okay?"

"Sure, no problem. Liam."

"Yeah, Brett?"

"Remember, the academy was founded in 1781 by John Phillips and his wife, Elizabeth, and the mission was to educate students under a Calvinist religious framework," Brett said, smiling and laughing.

"Screw you, Brett!"

"Remember, play nice with the parents too; you are graded as a guide."

"Yeah, yeah…"

Twenty minutes later at the admissions office, a long stretch limousine with New York license plates pulled in the driveway. The limo came to a stop at the front entrance of the admissions office, a tall platinum-haired woman, dressed in black, exited the back of the limo. In tow was a smaller man, about five feet nine inches tall, carrying what appeared to be a notebook. Finally, *she* exited the limo. All eyes in the admissions office were on her. A raven-haired, blue-eyed, slender, athletic-looking girl, she wore a long skirt with a white blouse and a thin black sweater.

"Come on, my dear, we are late," said Ms. Angela Rubin, who made the appointment.

"We wouldn't be if you didn't need so many bathroom breaks on the way up here."

"Then don't get old, dearie; don't get old."

"Ladies, we have a schedule to keep," said the little man.

They entered the admissions office, where they were served homemade donuts and hot apple cider.

"Ms. Rubin, I presume?"

"Yes, you must be Mr. Lowe."

"I am."

"My apologies for our tardiness. We simply did not anticipate the amount of traffic leaving New York."

"No problem at all. This young man," he said, pointing to Liam, "will be taking you around campus after our interview."

"That's fine. We will be staying at the Exeter Inn around the corner, so we'll be close by."

"Liam, this is Ms. Angela Rubin. And you, sir, are?"

"I am Ms. Rubin's executive assistant, Robert Martin."

"Okay, this is Mr. Martin. And this is our applicant, Ms. June Belle."

"Pleasure to meet you all."

"Okay, Ms. Belle, let's have a chat before I send you off with Mr. O'Hara."

Just then, Headmaster Johnson arrived.

"Angela, how are you?" he said as he kissed her continental style on both cheeks. "And you must be June."

"Yes, sir, pleasure to meet you."

"You know, June, I knew your father. I'm terribly sorry for your loss."

"Thank you, sir."

"Professor Miller."

"Yes, sir."

"Who will be interviewing, Ms. Belle?"

"I will be, sir."

"Well then, I am sure that this is just a formality. And who will be showing Ms. Belle around campus?"

"Well, she's spending the weekend with Ms. Laura Tate at Bankroft Hall."

"Oh, wonderful, she's an excellent student and one of our best field-hockey and lacrosse players."

"And Mr. O'Hara here will be showing Ms. Belle around campus," he said, pointing to Liam.

"Liam."

"Yes, sir."

"Let's stay out of trouble, okay?" he said with a wink.

"Yes, sir."

"Professor Miller, please call me after you are done with Ms. Belle."

"Will do, sir."

"Angela," he said, holding Angela's hand, "always a pleasure. Let me know if you need anything." Turning toward Mr. Martin, Headmaster Johnson extended his hand. "Mr. Martin, a pleasure as well. Ms. Belle, let's hope that you make the right decision and select Exeter over Andover and Choate."

"Well, this is the last school that I am visiting, and if all goes well, I'll weigh all my options."

"Just call me if you need anything."

June and Mr. Lowe went into the interview room.

"So, Liam, tell me about yourself. Are you a model?" asked Ms. Rubin as she glanced over her *Elle Magazine*.

"Excuse me?"

"I asked if you modeled?"

"Um, no, I'm afraid not."

"I like your cheekbones, your eyes, and you have good height. You're a bit too muscular, but I can work with that. Robert, take down his information."

"Ma'am, I appreciate your offer, but I really have no interest."

"Young man, do you know who this is? This is Angela Rubin. She heads the largest talent agency in the city. It's impossible to get an appointment with her. I should know since I keep her schedule, and you're saying what?"

"That sounds wonderful, and I mean no disrespect, but I really have no interest." Just then out of the corner of his eye, Liam saw the interview office door open. "Oh, look, it's June. She must be done with her interview."

"Young man."

"Yes, Mr. Martin?"

"Take this card should you change your mind or find your senses."

"Thank you, sir," he said as Mr. Martin handed him his card. "June, are you ready to go and see the campus?"

"Yes, just one moment please while I speak with Angela and Robert for a minute."

"Sure, no problem."

A couple of minutes later, they left the admissions office.

"It's Liam, right?" asked June.

"Yup."

"So how did you pull this detail?"

"Well, the normal campus-tour guides all fell ill with the flu. I was walking out of my chemistry class when Mr. Lowe, who is also the head of my dorm, called in some markers for me to give this tour."

"You're kidding."

"Nope, but I don't mind; the majority of classes are over anyway."

"What were the markers, if you don't mind me asking? And what did Mr. Johnson mean about staying out of trouble?"

"Nothing major, just a few curfew violations. I think that we're even now, though, so no big deal. Regarding the headmaster, that's a whole other story. Three days into transferring into Exeter this year, I got in a disagreement with some townies who were picking on another academy student. Well, enough about my indiscretions and me—and you, what's your story, Ms. June? Was that your mother and father who accompanied you here?"

"No, Angela is sort of an advisor, and Robert is her assistant. They are both close friends, and when my parents died in a car accident in France last year, they helped me a great deal."

"I'm so sorry; I didn't mean to pry. My apologies. Now I feel like shit—oops, I mean, bad."

"No, that's all right," she said as she laughed. "That's cute. They just watch over me and for my well-being. I am what is called an 'emancipated minor' since my parents' passing. You see, my family and I were in the entertainment industry, and I was homeschooled while we were on the road. I was just accepted to Yale for admission next year, but I decided to take a year off and go to prep school before Yale. I think this will give me an opportunity to better acclimate myself to kids my own age and the rigors of being in a classroom structure."

"Wow, already accepted to Yale, huh? Congrats! So you're coming here to do what?"

"I just want to get a feel for 'normal' school, I guess."

"That's cool, but this place is a grind. To our right, that big building over there is the library. It was donated by the class of 1945. The architect was some famous guy named Lewis Kahn, and it's one of the biggest libraries in the country, bigger than most college libraries, actually."

"Wait—so none of this is registering with you?" said June.

"I'm sorry. None of what?"

"Of who I am? Or what I do?"

"Sorry, no, are you someone famous or something? You know, my roommate would probably know you. He's an accomplished actor who won a Tony award. His name is Tom Humphreys. Have you heard of him?"

"Unfortunately, no. Has he done anything recently?"

"No, he's been busy with school. He's done some summer theater off Broadway, but nothing major because of his academic schedule. Hey, over there is the Phelps Science Center, where I can show you my Bunsen burner if you want?" he said with a smirk.

"No thanks, I'm good."

"And over there is the Forrestal-Bowled Arts Center, where you can practice music, sing, dance, perform theater, whatever. I take piano and guitar lessons there."

"Ah, so you're a musician? Me too," said June.

"Really, what do you play?"

"Well, I sing and can play the violin, piano, harmonica, and a little bit of the spoons."

"The spoons, huh? You'll have to show me some time," Liam said.

"Hey, if you think you can keep up, we can play," June said with a smile.

"Wow, cute and cocky."

"Liam O'Hara, are you hitting on me?"

"That depends."

"That depends on what?"

"Two things. First, do you have a boyfriend? If so, 'Guy Code' prohibits me from pursuing you any further."

"Interesting, a man with morals. Apparently you've never been outside of this area code because Guy Code rarely applies to the men I know. And the other thing is?" asked June.

"Second, and most importantly, is it working?"

"Wait, you're telling me *you* don't have a girlfriend here?"

"The short answer is no," he lamented.

"You're kidding me. Right?"

"I wish I were. I'm a pariah here. And at home, they don't understand my life here. It's a very complex catch-twenty-two."

"Pariah, huh?"

"Yeah, they think I'm some sort of thug from South Boston because I'm on full scholarship here and because of an incident with some townies last year," Liam said.

"What happened last year?"

"I got into it with a couple of townies because there were three guys picking on an academy kid."

"But I thought that you were defending another student?"

"I was, but when two cruisers come to your dorm on the third day of school and you get escorted out in cuffs, people talk and make assumptions."

"Yeah, I know what you mean. My theory on people like that is they are all like crickets. They make a lot of noise far away, but when you get right up on them, they become silent."

"Interesting philosophy. So over here are more dorms, and this one—Bankroft Hall—is where you'll be staying with Laura Tate. Let's walk in, but I am only allowed to stand in the foyer because it's a girls' dorm. They're quite strict about that policy."

"You're kidding me. Right?"

"Nope, no boys are allowed upstairs unless during school hours, with permission, and the door has to be open."

"Wow, it's like jail."

"This is *nothing* like jail. Trust me!"

"I'm sensing another story."

"That will have to be for another time. And there is Laura. Hi, Laura. This is June Belle, your roommate for the next two nights."

"Hi, June, pleasure to meet you. What are you doing with her, Liam?"

"And it's nice to see you too, Laura. I'm her tour guide around campus."

"Just as long as he keeps you away from campus security, you'll be fine, June. Liam, please have her back here by five o'clock. We're going to dinner, then to the movies, followed by the dance tonight with the girls. How's that sound, June?"

"Sounds great. Thanks," June said as we walked away from Bankroft Hall. "Well, you were right."

"I was right about what?"

"That she's a bitch!"

"I never said that!"

"It's okay; I was reading between the lines, especially the way she spoke to you. There was no need for that."

"Well, the fact is, if you're the prettiest girl in school, you can do what you want around here socially. Actually, she's dating a tennis player who was here last year but is now a freshman at Harvard."

"So do you think I'm prettier than her?"

"That's a loaded question."

"How so?"

"Well, you still haven't answered *my* question if you have a boyfriend or not."

"Okay. No, I do not. We broke up a couple of months ago."

"How long were you going out? Please tell me you've been on at least one date since you broke up with your old boyfriend." Liam hesitated as they continued to walk around campus. "And this is Kirkland House. Actually, I think I can show you this dorm house because it's being remodeled. This is the dorm that my current roommates and I want to live in next year. Let me just ask the house faculty, Professor Edwards, if we can take a quick look around."

Liam knocked on Professor Edwards's door.

"Yes, can I help you?"

"It's Liam O'Hara from your English class, sir."

"Yes, of course, Liam, what can I do for you?"

"Well, I'm on a school tour at the behest of Mr. Lowe and Headmaster Johnson, and I wanted to show Ms. Belle here what a house dorm looks like versus where she will be staying this weekend in the Bankroft dormitory with Laura Tate."

"Ah, Ms. Tate is a lovely girl. Sure, no problem, Liam. Please be quick, though, because the painters will be back in about twenty minutes to finish up the third floor."

"Thank you, Professor."

"No problem, Liam. Enjoy your visit, Ms. Belle."

"Thank you, sir."

"Yeah, Mr. Edwards is a great guy."

"If he's such a great teacher, what grade did you get in his class?"

"Let's just say that I did well."

"Well, huh?"

"Yeah, let's just leave it at that."

"Okay, okay, Mr. Brainiac. And yes, to answer your question, I have gone out on a few dates after my breakup. But why is that relevant?"

"Well, I'll tell you why. You never want to be the 'rebound guy.' The rebound guy is always compared to the previous boyfriend, and it rarely works out."

"Liam, do you ever think that you overanalyze the dating process?"

"That's exactly what my best friend's girlfriend, Sue, says!"

"Smart woman! You should listen to her."

"Well, you can meet her this weekend if you would like. She's coming up here with my best friend from home, Mikey, and my brother, Ray, to spend a couple of days and drive me back to Boston over break."

As they walked up to the third floor of Kirkland House, they reviewed each floor. "The first floor has a double, right next to the common room, where there is a house fridge and house TV. The second floor contains the house shower and another double suite."

"Two showers for how many people?"

"Eight people, and that's better than the twenty-five plus that currently use my dorm shower and bathroom."

"And these are the singles on the third floor."

"They look a bit small."

"They're awesome! Privacy, privacy, privacy."

"Hey, Liam."

"Yeah?"

"Do me a favor, and close your eyes while you imagine yourself here next year."

"What? Why?"

"Just do it. If you believe it, you will achieve it; just close your eyes and think about it."

"Okay, okay."

Just then, June moved close to Liam and whispered in his ear to keep his eyes closed. Then June softly caressed his cheeks, got on the tips of her toes, and then started to kiss him. Liam was paralyzed, but he somehow managed to move his left hand around June's waist and put his right hand to the base of her head as he guided her in a circular motion as they embraced.

"Liam, Ms. Belle, are you two still up there? asked Professor Edwards. "The painters are back."

"Yes, um, sir, we'll be right down."

As they walked back down to the entrance, they saw Professor Edwards, and Liam thanked him once again.

"Yes, thank you, Mr. Edwards," said June.

They now walked toward the gymnasium.

"June?"

"Yeah?"

"What was that?"

"Well, I wanted you to know that I was right."

"Right? Right about what?"

"First, that you are a great kisser! Second, we just christened the new dorm, and you had a girl in your room."

"You really need to come here next year."

"Well, things are looking up."

Just then they heard the rumblings of Mikey's Chevy Nova approaching firm down the street.

"There he is!" said Mikey.

"Hey, Liam," said Sue.

"Hi, Liam," said Ray.

"Guys, this is June. June is a prospective student next year. June, this is my best friend whom I told you about, Mikey. This is his girlfriend, Sue. And that young man over there is my brother, Ray."

"Nice to meet you all."

"Liam."

"Yeah, Mikey?"

"Don't even think about it."

"Think about what?"

"She's way, way out of your league!" Mikey said, smiling to embarrass him.

"Dude, seriously. This is what I'm talkin' about, Sue; he ruins my game! Look, guys, meet me back at my dorm. I'm going to drop off June back at admissions, and then we can catch up on the plans for tonight, okay? June, here is my card." Liam franticly scribbles his dorm phone number on the card. "Call me if you need anything tonight, after your visit, or if you are ever in town or just want to make out, whatever," Liam said with a devilish grin.

"You have a card?"

"Yeah, the card was a birthday gift from my roommates."

"Maybe I'll need one of those." June smiled.

"And at the risk of making myself vulnerable, I really want to meet up with you tonight. Try and lose Ms. America and the girls. We'll be at the same movie, followed by the dance, and then we can meet up at the after-hours food stop where everybody hangs out. It's called the Grill."

"Now that sounds like a plan. I'll look for you and your gang. And Liam…"

"Yeah?"

"You're a great kisser!"

"You're not so bad yourself," he said, blushing and walking away with a huge smile on his face, the bravado diminished.

Back at Liam's dorm, she was the one and only subject that the Southie gang wanted to talk about.

"Dude, wow! Now that was strong! Is a she a student here or what?"

"No, maybe next year. She's an interesting girl. Get this. She is already accepted to Yale for next year, but she wants to go to prep school for a year to acclimate herself to a more structured classroom environment."

"You're fucking kidding me!" said Mikey.

"Liam, she's beautiful. She looks familiar too," said Sue.

"Well, she alluded to the fact that she was in the entertainment industry, and both of her parents recently passed away in a car accident. She was homeschooled her entire life."

"Are you dating her, Liam?" asked Ray.

"No, Ray, we just met, but she does want to meet up with us tonight."

"Speaking of which, what's on the agenda this weekend, bro?"

"Well, movies and the dance tonight, followed by post-movie snacks at the Grill. I'll take Ray to my dorm, and you guys can head over to Portsmouth. Why don't you guys check in, relax, and swing by here at six p.m."

"And Saturday?"

"Well, I have my track meet at one o'clock, so come on over after breakfast, or get breakfast here, and we'll grab an early dinner in town, followed by another movie on campus. We'll leave for home right after breakfast on Sunday."

"Okay, that sounds like a plan. See you guys at six o'clock."

"Sue, remember, no booze for this guy. Mikey, you promised."

"Relax, I know what I promised. See you at six o'clock."

Later that day at Assembly Hall for the movies, Liam said, "Hey, guys."

"What's the movie, Liam?" asked Mikey.

"It's *Top Gun* tonight and *Stand by Me* tomorrow night," said Ray.

"Yeah, he's right. I heard good things about both," said Liam. "Come on, let's get good seats." They sat in the front row of the balcony. "We can also see who is coming and going."

"Hey look, Liam, isn't that June from earlier today? She's looking up at you."

June waved and mouthed "save me" as she looked to her left and then to her right, where Laura Tate and her field-hockey and lacrosse friends were surrounding her.

He held up his index finger as if to say, "One second, I'll be right down," and pointed to the corridor near the bathroom sign.

June winked and nodded.

He scurried down the flight of stairs to meet June at the bathroom.

"So how's it going with Ms. America?"

"Laura is nice—very insecure, but nice."

"Insecure? Her?"

"Well, she's very concerned about her image and where she goes to school next year."

"Aren't we all, though?"

"Yes and no. You, for example, are an open book in my opinion."

"I am, huh? Okay, give it your best shot."

"Okay, you are honest, sincere, a good friend to those who you let in, and you care deeply for others. However, I sense that there is a void somewhere, and I'm not quite sure where that is. It seems like you have a nice family, and your brother is adorable. How did I do?"

"Well, you are very perceptive, June. My mother passed away when I was seven, and then I lived with Mikey's family for a bit while my dad was away in Vietnam. When my dad got back from the war, he died a few years after that from cancer. I then was sort of adopted by a family friend just before I was to enter state foster care. There are a few other colorful moments in between, but that's pretty much me in a nutshell. I'm on scholarship here, and I don't come from money. I'm sorry if I don't fit into the 'Mayflower money' type that traditionally populates this school. Look, I'll understand if you don't want to hang out."

"Liam?"

"Yeah?" he said, looking at the ground very self-consciously.

"Can you just shut up for a minute while I kiss you!"

As she leaned into embrace Liam, a cheer from the upper deck of the balcony erupted. Some of the students thought the movie was about to start, but Liam's football teammates saw him and cheered him on. Just then, Laura Tate and her friends saw what was happening, and they quickly interrupted.

"Is everything okay here, June? Did he force himself on you?"

"What? No! Liam is a gentleman. He's far too shy to kiss me, so I attacked him," June said with a smile.

"June, we'll talk later," Liam said as he walked away and back to his seats with his friends.

"Count on it."

"June, do you know anything about that boy?"

"Just a little bit, why?"

"Well, he's like one of those transfer jocks that the school recruits to have good football teams."

"Were you recruited to play field hockey and lacrosse?"

"Yes, but that's different."

"How so?"

"I came here as a freshman, whereas Liam transferred in."

"So what's his story then, Laura? One of his English professors told me that he's very smart as well."

"I think he takes mostly jock classes. Girls, are any of you in Liam O'Hara's classes?"

"He's in my chemistry class and gets all As."

"The same with me in my Chinese and American history classes. He's a pretty bright kid."

"Well, Laura?" asked June.

"Okay, so he's not like some of the other jocks, but the first week of school, he almost got kicked out for being arrested. I think that's some sort of record, isn't it, girls?" They all laughed. "Look, the movie is starting. Let's just watch it, and then we can chat later at the dance."

As Liam made his way back to his seat in the balcony, John, Dave, and Joe from the football team were sitting next to Mikey, Sue, and Ray.

"Bro, up high!" John said and signaled for a high five. "Now that was impressive! I mean, look at her, and look at you."

"Why does everyone say that?" he said.

"Liam, what the hell was that? I mean, Dave and I thought that you were some sort of monk, and then you pull *that*? And does she have a sister?" asked Joe. Dave nodded.

"Liam, are you okay? This is a bit out of character for you," said Sue.

"Leave him alone," said Mikey, and he greeted me with a high five as well. "It's about time."

"About time for what?" he asked.

"That my skills rub off on you." They all started laughing.

"Shhh…the movie is starting," said Ray.

After the movie they all headed over to the dance.

"So what did you guys think?"

"I don't know about you guys, but Annapolis and flight school are now on my list of schools for next year," said John.

"Me too!" said Dave.

"Great effing movie!" exclaimed Joe.

"So, Ray, what did you think of the movie?" asked Liam.

"I want to be a pilot too!"

"Okay, guys, let's head over to the dance in the old gym. Sue, Mikey, did you guys like the show?"

"Yeah, it was great. Thanks for the invite."

"So let's all get a move on."

At the old gymnasium, June came over to say hello to the group Liam was with.

"Hello again. It's Mikey, Ray, and Sue. Right?"

"Correct," said Sue.

"So, Liam, how about a dance?"

"Oh, I really don't dance I'm afraid."

"Come on, be a sport."

"No, sorry! I'll make a fool of myself out there."

"Okay, but, Liam, a girl can only be rejected so many times—remember that. How about you, Ray?"

"Me? Really?"

"Yeah, sure, let's go."

"Come on, Mikey, let's join them," Sue said.

"Sorry, bro, duty calls," Mikey said to Liam as he headed to the dance floor with Sue.

"Dude, what are you thinking? Why aren't you on the dance floor with that girl?" asked John.

"Well, I thought that my brother might like to enjoy himself, and June asked him."

"Excuses, my friend, excuses. You had better enjoy the moment before she goes."

"Okay, next song I'm in."

As Eddie Murphy's song "Party All the Time" ended, June reached out her hand to Liam. Mikey, Sue, Ray, and the guys watched.

"Come on, Liam, I won't hurt you."

"I know that; I just don't want to step on your toes and hurt you!"

June said, "Let's go!" as REO Speedwagon's "Can't Fight This Feeling"—a slow dance—began.

"Okay, okay."

June put her hands around the back of Liam's neck, and he had his hands on her hips as he gazed in her eyes.

"Sorry if I'm a little rigid on the dance floor; I just don't have much practice," he said.

June leaned in and whispered in his ear, "Relax, just relax; think of dancing as a vertical expression of a horizontal desire."

Liam then moved his hands from June's hips to the lower part of her back, pushed her closer, and then he began to kiss her.

"Will you guys look at that? I don't think you can put a piece of paper between the two of them. What is this world coming to?" John said with a smile.

"More importantly, I'm not positive, but I believe that Jefferson Starship's song 'We Built This City' is a fast song, and they apparently are off beat," said Mikey as everyone laughed.

"No, I think they're creating their own beat," said Sue.

Just then the lights flickered on and off to signify that the dance would be over shortly.

"June, I'm taking the guys down to the Grill; do you want to come and join us?"

"Sure, I'll meet you there after I tell Laura where I am going."

"Do you want me to wait?"

"Sure, thanks."

"Laura, I'm going to head down to the Grill with Liam, my friend, Sue, and some of his friends, okay?"

"Well, we were all going to go together if you can wait a few minutes."

"I'm going to go now because I have to go to the Exeter Inn to pick up a few things if that's okay," asked Sue.

"Um, okay, no problem. We'll be there shortly."

"Thanks, Laura. I'll see you and the girls in a few."

"Do you really have to go to the Exeter Inn first?" asked Sue.

"No, I just said that. Those girls are boring. Let's get out of here and meet the boys," said June.

June and Sue left the gymnasium en route to the Grill, just a five-minute walk across campus.

"So, Liam has no idea, does he?"

"Idea? Idea about what?"

"Who you are?"

"Sorry, what do you mean?"

"Liam and my Mikey may not read *Vogue*, but I do."

"Guilty. How did you know?"

"You looked very familiar, but I couldn't place it until I saw you on the dance floor with Liam. That looked like the same move you used to draw in Anthony Michael Hall in that movie *First Time*. You're Juniper Belle Jones, aren't you?"

"Well, Brava! You got me. So, are you going to tell Liam?"

"I won't, but only if you promise that you will before the weekend is over."

"Thanks! I will. I just want to feel normal for one weekend. I promise I'll tell him tomorrow before I leave, okay?"

"Yeah, that works."

"Thanks, Sue!" June said, giving her a hug.

"The crazy thing is that his roommate has that poster of you on his wall with you in a stars-and-stripes bikini top, wearing fatigues. So he sees you every night."

"I was a blonde back then, so maybe that's why he doesn't recognize me. At any rate, I'll tell him tomorrow. Thanks again, Sue."

"Sure."

"Sue, can I ask you something?"

"Yeah sure, June, what would you like to know?"

She hesitated a moment. "What's Liam's story?"

"Well, since Liam seems to like you, I'll tell you a bit. You see, Mikey and Liam are like brothers. For example, when they were in the third grade, their school had a field trip to the Museum of Science; Mikey didn't have the money to go, so Liam said that he didn't have the money either because he didn't want Mikey to be alone and the only one not going on the trip. When Liam's mother passed away and his dad was still in Vietnam, Liam stayed with the Maguire family for several months. Then when Mike's dad went away to prison, Liam's dad took care of Mikey's family by paying rent, buying groceries, and helping with tuition when he could. When Liam's dad passed away, he was all over the place and almost became a ward of the state until a family friend took him in; Ray's father, Judge Mahoney.

"Those are just a few of the things that went on. There is more, but he should really tell you himself when the time is right. I just hope that you're not slumming for a weekend. That'll break his heart."

"No, I would never do something like that!" exclaimed June.

"Aren't you supposed to be dating someone from the New Kids or something like that?"

Shaking her head, June said, "No, that's all tabloid trash! After my parents' passing, I need to start a new chapter of my life."

"Well, here we are. This is the Grill," Sue said.

"Got it, and thank you, Sue."

Sue spotted the boys. "Hey, boys," called Sue.

"Girls, have a seat."

"June," asked John, "Liam says that you have already been accepted to Yale, but you want to go to prep school for a year anyway. Is that true? And if so, the infirmary is just across the street in case you have any brain damage."

She grinned. "Well, I have no head trauma; however, it is true. I was homeschooled for the past twelve years while I was on the road, so now I want to acclimate myself to a traditional classroom environment and the rigors of being in a normal school."

"You know, June, sometimes head trauma is delayed; let's just stick with that," John said with a smile.

"Okay, thanks—I guess."

Just then, his roommate Tom Humphreys ran into the Grill and interrupted, "Excuse me, guys. Liam, I need to talk to you, now. It's important!"

"Sure, is everything okay?"

"No, everything is not okay! Look, I wasn't snooping, but I did notice this card on your desk," he said, handing him Angela Rubin's card. "How did you get it? Did you find it on the street? Did you meet her? What? I need to know, and now!"

"Um, she was in the admissions office earlier today and she started up a conversation. She actually asked me if I wanted to model, if you can believe it? I even asked her if she knew you."

Eyes dilating, he said, "You did what? Now I'm mortified. You have to call her back."

"Well, it's a bit late now, don't you think?"

"No, not now, tomorrow morning. Why was she here anyway?"

Looking earnest Liam said, "June, do you have a second?" Liam asked as he waved her over to his table. "This is my roommate Tom Humphreys. He's the one who won a Tony award a few years ago that I told you about."

"Hi, nice to meet you, Tom," she said as he reached out his hand and kept staring at her and into her eyes.

"May I have my hand back, Tom?" June asked.

"Yes, of course, I'm sorry. You just look so familiar."

In walked Laura Tate and her friends. "Hey, June, the Grill is about to close, and we're heading back to the dorm. You ready to go?"

"Okay, boys, Sue, I have to run," said June. Turning to Liam she said, "Liam, how about breakfast at the Exeter Inn with Angela, Martin, and myself tomorrow morning? Say, seven-thirty?"

"Sure, I have a track meet later that morning, so no problem. Also, would you mind terribly if I bring Ray and Tom with me? I'll pay. And Tom would love to meet Angela and Martin in person."

"Don't worry about paying. That's no problem; see you there." She then kissed him on the cheek good-bye.

He headed back to his table with Mikey, Sue, Ray, and his teammates.

"Bro, you had better marry that one. She's a keeper!" said Mikey.

"Liam, Mikey's right; she's actually too good for you!" said John, and the rest of the guys laughed.

"Liam, can we talk?" Sue asked as she pointed to an empty corner table.

"See, guys, Sue will give me *real* advice."

"Yeah, what's up? Are you and Mikey enjoying yourselves?" asked Liam.

"Yeah, we always have a good time visiting you. It's about June. She's a lovely girl, and you shouldn't let her go."

"How do you know?"

"Trust me, I know."

"Okay, I trust you, but she and I just met."

"Liam, just go for it."

The following morning, they were meeting June for breakfast. There was no better breakfast in the state, with their homemade pancakes and cinnamon donuts.

"Good morning, Ms. Rubin, Mr. Martin, please forgive the intrusion; we were invited to breakfast by June," he said with a smile as he looked toward June.

"June, honey, is there anyone you didn't invite to breakfast?"

"Look, if it's a problem, Ms. Rubin, we'll just sit over here anyway."

"Angela! They are *my* guests!"

"Fine, sit down, boys."

"June, maybe this is a bad idea; we're going to go."

Tom cleared his throat.

A desperate looking Tom said, "Hi, Ms. Rubin. Tom Humphreys here. I'm a big fan of yours. Oh, and just in case we miss breakfast, here are some head shots and my CV." His words tended to run together.

"Young man, are you kidding me? I'm trying to have breakfast."

"We can discuss this awkward meeting all the way to the Oscars," Tom said and winked at Mr. Martin.

"Please don't leave, Liam. I want to talk to you before I have to go back to New York," said June.

"No, it was never a good idea to intrude anyway—my apologies."

"Just give me one minute to speak with Angela, please?"

"Okay."

Sounding miffed June said, "Angela! What are you doing? These are my guests!"

"Look, dear, we have to discuss these scripts," Angela said as she pointed to several scripts thrown around the breakfast table. "They all want you! This one here," she said as she picked up a thick script off the table, "is with Matt Dillon. This other one here"—lifting another script from her bag—"is with Julia Roberts!"

A tense June said, "Not the point, Angela! You're embarrassing me! Robert, speak with her!"

"Angela, let's give her five minutes; then we can review these scripts. We have a four-hour ride home."

"Liam, I'm so sorry! Please forgive my rude friends," June said as she turned to her left and glared at both Angela and Robert.

"Look, it's no big deal. We'll just eat at the cafeteria. I see that they have some business for you to review."

"Well, that's kind of what I wanted to tell you. Those items on the table are offers for work: some modeling, some movies, and some guest appearances."

"What?"

"Well, I kind of told you, but my full name is Juniper Belle Jones."

"The actress?"

She frowned a bit. "Remember, I'm a person first, and I just want to be normal. I just want to be an everyday student, so I use part of my legal name, 'June,' which is short for 'Juniper,' and my mother's maiden name, 'Belle.' I didn't want to mislead you any longer."

"Well, this is a lot to process. I mean, I wanted to ask you something. I even promised Sue, but this changes things, and I'm just going to make a fool of myself now."

"No, no, you won't. Never! Just ask. What do you want to ask me?"

Looking down at the floor and occasionally making eye contact, he said, "I know we just met, and I think that we...um..."

"The answer is yes."

"Yes to what? I didn't finish asking you anything. You can't possibly know what I was going to ask you?"

"Well, then, I'll ask you, Liam. I would like to keep seeing you. I know that we just met, but you are the most honest, sincere, and caring person I've ever met. I'm around superficial people all the time who want something from me. Then I look at you—you're different. I see the way you are with your friends, your brother, with me: that's special. I know that you live in Boston, and I live in New York, but let's give it a try. What do you say? You know, this may even work out *better*. We could get to know each other on a different level first."

"For the record, I was going to ask you that you know!"

"Noted. But there is one more thing."

"Sure, what's that?"

"If we are to try this, you have to promise me one thing."

"Sure. Name it."

"No, it's not that simple. You have to promise me that you will never, ever, lie to me—no matter how painful it may be. If you meet someone or think that you are protecting me from something, please promise me that you'll never lie to me."

"Okay, I promise."

"No, seriously, look me in the eye. I can only be around people I trust. The same rules apply for Angela and Robert—their manners aside."

Locking eyes with her, he said, "June, I promise to always be honest with you. Okay?"

"Yes!"

"And the same for you, okay?"

"Absolutely!" June said emphatically.

"I want you to have this as well. It's a small memento of this weekend."

"What is it?"

"My team sweatshirt. Hopefully this will help when you decide on which school to attend."

She did a double take. "I can't take this; it's your *team* sweatshirt."

"I know, but if you decide to go somewhere else, or if our paths never cross again, when you wear this sweatshirt, you'll think of me, and I hope that you'll at least have fond memories of our time together."

Sue smiled broadly. "Liam, you are too good to be true!"

"June, you have my card; give me a call when you are free. And how will I contact you?"

"You can reach me at two one two, triple five, two four five six. That's my pager. Or you can reach me anytime at home: two one two, triple five, one seven eight six. That's my private line and answering service, which I check daily. Here are Martin's and Angela's numbers as well."

Turning to Tom, June said, "Tom, it was a pleasure, and I'll make sure Angela looks at your envelope." June extended her hand in friendship.

"The pleasure was all mine, June, and thank you!"

With a coquettish smile, she said to Ray, "Ray, can I have a kiss good-bye?"

"You betcha!" June kissed Ray on the cheek and gave him a long hug. Then Ray turned to Liam and said, "See, Liam, that's how it's done."

Liam kissed June on the lips and promised to call one of the four numbers that she'd provided.

With a conspiratorial smile, she said, "One last thing, Liam. I'll be on MTV tonight for an interview around nine p.m. I'll try and signal you if you can watch."

"Um, okay. Will do. And good luck!"

Walking back to the campus and the cafeteria, Tom said, "Liam."

"Yeah, Tom."

"I owe you a ton! That was Angela Rubin, for goodness' sake! Angela freakin' Rubin!"

"I'm happy that you met her, really. And June said that she would make sure that Angela looks at your envelope." Liam winked at Tom. "Ray, we have to get going. Let's grab a quick bite and then meet up with Mikey and Sue before my track meet, and then let's go home, okay?"

"Great! Can I have pancakes, Liam?"

"You betcha, Ray," he said.

Later that day, riding home to Boston in Mikey's car after the track meet, Mikey said, "Bro, I didn't realize that you were *that* slow?"

"What? I came in third! And I'm racing against kids who are All–New England prep school in track!"

"Bro, I saw your time, and you're better than that!"

"Yeah, I know. I was distracted."

"June?" asked Sue.

"Yeah, she's a keeper. I hope she comes here next year."

"I have a sneaking suspicion that she will," said Sue with a smile.

Back home in Beacon Hill at the judge's brownstone where Mikey dropped Ray and Liam off, the judge greeted them.

"Ray, how was your visit?"

"Dad, I had the best time! The best! And Liam has a girlfriend."

"Liam, what's this?"

"Nothing really, I met a girl; that's all."

"Okay, tell me the details, Romeo."

"Romeo? Hardly! Her name is June Belle. She's some sort of model/actress/singer who lives in New York City. She was a homeschooled student who was recently admitted early decision to Yale. She decided to go to prep school for a year to better acclimate herself to a classroom environment."

"Wow, sounds like a lovely girl. I can't wait to meet her."

Ray gushed, "Dad, she's beautiful, and we all saw Liam kiss her."

Liam admonished jokingly, "That's just between brothers!"

"Oh yeah, sorry, Liam."

"Judge, do you mind if Mikey and Sue come over this evening? June is going to be on MTV, and she wanted Ray and Liam to watch."

"Sure, no problem, just unpack and start your laundry. I just don't want dirty clothes to start piling up. And that goes for you too, Ray."

"No problem, sir, we'll start all our laundry now. Thanks, Judge."

As nine p.m. approached, Ray made some popcorn, and Mikey and Sue joined them in the lounge to watch TV.

Mikey asked, "How is June going to signal you?"

"I'm not sure, but it's too soon for her to get a tattoo of my name," he said, smiling.

"More like the other way around, Liam," said Sue.

"Hey, there she is; there's June! Shhh…"

"What's that bruise on her neck? Is that a hickey, Liam?"

"No, nothing like that! Shut up, friggin' Mikey!"

"Forget the neck, do you see what she is wearing?" asked Sue.

"Who cares? What are you—a fashionista or something now?" said Mikey.

"No, you rude SOB! It's Liam's Exeter football sweatshirt with his number on it."

"Wait—shut up! No way!" said Liam.

"Next up on MTV's TRL is model, actress, and singer Juniper Jones in her *first* MTV interview since the tragic loss of her parents in a car accident in Paris just a few months ago. We'll be taking live questions from the audience, and we'll be right back."

"Now be quiet, guys; let's hear this. Please pass the popcorn, Ray," he said.

"Hi, this is Dave Holmes, and I'm back with MTV's TRL. In studio with me is the talented and scholarly Juniper Jones.

"Juniper, how are you doing since the passing of your parents a few months ago?"

"I'm doing as well as can be expected. I miss them every day, but I am thankful for my family friends like Angela Rubin and Robert Martin, who have been a tremendous support to me."

Looking at his notes, he said, "It says here that you have been accepted to Yale in the fall. Wow! Brains and beauty."

"Well, thank you, Dave. My acceptance to Yale is quite an accomplishment and one that I am very proud of. My parents stressed the importance of an education first."

"So when do you head to New Haven? This fall?"

"No, since I have been homeschooled for all these years, I decided to go to prep school for a year to better acclimate myself to a normal classroom setting."

"You mean you're going *back* to high school? Don't kids these days want to escape high school?"

"I suppose so, but I love school. I love learning new things, and meeting new people fascinates me."

"So where will you be spending the year before Yale?"

June put both hands on the base of her sweatshirt and stretched it out. "I'll be attending Phillips Exeter Academy, in Exeter, New Hampshire, next year."

"Well, congratulations, June! Now we have some questions from our studio audience. Are you okay with that?"

"Sure, Dave."

"Hi, Juniper, I'm Mary from Connecticut."

"Hi, Mary, what's your question?"

"I loved you in the movie *Only You* and the way you sang the title song on the soundtrack. Will you be doing any more movies or producing any more albums?"

"That's a great question, Mary, and thank you. I had some songs already completed on a new album that my parents were coproducing with my label, and I hope to finish it this summer. I've also been fortunate to have some follow-up movie script offers that I am reviewing, but I think I'm going to take a break from all that and modeling to focus on school for now."

"Thanks, Juniper."

"Another question."

"Hi, Juniper, I'm Conrad from Montreal."

"Hi, Conrad."

"I was wondering if you have a boyfriend. And if not, what is your opinion of Canadian men? Because I am available," Conrad said as he sat back down with a smile and got high fives from his friends.

"Well, I'm flattered; thank you. And to answer your question, Conrad, j'aime le Canada, et j'adore la population Canadienne, cependant, j'ai rencontré quelqu'un de très spécial sous le nom de Liam. Bonjour, mon amour," June said as she blew a kiss to the camera.

"I didn't know you spoke French, Juniper."

"A little."

"So what did you say?"

"I said that I love all Canadians, but that I am currently involved with someone."

"Really? That's a TRL scoop! With whom? Is he in the industry?"

"No, nobody in the industry, he's a civilian."

"Does he have a name?"

"His name is Liam, but that is all that I can tell you."

"Thanks for the scoop! And, Liam," Dave said, looking directly in the camera, "you are one lucky dude!"

"Well, that's all the time we have for now. Thanks so much for your time, Juniper. We all wish you well, and we look forward to your next album and movie."

"Thanks, Dave!" she said as she waved good-bye to the camera.

"Bro, you totally got a shout-out on friggin' MTV, *and* it was in French! If I didn't know how much of a loser you were, I'd be jealous," Mikey said with a smile.

"Shut up, Mikey!" Liam said.

"That was nice, Liam, very nice," said Sue.

"Thanks, Sue."

"How come she didn't say *my* name, Liam?" asked Ray.

"Well, I think because she didn't have enough time, buddy. We can call her and ask her tomorrow, okay?"

"Yeah, thanks, Liam."

THE PERFECT SUMMER

JUNE EVENTUALLY DECIDED TO ATTEND Exeter the following year over the objections of both Angela and Robert. They felt that since Choate was only two and a half hours outside New York City, June could still work if she wanted to. At the very least, Andover would only be a thirty-minute ride to Logan Airport and a forty-five-minute flight back to the city. Exeter, on the other hand, was an additional forty-five minutes north of Andover and that much more challenging to get to and from the city.

Over the next semester and most of the summer, June visited Liam several times up at Exeter and in Boston while she was living in New York modeling and reading scripts. Romance was in the air. As the school year ended and the summer progressed, Liam finished his internship at the Gardener Museum and focused for the rest of the summer on training for football and hanging out with Sue and Mikey.

The four friends became quite the foursome when June came to town. They would go out to the movies, go to the beach, attend Red Sox games, and talk about the future. Actually, Sue and June became really good friends too. June embraced the normalcy of her life and occasionally stayed over at Sue's house when she was in town because she really liked the feeling of waking up in a house versus a hotel.

Toward the end of the summer, Liam attended the Boston College, Notre Dame, and Stanford football camps. After his last camp in Palo Alto, Liam was rated the number three or four high-school quarterback in the nation, depending on which recruiting services coaches subscribed to. He never understood that type of rating. In his mind, it just meant that he had a bigger target on his chest. Not to mention, it seemed like at each camp the coaches emphasized that he had to work on his passing technique. He held over twenty-five Division I scholarship offers by the end of the summer. The question was if he would become a local hero like Doug Flutie and attend Boston College, or would he attend the national powerhouse Notre Dame?

Since it was their last night in town together, they decided to go out for pizza and hang out at the beach. They made a bonfire and just sat and talked throughout the night.

"You know, I wish we could hold on to this moment forever. Everything is perfect here," said June.

"Any time you want to change lives, you just let me know. There's an opening at the car wash for you." Mikey laughed, enjoying his own humor.

"No, I hear what you are saying, June. Good friends, good pizza, and a bonfire—it doesn't get much better than this," said Sue.

"Thanks, Sue. Hey, sorry to cut this short, but before it gets too late, Liam and I are going to head back," said June.

"But it's only seven p.m., and I don't want to leave yet, especially if June is staying with Sue," said Mikey.

Sue kicked sand at Mikey. "Shut up! They're going back to June's hotel."

"Oh...oh, yeah, I forgot."

They left the beach and drove back to the Four Seasons Hotel, where June was staying.

"Okay, June, give this handsome Irishman a hug. We'll visit you guys up at school later this semester," Mikey said as he hugged June.

"Liam, take care of her," said Sue.

As he hugged Sue, he whispered in her ear, "I will, but let me know if you or Mikey need anything, okay?"

With a tear in her eye, she said that she would.

"Bro," he said as Mikey winked and then nodded to him.

He nodded back and smiled.

As Mikey and Sue were about to drive away in his late-model Chevy Nova, which was in desperate need of a new engine, Sue winced when Mikey pulled out.

Mikey said to June, "Hey, June..."

"Yeah?"

"Just remember, it's not the type of car that you drive, as much as it is the size of the arm that hangs out the window that matters!" Mikey said as he flexed his left bicep out the window and, still grinning, drove away.

They walked into the hotel foyer, and there was an awkward, tense silence.

"Did he just say what I thought he said?" asked June.

"Yeah, he's priceless!" They both laughed, as did the doorman who let them in and had heard the exchange.

"So you told them!" he said to June as they walk toward June's room.

"Sorry, but I had to say something so that they wouldn't worry."

"That's fine, but I still have to be back home by midnight, per the judge."

"Don't worry; I'll be gentle."

"And don't think that you can take advantage of me because I'm a rookie at this," he said with a smile.

"Hey, I am too! It's just that I've had to role-play in a couple of films and fashion shoots, but I have no idea what I'm doing either."

"Okay because I secretly rented the movie *9 1/2 Weeks* the other day, but I'm still nervous; that's all."

"You know, we don't have to do this if you don't want to," said June.

"No, it's not that. I want to tell you something."

"What is it, Liam?"

As he gazed into her eyes, he murmured, "Whether we decide to do this tonight or not, I want you to know something. I love you,

Juniper Belle Jones. I love your smile, the fact that you don't judge me, my friends, or my family. I love how you see the world, your optimism, and of course your great choice in men," he said, smiling. "I don't have much to offer you, and I don't really expect you to feel the same way that I do."

June interrupted. "But, Liam—"

"Wait, I'm almost done. Where was I? Oh yeah, I don't want to scare you away, but should something ever happen to you, and I didn't get a chance to tell you how I felt, I could never forgive myself," he said and looked back up at her. "Okay, now I'm done."

"Liam O'Hara."

"Yeah, June?"

"Let's get inside quickly; I want to show you *just* how much I love you!" she said as she started to tear up and smiled through the tears.

The following morning, Ray, Liam, and June packed up the judge's Range Rover full of books, clothes, and snack food for the trip back to Exeter. Preseason football camp started one week before the rest of the student body arrived back to campus.

"Okay, guys, here we are, Kirkland House. Let's say hello to Professor Edwards and unpack. Liam and Ray, you get the trunk. June and I will start with the linens," said the judge.

As June brought up the first crate of linens, she asked, "I remember this room. Do you, Liam?"

"I do indeed! But the judge and Professor Edwards are right downstairs."

"We have all year, Liam," June said with a smile.

"Liam, this looks like the last of it," said the judge.

"Yeah, just put it over there, and I'll put it away later."

"Liam, I want to talk to you alone if you don't mind."

"Sure, Judge, what's up?"

"Well, Liam, this is your last year here at Exeter, and I want you to finish it strong without any distractions, if you know what I mean."

"Yes, sir."

"Don't get me wrong. June is a lovely and bright girl, but I want you to be focused on school first, football, and *then* extracurricular activities. Understand?"

"Yes, sir."

"Liam, your father would be very proud of all that you accomplished so far. Father Callahan and I only want the best for you."

"Yes, sir, I won't let you or Father Callahan down."

"Liam, just don't let yourself down with this opportunity."

"Understood, sir."

"By the way, have you decided yet between Boston College, Notre Dame, or Stanford yet?"

"No, not yet, I'll wait and see how this year plays out before I decide."

"Okay, let's go downstairs and say good-bye to Ray and June."

"How about a hug, Ray?" Liam said and whispered to him to take care of the judge.

"I will, Liam, I will. And can I visit you too?"

"Yes, of course, Ray, we'll figure out a weekend or two—just like last year. June, I'll see you soon."

"You bet."

"Judge, thanks again for everything," Liam said as he gave the old man a hug.

"Liam, we'll see you in a couple of weeks for the Andover scrimmage. Okay?"

"Yes, sir."

As the judge drove away, Liam looked at his watch and realized he had to hurry up to the gym for the first team meeting.

"John, Joe, Dave, how's it going?"

"Holy crap, Liam, what the hell have you been doing? Vitamin S or what?"

"No, John, it's all natural. You guys look healthy as well. How were your summers?"

"All good, bro. Ready to kick some ass here?" said Dave.

"Senior season, bro, game day, every day!" said Joe.

"I hear you, Joe. Hey, did we ever find a running back to replace Eric?"

"They got some PG kid in here late from Lynn. Who knows?"

All the new team members introduced themselves, and they get their issued equipment. After that they were all tested in the weight room and their forty-yard dash time.

"Hey, did you guys see that new running back from Lynn?"

"Yeah, I blinked and the friggin' kid was through his forty. What's his story?" asked Dave.

"I heard that he was all-state as a junior, and he blew out his ACL the last game of the season against Lynn English on Thanksgiving. I heard that he had offers from BC, Michigan, and Syracuse when he was a junior, but they withdrew their offers after his ACL tear."

"No shit?"

"Yeah, so now he's looking at UNH, UMASS, and some Ivies."

"Good, because we need something to keep defenses honest."

As they showered before dinner, the new tailback was staring at Liam.

"Dude, can I help you with something? You're creeping me out with all the staring."

"No, sorry, man, I...um...was looking at your ink."

"What about it?"

"Nothin', it's just that I think I've seen something like that tattoo before."

"I doubt it. Do you mind? I just want to finish my shower and go eat."

"Yeah, yeah, my bad. Sorry, dude."

Later that afternoon at dinner, the conversation got heated. "Hey look, Liam, it's your boyfriend from the shower."

"Shut up, Joe."

"Oh look, here he comes," said Dave.

"Pucker up, Liam," said John.

"Hey, guys. Liam, I remember where I saw that artwork from," said the new guy.

"Oh really, where?"

"You're from Southie, aren't you?"

"Yeah, how'd you know?"

"I'm Cameron Pedro from Lynn. We went to the Little League state finals together a few years back. Remember?"

"No way! How the hell are you?" Liam said as he gave Cam a hug.

"Good, man, how's that other kid? The pitcher."

"You mean Mikey?"

"Yeah, that's him. And that kid, Ray?"

"Both doing well, thanks for asking. Guys, this is Cameron Pedro. He's cool people from Lynn. We played Little League baseball against each other when I was younger."

"Hey, Cameron, nice to meet you. I'm John, this is Dave, and this is Joe."

"Hey, and Cam is fine," he said as he nodded to each of them.

"So, Cam, how'd you end up here?" asked Dave.

"Well, I was young for my grade in my other high school, Lynn Classical. I just turned seventeen over the summer, and one of my teachers recommended that I try prep school for a year to improve my chances to get into a better college. I had an injury at the end of my junior year, and most of the D-I schools shied away from me while I was rehabbing over most of my senior year. My only options were Connecticut, New Hampshire, U Mass, and U Maine. Some Ivies contacted me late and recommended a prep year as well; so here I am. How about you guys?"

"Dave came here as a freshman. Joe and John came in as sophomores, and I transferred in as a junior."

"Don't worry about getting any looks this year, Cam; plenty of scouts will be visiting our games to check out Mr. All-American, Liam."

"Whatever, John."

By the end of training camp, Cam quickly separated himself from the competition and earned the starting spot at tailback. With Cam's quickness and speed, it looked like they could make another run at the prep title. The scrimmage against Andover was just two weeks away.

In the interim, classes at school began, and June and Liam were inseparable. June was taking mostly literature, art, and writing classes, while he was finishing up some core requirements in math and in the sciences. In addition, June joined the field-hockey team as her requisite sport. Nevertheless, they managed to eat dinner together most nights, followed by studying at the library. Life at school was a bit of an adjustment for June since she was used to her independence. Liam could see that she liked it, though, and that she was making some new friends who shared her passion for writing and the arts as well.

THE ANDOVER SCRIMMAGE

THE GIRLS FIELD-HOCKEY TEAM WAS about to take the field against Proctor Academy, and June was on the sidelines in her new uniform. Liam waved to her as he got closer to the field. He was directed to a gated-off section of the field for family and fans. Other family members were wearing white buttons that read, "EXETER," on the top, and their daughter's number on the pin. He purchased three pins in anticipation of Ms. Angela and Mr. Rubin possibly showing up.

"Hey, Liam, what do you think of my uniform? Sexy isn't it?" June asked as she stepped on one toe with her stick in one hand like she was on a modeling shoot.

"Agreed! How's it looking for playing time today?"

"Well, the bad news is that some of the girls are sick with the flu. The good news is that they may have to play me!" June smiled. "Aw, you ordered three pins with my number? You're so sweet! Hey, I have to run. Coach Renee is calling us."

"Good luck!"

"Thanks," said June as she winked back at him.

The game was going back and forth, and June was actually playing quite well for her first organized game. The score was tied 2–2 with only four minutes left in the final period. Coach Renee decided to move June up to the forward position because they had to press more on offense, and Allison Union—the starting forward—was getting winded. Exeter won the next faceoff, and June ran up the right side

327

of the field where she saw an opening. Allison quickly passed it ahead to June as she saw her breaking away from the Proctor defender. June caught the ball and saw Laura Tate heading for the goal behind the last defender. June turned and drilled a pass through the defender's legs to Laura. Laura stopped the ball, wound up, and then whacked the ball past the goalie. The team ran to hug Laura for her goal and June for the assist. It turned out to be a great opening win for the team, led by Laura and June!

Exeter was just about to start the preseason scrimmage against Andover when they saw them take the field to warm up. Wow! They were huge! After four consecutive years of losing to their archrival Exeter, it looked like the Andover admissions committee decided to invest in a few more postgraduates (PGs) to reverse the losing tide and beef up their team. Even though they looked better than last year's team with Cam in the backfield, this would be a big challenge by the end of the year.

Andover was led by a two-time all-state PG linebacker from Hyannis, Massachusetts, named Nick Hirou. He was an imposing six-feet-two-inch linebacker, who was encouraged by a few Ivy League schools to do a postgraduate year if he wanted to attend one of the Ivies. He currently held scholarship offers from BC, Syracuse, Maryland, and North Carolina. He led the Andover team onto the field; he had painted black triangles around both of his eyes. He assumed this was some sort of sign to intimidate the opposition.

"I'm coming after you, number one. Yeah, you Mr. All-American. I'm going to bury you! This is my house!" said Hirou.

"Do you hear that shit, Liam?" asked John. "I'm going to knock him on his ass after the first play!"

And then from the sidelines, Hirou's father started to chime in as well.

"Go ahead, Mike, take him out!"

"Hey, Liam."

"Yeah, Cam?"

"You're not going to believe this, but that Hirou kid is that same ass-hole from Little League who started that shit with Ray at the banquet."

"No shit?"

"Yeah, that's him! I remembered him because his father was a prick too!"

"Let me see." He stopped on the field to look over at the Andover sideline. "No friggin' way! That *is* him!"

"Guys, let's get going and stop staring at them. Liam, line 'em up for warm-ups," said Coach Long.

"Guys, let's go. Line 'em up."

After calisthenics and warming up, the captains met at midfield. John and Liam represented Exeter, and Nick Hirou and their safety, Fletcher Johnson, represented Andover. They met the head referee at midfield.

"Okay, boys, this is a controlled scrimmage. You'll each have twenty plays on offense, followed by twenty plays on defense. We'll do that two times, and then it will be halftime. After the half, we will play a thirty-minute full scrimmage. Exeter, as the visiting team, you call the coin flip: heads or tails."

"Heads," said John.

"Heads it is, number sixty-five. Do you want the ball on offense or defense first?"

"We'll take offense first, sir."

"Andover, which end of the field would you like to defend?"

"The south end zone, sir," said Fletcher.

The referee signaled that Exeter would be on offense first and that Andover would defend the south end zone.

"Boys, shake hands, and let's have a clean game."

Liam shook Fletcher's hand first, and then Hirou stared at him while Liam extended my hand.

"Hey, dude, you gonna' shake hands or what?" he asked.

Hirou just stared at Liam and then turned away back to Andover's sidelines.

"What the hell is that all about?" he asked Fletcher.

"Watch your back, man. That kid is a few fries short of a Happy Meal. He's a nut on the field. Even against his own team, he goes full speed."

"Gotcha, thanks for the heads-up, Fletch."

After the first couple of sets of offensive downs, the team was starting to get into the rhythm of things. He consistently completed short outlet passes, followed by hard runs by Cam. He was leading the offense with great precision as we were marching up the field to score. The Andover defense could not get to him, so they decided to be more aggressive up the middle. Andover's strategy to stop this drive was to stack the linebackers right at the line of scrimmage and blitz on every down. As he approached the center, Hirou started screaming out defensive signals, and then he kept pointing at Liam.

Liam approached the center and started to call the signals.

"Ready—set—red seven—red seven…" But then the defense shifted right in the gaps between the center and the guards, so Liam had to change the play from a run up the middle to a play-action pass to the right side: "Check, check, check—red twenty-four—red twenty-four—set—hut—hut."

He took the ball from the center, faked the handoff to Cam, who blocked one of the blitzing linebackers, and then rolled out to his right and was looking for Joe to trail the play. Realizing that Joe was being held up at the line of scrimmage, Liam ran out-of-bounds. Two yards outside the Andover sidelines, the other blitzing linebacker (Hirou), who was trailing Liam on the play, hit Liam after the play was called dead by the referees. Hirou immediately got in his face.

"This is my house, All-American! My house, and don't you forget it!" He threw Liam to the ground again.

"Great hit, Mike!" said Hirou's father, who was clapping just a few yards away from him.

The referees missed Hirou's second hit as he was on the ground. John Caru came over and grabbed Hirou to get him off Liam.

"Thanks, John."

"What the hell is with that guy?"

"I have no idea. He keeps screaming, though. He's got issues."

The next play Liam told the offense that they were going on a delayed snap.

"Remember, guys: red fourteen on three, red fourteen on three, and nobody go offside! Ready?"

"Break," everyone chanted.

As soon as Liam broke the huddle, the linebackers shifted in the same gap position as the last play.

Liam immediately called a check to the play that was sent in from the sidelines.

"Ready—set—check, check, check forty-four—check forty-four—hut—hu—"

On the second "hut," Hirou broke through the line and hit Liam before the ball was snapped. The referee immediately threw the flag for an offside penalty, but not before Liam got knocked on his back. Liam immediately got up and went after Hirou.

The referee quickly separated them as Hirou kept yelling, "My house!"

"Okay, everyone, get in the huddle now!" Liam called as he motioned with his hands for everyone to hurry up. "I've had enough of this shit! This is what we're gonna do. Cam, we're going to run red fifteen. I'll fake the handoff to you, and then I want you to settle right behind of Hirou, okay?"

"Yeah, okay."

"John, I'm going to throw the ball right in Hirou's hands, about ten yards away and to your right, understand?"

"Yeah, but why?" asked John.

"So that you can go full speed and knock the shit out of him."

"Oh, this ought to be good," said Dave and Joe.

"Hey, I need you two to make sure John gets him. If John misses, you two clean up. So be ready."

"Forget that, I won't miss!"

"Okay, red fifteen on one, red fifteen on one—ready, break!"

As he approached the line, he looked at Hirou and smiled. This infuriated Hirou even more as he stepped back in his position, screaming the defensive calls.

Liam called the play, "Ready—set—red fifteen—red fifteen—hut."

Liam took the snap and faked the handoff to Cam on the left side of the line. Cam ran through the hole and sat right behind Hirou just as Liam instructed. John maintained his block for a second and then released his defender. Liam sat back in the pocket and threw the ball toward Cam. It was a perfect spiral pass that fell directly into Hirou's lap. Hirou caught the ball with wide-open eyes and started to head up the field. As Hirou took his first step forward, John was coming full speed from his blind side. He hit Hirou with such force that Hirou's helmet popped off, and we heard a snap as he fell to the ground. The referee quickly blew his whistle and designated that the ball was turned over to Andover. As the dust settled, Hirou was still on the ground, moaning when they were ready to start the next play. The referee blew the whistle again and called an injury time-out. The trainers ran onto the field and waved for a cart. It appeared that John had separated Hirou's shoulder, and he would be out for at least four to five weeks. As Hirou was being carted off the field and both teams were clapping, Liam paused and shouted to him that this was his *house* with a smile. Upon realizing what Liam said, Hirou flipped him the bird.

After the game, Liam met up with the judge and Ray.

"Hey, guys."

"Nice game, Liam!"

"Thanks, Ray."

"What was that all about, Liam?"

"You'll *never* believe this, but that linebacker was the same jerk from Hyannis who gave Ray a hard time in Little League."

"You're kidding."

"No, and get this. His father was the guy on the sidelines, cheering him on to kill me!"

"Well, then, serves him right, but I hope that the boy is okay, though."

"I was told that he had a concussion and a separated shoulder; that's all."

"Okay, maybe you'll see him at the end of the year then."

"Let's hope not!"

"It looks like you improved at running back. That will help you in the long run."

"Yeah, in the small-world category, the new running back is Cam Pedro. Cam played on the Lynn Little League team that won the state title. He was an all-state running back who had an ACL injury. He's looking at some local schools and some Ivies."

"Well, I like the way he runs. He makes kids miss, and he has a second gear."

"Hey, I have a second gear."

"Liam, my boy, you have a great arm, but when you run, your second gear is from slower to slow compared to that young man. I'd like to meet him."

"Sure, one second."

"Hey, Cam, you got a sec?"

"Yeah, what's up?"

"Do you remember Ray from Little League?"

"Sure, hi, Ray. How are you?"

"You had a great game, Cam! Nice running."

"Thanks, Ray!"

"And this is Judge Mahoney, my adoptive parent. Please bear with him; he's getting old, and his eyesight is going; he called me slow compared to you. Cam, tell them the truth: Who would win in a forty-yard dash?"

"You would, Liam, if I gave you a twenty-yard head start," Cam said with a smile.

"Nice game, young man."

"Thank you, sir."

"Liam tells me that you are looking at some Ivies?"

"Yes, sir. Coach Carlson, the head assistant coach from Harvard, recommended that I take a postgraduate year, and they would consider me if my test scores improve."

"Well, if that's any indication of what my alma mater can expect, then they should accept you right now."

"Thank you, sir. I am trying."

"Liam, on the other hand, won't even consider the Ivies. He's stuck on Stanford, Boston College, and Notre Dame."

"All great schools, sir."

"Yeah, don't encourage him. Okay, boys, we have to get back. Remember, study hard and stay out of trouble."

"Yes, sir."

"Judge?"

"Yes, Liam?"

"I didn't see Mikey or Sue. Any word from them?"

"No, sorry, Liam. Father Callahan sends his regards, though. He had several baptisms to attend to and couldn't make it."

"Okay, please send him my best."

"Will do."

"Ray, I have to go. Can I get a hug?"

They embraced.

"We'll see you in a couple of weeks for the season opener."

"Okay, guys, see you then. Thanks again for coming."

THE ANDOVER GAME

As the season progressed, Exeter remained undefeated, and more and more schools came recruiting Liam. Going into the final game of the season, they were 8–0, and Andover was undefeated as well. This game was being hyped throughout New England because it boasted over fifteen players going to Division I or I-AA schools. Scouts from all over the country were going to be there. Exeter was led by Liam, who was one of the highest-rated quarterback in the nation, and Cam, the leading rusher in the league. Andover was led by Massachusetts High School All-American Nick Hirou, who made it back to action two weeks after his preseason shoulder injury.

It was a cold and rain-soaked day in Andover, Massachusetts. The running game was stifled due to the muddy field conditions, and the receivers were slipping all over the field. Nick Hirou, the Andover middle linebacker, was playing like a man who was possessed. Every time Exeter gave the ball to Cam, he was sloshing around in the mud and didn't get very far off the line of scrimmage. Hirou kept screaming at Liam that this was his house.

It was a 0–0 tie late in the fourth quarter with the rain still coming down in buckets. It was fourth down with two yards to go for a first down but time was running out. The ball was on the Andover thirty-yard line, and there was less than forty seconds left on the clock. Liam called a naked bootleg to the left, and he told Cam to run up the right sideline instead of faking the run up the middle. Liam ran the play exactly as Liam designed. Liam faked the handoff to Cam on the right and rolled out to his left. Hirou immediately chased after Liam because he saw that Liam had no blockers to protect him. Just then Liam saw Cam breaking free up the right sideline. Liam stood his ground and threw a perfect spiral up the right sideline. As Liam threw the ball, Hirou hit Liam with such force that he knocked the wind right out of Liam. Liam could not see the end of the play because his face was buried in the mud. All he could hear were the screams from the Exeter sidelines. Cam caught the ball, and Exeter beat Andover 7–0.

After the game, Liam was handed the MVP trophy by Coach Long, but he gave it to Cam instead because he said that Cam really earned it.

Unfortunately, Liam could not celebrate the win with his teammates on campus just yet because he had to go to Andover's Isham Health Center for x-rays on his ribs. As they left the field, June was cheering so much she practically lost her voice.

"Are you coming back on the bus, Liam?"

"No, I have to go to the campus infirmary first for x-rays."

"Hey, bro, nice game!"

"Mikey! You made it!"

"Of course, I did. You think I'd miss your last high-school game?" They hugged.

"Sue, thanks for coming too," Liam said as he kissed her on the cheek.

"June, we'll wait, and then we can drive you back to campus if you want," said Mikey.

"Oh, will you? Thanks so much."

"June, you'll need permission from whomever you came with. Just tell them that we'll take you back."

"Thanks, Judge."

"Hey, Ray, buddy, why are you crying?"

"Because you're hurt, Liam."

"No, I'm fine. Here, take my game shirt; it's yours now. Give me a hug; I'm fine."

"He's all right, Liam. He's just emotional about hospitals; that's all."

"Liam, nice game, and you're welcome."

"Father Callahan! Thanks for coming! What is it that I should be thankful for?"

"My prayers, young man, my prayers. To think that a Statue of Liberty trick play like that would work in this weather required divine intervention, my boy."

"Then by all means, Father, thank you too!"

Later that evening they all went out to dinner at the Exeter Inn to celebrate the win. Liam's arm was wrapped in an Ace bandage and soft cast to keep it immobile. Just before dinner was about to be served, he proposed a toast.

"To my immediate family," he said as he nodded to the judge, Ray, and Father Callahan, "my best friends"—nodding to Mikey and Sue—"and to my new family." He nodded to June. "I want to thank you all for your support, guidance, and friendship. A few short years ago, I was thrust into a position where I could have been a victim and ended up on the streets. However, I was saved. I was saved by my best friend for always being there for me during thick and thin. To Father Callahan, who took me in when my father passed. To Judge Mahoney and Ray, for allowing me to become a part of their family. And finally, to June, who taught me how to love and trust outsiders again. For this I am forever grateful and blessed to have you all part of my life. Please raise your glasses as we celebrate, and I thank all of you!"

"Wonderful toast, my boy, wonderful," said the judge.

"Thank you, Judge. By the way, I need to speak to you about something over break if you don't mind."

"Yes, by all means. Is everything okay?"

"Yes, everything is fine. I just need to discuss a personal matter; that's all."

"Okay, my boy, whenever you are ready."

Liam then made his way around the table to thank everyone in person.

"Mikey, Sue, thanks for coming today. I'll need to speak to you both when I get home next week on break. Okay?"

"Sure. Is everything okay?" asked Mikey.

"Yeah, I just want to go over some legal papers that I need you to sign, Mikey, just in case something happens to me."

"What the hell are you talking about?"

"Look, I don't want to discuss it here and now; it's just in case something happens to me. Basically, I want part of my estate to go to you and Sue."

"Estate? And why her?" Mikey asked with a smile.

"It's just some money my dad left me, and if you two get married, I would want you guys to start off on the right foot."

"Um, I guess so, sure," said Mikey.

Sue rolled her eyes. "Who *are* you? Your best friend is making a kind gesture, and all you have to say is 'um'? Liam, that is a very generous offer. Let's not distract from this evening. We can talk about it next week when you get home if you still want to."

"Great, thanks, guys."

"Hey, beautiful."

June whispered in his ear, "Liam, that was an amazing toast, thank you. I want to be alone with you, take you away to the Four Seasons in Boston, and rip off all your clothes."

"Um, great idea, but I'm wounded, and I can't really move."

"Don't worry; I'll do all the work," June said, with a coquettish smile.

Liam stepped back and paused as he gazed at June. "If I could, I would drop to one knee and propose to you after a comment like that!" he said, blushing.

"So, Ray, you didn't want to wait and wash that shirt, huh?"

"No, I wanted to wear it now."

"You got it, buddy!"

A Change Of Heart

EARLY THE FOLLOWING WEEK, IN Coach Long's office, the Harvard assistant coach, Coach Carlson, was visiting.

"Coach Carlson, this is my friend, Liam, Liam O'Hara. He's the quarterback on our team."

"Please, I know Liam from his camp at Stanford last summer."

"Coach, nice to see you again."

"You had a great season, Liam."

"I was only as good as my man Cam here running the ball."

"Yes, Cam had a great season, and that's what I want to talk to him about."

"Well, I'll leave you to it. I have to get a lift in. Let me know how it turns out."

After about forty-five minutes, Liam met up with Cam in the weight room.

"Well, how'd it go?" he asked.

"Good news, bad news, I guess."

"What's that mean?"

"They really like me, and they said that they can get me in, but my bandwidth is low, and they usually reserve those lower bandwidth slots for linemen. They still want me to come on an official visit during our winter break in a few weeks, just in case any of their linemen fall out or go somewhere else."

"Hey, that's good news! What are the other Ivies saying?"

"Pretty much the same thing. This sucks. It's funny. Right now, I only have offers from U Mass, UNH, and UCONN. However, if my academic index were just a few points higher, I would have my choice between U Mass or Harvard, UNH or Dartmouth, UCONN or Yale. Pretty extreme choices, huh?"

"Gee, when you put it like that, I guess it is messed up."

"All I can do is pray, wait, and see."

"Sorry, Cam, I wish there was something I could do."

"Yeah, me too. Hey, enough of this self-pity crap. Do you think June will dance with me tonight at the Spring Fling?"

"You know that she's my girlfriend. Right?"

"Yeah, but only because she hasn't experienced my moves on the dance floor."

"Shut up!" Liam said as he punched Cam in the arm. They exchanged silly grins.

Winter Break Begins

THE JUDGE MIGHT HAVE BEEN wondering why Liam wanted to talk to him in person. It was usually something more than mundane if he knew Liam.

"Hey, Judge, you got a minute?"

"Sure, Liam, how can I help you?"

"A couple of things really. First, the school is offering a trip to Ireland to visit Dublin and Trinity College for a week. I was wondering if it would be okay to go. I mean, if I have enough money saved up, what do you think?"

"Will June be going?"

"No, she'll be in Japan on a photo shoot throughout this break."

"Are you sure?"

"Yes, sir. See, even check out this postcard from Tokyo."

"Well, never worry about money, my boy. I'll talk with you about that later. Yes, you can go on the trip. When is it?"

"In two weeks."

"Sure, no problem. I'll send the deposit in tomorrow morning. What else?"

"Well, I heard about your incident a few weeks back, and I want to talk to you about it."

"What would that be, Liam?"

"Your mini-stroke."

"Who told you about that?"

"Never mind, I just heard; that's all."

"Well, I'm fine now as you can see, and there is no need to worry Raymond, okay?"

"Yes, sir, I won't, but that's what I wanted to talk to you about. I want you to know that should anything ever happen to you, I'll take care of Ray. I'll make sure that he will always be with me—no group homes, not a ward of the state, nothing like that."

"Liam, that is very generous, but you must live your own life."

"With all due respect, Judge, Ray is family."

"Liam, my boy, you are a generous soul. We can cross that bridge when it comes upon us. However, I will take what you said into consideration because Ray loves you too. And I thank you for that; you made my day. So—on to a more pleasant topic. Have you decided about school next year? South Bend, Palo Alto, Los Angeles, Chestnut Hill, where?"

"No, not yet, Judge."

"Any plans for tonight?"

"Yes, sir, I'm going to Cambridge to catch up with Cam, who is on a recruiting visit to Harvard."

"Okay, be good and try to be home by midnight."

"Will do, sir."

At the Harvard-Columbia basketball game, Liam walked into the Lavietes Pavilion and spotted Cam. "Hey, Cam."

"Liam, what's up? How's it going? What are you doing here?"

"I had a free night and wanted to catch a game."

"Hey, look who else is here on a visit. Fletcher Johnson from Andover."

"Hey, Fletch, how's it going?"

"And this is our host for the weekend, Art Irons, from Charlestown. He's the middle linebacker and captain next year."

"Art, nice to meet you."

"So you're what a top quarterback in the country looks like, huh?"

"Well, let's just say that I was lucky when they tested a few of us over last summer."

"And modest too."

"As a first-hand witness of what he has done over the past two years," said Fletcher, "I can assure you that he is the real deal. He's got offers from Stanford, USC, BC, Notre Dame, Miami, and UCLA."

"Wow, those are some big offers. But as far as you go, Fletcher, either he's that good or you're just that bad as a safety."

"No, it's not that; whenever we played Andover, I only threw away from where Fletcher was on the field. He was too fast and hit too hard, so I had to stay away from wherever he lined up." Liam winked to Fletcher.

"So, Art, how did you make it to Harvard via Charleston?" asked Liam.

"I prepped at Choate for three years."

"Ah, I see."

"Look, we're all going to a recruit party afterward. Do you wanna come by?" said Art.

"Sure, if it's not a problem, but I have a midnight curfew."

"What are you, twelve?"

"No, I just respect my household."

"Whatever, we're leaving in a few."

"You sure you don't mind?"

"Nope, not at all, in fact, I'm going to tell our current QB that you're thinking of coming here. Maybe he'll transfer. Ha!"

As they entered the Harvard campus and then the Wigglesworth Dorm, the party was in full swing. They had kegs of beer, a full bar, and lots of girls from neighboring colleges. Art asked, "Do you want to drink?"

"No, I'm good. I have to drive home tonight."

"Yeah, but that's in four or five hours, or you could crash here if you want."

"Thanks, but some other time."

"Cam, what are you drinking?"

"Soda water. I don't want to be hungover when I speak with the coaches tomorrow for my one on one."

"What time is that?"

"We're meeting in their offices for breakfast at nine o'clock, and my meeting is the last one at eleven o'clock. Basically, they tell us at that time who accepted a slot and who didn't or is still waiting."

"Well, I'm going to head out," Liam said. "I have Mass in the morning, and then I have to drop something off in Cambridge. Do you need a ride home or want to grab lunch?"

"Sure, Liam, let's grab lunch. It'll probably be my last lunch in Cambridge for quite some time, but sure."

"Great, I'll pick you up at the coach's offices."

"Cool. Drive safely, my friend," he said as they shook hands and embraced.

After lunch Liam said, "Fletch, I have to run. Good luck with the coaches tomorrow."

"Thanks, Liam, let's catch up soon."

"Thanks for the invite. I'm going to head out."

"Hey, man, the offer still stands. If you want to stay, you can have my bed, and I'll sleep over in my girlfriend's dorm."

"Thanks, but I'm good. Best of luck next year."

"Thanks, and good luck with your decision."

"Thanks!"

On the way out to his car, he started to open the Wigglesworth Dorm door. He saw a girl waiting outside, trying to get in. She grumbled, "Great, *finally* someone is here to let me in. I've been banging on the door forever, but those idiot football players have their music up so loud that nobody can hear me ringing the doorbell."

"I'm sorry; I can't just let anyone into this dorm. Do you have an ID?"

"No, because I left my wallet inside my dorm. I live on the second floor. Look, you can see that I'm a student here; this is my basketball team jacket."

"What's your name and phone number then?"

"Wait—are you a student here?"

"No, I just wanted to give a pretty girl a hard time; that's all."

"Grow up!" she yelled at Liam.

"Does that mean no name or number?"

"In your dreams—now get out of my way."

"So angry, so angry," he quipped. "Have a nice night."

At ten thirty the following morning, Liam entered the Malkin Athletic Center and greeted the student checking IDs. "Hi, I'm here to see Coach Corbin."

"Your name, please."

"Liam O'Hara."

"Hey, aren't you that kid from last night inside the Wigglesworth Dorm?"

"Oh, you're the basketball player from last night. I believe that I'm at a disadvantage. You now know my name, but I'm afraid that I don't know yours."

"And you won't. Sorry, Liam," she said with a fake upset look on her face, "but your name is not on the list. You'll have to call somebody."

"So it's gonna be like that, huh?" he said, grinning.

"Yeah, it is. Just like that!"

"Okay, can you just please give Coach Carlson this card and tell him that I am outside. It's important."

"You have your own business card, and you're only in high school?"

"Get off your pedestal; you were a senior just last year."

"You just wait here, and I'll see what they say."

"Thanks, Mary."

"My name is not Mary!"

"Okay fine, Kim."

"Zero for two, Liam."

"Hey, I'm tryin'—"

"Shut up!"

Two minutes later, the student returned and said, "Well, they're in the middle of seeing some recruits, but they said they will see you at eleven o'clock. They said you can wait in their offices."

"See, Karen, I told you so."

"It's not Karen either."

"Look, I'll be in this meeting for a bit. If you're still here when I get out, how about lunch?"

"What if I said I had a boyfriend?"

"Then I'd say, 'Lucky guy.' You have my card; call me when you are free."

"You're pretty cocky."

"Hey, I just like meeting new people. That's all, Sharon."

"It's not Sharon either."

"Yes, but I must be getting closer," he said, smiling as he walked into the coach's office.

"Liam, I'm done here. We can grab lunch now if you want," said a very sullen Cam.

"So what did Coach Carlson say?" asked Liam.

"Nothing much, the same thing that he said up at Exeter, that they really like me, they want me, but there are no more slots available I'm afraid." Cam put his head down between his legs and was on the verge of tears.

"Hey, don't worry about it, Cam."

"Give me five minutes, okay? I just need to speak with him quickly."

Liam knocked on Coach Carlson's door.

"Coach Carlson, do you have a minute?"

"Sure, Liam, come into my office. Have a seat."

"Thanks."

"How are your ribs?"

"On the mend, thanks."

"So how can I help you, Liam?"

"Well, it's how I can help you, Coach."

"How's that?"

"Here is my application to Harvard. I am either valedictorian or salutatorian of my senior class at Exeter, and I scored a fifteen ninety on my SATs. That score is in the ninety-fifth percentile of all test takers."

"Is this some kind of joke?"

"Nope, there are just a couple of things that I would require in return."

"What's that?"

"First, that my application is not made public until I notify Coach Williams at Stanford and Coach Long at Exeter."

"Okay, I have no problem with that."

"And second, I will only apply if you accept Cam Pedro as well. My GPA and my SAT scores put me at the highest bandwidth of incoming athletes, so this should put him back in the mix for admissions."

"Did Cam put you up to this? We can't barter admissions. You know that."

"No, Cam doesn't even know why I am here. Coach, I understand how the academic index works, and I also understand how you calculated Cam's position."

"Liam, like I said, we don't barter admissions."

"Coach, you'll be getting one of the top-rated QBs in the country, a very high GPA, and near perfect SAT scores. It's a win-win for you and Harvard. Here's the thing. I'm going to need your answer by Wednesday of next week; otherwise, Cam and I will be driving down to New Haven, and we'll see what they have to say. Based on the fact that they lost to you three years in a row, I suspect that they may be interested in this offer. And remember, Yale took Art Morris from Exeter late last year after he declined BC, Northwestern, and Syracuse; and he started as a freshman."

"How do I know that you won't change your mind about Stanford? You're their number-one recruit, you know."

"May I use your phone?"

"Sure."

Liam started dialing Stanford's coaching office.

"Good morning, Coach Williams; this is Liam O'Hara from Phillips Exeter. I'm leaving a message about my decision to play football next year. I've decided *not* to accept your generous scholarship offer. There were several personal factors that played into this decision, and ultimately, I need to do what's best for me and my family. I will be home later today should you wish to discuss this further."

"Okay, now I'm listening. But why else are you making this decision?"

"Well, my adoptive parent, Judge Mahoney, suffered a ministroke a few weeks back, and I want to stay closer to home should something happen again. That means that Yale, Dartmouth, BC, and Brown are all in the mix if I have to look elsewhere."

"Well, I'll tell you what, Liam. This may change things a bit. Let me speak with Coach Russell, and I'll let you know our decision."

"Coach, respectfully, you have until Wednesday. I have to call Coach Long next, so please keep this between yourself and Coach Russell."

"Okay, Liam, will do."

"Thanks, Coach. It was nice seeing you again."

"Yes, by all means, thanks, Liam. We'll try to let you know where we stand, by early next week."

"Thanks, Coach."

As Liam exited Coach Carlson's office, he turned and said, "Coach, look forward to hearing from you."

"Will do, Liam." And then he looked down at Cam. "Hey Cam, chin up."

"Yes, Coach, thanks."

"What was that all about, Liam?"

"One second, Cam."

"Melissa, I'll be waiting for your call."

"It's not Melissa either! Are you done trying to beg your way in here?"

"That's funny!" They're begging me not to go to Stanford. See you around."

"Don't hold your breath."

Liam smiled as they left the Malkin Athletic Center, and they got in Liam's car.

"What was that all about?" asked Cam.

"Nothing, I was just giving her a hard time; that's all."

"Hey, let's eat here at the restaurant, Nubar."

"Naw, it looks too expensive," said Cam.

"No worries, it's on me. We need to celebrate."

"Celebrate what? Are you kidding me? Now my college choices consist of UCONN, U Mass, UNH, and URI."

They sat down at a table in Nubar.

"So what's up?" asked Cam.

"Good news! I met with Coach Carlson and told him that I would be applying to Harvard."

"You're kidding! What about Stanford, ND, and BC?"

"Nope, none of the above."

"Well, congrats, I guess. Great, now that's one more person who takes a football slot. I'm not sure how that helps me?"

"I told them that I will *only* attend Harvard if they accept you as well. It's a package deal or nothing."

"You're kidding. Right?"

"Nope, and if they don't get back to us by this Wednesday, then you and I are headed down to New Haven for the same offer with Coach Carmine."

"Liam, I can't have you do that. Call him back and tell him that I'm not part of this deal. They might think that I put you up to it."

"Too late, I told him that you had nothing to do with this. It was *my* decision alone and my proposal."

"Liam, please, you can't do that. Why? You don't even really know me."

"Did you hit that prick Hirou *twice* in the Little League finals?"

"Yeah, why?"

"That's all I need to know. Shut up and let's just order lunch. I'll tell the judge my decision this afternoon, and let's see what he can do behind the scenes to help us as well."

"Liam, I don't know what to say?"

"Well, if things work out, I'm sure I'll hold this over your head forever," Liam said with a wink. "Just keep it between us because I haven't told Coach Long or the judge yet."

"Hey, even if things don't work out, I appreciate what you're doing, Liam."

"Forget it, let's order. I heard that the burgers here are fantastic!"

Later that day, when Liam got home, he sat down to talk to the judge about his decision. "Judge," he said.

"Yes, Liam."

"Do you have a minute?"

"Sure, Liam, what's going on?"

"I thought that you would want to know that I've narrowed my decision as far as schools go. I met with Coach Carlson at Harvard and submitted my application for admission."

"You're kidding me. What about Stanford? Notre Dame? Miami or Boston College?"

"Well, I decided that I wanted to be closer to home and my family. The only caveat is that I told Coach Carlson that I would *only* attend Harvard if they accepted Cam as well."

"Liam, I don't think that the coaches can promise that. And this decision of yours doesn't have anything to do with what we discussed the other day, does it?"

"The Harvard coaches told Cam that they really liked him, but that his academic index, his AI, was too low. They use those lower-band slots for linemen. That tells me that they can accept him, but they have different priorities. With my high AI, this should offset Cam's lower AI. And yes, it did factor in my decision, but Stanford was too far away, and Notre Dame is in the middle of nowhere. The staff at BC didn't thrill me either."

"That's a big gamble, Liam."

"Well, I'm making the same offer to Yale on Wednesday if Harvard says no. I was hoping that you could speak with some of your friends on the football committee too. The reality is that landing a five-star recruit would speak volumes to either program."

"Okay, Liam, I'll make some calls, but no promises."

Later that afternoon in the judge's private study, he called the head of the Harvard Football Committee.

"Hello, this is Michael Mahoney for Robert Burke."

"Judge, is that you?"

"Yes, Bob."

"I hope that you are calling about your boy, Liam. Has he come to his senses and turned down Stanford, Notre Dame, and BC to play for us?"

"Well, that's the reason I'm calling. The answer to your question is yes and no."

"What does that mean?"

"You see, Liam just dropped off his Harvard application to the coach's office."

"You're kidding. That's great!"

"Agreed, but there is a catch."

"A catch? What catch?"

"Well, between Liam's grades and his SAT scores, his calculated academic index puts him somewhere around the ninety-ninth percentile of all incoming freshmen. That's not the problem. He wants his

Exeter teammate to be admitted with him. The young man's name is Cam Pedro. He is at Exeter now and is a heck of a running back from Lynn, Massachusetts. Coach Carlson said that they like him a lot; however, he would be a low-band kid, and the staff usually holds those slots for linemen."

"Judge, you know we can't play games like this."

"I know; I know—that's what I told Liam. The reality is that Liam's high AI should offset Cam's average AI. I'm just keeping you in the loop as to what *can* happen with a little nudge by the football committee. If it doesn't work out, the boys are going to try New Haven. I'll be damned if that isn't the type of thing that would ignite recruiting at Yale."

"Yale? Come, Judge! What the hell is that?"

"I know. I just don't want our hubris to ruin a good opportunity here. Remember what happened to the Juron kid out of Swampscott a few years ago. We were messing around with his admissions, and he finally said, 'Screw you; I'm going to Yale.' We all know how that ended. He was a four-time All-Ivy and two-time All-American who beat us three out of four years. And then he went on to play several years in the pros."

"Okay, I'll make some inquiries. Are you sure if we get both of them in, they'll come? I mean, I don't want Liam to all of a sudden change his mind and end up in Palo Alto, and I'll have egg on my face. He's Stanford's number-one recruit, you know."

"One, you have my word. Two, it is my understanding that Liam already called the Stanford staff while in Coach Carlson's office and said that he would be playing elsewhere."

"Well, if that's the case, I'll see what I can do. No promises, though, Judge."

"Understood, Bob. Please keep me posted."

"Will do."

"Thanks again, Bob."

Two weeks later while on break, Liam called Cam to check in on him and see how he was doing.

"Cam, it's Liam. Any word from Harvard?"

"No, you?"

"No."

"I guess your bluff didn't work."

"It wasn't a bluff. I'm picking you up, and we'll go to New Haven tomorrow if we have to."

The doorbell rang at Cam's house.

"Liam, hold on; someone is at the door. One sec."

"An envelope here for a Cameron Pedro," said the Federal Express delivery man.

"Who is it from?"

"You'll have to read it to find out, sir. I just need you to sign here."

"Okay, thanks."

As Liam was waiting on the phone for Cam to return, the doorbell rang.

"Cam."

"Yeah?"

"Now someone is at my door. Hold on."

"Package here for a Liam O'Hara."

"Yeah, that's me."

"Please sign here, sir."

"Sure, thanks!"

"Cam, who is your package from?"

"The Harvard football office. And you, Liam, who is your package from?"

"The same—the Harvard football office."

"No way!"

"What is it?"

"I'm not sure, but I think, or rather hope, I know what it is." said Cam.

They both ripped open the FedEx envelopes.

"What's yours say, Liam?"

"It's a Letter of Likelihood from Harvard admissions."

"How about yours?"

"The same!"

"What does that mean?"

"Well, that means that we'll be accepted, provided that we maintain good academic standing for the remaining two semesters at Exeter and if we stay out of any trouble."

"You're kidding me!"

"Nope! We should be getting formal letters of acceptance in a few weeks."

"Do you think I can tell my mom?"

"I'd wait until the formal letter comes from admissions and let her open it. What do you think?"

"That's a great idea. And, Liam..."

"Yeah, Cam?"

"This completely changed my life, you know? I mean I owe you a lot. Nobody has ever done something like this for me."

"Cam, you don't owe me anything. We're all good. Just start getting ready for next year and prove to them that you are worth the price of admission!"

"I'm going to be a beast next year, Liam, a beast!"

Later that week Liam's doorbell rang; it was Sue and Mikey.

"Mikey, Sue, come on in. I'm leaving for a school trip to Dublin tomorrow for a week, and I wanted to tell you both something. I've decided to stay local for college."

"See, I told you, Sue; he's friggin' goin' to BC!"

"Nope."

"BU?"

"Nope."

"No way, you're going to be one of those assholes at Harvard."

"Yup."

"Congrats, Liam!" Sue gave him a hug and a kiss on the cheek.

"Yeah, bro, nice job! Your mom and dad would be proud."

"Thanks, Mikey! I think that they would be too."

"Come on; let's grab a bite now because I have to get up early tomorrow."

Return From Dublin

The following week at Logan Airport, the judge and Ray picked Liam up from his trip.

"Hey, Judge; hey, Ray! I missed you guys."

"How was your trip, my boy?"

"Fantastic, Judge! I really need to travel more."

"What did you get me, Liam?"

"Raymond! That is rude."

"Sorry, Liam."

"No problem, Ray—here. This is saltwater taffy that is a specialty of the Cork region that I visited."

"Gee, thanks, Liam."

"Thanks again, Judge, for picking me up at the airport."

"Nonsense, my boy."

"Hey, this is for you, Judge. And one for you, Ray. I also have one for Father Callahan as well."

"Liam, these hand-knit sweaters from Cork are beautiful. You are far too generous."

"No, not at all, Judge, it's the least that I could do."

"Well, let's get settled and do some laundry. Is Tommy Demps still planning on driving you up to Exeter tomorrow?"

"Yes, sir, we're stopping by to see Mr. Maguire as well."

"Okay, just be safe."

"Yes, sir."

"Before you go, we need to chat tonight, though, okay?"

"Sure, Judge. Everything okay?"

"Everything is fine, Liam."

"Judge, any word from June?"

"Sorry, Liam, no word, but you did get a postcard from Tokyo."

"Thanks, Judge."

Later that night the judge called Liam to his study for a discussion. Liam knocked.

"Please shut the doors, Liam."

"Yes, sir. This sounds serious."

"Yes and no, Liam."

"Have a seat. It's about your turning eighteen, your inheritance, and your father's wishes."

"This does sound serious."

"Well, it is, young man, and you have some decisions to make. When you turned eighteen a few months ago, you became a legal adult. That means, if you would like, you do not have to be under my guardianship any longer. Know this, though: when we took you into this house, we expected you to be a permanent part of this family, if you wanted."

"Just so that I'm hearing you correctly, I can stay as long as I want, or leave if I want. Is that correct?"

"Yes, in a manner of speaking."

"Do you want me to leave, Judge?"

"Heavens no! We want you to stay for as long as you want. As far as Raymond and I are concerned, you are family, my boy."

"Phew! That's a relief because I want to stay! And remember what I said that if something ever happens to you, I promise you that I'll take care of Ray."

"Liam, you have no idea what that means to me. However, you may have a change of heart after I tell you this. You know that your father left you a little money to get started in life. Well, it is in a trust, and you get it when you turn nineteen next year. It's a little over two hundred twenty thousand dollars from his savings, military benefits, and life insurance."

"Wow! That's a lot of money."

"It is indeed. Do you remember H. D. Daniels and the Daniels family?"

"Yes, of course, they are that family from Texas who came to my dad's funeral."

"Are you aware of the story how your dad knows one of the most powerful families in the United States?"

"No, not exactly. I believe they served together over in Vietnam or something like that."

"That is correct. What happened is that your dad's platoon, which was being led by H. D. Daniels Jr., was captured by the North Vietnamese while on a routine recon mission. They were led off to a prison camp just north of the thirty-eighth parallel. While at the camp, your father took care of H. D. Jr. while he was sick and nursed him back to health. Otherwise, the North Vietnamese would have shot him on the spot because he could not work. About two months into their capture, your father escaped and tried to get help. While Declan was laid up in the American hospital in Saigon, H. D. Sr. visited your father to find out what he could about his son. Since this was your father's second tour, and he was now a *former* POW, he was being sent home as a hero for escaping the North Vietnamese. H. D. Sr. made your father a proposition. He offered your father one million dollars in cash to go back and try and help free his son since the military would not go through Cambodia or go north of the thirty-eighth parallel to rescue his platoon. Declan told H. D. Sr. to "stuff it" and said that he would do it for free as soon as he was released from the hospital. As H. D. Sr. tells the story, Declan told him that he was impugning his South Boston Irish integrity by offering him that money—and that of all marines. Both men were stubborn, so they made a compromise. If anything were to happen to your father during this rescue mission,

HD would put that million dollars in a trust fund for you until the age of twenty-one. Your father eventually led the mission back to the North Vietnamese prison camp. He freed everyone in his platoon who was still alive, including H. D. Jr. At your father's funeral, H. D. Sr. advised me and Father Callahan that he'd put money aside in a trust for you. We are not quite sure of its value, but it is substantial, and you will have access to it when you turn twenty-one."

"Are you serious?"

"Completely."

"No way! But why? My father came back from the mission."

"Yes, I know, but HD felt that he owed your father a great debt."

"Wow! That's unbelievable! So we were rich all this time?"

"I'm afraid so, but the rules of the trust state that you cannot have access to any of the money until you turn twenty-one. I would highly recommend that you say nothing of this to *anyone* until you turn of age."

"Should I not take the money, Judge?"

"No, I don't think your father would mind. It will give you a head start in life. If you look in your bank account now, you will see your new available funds that your father left for you. These are supposed to be used for clothing, books, and any other immediate needs that you may have. I just want you to be responsible, Liam."

"Yes, Judge, I understand."

"Now go to bed and get some rest; it's been a long day."

"Yes, sir."

The following morning, Liam packed up his remaining books and clothes in his bag and was ready to head back to school.

"Judge, Ray, there's my ride."

"Do you have everything you need, Liam?"

"Yes, sir. How about a hug, Ray?"

"You betcha."

"Ray, I want you to spend the weekend again in a few weeks, okay?"

"Is it okay, Dad?"

"As long as Liam has all his work done, then yes."

"Okay, Liam, in a few weeks."

"You betcha, Ray," he said as he walked out his door.

Middlesex Jail

Tommy Demps made arrangements with Liam to go see Big Mike in jail. Mike was glad to see them. "Is that ADA Demps over there?" asked Big Mike.

"Hey, Mike," Tommy said.

"And, Liam, you look more and more like your father each day! Give me a hug!" Big Mike and Liam hugged. "So, Liam, I heard that you have some news."

"Yes, Mr. Maguire, I'll be going to Harvard in the fall."

"Great! Your parents would be so proud, Liam. I'm proud of you!"

"Thanks, Mr. Maguire. So how are you? My father wanted to make sure that you had enough money in your canteen."

"Yes, Tommy took care of all that. Thanks."

"Is there anything else you need?"

"No, all good here. How's Mikey?"

Liam tensed up. His mouth drew tight. "Well, I'm not sure. He's fallen off the radar a bit, sir."

"Tommy?"

"Yeah, Mike, I heard he left the car wash and is boosting cars with Colin O'Neil's crew."

Big Mike was obviously upset. "Liam, you know anything about this?"

"No, sir!"

"Tommy, this is how it starts, and then he'll go on jobs, and then he'll fuckin' end up in here. What does his girlfriend, Sue, know?"

"Not sure, Mike."

"Nothing, I would imagine, Mr. Maguire. What I mean is, she would tell me if she knew anything like that. I told Mikey if he ever needed money that all he has to do is ask. You guys are family to me."

Big mike was shaking his head. "Thanks, son, but his dumb pride is going to get him in the can. Is he staying away from those Winter Hill shitheads? Liam, if you are in touch with Mikey, don't tell him that we're talking about him, okay? I'll take care of that Colin O'Neil."

"Yes, sir."

"Liam, I mean it! Not a word! This is going to be tough love, but we can't have him end up in this place."

"Yes, sir."

"How are you doing, Liam? Do you need anything?"

"No, sir, I am well provided for by the judge."

"Great, Liam. Can you please give me and Tommy here a minute?"

"Yes, of course, great seeing you, sir."

"You too, and I'll see you outside of these walls in about eighteen months."

Tommy and Mike talked privately for another ten minutes.

"Mike, you know that sooner or later those two worlds overlap. What do you want me to do? Have him picked up?"

"Yeah, Tommy, pick him up, would you? Put him in the can for a night or two, and see if he gets the message."

"Consider it done, Mike."

"Hey, Tommy?"

"Yeah, Mike?"

"You know I'm grateful for everything you've done here. Right?"

"You can take me to dinner in eighteen months. Okay?" said Tommy.

"You bet! I'll take you to the finest drive-through in the state."

Grinning, Tommy said, "That sounds like a plan, Mike. Remember, get in touch with me if you need anything, okay?"

At that, they left the prison and started heading back to Exeter.

"Listen, Liam, you can't afford to get mixed up in Mikey's shit right now. You got that? Let Mikey run his path. I'm on it, okay?" said Tommy.

"But hey, Tommy, he's my best friend."

"You heard Big Mike!"

"I did."

"He has to *want* to change, or he's going to end up owing the wrong people, in jail, or dead."

"Well, between all of us, none of that should happen."

"Agreed, but some things are out of our control. You get me?"

"Got it, Tommy."

"Just focus on staying in school, graduating, and maybe helping him out with a job or something down the road."

"That's always been our plan. Whoever made it big would help the other one out."

"That's a good code. Your father and Big Mike were like that."

Spring Semester

BACK ON CAMPUS HE HURRIED back to his dorm room.

"So, boys, what's the verdict? Where are you guys going next year? I'm sure that you got your letters by now."

"Brett?"

Brett held a hand up. "Wait, Liam, first, you got a message from June; she said that she'll be back tomorrow with some news."

"Thanks, Brett."

"Well, to answer your question, Liam, it's Stanford. My dad likes the tuition-exempt status that he gets as Provost. It was either that or pay thirty to forty grand a year at Yale."

"Congrats, brother, that's great!"

"Tom, you?"

"Columbia, early decision! And I can still do theater!"

"Fantastic, Tom! I'll only be a few hours away by train when you catch on to another production. Hey, in advance, I just want you to know that I'm not paying for tickets to any of your shows," Liam said with a smile.

"Liam, how about you? Will you be joining me at Stanford?"

"Yeah, Liam, I told my dad that you were leaning toward Notre Dame; what's up?"

"No, I decided on Cambridge late."

His jaw dropped. "No way, Harvard? When did that come into play? I didn't even know you applied?"

"It was a last-minute decision. I filled out my application in the waiting room of the Athletic Department, and I submitted my application on the spot."

"What?"

"Yeah, I literally decided to apply on the spot."

"Well, congrats, Liam, you earned it. But why?" asked Brett.

Liam lapsed solemn. "The judge recently suffered what's called a transient ischemic attack, which is like a mini-stroke. So, I wanted to be closer to home just in case anything happened again. I also wanted to be closer to Ray, Mikey, and June. Not to mention, some of those guys on the Stanford football team were a joke. It's a jock school—the Duke of the West Coast in my opinion. No offense, Brett. For serious students, like you, it's great. And now Tom and I have a place to visit out west during our spring breaks."

"Hey, guys, I have to run and meet Headmaster Johnson and his wife with my folks before dinner. Are you guys free tonight? My mother and father would like to take us all out to the Exeter Inn for dinner. If you're interested, meet us at the inn at six o'clock sharp. You know my parents, so don't be late."

"I'm in," said Tom.

"Free food, I'm in too," he said.

Later that evening Brett and Liam walked over to the Exeter Inn for dinner with the Welch family.

"So, boys, Brett here tells me that you've decided on schools for next year."

"Yes, sir."

"I'll be going to Columbia, and Liam here decided on Harvard just last week."

"Yes, that's correct, sir. And thank you both for having us to dinner this evening," Liam said.

"Liam, I'm afraid that Coach Williams will be disappointed in your decision."

"Yes, sir, he told me as much. Ultimately, it was a health matter at home as much as anything else that made my decision a little easier. You see, the judge suffered a mini-stroke a few months ago, and I felt that I needed to be closer to home for both him and Ray just in case something happened again."

"Well, a full-ride scholarship is tough to pass up."

"It is, sir, but an old family friend has agreed to pay my way just as long as I work in one of his offices for a couple of summers."

"Well, that's quite a generous offer. Where will you be working?"

Liam added, "I'll have my choice of offices in Dallas, New York, San Francisco, Boston, Moscow, London, Madrid, or Beijing."

"Those are some fine options. What company will this be with?"

"Well, the family owns a few businesses, so I may do something with international economics, shipping, technology, or art. I just haven't decided. The Daniels family doesn't need a decision until later this year."

"Daniels family? As in H. D. Daniels?"

Liam looked up. "Yes, do you know them?"

"Of course, everyone should know them. And so how is it that *you* know them?"

"Dad, come on. What's with the third degree? We're trying to have dinner here."

"Yes, Henry, let's let the boy breathe," said Brett's mother, Helen.

"No, that's fine. My father was in his son's platoon in Vietnam."

"I'm sure there were plenty of men in his platoon. Your father must have made quite an impression."

"He did and with HD's father as well. Mr. Daniels told me what my father did. However, it is still classified, so I am not at liberty to discuss it."

"Thank goodness! Can we order now?" said Brett.

"Relax, Brett, it's a preordered meal. We're having surf and turf. You boys okay with that?"

"Yes, sir," Tom and Liam said in unison.

He had some interesting news. "Fine, I'll change the subject. You know, boys, I had a very interesting conversation with Headmaster Johnson this evening. It seems that going into this last semester, Brett and Liam here are neck and neck with their GPAs for the honor of valedictorian."

"Seriously? That's a big thing here?" he asked.

"Yes, Liam, it is. In fact Brett's great-grandfather, my father, and I were all valedictorians here."

"Dude, no pressure on you, eh?" said Tom.

"You have no idea."

"So what do you think about that, Liam?"

"Sorry, what do I think about what?"

"The fairness of a transfer student being allowed to compete against a four-year student to earn the distinction of valedictorian."

"Oh, my apologies, I missed the first part of that question. Well, if your question is, Do I think that it's fair for me to be considered for the honor of valedictorian as a transfer student? I think your question would be better served if it were posed to the academic advisory committee."

"Yes, I understand that, but what is *your* feeling on the matter?"

"My feeling is that far too much emphasis is given to something so superficial."

"Superficial? How is being recognized with the highest GPA in the classroom superficial?"

"I would rather be recognized for my citizenship, academic discipline, and class leadership."

Brett's mother chimed in. "Thank you, Liam, my sentiments exactly! Henry, now please let the boys eat."

"Yes, of course."

After dinner, Brett and Liam walked back to Kirkland House.

Brett said, shrugging, "Liam, I'm sorry for my dad."

"No big deal, Brett. Hey, why didn't you tell me about the valedictorian thing?"

"That's my cross to bear, not yours."

"Brett, are you sure that your dad wasn't talking about me being in contention for valedictorian?" said Tom.

"Yeah right," Liam said as he and Brett both laughed.

Later the next day, Cam was called out of his history class for an emergency call; his mother needed to speak to him immediately.

"Mom, what's wrong? I just got pulled out of class. Did something happen? Is Joey (Cam's little brother) okay? Dad? What?"

He heard sniffling and crying in the background. "Ma, I hear you crying; what's going on? Do I need to come home? Is Dad okay? Are you okay?"

"No, no, it's nothing like that."

Still, Cam heard more tears. "Then what is it, Mom? You're scaring me!"

"You got in!"

"What? What did you say?"

"You got into Harvard! You're going to Harvard, and all we have to pay is three thousand dollars a year. You're going to Harvard!"

"Okay, is that it, Ma?"

"Yes, that's it. I'm so happy for you."

"I know, Ma. It was a lot of hard work and sacrifice on everyone's part. I have to get back to class now, okay. I love you."

"I love you too, Cameron. Stay out of trouble up there."

"Yeah, I know, Ma. I love you too. I'll call you later tonight after class."

At breakfast the following morning, Liam saw June sitting at a table by herself. He quickly jumped out of the breakfast line and ran to her table.

"June! Where have you been? I've been calling your dorm, going to your classes, and leaving messages everywhere. I've been carrying this thing around with me everywhere just looking for you. Do you like it? I've missed you so much, and we have to catch up about your trip to Japan."

"Wait—we have to talk, Liam."

"Tell me about it. I have some *big* news to tell you! First, do you like the sweater?"

"It's beautiful. Thank you," June said, her voice unusually sullen.

"What's wrong, June? Did something happen while I was away? Are you oaky?" Liam asked.

"Yes, but I need to talk to you alone."

"Sure, let's go to the library, where it's quiet."

They walked silently toward the library and found a quiet corner of the reading room to talk.

"I have to tell you, June, you're freaking me out here. What's up?" Liam asked as they settled down on the second floor of the library.

"I have to tell you something, but I don't want you to get angry."

"I can't promise that. What is it? Just say it, June."

"Remember when we said to each other that we promised to tell each other the truth?"

"Yeah, well?"

"Well, when I was in Japan a few weeks ago doing that photo shoot and a commercial, I met up with my old boyfriend, Jamie Crown."

"The kid from that boy band from Chicago, Chi-Five?"

"Yes, we worked together when we were younger and dated before my parents' accident."

"So what happened?"

"Well, I kept calling you. You weren't around. I was feeling lonely, and we were reminiscing about my parents since it was the anniversary of their accident. I was feeling vulnerable, and we...we, well...we fooled around."

Liam's face dropped. "You did what? I trusted you with everything!"

"Liam, I felt horrible the next morning, and I didn't want to talk about this over the phone. I needed to talk to you in person and explain myself."

His eyes pleading, he said, "You're kidding. Right?"

"No, I'm sorry; I am not. It happened, and I'm not proud of myself."

"Did you sleep with him?"

"No!" she said emphatically.

"Then what? You just kissed him?"

She squirmed and hesitated. "I told you, we fooled around a bit, but I don't want to get into it."

"That's convenient for you! Is that it?"

"Yes, but I want to talk to you. We promised to be honest with each other."

He now got adamant. "Yes, we did. I've decided to go to Harvard to be closer to you, the judge, and Ray. Now I'm second-guessing that decision! Enjoy your sweater."

Liam got up and walked away as June called after him, "Liam, what about us? I want to talk to you."

Without looking back he said, "I'll let you know when we can talk about this. It's too much to process right now. I'll tell you one thing, though. I feel betrayed!"

"Liam, wait."

"No, I have to go."

"But, Liam…"

Shrugging, he added, "I'll call you when I'm ready to talk."

The following morning there was a loud knock on Liam's door.

"Liam, you up?" John loudly asked through the dorm room door.

"John? Is that you?"

"Yeah, what's up? Everything okay? It's early," Liam said.

"Just open the door."

John came in. He was holding a magazine. "Bro, did you see this? My girl gave me this article from *Star* magazine with June in it. And your girl is all over another dude—that boy band zero from Chi-Five!

This may just mean that she's gay. I knew it; you flipped her. Just so that we're clear, under normal circumstances I would copy the article and paste this all over the gym, along with some *great* captions. However, I know how much June means to you, so I decided against it."

"Let me see that." Liam ripped the magazine out of his hand. "Yeah, she told me about it last night."

"Does that mean I can tell you some of the captions that I thought up?" John asked with a smirk.

"No! What is wrong with you?"

"You're kidding. Right? This is like a fat kid with a box of cookies and you tell him he's on a diet and not to eat."

"No! I have to go for a run."

"Wait—how did you leave it with June? That's a serious question. I only ask because we're all going to want to know how to treat her."

"What do you mean?"

"Look, we're all friends with her, but we were friends with you first. If she's betrayed you and it's over, then fuck her! She's dead to us. If you're working through this, we'll acknowledge her but not engage her. And if things are cool with her, then we're all good. I'll tell you what, bro; for now, fuck her! I mean she's cool and everything, even easy on the eyes, but this is some real bullshit."

"Thanks, John, I think."

"No worries, Liam. The other guys feel the same way."

"How does everyone know already?"

"Are you kidding? I told them. This is huge! Cam was especially upset and wanted to know if you and June were finished?"

"That's nice of him."

"Well, he just wanted to know how long he would have to wait before he could ask her out," John said with a laugh.

"Screw you, John!"

"What?"

"Let's go; I have to go for a run and clear my head before class."

As John and Liam left Kirkland House, June was on the steps, waiting for him.

"Liam, can we talk about this?"

"June, I have to go for a run. We'll talk later."

"You promise?"

"Yeah, later," he said, putting his Sony Walkman headset on and starting to run.

"Okay, later," said June.

"John, do you have a minute?"

"For what?"

"How bad is it?"

"Bad!"

"How bad?"

"Look, Liam's not like the rest of us. He only lets a few people in his life because he's either been burned, beaten, or betrayed in the past. You know that. You were something special to him. I mean, he talked about a life with you. And what do you do? This shit to him!" John said, pointing to the *Star* magazine article.

At that June started to cry. "He doesn't deserve that! I'm sorry, but I have to go."

John took two steps and then turned around. "And another thing. I don't mean to be unkind, but you fucked up! This type of person comes along once in a lifetime, and you blew it! He never wanted *anything* from you, or anyone else, just friendship and loyalty. You betrayed him on both fronts." John walked away as June continued to cry.

After class Liam headed over to the gym to lift and work through his anger before baseball practice, when Coach Long appeared.

"Liam."

"Yeah, Coach?"

"Everything okay? I mean you're hitting those weights pretty hard."

"Yeah, just getting ready for baseball practice in a few, I guess."

"Well, it looks like something else. You second-guessing Harvard?"

"No, nothing like that at all."

"Everything okay at home?"

"Yes and no."

"Come on, let's go to my office. If you get any bigger, the Harvard coaches will put you at defensive end."

They went into his office. "Here, sit down. So what's going on with you, Liam? Everything okay at home?"

"It's June, Coach."

"Your girlfriend, June?"

"Yeah, well, I'm not so sure."

"Why?"

"Take a look at this," Liam said and handed the coach the *Star Magazine* article.

"I see. You know, Liam, maybe it's a good time to take a break and just focus on yourself for a while."

"I thought about that, Coach, but it just hurts every time I see her. I get this feeling in the pit of my stomach."

"I know, son. It may seem bad now, but give it time. The one thing you should do is forgive her. I'm sure she realizes what she did was a mistake, but you can forgive her and move on if you want."

"Forgive?"

"Yes. What would Father Callahan say?"

He pondered that for a while and then said, "You're right. And then move on. Thanks, Coach. I appreciate the talk. Sorry, but I have to run. I have to get to baseball practice in a few minutes."

"Any time, Liam. Hey, I heard that there will be some Major League scouts at the game against Choate tomorrow."

"Yeah, I heard the same thing."

"Good luck on the mound, Liam."

"Thanks, Coach."

The following day against Choate, John, Dave, and Joe were all at the game, and June was there as well.

"Hey, guys, did the game start yet?"

"What's up, Cam? Yeah, just started."

Cam nodded back to the guys.

"Hey, Cam," said June.

"Hey," he said as he nodded to June and sat between the guys and June.

"How's our guy doing?" asked Cam.

"He's got a no-hitter through five, and they clocked him at ninety-three last inning," said Dave.

"You're shittin' me!"

"Nope, they're right," said a voice from the top of the stands.

"And you are?" asked Joe.

"I'm Frank Nicossia, a scout for the New York Yankees. So where did Liam sign to play football next year?"

"Harvard, why?"

"Because we may be interested in signing him."

"No way!"

"Yeah way."

"No, I mean he would *never* sign with any New York team!"

"Why is that?"

"Because he's from Boston, and he hates the Yankees."

"Well, this is a little different, young man. I'm talking about a professional baseball contract and a big signing bonus."

He shrugged. "Okay, you'll see, but don't say I didn't warn you."

After the game as Liam was walking back to the gymnasium to take a shower, the man approached.

"Hi, Liam, my name is Frank Nicossia; I'm with the New York Yankees."

"Hey, nice to meet you. What is it exactly that you do?"

"I'm a scout."

"Great job! Bad team." Liam said with a smirk.

"Ha! Pretty funny, kid."

"This is my baseball coach, Mark Decker."

"Coach, pleasure to meet you," he said as we shook hands.

"The same. I got your message that you would be coming to see Liam pitch. So what'd you think? As advertised or what?"

"Well, six four coming off the mound with that ninety-two-plus fastball is quite impressive."

"So how can I help you, Mr. Nicossia?"

"What would you say if we were interested in drafting you?"

"Respectfully, I'd say, save your pick. I'd never play for anything that has to do with New York."

"You're kidding, right?"

"No, not at all, I was there in 1978: Bucky friggin' Dent!" he intoned. "Listen, I couldn't walk the streets of Southie if I were drafted by the Yankees, so don't bother."

"Coach? He can't possibly be serious."

"I tried to tell you this over the phone, Frank. Save your pick; Liam won't change his mind."

"Well, what if we draft you anyway, young man?"

"I would rather play professional softball in Alaska than play for the Yankees, Mr. Nicossia."

"Well, I'll tell the front office, but this is a new one to me. Best of luck to you, young man."

"And to you as well, sir," he said as Mr. Nicossia walked away. "Hey, Mr. Nicossia."

"Yeah?"

"There is a pitcher at Deerfield Academy by the name of Peter Kerr who you might be interested in as well."

"Kerr, huh?"

"Yeah, Peter Kerr, he throws ninety-plus and is a lefty."

"Thanks for the heads-up."

"If you sign him, can we split the commission?"

"I'm not on commission, but I can get you tickets to any game that you are in New York for, no problem."

"Then it's a deal. Good luck!"

The next day, in the school's newspaper, the *Exonian*, the headline read, "O'HARA THROWS NO-HITTER AGAINST CHOATE AND STRIKES OUT NEW YORK YANKEES TOO."

As soon as the article hit the school, it eventually found its way to the local newspaper the *Seabrook Times* and then to the state paper, the *Portsmouth Herald* and finally to the *Boston Globe*, where the article went national.

SOUTHIE PREP BASEBALL STAR REJECTS NEW YORK YANKEES OFFER BECAUSE THEY ARE THE YANKEES
Eighteen-year-old Liam O'Hara, after throwing a no-hitter against the Choate School, was approached by a scout from the New York Yankees about their interest in signing him to a professional minor-league baseball contract. O'Hara's response was that he would rather play professional softball in Alaska than have anything to do with the Yankees! Once again, Southie's finest rising to the top! Mr. O'Hara will be attending Harvard in the fall and is rated the number-four prep quarterback in the country.

After that article hit the newswire, Liam received several boxes of hate mail from New York Yankee fans, exclaiming that he wasn't good enough for the Yankees anyway. Then there were several boxes full of pro–Red Sox mail from all over New England as well as a hand-written internship offer from the owner of the Red Sox, Jean Yawkey, herself. Finally, he received a tryout offer from the Juneau Polar Bears in the Alaskan Miner's Softball League.

The following morning June was once again at the steps of Kirkland House, waiting to speak with him. Finally, he decided that enough was enough, and they would talk through this issue.

"One thing is for sure: you're persistent."

"I am. And you are worth it. So do you think that we can we talk today?"

"Yes, let's go to the library before assembly."

"Really?"

"Yes, let's finally talk."

As they settled in at the second-floor table of the library, he pulled out a chair for June. "This looks serious," said June.

"It is for me."

"I was just trying to bring a little levity to this discussion, Liam; that's all."

"Well, you're failing."

"Okay, then you talk. This is your meeting."

Gazing into her eyes, he said, "I want you to know two things. First, I love you and will always love you because you represented a part of my life that saved me in many ways." June started to tear up. "Second, I forgive you. I appreciate your honesty, but I cannot forget that act of betrayal. I trusted you with everything—my feelings, my emotions, and my heart—and you trampled on that trust. You, of all people— you made me feel like a fool!"

"No, no! Liam, I'm sorry! I'm so sorry! It was a mistake. Please Liam, please...I love you." June began to sob hard.

"I love you too, but I need a break to think things through. I mean, I changed my life for you. I decided to go to school on the east coast to be closer to you as opposed to going to Stanford. I was even talking about starting a family with you. I know that sounds stupid, but that's what you meant to me."

"Meant?"

"I don't know. I still love you very much, but things have changed."

"Liam, I apologized. I'm sorry that happened. It was really noth-ing, but it happened. I wish I could go back in time and change things, but I can't. I'm *not* trying to make excuses, but I was vulnerable, and it was the anniversary of my parent's accident. I can only apologize and say I'm sorry. I promise you that it will never happen again."

"I know, and I believe you. It's something I have to work through."

"What does that mean for us?"

"It means I still need time to think things through. I'm not going to date people or anything like that. I mean, we're graduating in a couple of months, so I need to figure things out."

"Okay, so there is hope. We're not done."

"Yes, there is hope. I think we need to start over and work on some things. Does that make sense?"

"Yes, I understand. I'll do anything. Liam, I can't lose you! Can I have a hug? I've wanted to hold you since I got back."

"Of course," he whispered in her ear that he would always love her, and she smiled.

A couple of weeks later, he met up with John, who had a question. "Dude, you and June still on the outs?"

"No, we're working through things. Why?"

"Just askin', that's all. She's sunbathing with some other girls out by Bankroft, and a crowd is gathering along the south side of Wentworth Hall, staring at them."

"What do you mean?"

"Well, let me see—your amazingly hot friend or girlfriend or whatever is sunbathing with her dorm mates, and a bunch of prepubescent boys are staring at them outside of their dorm windows. How's that for simplicity?"

"Wow, I can see what you're talking about from here. She is hot, isn't she?"

"Smokin'! And I have to tell you, if you don't get back with her full time, the guys and I think that you *must* be gay."

"Thanks for the vote of confidence."

"What? And you can't see that logic?"

He grinned. As he peered over by the Bankroft dorm lawn once again, he said, "No, I guess you and the guys are right."

"Did you hear what else she's doing?"

"No, what?"

"She's performing on campus next week in Assembly Hall. And get this: she's going to premiere her new song and her latest video."

"June mentioned that she may have to go to New York to do that, but nothing about doing it here."

"Well, she is, and June demanded that a hundred percent of all the proceeds be donated to financial aid here at Exeter. Headmaster Johnson is ecstatic!"

"Wow, that's generous."

"I'll say! That's a few hundred grand, easy."

One week later, the night of the event, June called up Mikey, Ray, and Sue to attend as well. They would all sit with Liam in the reserved section, which was earmarked for distinguished alumni, faculty/staff, the headmaster, MTV personnel, Angela Rubin and Robert Martin, and a few select friends.

"Good evening, Angela, Robert," he said, nodding to them.

"Liam, was this your idea?" asked Angela.

"No, why?"

"Because it's brilliant! It shows June's vulnerability, her dedication to education, and her generosity by giving back to others."

"How's her new video look?" he asked.

"You mean you haven't seen it?" asked Robert.

"No, why?"

"Oh nothing, you'll be surprised."

"Bro, great seats, huh? This is better than the seats that we get at the Boston Garden," said Mikey.

"I'm just glad that you guys could make it. I haven't seen you both in forever."

"Yeah, this is fantastic, Liam! And June even put us up at the Exeter Inn tonight," said Sue.

"Yeah, I heard. That is very nice of her."

"And, Ray, are you happy to be here this weekend?"

"You betcha, Liam!"

"Okay, quiet, it's about to start."

As the curtain pulled back, June started playing her hit song "Forever You" accompanied by the Phillips Exeter Academy Chorus and Orchestra. June was playing the piano and singing. Her voice proved to be magical, and the audience in Assembly Hall was mesmerized. Outside the building, on the Assembly Hall lawn, there were two large screens set up so that the overflow of students and people from the town could share in the event. The entire student body was cheering for every song. Finally, June went backstage to put on Liam's "Exeter Football 1" sweatshirt and dedicated her final song to him.

"Before playing this debut video, I would like to take this opportunity to thank MTV, the faculty and staff at Exeter, Headmaster Johnson, the *undefeated* girls field-hockey team—sorry, a shameless plug, but you girls rock! But most importantly, I want to dedicate this next song and world premiere video to the one true love of my life, Liam O'Hara."

June's song and video, "Not over You," premiered number one on the pop charts after her performance.

The video was a montage of June singing and pictures of their time together in and around the Boston area last summer. There were pictures and home videos from our time at the beach, watching the Red Sox, walking around Southie, and from her time at Exeter. There were pictures of Mikey and Liam playing basketball, June kissing Ray on the cheek, Sue and June at the beach, the Exeter girls field-hockey team, pictures from the Andover-Exeter football game, and of course pictures of June and Liam together throughout the year. The final fade-out picture was of Liam holding a blanket around June, and Mikey holding a blanket around Sue, with a bonfire in the foreground at Crane's Beach in Ipswich last summer. It was all very romantic.

As soon as the song concluded, the entire assembly stood up and cheered! There was a loud roar from outside on the lawn as well. Even the MTV hosts stood up in amazement of the video. June ran off stage and into his arms as they kissed and he twirled her around. All the while the cameras were filming. By the end of the evening, the switchboard in New York City blew up with responses to the concert and the video. Everyone met up at the Grill later that evening.

"Great job, June!" everyone said when they walked by their table.

"June, I didn't realize you had those chops," said John.

"Thanks, Mikey and Sue, for coming."

"There is just one more thing, June."

"Yeah, Mikey?"

"I don't recall giving you permission to use my pictures or images for your video. My attorney will be in touch with you early next week," Mikey said, laughing.

"Hey, Mikey's right! What sort of compensation are we entitled to?" Liam asked.

June whispered in his ear. "I have a room at the Exeter Inn; you can have me there all night."

"Check please! I'm good! Forget it! Suit dropped!" he said with a smile. "Ray, why does the whole world get to see you kissing my girlfriend?"

"Because June said that I'm a better kisser!" Ray smiled, and the entire table laughed.

VALEDICTORIAN

WITH ONE WEEK BEFORE GRADUATION and one final exam in physics left, both Brett and Liam remained neck and neck on their GPAs for valedictorian. Both were summoned to Headmaster Johnson's house to meet him and Professor Ellis from the Physics Department. The professor greeted them, "Gentlemen, how are you both?"

"Fine, sir," Liam said.

"I'm well, sir."

"Boys, do you know the reason why we brought you here today?" asked Headmaster Johnson.

"No, sir."

"Me neither, sir," said Brett.

"Well, I want to first congratulate both of you on your exemplary academic work throughout your tenure here at the academy."

"Thank you, sir."

"Yes, thank you."

"The reason why I have you both here today is because as it stands now, you two are in a statistical dead heat for the honor of valedictorian. As you know, the individual who earns this distinction will be afforded the opportunity to address his peers during the commencement address on graduation day. Professor Ellis is here because you both have one test left in his physics class, which he says that you both are doing excellent work. Both Mr. Ellis and I have discussed this, and we are comfortable offering you both the opportunity to be covaledictorians if you want. Or you can roll the dice on the last exam, and we may very well find our way back here in a week. What are your thoughts, boys?"

"I'm good with whatever you want to do, Brett. I know how important it is to you."

"Me too. I don't have a preference, sir."

"Okay then, since neither of you wishes to exercise the covaledictorian option, it will be up to the last exam. Boys, I wish you the best of luck," said Headmaster Johnson.

"Thank you, sir."

"Yes, thank you both."

"Do you boys need me to call your dorms if you get back late?"

"No, sir, we're right around the corner. We live in Kirkland House."

"You mean you both live in the same house too?"

"Yes, sir."

"Well, that must make for interesting discussions around the common-room fireplace, eh, boys?"

Both Brett and Liam smiled.

"Okay, boys, that's all. Let's talk next week."

"Headmaster Johnson, Professor Ellis, before we leave, may I have a word with you both in private?"

"Yes, of course, Liam."

"Brett, I'll just be a minute. We can walk back together when I am done."

Brett stepped out.

"Yes, Liam, how can we help you?"

"Dr. Johnson, Professor Ellis, I believe that Brett deserves the distinction of valedictorian more than me."

"That's very noble of you, young man, but that's not how things work here I'm afraid, Liam."

"With all due respect, sir, Brett has been here all four years, and I have just been here a little over two. Exeter has been very good to me, and I appreciate all the scholastic opportunities and athletic honors that it has afforded me. However, this particular honor means far more to Brett and his family than it does to me. With respect to Professor Ellis, I could tank the last exam, but that wouldn't be fair to him since he is an excellent teacher."

"Liam, does this have *anything* to do with Brett's father?"

"No, sir, but Brett does have a legacy to live up to, and I do not."

"Thank you, son. Let's just wait until after the exam next week, and then we can make a decision."

"Yes, sir, but I will not change my mind. Thank you both for your time," Liam said and exited Dr. Johnson's study.

"So what do you think of that, Eli?" said Headmaster Johnson.

"I think that they'll both ace the exam, without question. These two have been once-in-a-lifetime students whom I could see both having very successful careers in physics or related fields if they so choose."

"They're that good?"

"Yes, that good. And that was a very selfless act by Mr. O'Hara."

"Agreed. At very least he will be honored at graduation for his service toward the school."

Walking back to Kirkland House, they started discussing their visit.

"Liam, what was that all about?" asked Brett.

"Nothing, why? I just asked for more graduation tickets for my extended family."

"Shut up! What did you *really* say to Dr. Johnson and Professor Ellis?"

"I asked them if they would mind listening to the draft of my valedictorian speech," he said with a laugh.

"Shut up. You're a jerk! Seriously, what did you say?"

"Okay, seriously, I told them that you deserved the honor more than me. The exam this week will mean nothing because I expect us both to do well. You've been here all four years, and I've been here just a little over two."

"Liam, that's not you talking; that's my dad talking."

"Yes and no. I mean, I think he has a point. The biggest issue is that I don't really care, and it would mean so much more for your family, seriously."

"Liam, I'm fine with covaledictorians."

"Yeah, I know, but it's no big deal to me. I've done just fine here, and I'm happy that you and Brett are my friends. Not to mention, now your dad can stop calling the house to see if you won it yet."

"Shut up!" Brett said as he hit Liam on the shoulder. "No matter how the exam goes tomorrow, Liam, I know you well enough that I can't change your mind, so all I'm going to say is thanks."

"No problem, Brett."

One week later, graduation day arrived, and Headmaster Johnson was handing out individual awards to graduating seniors.

"And this next award is bestowed each year by the Aurelian Honor Society of Yale University to the member of the senior class who best combines the highest standards of character and leadership with excellence in his studies and in athletics. I am proud to bestow this year's Yale Cup on Liam O'Hara."

Liam received a standing ovation and cheers from his teammates and friends as he walked across the stage, shook hands with Headmaster Johnson, and raised the Yale Cup over his head.

"Our last and final award is the Faculty Prize for Academic Excellence. This award is given each year to the student who has attended the academy for two or more years and is recognized on the basis of holding first rank in their class. This year's valedictorian and commencement speaker is Brett Irving Welch III."

Brett received a standing ovation from the class, and Mr. Welch cheered and clapped the loudest. Liam didn't think he ever saw Mr. Welch so animated about anything Brett had accomplished since he had known him. Seeing the expression on Mr. Welch's face just reinforced Liam's decision to skip two questions on the last physics exam. Brett shook Headmaster Johnson's hand and was now headed to the podium to deliver the commencement address.

"Headmaster Johnson, distinguished Exeter faculty and staff, parents, and, of course, the class of 1987, I would first like to thank you all for helping guide us to this great day. To the parents out there who have sacrificed so much to make this special day happen, we thank you. To the faculty and staff who have constantly challenged us both inside and outside of the classroom, we thank you. To my classmates, who continuously push the limits of academic excellence, I thank you.

"As we cross this stage today, armed with our Exeter diplomas, we close an important chapter of our lives. Four years ago, we were brought to the academy as shy and timid thirteen- and fourteen-year-olds. Today, we are confident and mature seventeen- and eighteen-year-old adults ready to embark on the next phase of our lives. This time, however, we are armed with the knowledge and conviction of an Exeter education. The lessons that we learned in the classroom will serve us throughout our academic careers; however, the lessons we learned from our peers will carry us through our lifetimes.

"As I look across this stage, I see classmates who are the sons and daughters of families from Fortune 500 companies, heads of state, diplomats, leaders in academia (myself included), 'new money,' 'old money,' and so on. What I have learned from this group of classmates is that Brooks Brothers and J Press are acceptable clothiers, that a 1982 Domaine Romane Conti is a superior vintage to that of a 1980 Chateau Lafite Rothschild, and that traveling from the east side of New York City to the west side of New York City may require a passport.

"Remarkably, I have learned the most in my time here at Exeter from my two roommates: one, an Upper East Side thespian, and the other, an orphan from South Boston. Tom, who is an accomplished actor, taught me a greater appreciation for the arts and theater. He taught me that it is okay to fail and that perfection should be left to God. However, I still contend that my charcoal interpretation of Degas's *Dancers* deserved a better grade than his. Professor Grogan, it's still not too late to adjust those grades!

"My other roommate, Liam O'Hara is from a gritty part of South Boston. When I first met Liam, I thought that he was just another dumb jock admitted to help the football program. Clearly, I couldn't have been more wrong. Although he unmistakably excelled on the athletic field, he proved to be a brilliant peer in the classroom as well. His passion for physics, the classics, and mastering Chinese consistently challenged me to want more out of my time here at Exeter. Liam taught me humility, compassion, acceptance, and that friendship can come in many shapes and sizes. This was no more evident than when our debate team was in a match against Andover a few weeks ago. Liam brought in a cardboard sign to psych Andover out. The sign read, 'Andoverum dolor Vadam, id est bonus, utrum ipsa esset, aliquando pro nobis,' which loosely translates to 'Andover team—it's all right, it's okay, you're going to work for us some day.' I even think the judges were intimidated by Liam's presence. By the way, we beat Andover six to five in points.

"The lessons that we have learned and the friendships that we have forged at this great institution will last a lifetime. For this we are forever grateful. It is important that we bring the core values that Exeter has taught us to the next chapters of our lives and beyond. I know that I will.

"Once again, I thank you all for your sacrifices, your dedication, and for your time this afternoon. I wish you all nothing but professional success, sound health, and most importantly personal happiness in the years to come."

Brett received a standing ovation. As he walked off stage, Liam thanked him for his kind words and pulled Tom aside to take our pictures together.

"Hey, Tom, Brett, how about a picture before we leave for the summer?"

"Excellent idea, Liam," said Brett's mother. "Now, you boys come over here."

Mrs. Welch whispered in Liam's ear, "Thank you for what you did for Brett."

Liam smiled.

"Thanks, guys! You have my numbers. Keep in touch."

"Liam, do you have a moment?" asked Mr. Welch.

"Yeah, sure."

"Well, Liam, congratulations on winning the Yale Cup. That's quite an honor. That was too bad about that last physics exam, though."

"Thank you, sir. And yes, it was too bad, but Brett got what he earned. And it was a great speech."

"He did work very hard, and I am very proud of Brett, but I will always remember your sacrifice, young man."

"Thank you, sir."

"Have a nice summer, Liam. I hope we see you soon."

"Thank you, sir."

Liam ran over to his other friends and called for June. "June, come here. Let's take a picture together, and then let me take a few of you with Angela and Martin."

"Okay, line up right here in front of Assembly Hall. Come on, Angela, it's okay to smile; that's it, Martin! See, beautiful picture! On three say, 'I hate New Hampshire!'" They all smiled.

"June, come over here and take some pics with me and the guys."

Then Father C., Judge Mahoney, Ray, Mikey, and Sue all circled around for a group picture. "Okay, June, last round of pictures, I promise; let's call this one 'Southie.' Thanks, guys."

"Okay, now one with me, the judge, and Ray."

"One with me and Ray."

"One with me and Father Callahan."

"One with me and Mikey and Sue."

"Last one, I promise…"

"One with me and Mikey. Come on, smile, brother!" he said as they took their last picture.

"Hey, Mikey."

"Yeah, bro, what's up?"

"I need to talk to you when we get home."

"Yeah sure, when you get settled, give me a call, and we'll go out."

"Good. Will do. And thanks for coming, Mikey! Seriously, thanks. It means a lot to me."

"I know. That's why I am here, bro."

Summer Before Freshman Year

It was a warm June day, and Father Callahan and Liam decided to grab a bite at Ray's Pizzeria and catch up.

"So it's Harvard, huh?" said Father Callahan.

"Yeah."

"What's the plan there?"

"I dunno? Prelaw? Premed? Public service—maybe the CIA, Foreign Service, NSA? We'll see. If I decide to go to law school, I'll just go into practice with Tommy Demps," Liam said with a smirk.

"Well, you may need to go to law school if you want to keep Mikey on the straight and narrow."

"Yeah, I thought about that. Speaking of which, what's going on with him these days?"

"He's straying from the path I'm afraid."

"How so?"

"Well, he quit his job at the car wash when the hospitals were hiring again, and his mother went back to work."

"So, Father, what's Mikey doin' now?"

"He deals in 'used cars.'"

"With whom?"

"I heard that he's working for Frankie Hayes."

"Who is paying the tax to Connor?"

"Frankie covers that out of his end so that Mikey's name is not in the mix. Even so, Mikey has earned quite a reputation for himself these past few months," said Father Callahan.

"How so?" he asked, his jaw slack.

"He's floating a lot of cash around the neighborhood and driving a new car that's paid for in full."

"What happened to my dad's Chevy Nova?"

"Maggie drives it to and from work. Don't worry about that car; it's still in great, condition," said Father Callahan.

Looking downcast Liam said, "So, Father, he's taking contract jobs now with Frankie?"

"Afraid so, Liam."

"I'll talk to him."

Liam returned to the judge's brownstone later that day.

"Liam."

"Yes, Judge?"

"This came for you the other day from Harvard housing."

"Housing? It must be my dorm room next year and my roommates."

He opened the envelope.

"Hey look, Judge, I'll be living with Cam and a guy named Sam Collins from San Diego and Peter Newton from Providence."

"What housing did you get?"

"Hollis Hall. How is that?"

"Right in the Yard."

"Did you live there?"

"No, I lived right next to it in Gray's Hall; we had bigger rooms," the judge said with a smile.

"I have to call Cam."

"Go ahead, and give Cam my best."

"Will do, Judge."

Later that evening he got in touch with Cam.

"Good evening, may I please speak with Cam?"

"May I ask who is calling, please?"

"This is Liam, Liam O'Hara."

"Oh, hi, Liam, this is Mrs. Pedro."

"How are you, Mrs. Pedro?"

"Wonderful, Liam. We're so proud of Cameron."

"You should be. He worked very hard last year at Exeter, and he'll do great next year at Harvard."

"Oh, we hope so. Here he is. Cameron, it's Liam. Nice speaking with you, Liam."

"You too, Mrs. Pedro."

"Hey, Liam, what's up?"

"First of all, how is it that your mother is so nice and you're such a jackass?"

"You just like her cooking."

"Correct. But nevertheless, she's so nice. Did you get housing yet?"

"No, why? You?"

"Yeah."

"And?"

"We're roommates!"

"You're kidding."

"Nope, we are!"

"That's awesome! Is it just us, or anyone else?"

"We're in a dorm called Hollis House with two other dudes: one guy from Providence and another guy from San Diego."

"Cool, we'll make it work. Great news, my man! So what's up with you?"

"Nothing much. I just got back from a trip abroad with June."

"She asked about me, didn't she? I see the way she looked at me when you're not around, you know."

"You should take medication for those delusions, Cam, seriously."

"Sorry to cut this short, Liam, but I have to run. I have to get ready for work at Stop & Shop. Those groceries won't bag themselves, you know. Let's talk tomorrow."

"Sounds good," Liam said.

DR. PHILLIPS

LIAM'S SURPRISE GRADUATION GIFT FROM the judge was a trip to Europe to visit Ireland, France, and Italy. Since Liam would be working at the Gardner Museum again this summer, the judge thought that it would be a good idea for Liam to be exposed to different types of cultures and museums. Prior to going abroad, Liam mapped out his trip with Dr. Robert Phillips, the curator of the Gardner Museum. Upon Liam's return home, he was armed with a wealth of knowledge from all the classical artists and museums alike. The following day, Liam went back to his summer job at the museum.

In the hall outside his office, Liam found his boss. "Dr. Phillips?"

"Yes, Liam?"

"Do you have a minute?"

"I sure do; come into my office, and tell me all about your trip. Were my colleagues helpful to you?"

Liam's enthusiasm was written on his face. "Helpful? They were amazing! The lines to get in the exhibits at the Louvre and the Uffizi were both a city block long. When we announced who we were at the security check-in like you said, they walked us through the lines like we were royalty. It was amazing! Each curator took us behind the scenes on their restoration projects. For example, in the Louvre, Dr. Catan and his staff were working on several eighteenth-century impressionist pieces, and we were fortunate to get close to some of Claude Monet's works that they were restoring. In addition, the wing where the *Mona Lisa* was on display was being updated with a new security system, so it wasn't open to the public. Nevertheless, we were fortunate to have a private showing. In Florence, Dr. Capone's staff was primarily working on sculptures. They were focusing in on several pieces by Donatello from the early Renaissance period. It was amazing to see what these modern-day artists can do to make such repairs look so seamless. Naturally, we got to see the *David*, except we didn't have to deal with being roped off; we were fortunate enough to view him up close and personal. I can't thank you enough! Please accept this small token of my gratitude."

Dr. Phillips opened his gift, and his jaw dropped. "Liam, this is a sterling silver Mont Blanc pen! I can't accept this. It is far too generous of a gift."

Liam was firm. "Then please accept it as a sign of our gratitude and a partial retirement gift as well."

"Well, under those circumstances, I am humbled and honored. Thank you."

"Wait, there is more; look at the bottom of the envelope."

"What is this? Red Sox–Yankees tickets?"

Smiling he said, "They are! I know how much you and your wife like the Red Sox, so we got you a pair of tickets right next to the Red Sox dugout. The only person obstructing your view will be the umpire. So enjoy."

"Thank you, Liam. Thank you, the judge, and Raymond for your generosity. These are such wonderful and completely unexpected gifts."

"I'll tell the judge and Ray that you like them."

"I'll call the judge as well."

"So what else did Dr. Catan and Dr. Capone say?"

"They both told me that they worked under you when you were curator at the National Museum in Washington prior to taking your post here about ten years ago."

"That is correct."

"So why did you leave the National Museum?"

"Well, the Gardner Museum was going through some changes. Actually, they were getting some very bad press across the country and internationally, so they called me in to calm the art community. You see, Mrs. Gardner and her husband, Jack, were great patrons of the arts. As you know from the museum tours, she and her husband acquired many works of art from the masters throughout the world but mostly in Europe. These pieces ranged from Matisse, to Rembrandts, to Raphaels, and sculptures by Luigi Ontani and Degas, just to name a few. Their collection still remains one of the largest private collections amassed in the world.

"The issue is that a lot of these pieces were bought on what could be construed as the black market at the time of sale. Each piece of art has a *legal* bill of sale and province; however, these types of sales were supposed to be kept within the country of origin. That is why most of these pieces were purchased by third parties. In this case, two nefarious art advisors to Mrs. Gardner by the names of Branson Smithe and Samuel Aarons acted on her behalf. Basically, they would purchase the pieces and then have them shipped to the Gardners in the United States. It would be the equivalent of purchasing renowned antiquities from Egypt, Italy, or Greece today. They are all considered property of their respective country, except if they are in private collections and have the appropriate documentation. So I established our artist-in-residence program here at the museum to encourage, preserve, and support fledgling artists, sculptors, and the overall development of the arts."

"Yeah, those programs are great! You really get to see some up-and-coming artists."

"So as you can see, Liam, it's quite a balancing act."

"Yeah, back to these lawsuits, what about the British and all the Egyptian, Greek, and Roman antiquities that they have on permanent display in the Natural History Museum in London? We saw a lot of artifacts and paintings there a few weeks ago."

"Excellent question, Liam. Most of those particular pieces were pillaged during some type of occupancy. In fact, there is current litigation in international courts to bring those pieces back to their country of origin. Similarly, there has been some discussion about several of the Gardner's pieces. Some families contest that these pieces were stolen and then sold on the black market. Others contend that some pieces were prohibited from leaving their country of origin at the time of purchase and then illegally smuggled into the United States. I came here to try and refute those claims based on my knowledge and understanding of the archived paperwork we have here."

"Wow, that sounds fascinating!"

"It's a lot of work. Fortunately, the Gardner's kept meticulous records."

"And what have you unearthed thus far?" he asked.

"Well, to be completely honest, some of these inquiries do have some merit. It all depends on how we want to contest the ownership in court. On the one hand, some of the initial purchases represented defective titles or provinces, which means they were bought against the law of the state of origin or transported out of the country by dubious means. On the other hand, you must take into consideration what they represent in their current state. The Gardner's trust stipulates that they are to be shown for the greater good of all. Taking this argument one step further, even if we were to concede ownership to an individual or state, who would compensate the museum? And for how much? Arguably, individuals (and even some countries) cannot afford the current value of some of these pieces. They range in the tens or even hundreds of millions of dollars. So even if you concede to some type of no-fault exchange, compensation would have to be made to the museum one way or another."

"So you are curator, investigator, appraiser, and a diplomat all rolled up in one?"

"Sometimes, Liam, I have to wear many hats." Dr. Phillips looked at his watch. "Oh, look at the hour; we're about to open. Let's get to our stations."

"Yes, sir, and thanks again, Dr. Phillips."

"Any time, Liam. Any time."

New Teammates

As they walked into the Yard, Cam and Liam were awestruck. They'd been here several times before; however, the reality of what was ahead of them was just settling in. As Cam and Liam made their way to their dorm rooms on the third floor of Hollis House, they were told to report to the Malkin Athletic Center (a.k.a. "the Mak") by 1:00 p.m. At that time, they would be introduced to their new teammates, their position coach, and meet the entire coaching staff as well. Cam and Liam started to walk over to the Mak at around noon so that they would not be late for their first meeting and they could check out the lay of the land.

"Dude, I still can't believe that I'm here—we're here!"

"Relax, Cam, you deserve to be here. Nobody did you any favors to get here; you earned your spot. You worked hard in school at Lynn Classical and even harder at Exeter. On the other hand, the team did need a five-ten Mexican running back for diversity's sake, and you filled the spot. Don't run away from it—embrace it!" Liam said, laughing.

"Screw you, Liam! And why do you keep calling me Mexican? You know that I'm Puerto Rican! And another thing, I'm five eleven, not five ten," Cam said with a smile as he stood on the tips of his toes.

"Okay, shoot me for being off by a few geographical miles and an inch."

As they walked toward the Anderson Memorial Bridge to their meeting, Liam continued, "Seriously, though, Cam, you can't let this place define you. It's only a part of who you are. You don't want to go through life where people say, 'Hey, there's Cam Pedro; he went to Harvard.' You want them to say, 'Hey, there's Cam, the successful attorney/businessman, who also attended Harvard.' Get it?"

"Yeah, I get it. You're right, thanks!" he said as they kept walking through Harvard Square.

"Hey, Liam, remember that café over there? Nubar, isn't it? I thought that was my last meal in Cambridge for a while. I thought that I was headed off to either U Mass or UNH or something."

"Yeah, I remember. Now you are here, and that was an expensive lunch. You owe me!"

"Shut up!"

Cam and Liam approached the Mak and saw a large group of athletes gathering at the entrance. Most of the guys were wearing their high-school letterman's jackets from around the country. The sign at the entrance said for football players to report to the main gymnasium and sit in the stands.

Once they all filed into the gymnasium and sat in the stands, Coach Carlson took over.

"All right, gentlemen, settle down," he said, waiting until the gymnasium was silent. "Gentlemen, when you hear a coach speaking, I do not want to hear a word from those stands. Are we clear?"

They all answered with various affirmative grunts.

"Gentlemen, your proper response when a coach speaks to you is one of two answers: 'Yes, Coach,' or 'No, Coach.' Are we clear?"

"Yes, Coach," the team yelled from the stands.

"I said, 'Are we clear'?"

"Yes, Coach!" came the response louder from the stands.

"Gentlemen, try and act like you want to be here and act like you want to play football for the *Harvard Crimson*. I asked you a question. Are we clear?"

"Yes, Coach!" screamed all the players from the stands. With the forced enthusiasm of a marine-recruit platoon.

"Now that's more like it! Thank you. Gentlemen, most of you know me, but for those who do not, my name is Coach Carlson. I am the head assistant coach for Harvard football, and I will be running this orientation. Now I would like each of you to introduce yourselves to your new teammates. Please stand up and state your name, the position that you were recruited to play when you came in for your official visit, and where you currently reside. Please start from the first row from my left."

"Peter Thomas, kicker, St. Paul, Minnesota."

"Paul Lang, defensive end, Palo Alto, California."

"Jim Teatom, defensive back, Massapequa, New York."

"Cam Pedro, running back, Lynn, Massachusetts."

"Liam O'Hara, quarterback, Boston, Massachusetts," and so on.

As the last player stated his information, Coach Carlson took the stand again. "Gentlemen, please take a look to your left, and then take a look to your right." He paused. "These are the young men who will be your best friends over the next four years. You will shed blood, sweat, and even tears together on the football field. Take the time to get to know one another now because the friendships that you forge in practice, on the field, in the weight room, and in the class room will last you a lifetime." He then added, "The next part of this presentation will be led by Coach Kyle Coburn."

"Gentlemen, my name is Coach Coburn, and I coach the hardest working, the hardest hitting, meanest SOB defensive backs in the Ivy League! Let me tell you a little bit about myself so that you know that I understand what it takes to succeed. I was an All-American defensive back out of the University of Florida and played three years in the NFL with the Tampa Bay Bucs. I hold a master's degree in education from Harvard, and I am working toward my PhD. Rest assured, gentlemen, I know what it takes to excel in the classroom and on the field. I expect a maximum effort on and off the field from each of you as well."

Coach Coburn then flipped over a chalkboard, and in big chalk was written the number .0001. "Gentlemen, who knows what this number represents?"

Silence filled the room.

"That number represents one percent of one percent. That number is you, gentlemen! You are the best of the best and the brightest of the brightest that this country has to offer. It is an honor and a privilege to be a part of Harvard University and Harvard football! Now what does that mean?" He paused and then continued, "Anyone?" He asked again and then said, "It means don't screw it up! First, we *expect* you to be prepared in the classroom! You have plenty of academic support from the athletic department, the coaches, the school, and, I hope, from thirty of your new best friends. Second, we expect you to be prepared every time that you step on the football field. Practice to be perfect every day; otherwise, you or your teammate will get hurt! Lastly, don't screw this opportunity up by drinking or doing drugs— none of you are twenty-one, so I expect none of you to be drinking. And doing any sort of drugs is stupid! It's that simple! If you *must* drink, do it on your own time at home, not here, where you will embarrass the university, the team, and yourself."

Coach Coburn went on to explain what the coach's expectations of them were going to be.

"Our expectations of you young men are very simple. As freshmen, you are responsible to assist the volunteer managers for practice setup and teardown. We expect you to come to practice early when it is your position's day to assist with equipment and setup. After practice, you will assist with equipment breakdown as well. This will be on a rotating schedule starting with the quarterbacks for the offense and the defensive backs for the defense.

"You will treat the trainers who tape you and tend to your injuries with the same respect afforded to the coaching staff. Are we clear?"

"Yes, Coach!" the team screamed.

"Regarding *time*, we *expect* you to be on time at all times. This means to be on time to all meetings, workout sessions, training room, rehab, study halls, and games, or you will be running gassers as punishment after practice. *On time* to this staff means to be there ten minutes ahead of your scheduled appointment. If you are going to be late, for whatever reason, you must call your position coach, one of the team captains," Coach Coburn said and pointed to his left, to Art Irons, a linebacker, and Darren Thomas, a wide receiver, "or someone on the training staff. Telling your teammate that you will be late does not count. Being late for a bus trip is inexcusable! We will leave you behind, trust me; just ask Peter Hamilton, our All-Ivy kicker for the past two years. Just before the Princeton trip, Pete decided to get off the bus at the last minute to get a can of soda at the local deli. As he was approaching the bus, we closed the door and drove away. When other people count on you, you have a responsibility to yourself and your teammates to be on time. It's that simple." As Coach Coburn concluded his remarks, he said, "Gentlemen, remember these five simple rules, and you will succeed here at Harvard. Rule number one: your first priority is your family and your faith. Rule number two: be prepared in the classroom. Rule number three: respect your teammates, coaching and training staff, and your peers. Rule number four: no drinking or drugs. And rule number five: be on time! If you follow these five simple rules, you will have a successful time here at Harvard. Are we clear, gentlemen?"

"Yes, Coach!" said the team in unison.

"Any questions?"

There was a pause.

"Okay then, let's divide into two lines. Offense to my left, defense to my right. The offense will go take their physicals, while the defense tests out in the weight room and on the track. Let's go! Let's go! Let's go!"

PRESEASON CAMP

AT THE BEGINNING OF CAMP, every freshman is on the lowest rung on the ladder of their position. Currently, Liam resided as the number-six quarterback on the depth chart. Cam was the fifth running back listed on his depth chart. The difference was that everybody was talking about Cam's forty-yard-dash time of 4.39 (versus Liam's 4.68).

As camp progressed, Cam and Liam separated themselves from the competition immediately. Once Liam learned the system and was familiar with all the plays, recognized defensive patterns, and could call audibles at the line of scrimmage, everything came together. Cam was blowing people away with his speed and agility. Typically, freshmen do not play right away. However, Cam was doing so well that it would be tough to keep him off the field as a freshman. If for nothing else, Liam expected Cam to play special teams just so that they could get the ball in his hands.

Toward the end of camp, Liam moved up to the number three slot on the depth chart. This was largely due to the fact that nobody could match the velocity and precision of Liam's throwing arm. In fact, Liam was throwing the ball with such accuracy and speed that he broke two different wide receiver's fingers, trying to catch his passes. The good news was that Harvard traveled three quarterbacks, so Liam would be on the taxi squad for away games.

Cam was the biggest surprise at camp. His ability was not a surprise to Liam. But to the staff and the rest of the team, he made a major statement. Cam was now splitting time as the number two/three tailback, and he was number-one punt returner and kickoff returner.

All position players were called into their respective coach's office for their weekly update. Liam waited for Cam at the Mak until his meeting was over so that they could walk back to our dorm together.

"How'd it go, Liam?" asked Cam.

"Good, I guess. I told Coach Carlson that I wanted to change positions and move to wide receiver. I told him that I would still be a reserve quarterback, but that I just wanted to get on the field anyway that I could since we are thin at the receiver position."

"And?"

"Coach Carlson said that he would keep an open mind. How about you?"

"Nothing really. They want me to have a better command of picking up blitzes and when we call audibles on the line; that's all."

"Yeah, well you better; otherwise, I get killed!"

"Shut up!"

THE GAME

HARVARD STARTED THE YEAR WITH an opening loss to Holy Cross 7–21, followed by a tight win against Brown 14–13. Unfortunately, the Brown win cost Harvard their number-one wide receiver, Wally Grace, with a torn ACL. At that point, Liam started to get into the wide-receiver rotation more often. Cam, on the other hand, was doing a great job on special teams and at running back. He ran back punts against Columbia, Brown, Leigh, and Dartmouth all for scores.

By the end of the year, both Cam and Liam were in steady rotations as they were outperforming most of the upperclassmen in their respective positions. The final game of the year was an 8–1 Harvard team versus a 9–0 Yale team. Whoever won this game would be crowned Ivy League Champions!

Liam thought that he had some idea of the magnitude of the Harvard-Yale game on the basis of his experience playing Andover every year; however, he quickly learned that paled in comparison to what he was experiencing this week. The week leading up to the Yale game was like what you would expect leading up to the Michigan-Ohio state game, or the Stanford-Cal game. Throughout the university there were "Harvard Beat Yale" bed sheets hanging from dorm windows, posters mocking Yale University and their bulldog mascot "Handsome Dan," and articles in the *Harvard Crimson* newspaper mocking Yale students. Game week's practice was really focused and crisp. They did minimal hitting during this week to avoid any unnecessary injuries. Coach Carlson kept reinforcing the fact that we will *not* lose this Ivy Championship on our home field! The local and school newspapers ran feature articles on the seniors participating in their last game against Yale. The anticipated attendance for this week's game was projected to be around sixty-five to seventy thousand people. Liam received calls all week from his roommates at Exeter, Brett and Tom, past coaches, friends, and even a card from Mr. Maguire all wishing him good luck. Even Tommy Demps stopped by practice to say hello. "It's amazing what an ADA badge can do for you," Tommy said with a wink.

While they were stretching out across the field for warm-ups, they could see that the stadium was starting to fill up. By the time they returned from their locker room for final pregame instructions, the stadium was about three-fourth full. Just before kickoff the seniors were announced and acknowledged by the crowd. Fans were screaming from all over the stadium! Liam tried to locate June, the Judge, Ray, and Father Callahan; however, to no avail. They won the coin toss and elected to receive the ball in the second half.

By the end of the first quarter, the score was Yale three and Harvard zero. Cam was having a good game so far, averaging about four and a half to five yards per carry, and he returned one punt thirty-five yards before Ricky Woods, the senior tailback, fumbled it away on the next set of downs. Liam caught four passes for sixty yards and was having a good game so far.

Toward the middle of the second quarter, Yale punted the ball and pinned the opponents down on their own four-yard line. The first play of the series came in as a quick pass to Liam and got as much yardage strait up-field as possible. Liam gained nine yards. Cam ran the ball the following play for three yards and a first down. They did another quick pass to Liam, gaining an additional eight yards. The ball was

Gregory M. Abbruzzese

now on their own twenty-four-yard line with a little over eight minutes left in the half.

Matt came in the huddle and called the play. "Trips right forty-two stretch on two. Trips right forty-two stretch on two." Matt paused. "Listen, Cam, sprint down the field as quick as you can, and Liam will put the ball right in your arms. Make it happen, Liam!"

"Just keep running, Cam," said Liam.

Matt took the snap, quickly turned to his right, and threw the ball to Liam behind the line of scrimmage. Liam tucked the ball under his arm as if he were going to run the ball, and then took one step backward and fired the ball all the way down to the Yale forty-yard line on a rope. He actually hit Cam in stride as he was running up the sideline. The strength and precision of Liam's arm was like that of a professional quarterback! The crowds on both sides of the stadium were in awe of what they just witnessed. Five plays later Harvard scored and made the extra point. Harvard was now leading 7–3 with under four minutes left in the half.

As the third quarter drew to a close, Liam scored on the last play of the quarter. It was a 25-yard slant across the middle of the field. After several scores by Yale, Harvard narrowed Yale's lead to 31–25 with one quarter left. Liam was having the best game of his career thus far with one touchdown, over 160 receiving yards, and 55 passing yards.

There was only thirty seconds left in the fourth quarter with the ball on the Yale eight-yard line and only time left for one last play. Matt pulled everyone together.

"Guys we're only going to get one last shot at this, so let's make it happen! Seniors, this is your last frigging game, so push it! Underclassmen, you don't want to be the team that lost to Yale on your home field, so let's go!" said Matt. "Everyone *hold your blocks*! Trips left forty-four fade right on one. Forty-four fade right on one. And Liam, don't drop the ball!"

"Ready, set, trips forty-four, trips forty-four, set hut."

408

Liam quickly ran off the line of scrimmage as if his route was going to be a slant across the middle. Both the safety and defensive back bit on his fake. Liam then planted his left foot and took off in a forty-five degree angle for the back pylon in the end zone. He had a step on both the defensive back and the safety, who were supposed to be covering him. However, the Yale linebacker quickly realized what was happening, and he reacted by immediately chasing after Liam. Matt threw the ball high in the air, and Liam went up for the ball at its height. It almost seemed like things were going in slow motion. Liam grabbed the ball, pulled it into his chest to protect it as he was heading back down to the ground. All of a sudden, he felt his legs being cut from underneath me. It was the trailing linebacker. He hit Liam with such force that he spun him upside down, and Liam landed on his head. At that point Liam became numb on the entire left side of his body. In the distance Liam could hear the crowd screaming, but he did not know why? Was it the Harvard crowd because he scored, or was it the Yale crowd because he dropped the ball? As Liam rolled over to his right, he could see the head referee raise both his hands for a touchdown, and he smiled. The ref asked Liam for the ball as his teammates were coming over to congratulate him, but Liam told him that he couldn't move his left side. The referee quickly blew his whistle and waived off all celebrations. He pointed to the Harvard head trainer and waved for the ambulance immediately.

"Son, you're going to be all right. You held on to that ball like it was a newborn child. That was one hell of a catch."

"Thanks! But Ref, I can't feel my left side at all."

"Son, don't worry, it's probably just a burner. You'll be just fine."

The entire offense was surrounding Liam as the ambulance made it to the end zone on the Yale side of the field. In the stands the judge's cheers turned into gasps of concern.

"Father, please see that Raymond gets home okay. I'm going to go to the hospital with Liam. Here are my keys."

"Of Course, Judge, of course."

"Ray, June," he said, as the judge gained his composure, "Liam will be fine; this is just precautionary. June, you can meet me at Mass General. I'm sure that's where they will take."

"Yes, Judge."

The judge made his way down through the stands to the sidelines, but security was blocking him from getting on the field. Tommy Demps, who was at the game with his sons as Liam's guest, saw that the security guard was giving the judge a hard time about getting access to Liam. Tommy came over and flashed his ADA badge. The security guard didn't budge until Tommy explained to the guard that he had two choices: either he lets the judge pass through or he can join the player in the ambulance.

"Thanks, Tommy."

"No problem, Judge! Tell Liam that he's in our prayers."

"Will do." The judge ran across the field.

As Liam was being immobilized on the gurney, Matt came over to check on him.

"You okay, Liam?"

"You threw the ball too high!" Liam laughed.

"Sorry about that, but you held on to it!"

"Please step away, young man; we have to get him in the ambulance," said the EMT.

Just before they wheeled Liam off to the ambulance, Liam saw a Yale uniform, number seventy-four, coming toward him through a sea of Harvard players.

It was Dan Morris, his former Exeter teammate. Dan grabbed Liam's hand and quickly said a prayer over him.

"Thanks, Dan."

"I hope you're okay, Liam. I'll see you after the game."

"Hey, Dan," he said as they wheeled him away.

"Yeah, Liam?"

"Do me a favor—do you think you can go offside next series." Dan smiled.

Harvard beat Yale 32–31, and Harvard was crowned Ivy League Champions. Liam earned Second Team All-Ivy as a receiver and the Rookie of the Year honors as well. Cam earned First Team All-Ivy for his Special Teams play and Honorable Mention for Running Back.

MASS GENERAL HOSPITAL

By the time the ambulance got to Mass General, Liam started to get some feeling back in his left toes. His left arm, shoulder, hip, and leg were still numb, though.

"Judge, do you know who won the game?"

"No, no, I don't, Liam. How are you feeling?"

"Like a truck ran over me."

A doctor walked into his room.

"Judge Mahoney?"

"Yes."

"Is this your son?"

"Yes, yes, he is."

"May I talk with you for a moment outside, sir?"

The judge and the doctor left the room and talked in the hallway.

"Doctor, what's going on?"

"Well, we're going to have to run some additional neurological tests and an MRI, but there seems to be some pressure on the base of his spine that is causing this numbness. I suspect that Liam has some sort of microfracture and a dislocation of his cervical spine. It was caused by the way his head landed after being hit. It also appears that it may have come from a previous injury. Has Liam experienced something like this before?"

"Yes, last year, but it was attributed to it just being a burner."

"I see. The good news is that he is aware of his surroundings, and there appears to be no loss of memory."

"But what does that mean if there is a microfracture and a dislocation of his spine?"

"Well, let's get all the facts first before we speculate on what can or cannot happen. Again, we're going to keep him overnight, and then we should have some more answers in the morning."

"Yes, I understand that, but what if that were the case?"

"Then football would not be an option going forward I'm afraid."

"I see. Thank you, Doctor. We'll be right here awaiting the results of the test."

The judge walked back into Liam's room.

"Liam?"

"Yes, Judge?"

"Are you up to receive some visitors?"

"Yes, of course, but can they be short? My head feels like it is exploding."

"Yes, I'll tell them as much."

"Hey, look who it is—Father Callahan, June, and Ray!"

"Ray, why are you crying?"

"Because you're hurt, Liam."

Nurse Ellen came in to change his IV.

"Ray, I am not hurt! They just want to run some tests; that's all. Now stop that. I'll be home tomorrow. We need to start preparing for our summer vacation with June."

"Absolutely! Ray and I will do that tonight, and then we'll show Liam our plans tomorrow when he gets home."

"See, Ray, I'll be home tomorrow. Will you and June go get me some fig squares? You know the ones I like from Newman's Bakery in Southie."

"You betcha, Liam," Ray said, smiling.

"Father, thanks for coming. I see your prayers to keep me safe didn't work," Liam said with a smile.

"You are still alive, aren't you, Liam?"

"Yes."

"Then you owe me." Everyone in the room laughed.

"I guess I do. I'll see you at Mass this weekend, Father."

Father Callahan, June, and Ray left the room. The nurse had a question for Liam.

"Liam?"

"Yes, Nurse Ellen?"

"Was that your girlfriend who just left?"

"Yeah, her name is June. Why?"

"You must be one hell of a football player then." Everyone laughed.

Just then the door opened. He feigned surprise and astonishment. "Oh no, look what the cat dragged in? Mikey Maguire? I thought that you fell off the face of the earth."

"Some of us have jobs, Liam. The car-wash business has an unforgiving schedule, but I made it to your game today. Great game, bro!"

"Yes, great game, Liam," said Sue as she gave him a hug.

"Guys, thanks for coming! I mean it, Mikey! I have winter break in a week or so; how about dinner?"

"Absolutely! I'll have June come over, and we'll all catch up."

"Liam, there are a couple of players here to see you as well."

"Okay, give me a minute, please."

As Mikey and Sue left, some Harvard teammates arrived.

"Hey, look who it is, Matt, Art, Darren, and my man Cam. I heard that we won!"

"We did, thanks to you!" said Cam.

"No, I heard Art over there made some key stops on Yale's last drive of the game. What are you guys doing here anyway?"

"Just checking in on you—that's all," said Matt.

"I'm fine! Go celebrate, for goodness' sake—but not too much, though. I want to celebrate with you guys too when I get out of here."

"No problem with that, Liam!" said Art. "Just get better. Hey, we have this for you." Art handed Liam a ball. "It's signed by everyone on the team."

"The game ball?"

"Well, it's one of twenty balls used in the game, but yeah, it's *a* game ball," Cam said with a smile.

"Thanks for stopping by, guys. I'll see you on campus in a day or two. Cam, can you take my gear out of my locker and put it back in our suite."

"Already did that, and thanks for the cab money that I found in your pants pocket."

"You're unbelievable," Liam said.

"And honest that I told you about it."

"Yes, that's true. See you back at the suite."

"Yeah, see you in a day or two." Cam left the room.

The judge said, "Liam, it's Dan Morris from Yale and one of his teammates. They're in the hallway, and they would like to speak with you if you are up for it."

"Hey, Dan, shouldn't you guys be heading home to New Haven by now?"

"Yeah, the last bus left a little while ago, but I wanted to see how you were doing. Liam, this is Walter Woods, our middle linebacker. Walt's the one who hit you—cleanly I might add—and he wanted to come by and see for himself if you were okay."

Liam could see that Walt was very emotional about this visit as he couldn't look him in the eye without tearing up, so Liam cut him off before he could say anything.

"You know what I like about you Yalies?"

"What's that, Liam?" asked Dan.

"How well you do your ventriloquist acts. Is that a required class for freshmen or something? I mean, I see Walt over there, but all I hear is Dan's voice."

Everyone in the room laughed.

"Hey, Walt, I'm Liam; nice to meet you," Liam said as he extended his hand.

"I'm so sorry, Liam. I never meant for something like this to happen," said Walt.

"Hey, I know that. Walt, look at the base of the left side of my bed. See that. I can wiggle all my toes. The rest is just rehab."

"You know, Liam, this is kinda your own fault when you think about it," said Dan.

"Okay, Dan, how's that? This ought to be good."

"Well, if you'd have just dropped the ball, you could have freed up your hands to land on the ground properly. That way, we could have won the game and the Ivy League Championship. But what did you do? You *selfishly* held on to the ball. I have no sympathy for you if you do something like that." Everyone laughed again.

"Judge, how can I argue with logic like that? Walt, we're good, okay?"

Walt nodded as he bit his lip so that he wouldn't tear up.

"This is for you, Liam," said Dan.

"Your game shirt, Dan?"

"Yeah, we're getting new ones anyway next year, but you played well today, so here is an additional memento of the occasion. It will be your only win and only championship, my friend. So enjoy it while you still can!"

"Hey, guys, can you do me a favor?"

"Sure, what?"

"Please sign this ball. All my teammates signed it, and I would be honored if you two would do the same."

Dan and Walt signed the ball and left to go back to New Haven.

"Thanks, guys," Liam said to them on their way out.

"Liam, Coach Russell and Coach Carlson are here to see you," said the judge.

"Coach…coach." Liam started to tear up.

"What's wrong, Liam? Are you in pain or something?" asked Coach Russell.

"No, Coach, I just let you down."

"Let me down? You saved the game!" said Coach Russell.

"Thanks, Coach, but I know what the doctor is saying. Based on this injury, I may not be able to play football again. I let you and Coach Carlson down."

"First of all, Liam, we don't know any of that until all the tests are complete. Secondly, we *just* planned on letting you play quarterback this year, and you earned All-Ivy honors at wide receiver and Rookie of the Year! You just almost single-handedly beat Yale, and recruiting is off the charts after you decommitted from Stanford last year. Our investment in you has paid off tenfold, so don't worry about that; just get better!"

"Yes, Coach."

"Not to mention, you squeezed us to admit Cam, and he's All-Ivy as well," Coach Carlson said with a wink.

"We'll see you at the banquet in a few days. Okay, son?"

"Yes, Coach."

The following morning, Liam, the judge, and Father Callahan met with the hospital neurologist and the orthopedic spine specialist.

"Liam, how are you feeling? I heard you had a great game yesterday."

"Thanks, Doctor, but it really was a team effort."

"That's great, Liam. I see that you are humble too. How's your left side feeling today? I see that you have much better range of motion in your arms and legs. Is the sensitivity coming back?"

"Yes, Doctor, I feel a lot better."

"Well, Liam, this is what we are seeing; here, let me show you." He put his x-ray up on the light box and pointed to the areas of concern. "See, here, here, and here. Based on the hit you took, there is pressure being put on your nerves. Our recommendation would be to have corrective surgery to ensure that pressure will be taken off the nerves permanently."

"What does this mean as far as football goes?"

"I think that we have to keep things in perspective here, Liam. You could have easily been paralyzed with the type of hit you took yesterday. By having this surgery now, you will be able to lead a normal and pain-free life. However, I'm afraid football is out of the question due to the nature of this injury. If you get hit there again, you could be permanently paralyzed."

"Doctor, what about running and other activities?"

"Excellent question, Judge. As long as he isn't participating in a contact sport, he should be fine."

"How about baseball?" the judge continued.

"That is up to you, but I don't necessarily see an issue with that," the doctor said.

"Okay, Liam, we have options. That's what's important."

"Yes, sir." Liam paused. "Judge, Father, Doctor, may I have a minute please?"

"Sure, son," said the judge. All three left the room.

Liam began to cry as he absorbed the news. There was a knock at the door. It was Father Callahan. He, it seemed, had talked to the doctor, and he sensed Liam's pain. "Liam, son, let's look at the positives here," said Father Callahan. "The sooner you have this surgery, the sooner you can begin to pitch again and maybe run track and field for Harvard. Don't give up, son; it's not in your nature." At that Liam started crying again, and Father Callahan hugged him.

"I know, Father," he said, his shoulders still heaving. "Okay, send them back in."

"Okay, Liam, we can have the surgery during your semester break in a week, and you can start rehabilitation approximately one to two weeks afterward, depending on how it goes and how you are feeling."

"Thank you, Doctor."

"Are you okay, Liam?" asks the judge.

"Yes, Judge, I just had more in the tank; that's all."

"I know, son. The important thing here is that you'll be able to live a normal life without any pain. When is the football banquet?"

"Next week."

"Well, let's tell the coaches before the banquet and thank them for everything."

"Yes, sir."

"You know you probably could still be a part of the program if you wanted to assist the coaches."

"I know. I thought about that. We'll see."

THE FOOTBALL BANQUET

THE EVENING OF THE FOOTBALL banquet came, and Liam was extremely nervous because he knew that he wasn't going to be able to play the game that he loved anymore. As Coach Russell stood up to give his closing remarks, the room fell silent.

"Gentlemen, I need your attention one more time, please. There are three more items on the agenda that I would like to address before we say good-bye for the remainder of the semester. First, to the freshmen, sophomores, and juniors, your position coaches will be on the road, recruiting for the next couple of weeks. Do not be discouraged if they don't get back to you right away. Just follow your off-season conditioning routine with your respective strength and conditioning coach. If you have any questions or concerns, they will get back to you when they are free. Second, I have the honor of naming the captains for next year's team. They are two young men who exemplify what it means to be a student, an athlete, and a teammate. I would like to introduce you to next year's captains, Willie Morgan and Sean Treadeaux."

Both players came up to the center of the banquet table and took pictures with Coach Russell. Then Liam got really nervous because he knew that it was time for him to speak.

"Gentlemen, there is one last item on the agenda, and then you can go. Finally, Liam O'Hara would like to say a few words to you all, Liam…"

"Thank you, Coach Russell," Liam said as he walked to the podium and could feel his legs shaking. Liam took his speech out of his left jacket pocket and cleared his throat. "By now, most of you have heard that, due to the nature of my spinal injury, I will be unable to continue to play football—the game I love. I don't really blame Matt, but did he really have to throw the ball that high?" The audience laughed. "I recently told my roommate, Cam, that Harvard College and Harvard football do not define who we are as a person. Rather, it is a piece of a bigger puzzle in life. I am thankful for the opportunity that I had to play for this university, but more importantly to play with you, my teammates." Liam began to tear up since this was a big piece of his puzzle. "I really wish that I could play with you guys a few more years because I know I still have more football in me. I also know that the only person happy that I can't play next year is Ryan Bells so that he doesn't have to transfer." Again the audience laughed. "Please raise your glasses. I want you all to know that it was an honor and a privilege to suit up and play side by side with each of you. For that I am forever grateful, and I thank you all." As he choked up and began to cry, Coach Russell hugged him.

The entire team stood up and gave Liam a standing ovation. Coach Russell had one last thing to say before dismissing the team.

"Thank you, Liam, and the feeling is mutual from all of us. So for the next three years, the number one will not be worn by any member of the Harvard football team until you graduate." The team gave the coach and Liam a standing ovation.

After the banquet, this year's captains, Art Irons and Darren Thomas, stopped Liam as he was about to leave with the judge and Ray. "Liam, we have something for you."

"What's this?"

Liam unwrapped what appeared to be a small pole. He immediately started to laugh as it was a custom walking cane painted over with the Harvard shield and Harvard football logo. In addition, each member of the team and coaching staff had signed it. Liam's jaw dropped.

"Now that is priceless! Thanks, guys," he said and gave each of them a hug.

Two weeks later Liam had successful surgery on his neck. He started rehabilitation about a week after the surgery so that he could evaluate his options. Liam decided to take the winter season off and think about what he wanted to do: baseball or track and field. While on break, Liam decided to catch up with Mikey and visit Mr. Maguire as well.

The Heist
(Continued...)

March 17, 7:22 p.m. A patrol car was approaching.

"Eagle One, Eagle One, you've got vultures on your six."

"Roger that, Eagle Two, can you clip its wings?" asked Tommy.

"Affirmative, Eagle One, but need the call now!" Joey exclaimed.

Tommy looks at Mike for confirmation.

"Take the shot," said Mike.

"Eagle Two, clip one of its wings now!"

"Affirmative, Eagle One. Affirmative." Joey took one shot with his rifle and silencer and hit the squad car's front right tire, stopping it on the corner of Louis Prang Street and Huntington Avenue. They were two blocks away from Mike and Tommy's position. The officer got out of his car and saw a flat tire. Not suspecting anything, the officer called in for a tow.

"How's the weather *now*, Eagle Two?"

"Clear skies, Eagle One, clear skies."

"See you at the nest, Eagle Two."

"Affirmative, Eagle One."

"We're good to go, Mike. Take Palace Road to Tremont Street to Melnea Cass Boulevard to the South Boston Bypass Road to the Shamrock Car Wash."

"I've got your six clear through the exit, Eagle One. No more vultures in sight."

"Affirmative, Eagle Two. Go back to the nest once we are clear."

"Affirmative, Eagle One."

At quarter to eight, back at the Shamrock Car Wash, Mike said, "Tommy, you good?"

"Yup, all set."

"Give me all your clothes and your shoes. I need to put everything in that barrel of acid," said Big Mike.

"Here you go. Liam put the bags away behind the soda machine."

"Perfect."

"Let's change the license plates, put the Shamrock Car Wash stickers back on the car, and when Joe comes back, we're out."

Ten minutes later Joe entered and asked, "Are we clean?"

"Yup, you?"

"All good on my end, and I left those cigarette butts just like we discussed."

"Perfect!"

"Let's go," said Joe.

"We can't. We have to break Mike's left arm."

"Are you serious?"

"He's right; we have to," said Mike.

"I thought that the casts were enough."

"We can't leave anything to chance, or we're all going inside for a long, long time," said Mike.

"Okay, straighten out your arm, Mike."

"Mike, on three I'm going to hit your arm with this wrench, okay?"

"Shit! Okay!"

"One...two—"

Whack!

"What happened to fucking three!" Big Mike screamed.

"It's better if you didn't see it coming," said Tommy.

"Okay, *now* can we go?" asked Uncle Joey.

Fifty minutes later at the Amesbury bus depot fifty-five miles away, Mike parked the car, opened the trunk, and took both bikes out. Tommy and Joe would now bike back over the New Hampshire border to Seabrook train station, where their car was parked. Mike headed back to the Shamrock Car Wash to drop off the car and then headed home to quickly recast his arm and pick up Mikey at the police station.

Ninety minutes later Big Mike arrived home.

"Mike, are you okay? Did everything go as planned?" Mrs. Maguire asked, relieved to see him home.

"Maggie, just like I promised you, nobody got hurt. We were in and out, and I really need you to recast my arm the exact way you had it before. No more questions please, or you'll be complicit."

"Okay, yes, I understand."

"Did the police call?"

"Yes, about thirty minutes ago. We can pick up Mikey at central booking downtown after ten p.m."

"Okay then, let's get going and get that blow dryer to make this cast hard so that we can pick Mikey up."

At quarter after eleven, at the South Boston BPD station, Big Mike walked up to the desk sergeant and said, "Mike Maguire to bail out Mike Maguire, Jr."

"One minute, sir."

"Mike Maguire, Jr. was brought in on a three zero nine D and D; he can be released into your care. Here he comes now."

"Mikey, come here. Are you okay?" his mother asked as she hugged him.

"You stupid little shit!" As Big Mike hit Mikey across the top of his head. "I told you to stay out of trouble."

"But...Dad—"

"Shut your mouth until we get home! Get in that car. Now!"

Back on the highway, heading home to South Boston, Mikey and Big Mike were in a great mood and reveling in their success.

"You know, Mikey, I scare myself with how good my acting skills are," said Big Mike proudly.

"Well, that hit was real," Mikey said as he touched his head softly where he was struck.

Big Mike grinned. "I'm a method actor, Mikey. I have to make things look real."

"Well done then, because I still have a headache!"

"And you were brilliant, my boy! All you have to do is square yourself with Father Callahan, and then you're good."

"I'm not sure what's worse, jail or Father Callahan," said Mikey.

"That's a tough one, my boy."

The following day the sensational robbery was all over the media. Headlines in the *Boston Globe* read, "LARGEST HEIST EVER! $500 MILLION STOLEN." The *Herald's* cover read, "$300–$500 MILLION GONE!" Even in the ER room where Mike was being x-rayed again, everyone was talking about the robbery. Mike had returned the following day to the hospital, where Dr. Franz was reviewing Mike's break and looking at an updated x-ray. "Well, Mr. Maguire, it's been a week and a half, and your break doesn't look like it's healing at all. Are you still using it at work?"

"Afraid so, Doc."

"Well, stop it. Stop it immediately, or we'll have to put a plate in your arm if this is the way that it's going to heal."

"I will, Doc. No more lifting for six to eight weeks."

"Okay then. Would you like some pain medication?"

"No thanks, Doc. I have to see my PO in a few days, and I have to give him a sample."

"But you'll have a prescription, or I can call him."

"No, that's fine, Doc. I'll be fine. Appreciate it, though."

"Remember, Mr. Maguire, stop using your left arm at work."

"Will do, Doc. Thanks again."

Two days later in Portsmouth, after leaving Attorney Duncan McDonald's office and discussing setting up a satellite car wash in Portsmouth, Liam reviewed the business plans with the team.

"I thought that the franchise was just part of that cover," said Uncle Joe.

"No, not at all; I've already instructed Tommy to purchase that empty lot we discussed with Mr. McDonald, and here are the final blueprints for a car wash and oil-change shop."

"Seriously?" both Uncle Joe and Uncle Tommy said at the same time.

"Yeah, I'm dead serious. This is business as usual, just like we discussed. We're going to build one up here, and I want you guys to run it. You can still have your construction business, but we'll be partners in this new venture. I'll own fifty-one percent, and these papers say you two together will own forty-nine percent. On the bottom are your salaries, with the potential of quarterly bonuses as soon as we start making a profit."

"How much do we have to put down?"

"Nothing. Your percentage is derived by running the business. Big Mike and Mikey are already turning a profit after just a little over a year into it in South Boston. We'll be expanding the South Boston location to include an oil-and-lube-changing station in the next few months. Speaking of which, we'll need your construction company to do the expansion. Can you do that?"

"Sure, Liam." Uncle Tommy and Uncle Joey exchanged a happy smile.

"Okay, now that *that* is settled, can we finally order lunch, for goodness' sake?" said Tommy Demps as everyone laughed.

"Wow! This is a really good steak," said Mike.

"Sure is! How's your lobster, Tom?"

"Maine's finest. I'm going to bring the family back here in a few weeks."

"So, did you guys hear about that robbery at the Gardner Museum?"

"Yeah, why?" asked Big Mike as the table lapsed silent.

"They're bringing everyone in, and I mean everyone, Mike. I bet they'll even reach out to you with some questions. My office has our money on Quinn and his crew. Nothing happens in this town without his say-so or without him getting a cut."

"What do they have, Tom?" asked Joe.

"Nothing really. They have a couple of size-nine and size-ten boot prints. Two, maybe three guys—they had fake BPD uniforms and pushed their way into the museum. One guy had a tattoo of a jaguar or something like that on his right forearm. Mike, you know anyone in the joint like that?"

"Nope. Plenty of tigers and lions, though."

"Yeah, me too; I never saw a black jaguar at Walpole, and nothing is on record with the gang units."

"So anything else, Tom?" he asked.

"Nope, BPD is stumped. They're checking the local fences, and they even have the FBI and Interpol involved."

"Sounds serious."

"It is, but they don't have anything on scene. There is one thing, though."

"What's that?"

"A statie who was lost was trying to get back to his barracks in Framingham, and he took a wrong turn off Huntington Avenue. This was just a few blocks from the museum around the estimated time of the robbery. He popped a tire. One guy at the garage thinks it's a bullet hole, but the statie says he never heard a shot."

"A bullet hole?"

"Yeah, go figure. Anyway, if they can't figure this one out in the next few weeks or so, the FBI will take over. The art is just worth too much. This crew is a group of master thieves. Some people think that they're out-of-towners."

"What's the reward up to?" asked Mikey.

"I think fifty grand."

"Fifty grand on five hundred million dollars' worth of art?"

Tommy Demps had something to say about that. "Yeah, I know, right. It should at least be one to ten million. Those insurance companies are notoriously cheap bastards. After a month or two, the reward will be up to a million or two. The insurance company thinks that because this is such a high-profile case that BPD will solve it. Unfortunately, my friends who are still in the ADA's office say that they have no clue, though."

Three weeks later the robbery was still all over the local and national news. The usual suspects were brought in, and everyone thought that it was Quinn and his crew who'd pulled the job. They even brought Big Mike in for questioning, but since he didn't have any tattoos, he was in a cast for over two and a half weeks, and he was on tape bailing out his son from BPD custody, he was quickly eliminated. There were leads being called in from all over the world, looking for the reward, but they turned up nothing substantial.

ONE YEAR LATER

ON THE ONE-YEAR ANNIVERSARY OF the Gardner robbery, the FBI's Art and Cultural Crimes division took over the case from BPD's Major Crimes Unit, and then things started to heat up throughout the Boston underworld. The FBI started by relisting all the stolen goods and even sent out forensic profiles of the criminals to the media. The insurance company agreed to increase their reward from $50,000 to $1.5 million.

Liam was nearing the end of his sophomore year when his freshman art-history teacher, Professor Kirk Powell, who was on sabbatical, read the FYI's article about the theft and remembered Liam's paper from the year prior. Liam's paper was about the Gardner Museum and these exact thirteen pieces of art. In Liam's paper, he went on to describe how those pieces were all part of a class-action lawsuit against the museum. Professor Powell read that FBI special agent Charles Kent was now in charge of the Gardner Museum investigation. Professor Powell decided to reach out to Agent Kent, but before he did so, Agent Kent tried to shake some local branches to see if any leaves would fall.

FBI headquarters downtown Boston.
"Agent Kent?"
"Yes."
"Your ten o'clock is here," said his assistant, Carmen.

"I'll be right down; thank you, Carmen." Two minutes later, Special Agent Kent of the FBI walked back to ask Carmen, "Hey, Carmen, so where are they?"

"They're in Interrogation Room One, Agent Kent. It's down the hall to your right."

"I told you, Carmen, 'Charlie' is fine."

"Yes, sir, Charlie it is. I'll remember next time."

Agent Kent entered Interrogation Room One.

"Ah, gentlemen, don't get up. I'll just sit over here," Agent Kent said as he paused to sit down across from Connor Quinn. "Mr. Quinn, now this *is* truly a pleasure. Your agency file is quite a read."

Agent Kent plopped Connor Quinn's thick file on the table.

"It says here that you actually served time at Alcatraz. That's a first for me. I only saw it as a tourist attraction myself, and to think you got to actually live there, wow! So how was the food at Alcatraz? I mean, to think that you got to see the whole United States on the taxpayer's dime? Let me see, you've been locked up in Boston, New York, Atlanta, San Francisco, and Leavenworth."

"You forgot that I spent a year at Angola," Quinn said with a smile.

"Thanks, I'll add it to the file," Agent Kent said as he made a notation on Quinn's file. "And you, Mr. Canti," he said, again plopping a file on the table on top of Connor's file and looking to his left, "you are no slouch yourself: several indictments for murder, racketeering, and drug trafficking, with only one conviction. Bravo to your attorney, Mr. Canti!" Then, turning to his right and putting another file on top of the pile, Agent Kent said, "And finally, we have you, Mr. Webster. You're not too shabby in your own right. Multiple arrests for B and E, several jewelry heists, and one Federal Reserve job."

"All accusations, cop. No convictions!" said Colin Webster.

"As I was about to say, no convictions. It appears you have the best attorney out of the bunch, Mr. Webster."

"That's great. So you can read, Agent Kent; now what is this all about? Why did you call us down here? And what division of the FBI did you say that you are with?" asked Connor's attorney, Patrick Baker.

"I'm with Art Crimes Division."

"Did you say Art Crimes?"

"Yes, that's correct."

"You're not Organized Crime? This isn't a RICO inquiry?"

"No, not today at least."

"So what the hell do you want with us?" asked Connor.

"One year ago this week was the Gardner Museum robbery; do you remember that?"

"Yeah, so? What does that have to do with us?"

"It is my understanding that nothing happens in Boston without you either knowing about it or being a part of it, Mr. Quinn."

Connor grinned. "You give me far too much credit, Agent Kent. I am but a humble tavern owner. Come by the Triple O, and the first round is on me."

"Thanks, but no thanks, Connor."

"Again, what does this have to do with us?" asked Connor.

"Well, funny that you should ask, Connor. You see, there was a pile of cigarette butts found just outside the museum the night of the robbery. They were next to the alley where the thieves took off after the robbery. Guess whose fingerprints were on those butts? Anyone? Anyone?" Agent Kent paused. "Okay, then I'll tell you: ding, ding, ding—they belong to Mr. Webster over there. So then we got to thinking: this was probably a three- or four-man job: two inside guys, maybe one getaway driver, and maybe one lookout. It so happens that the apartment complex across the street was broken into the same night as the robbery. During our investigation we found out that the rooftop has excellent sight lines of the museum and all its entrances and exits leading to and from that alley. And guess what we found on *that* rooftop?" he asked and paused again. "No, save your guesses: another pile of cigarette butts. Now guess who *these* cigarette butts belonged to?

Anyone—anyone—well, since there is only one man left in the room, those fingerprints belonged to you, Mr. Canti."

"Big fucking deal, cop; we didn't do it!"

Kent was enjoying himself. "No, that's where you're wrong. I think you did have something to do with it. The only question is why you all haven't been brought in for questioning before this?"

Carmen knocked on the interrogation room door.

"Yes?"

"Agent Kent, you have a phone call."

"Please take a message, Carmen; I'm busy entertaining friends," Agent Kent said as he smiled.

"The call is urgent, sir."

"This is a bullshit fishing exhibition. Charge us, or we're out of here, Agent Kent," said the attorney Baker.

"Don't worry, Mr. Baker; Mr. Kent doesn't really have a phone call; he's about to be ripped a new ass for taking us in," said Connor.

"We'll see about that, Connor. One moment, boys, I'll be right back."

Agent Carey was standing outside and grabbed Agent Kent's arm. "Who the hell do you think you are?"

"Excuse me? And you are?" Agent Kent said.

"I'm Senior Agent Joe Carey, and I'm your boss's boss! Did you pull the files of Connor Quinn?" he snarled.

"Yes, for my interview."

"Did you see that it was flagged?"

"I did, but this isn't a RICO inquiry; it's for the Gardner Museum theft."

"Are you *that* fucking stupid? He's my CI, and you drag him in for questioning?"

Kent planted his feet. "So if he's involved in this robbery, does that mean that he and his crew get a pass?"

Agent Kent's supervisor, Nick Williams, arrived, looking worried. "Joe, what's this all about?"

"This fucking moron brought in *my* CI and his crew for questioning about that Gardner thing without my okay," Agent Carey said.

"Charlie, you know protocol here."

"Not to mention, Nick, if he bothered to read that file, I had Connor and his crew under surveillance during the time of that robbery."

"That's interesting because there is no paperwork or record of surveillance until one month *after* this file began."

Agent Carey bristled. "What are you saying, you little shit?"

Kent was firm in his response. I'm saying that you are either lousy at paperwork, or you're looking the other way."

"Nick, are you going to let him talk to me like that?" asked Agent Carey.

Shaking his head Nick said, "Charlie, step back here. I've known Joe for over fifteen years. He's got more decorations than a Christmas tree for Christ's sake. Don't question his integrity like that."

"I'm not, Nick, the evidence is!"

"Nick, I am ordering you to release them, now!" said Senior Agent Carey.

"Charlie, let them go. There are other leads that you should be following. What about that professor from Harvard and that lead?"

"That's a bullshit lead. Okay, I'll do it," and turning to Agent Carey, he said, "but this isn't over, Carey."

Reentering Interrogation Room One, Kent looked disappointed. "Gentlemen, it appears that I have been instructed to let you go," said Agent Kent.

"Enjoy your next post in Antarctica, Agent Kent," Connor said with a smirk.

"You know, Connor, you may be very good at what you do in Southie—murder, drug dealing, and loan-sharking—but you are an absolute moron when it comes to the FBI. Our charter only allows us to operate within the fifty US states. And by the way, Antarctica is a continent, not a state."

"Fuck you; then enjoy Alaska!"

"Very eloquent, Connor, now rush off to the next Mensa meeting with your two friends here."

"The next time you bring us in here for some bullshit like this, I'll sue you for harassment!"

"Noted, honorable esquire Baker."

Two hours later Connor called Agent Carey.

"Are you fucking shitting me?"

"Connor?"

"Who else do you fucking think this is?"

"Hey, I got you, Colin, and Tony out of there right away!"

"You fucking idiot! We never should have been brought in for questioning in the first place. You're supposed to guard against this type of shit, you fucking moron!"

Carey was uncharacteristically candid in talking to Connor. "Here's a news flash for you, Connor; they have pretty compelling circumstantial evidence against your guys. It's pretty tough to explain all those cigarette butts in the alley and on the rooftop. Tony and Colin were either in on it or they were planning something. How the hell do you explain that?"

"They were set up! I was with Tony that night, playing the puppies at Wonderland after the parade."

"What about Colin?"

"He said that he was with some whore."

"Do you believe him?"

"Tony believes him, and that's good enough for me. Didn't you say that you had us all under surveillance that night anyway?"

"Yeah, but nothing on Colin."

"You better find out who stole the artwork or get the art back. That Agent Kent is like a rabid dog with a bone. He was specifically chosen by the Director himself to locate that art."

"I'll look into it. You do the same, but keep that fucking Agent Kent off my back!"

"Yeah, I'll do my best. Just stay off the radar until all this blows over."

Back in Agent Kent's office, Charlie called his secretary, "Carmen, can you please bring me in the file that just came in from that Harvard professor?"

"Yes, Agent Kent—I mean, Charlie. One moment please."

"Thank you, Carmen."

"Here you go, Charlie," Carmen said with a smile.

He opened the file and read the notes while calling the professor.

"Professor Kirk Powell, please."

"Speaking."

"Professor Powell, my name is Special Agent Kent, and I am with the FBI."

"Yes, how can I help you?" Professor Powell said.

"You sent us a note about the Gardner robbery along with a paper from one of your former students, a Liam O'Hara."

"Yes, I did. I sent you the paper because I found it odd that my student basically wrote about a crime that would happen a little over a year after the paper was submitted. Of all the artwork in that museum, he only wrote about the thirteen pieces that were eventually stolen. I found that quite peculiar."

"What type of kid is this Liam O'Hara?"

"Well, he's an excellent student and apparently a top-notch athlete."

"What I mean is, do you think that he has a dark side? Do you think that he is capable of something like that?"

"I would like to think no, but one can never tell. He grew up here in South Boston, and he might know people of ill repute, but I have no idea. I'd hate to condemn the boy simply because of his zip code."

"Well, thank you, Professor; I'll take this all into consideration and get back to you."

"Excuse me, Agent Kent, is it?"

"Yes."

"I was told of a reward if the thieves are unearthed."

"Yes, that's correct."

"Well, you have my name and contact information."

"I do. If anything comes of it, I will let you know."

"Thank you, Agent Kent."

"And you as well, Professor."

As he hung up the phone, Agent Kent called his secretary with a new request, "Carmen, can you call Harvard's general information and get the number for a student by the name of Liam O'Hara? When you get it, please dial the number and just transfer it to me."

"Will do, Charlie."

"Thanks, Carmen."

Five minutes later, Carmen said, "Charlie, here you go."

The phone rang, and a voice on the other end answered, "Hello?"

"Hi, my name is Special Agent Charles Kent with the FBI. I'm trying to reach a Liam O'Hara. May I please speak with him?"

"I'm afraid that he's not in right now; may I take a message?"

"Sure, please tell him that Special Agent Charles Kent called, and if he can call me back when he gets in, that would be great."

"Sure, what's your number, Agent Kent?"

"My direct line is six one seven, seven four two, double five double three. Please have him call me when he gets in or sometime tomorrow."

"Okay, will do. Is there any message?"

"No, my business is of a personal nature."

"Got it, thanks."

Liam got the message, took a deep breath, and called the following morning. "This is Liam O'Hara for Agent Kent."

"Mr. O'Hara, this is Special Agent Kent. Thank you for calling me back."

"Sure, no problem. How can I help you, Agent Kent?"

"Well, I was wondering if you could come in for a chat."

"A chat? A chat about what?"

"We can discuss that when you come down here. How about eleven a.m.?"

"Um, okay. How about we meet at the cafeteria on the main floor?"

"Sure, we can start there. Do you know where it is?"

"Yeah, I've been there before."

"Great, see you then." Agent Kent hung up the phone.

"Carmen."

"Yes, Charlie?"

"Can you please check the system and see if there is a file on a Liam O'Hara?"

"Yes, sir."

Twenty minutes later, Carmen returned. "There is no specific file on Mr. Liam O'Hara, but there is one for what appears to be his father, a Declan O'Hara."

"Please bring it in; thank you."

Later that morning in the cafeteria of the FBI, where Liam was to meet Agent Kent, he was sitting alone in a corner.

"Mr. O'Hara?"

"Yes, you must be Agent Kent." Liam extended his hand.

"I think that we might be more comfortable upstairs in my office. What do you say we move this discussion to a more private setting?"

"Upstairs? I don't think so."

"I beg your pardon."

"I think that you heard me. You asked me here to talk, so here I am. If you want to interrogate me, then I'll have my attorney contact you, and we can discuss the terms."

"You need an attorney? Just to talk? You know that makes one look guilty."

"Save it, Agent Kent. Guilty of what? You didn't even tell me *why* I was summoned. And by the way, I would never go into a gunfight with just a knife."

"Interesting choice of words, Liam."

"It's an old Southie saying from Howie Winter—his words, not mine, Agent Kent."

"Why so cynical, Liam?"

"Agent Kent, have you met a fellow agent by the name of Joe Carey?"

"I have."

"Then you know why," Liam said.

"Looking at your dad's file, I can see that, Liam. What was their involvement together?"

"Ask Agent Carey; he can best answer that question."

"But I'm asking you."

"I can't tell you what I don't know, Agent Kent. You'll have to ask Agent Carey what goes on in his mind. Not to mention, you have my father's file right in front of you, don't you?"

Agent Kent nodded and said, "Yes, I do."

"Then perhaps you can tell me what the interest regarding my father was all about? This standoff with my dad and Agent Carey will only come to light if something happens to me. And if anything does happen to me, then Pandora's box opens wide up. It's a deal my dad made years ago." He paused. "Is that what this is all about?"

"No, I'd like to ask you some questions about the Gardner Museum robbery."

"Gardner Museum robbery? You're kidding me, right?"

"No, in fact I'm quite serious."

"Okay, what questions do you have?"

"Well, your freshman-year art-history professor, Professor Powell, sent me your final exam paper."

"And?"

"Well, in your paper you talked about several pieces from the Gardner Museum that had litigation against them. Ironically, those were the only pieces that were stolen from the museum."

"I believe that I earned an A on that paper and in the class if memory serves."

"You did, but I would *not* have considered it an A paper."

"So you're an FBI agent and a critic?"

"No, an undergraduate English major from Princeton."

"Well, everyone needs a safety school, Agent Kent," Liam said, smiling. "I believe the paper that I wrote was about why the museum was being sued for these pieces and not about the pieces themselves."

"That's correct, but don't you find it odd that these thirteen pieces were the only ones stolen from the museum?"

"Odd? No. A coincidence? Yes. But maybe that's the lead you should be chasing: the story behind the pieces, and not just the pieces themselves. I mean, there were several Raphaels, Matisses, and Botticellis that were far more valuable—and accessible—that the thieves passed on."

"Wow, you know quite a bit about the museum. Is that your theory?"

"My theory? No, it's *a* theory, though, and I just read a lot."

"I see."

"Well, if you do follow my theory, and you eventually find out who stole the artwork, then I expect a piece of the reward."

"I'll keep that in mind."

"Anything else, Agent Kent?"

"I read your father's file, most of which has been redacted by the State Department, and I'm curious about a few things."

"About what?"

"What's your relationship with your father's best friend, Mike Maguire?"

"He's my best friend's father. Why?"

"Well, I see that you've visited him on several occasions at Walpole and at Middleton."

"And?"

"Why is that?"

At that moment, Judge Mahoney entered the cafeteria. "Liam, let's go."

"Can I help you, sir?" Agent Kent asked, surprised at the judge's arrival.

"My name is Michael Mahoney, Federal Judge Michael Mahoney, and Liam is my son. And your name, sir?"

"Special Agent Kent."

"Well, Agent Kent, you are formally notified that if you have any additional questions for Mr. O'Hara, you need to call me first. Is that understood?" Agent Kent nodded. "Let's go, Liam."

"It was a pleasure, Agent Kent."

"The same, Liam. I am sure that we will be in touch," Agent Kent said with a smile. "And will do, Judge Mahoney," Agent Kent said as the judge and Liam started to walk out of the building.

"What was that all about, Liam?"

"How did you know I was here, Judge?"

"Ray and I called your dorm to see what time your baseball game against Brown was today?" As the judge pointed to ray for confirmation. "Cam told us where you were. Why didn't you call me? And what did Special Agent Kent want?"

"I didn't call you because I didn't know what this was all about, and I didn't want to bother you. He just asked me some questions about my dad, Mr. Maguire, and the Gardner Museum robbery."

"But why did he want to speak with you about that?"

"I don't know. Do you remember the paper I wrote my freshman year? The one about the museum and the lawsuits?"

"I think so."

"It was my first A at Harvard, and I mailed it home to you."

"Oh yes, of course, I remember now. The thirteen pieces. Right? Actually, I think I still have it."

"Exactly. Well, apparently Professor Powell sent a copy of my paper to the FBI because he thought it was suspicious. Professor Powell noted that the pieces that I wrote about were the only ones stolen—and nothing else. I explained to Agent Kent that my paper wasn't about the pieces; rather, it was about the lawsuits surrounding the pieces."

"I see. So how did you leave it?"

"I don't know; you came in."

"Well, let's see what he says. Call me immediately if he contacts you again, understand?" said the judge.

"Yes, sir."

"So what time is the game today?"

"Four o'clock in Providence."

"Great, we'll see you there, and then we all can go out to dinner afterward. I know a nice little Italian spot called Al Forno in Providence's Little Italy. Then we'll drive you back to campus."

"Perfect, thanks, Judge! See you at four o'clock."

Back in his dorm room, Liam called Big Mike.

"Mr. Maguire? It's Liam."

"Hey, Liam, what's up?"

"We need to chat about the car wash expansion in Portsmouth. How does tomorrow look at ten a.m.?"

"Good, see you then."

The following morning, Liam went to the car wash to meet with Big Mike.

"Hey, Mr. Maguire."

"Hey, Liam, what's up?"

"Can you turn up that radio a bit, please?"

"Yeah sure."

"What's up?"

"I got called in by the FBI about the Gardner thing."

"What? How?"

"Because of a paper I wrote about the museum when I was a freshman. My friggin' art-history professor sent a copy of it to the FBI, and they called me the other day."

"What'd you say?"

"Nothing! I just said that it was a coincidence. That's all. I told him that I wrote about was the lawsuit against the museum, not the pieces that were stolen."

"Good! And?"

"The judge bought it, but not Agent Kent."

"Now what?"

"Nothing, I just wanted to keep you in the loop and for you to give Mikey the heads-up as well. We're covered because we have solid alibis. You too, but I just wanted you to know; that's all."

"Okay, thanks! Call me if the heat gets turned up."

"Where is the artwork anyway?"

"Don't worry about it; the pieces are safe. And if you don't know where they are, you're not lying."

Three weeks later there was a knock at the judge's home.

"Judge, Special Agent Kent from the FBI here; can I speak with you?"

"Yes, of course, Agent Kent, how can I help you?"

"I would like to speak with you and Liam again about this Gardner thing if I may."

"Are you making a formal inquiry?"

"I am."

"You know, Agent Kent, you had better know what you are doing. False accusations like this can lead to a shortened career."

"Thanks for the advice, Judge; I'll keep that in mind when I complete my report. How does tomorrow look at ten a.m. in my office?"

"We'll see you there."

At ten o'clock the following morning, the judge and Liam arrived at the receptionist desk of Agent Kent's office.

"Liam O'Hara to see Agent Kent, please."

"I'll call him now. Please take a seat."

Two minutes later the meeting was under way.

"Liam, nice to see you again. Where's the judge?"

"He had something come up at the last minute in court. He wants us to reschedule, but I think I'm good to answer a few questions."

"Are you sure? Because if so, I'll need you to sign a waiver."

"No problem."

"Okay, let's get started, and the sooner that we're through with this, the sooner I can cross you off the list of suspects."

They both walked into Interrogation Room One.

"Wow, this room hasn't changed a bit. You guys really could have at least repainted it."

"You've been here before?"

"We already went through this, Agent Kent. Speak with that jackass, Agent Carey."

"I will. How about we start with something easy? Do you remember where you were on the evening of March seventeenth of last year?"

"March seventeenth? Wasn't that the day of the Saint Patrick's Day parade?"

"Yes, that's correct."

"Well, then, I went to the Saint Patty's Day parade in Southie with my best friend, Mikey Maguire, and then I came back to campus to study."

"Did anybody see you? I mean, can anybody verify your whereabouts?"

"Here, let me see something." Liam reached into his back pocket and takes out his wallet. Liam pulled out a bent-and-worn picture that was lodged between a picture of his father and a picture with the judge, Ray, and June. "This is a picture of me and Mikey at the parade last year. I also remember that I lost my dorm ID on my way back to school from the parade that night. Since I couldn't get into my dorm, I had to go to Harvard security to have them issue me a new ID. After that I ordered Chinese food for my roommate and myself. You can contact Harvard security to verify my lost ID. I suppose you can contact Visa to verify my order of wonton soup," Liam said with a smile.

"That's a pretty big coincidence to have a picture like that readily available and you lost your campus ID on the same night, don't you think?"

"Do you have picture of your family? In your wallet, Agent Kent?"

"I do."

"See, I always keep pictures of my family with me."

"Okay, so what happened to your best friend?" asked Agent Kent.

"What do you mean?"

"Were you both together all day and night?"

"Ask BPD; he was brought in on a D and D while he was at the parade. They kept him in the tank until Mr. and Mrs. Maguire got him out later that evening. BPD should have a record of all that," Liam said.

"You wouldn't happen to know where Mike's father was, would you?"

"No, home I guess, like most nights. He was nursing his broken arm that he'd suffered a couple of weeks prior at work, I assume."

Agent Kent took notes.

"Okay, now that that's settled, did you work at the museum in the summers from 1987 to 1989."

"I did."

"In what capacity did you work there?"

"I led tours, picked up trash in and around the museum grounds, and gathered art supplies for the artists-in-residence program, stuff like that."

"What about security?"

"What about it?"

"Did you ever work security at the museum?"

"No."

"You know you have to answer me truthfully, Liam. I'm a federal officer. Otherwise, I can arrest you."

"Give it your best shot. I have been answering you truthfully." Liam paused. He put on his game face. "May I ask *you* a question, Special Agent Kent?"

"Yes, of course, Liam, what is it?"

"Were you part of a developmentally delayed recruiting drive that the FBI was conducting a few years ago when you received your badge?"

"Really, that's your play? Being a wiseass? Not a good move, my friend. How about I stick you up at Walpole with rapists, pedophiles, and murderers for the next ten to fifteen years, and you'll be somebody's property within a week. See how you like that."

"I heard that they were getting cable up there? Is that true? Hey, is King Jose' still running the show up there? If so, I'm good. It would be nice to see him again. It's been far too long."

"Funny, kid! My other option is to put you in an underground prison, like Henri Charriere, where your only friend will be the cockroaches that you catch. Try talking to them for a couple of years, and see how you like that."

"Look at you, Agent Kent, with that *Papillon* reference. And here I thought you were just an illiterate simpleton. Did you like his memoir? I read it in the original French print. The English translation is a bit darker, don't you think? Wait." Liam paused. "Or did you just see the movie? That must be it since there were no pictures in his memoir."

Just then the judge walked in, looking angered. "Agent Kent, I specifically told you to not question Liam outside of my presence, did I not?"

"Yes, you did, Judge, but he signed a waiver."

"Poison fruit, Agent Kent, you know that. Anything that Liam may have said up until this point is inadmissible."

"My apologies, Judge. May we proceed now?"

"No, we may not! I need to speak with my client."

Ten minutes later, after the judge and Liam had spoken, the judge turned to Agent Kent and said, "Agent Kent, we may proceed if you wish to do so. Your interview may start now. The time is ten thirty-eight a.m. Please proceed."

"Okay, thank you, Judge; let's move on."

"Yes, let's. Now why exactly am I here? I mean, what would I have to gain from robbing the museum?" Liam asked.

"Well, do the terms 'money' and 'greed' come to mind? You were an orphaned kid, and you see money all around you at Harvard, home, and with your prep-school friends."

"You don't do your homework, do you, Agent Kent?" said the judge.

"What does that mean?"

"That means you need to do your due diligence, Agent Kent. Liam has a trust fund that was set up for him by H. D. Daniels on his father's behalf; so *money* or *greed* would not be his motive."

"I was not aware of that. Are you serious?"

"Yes, I am. And as far as I can see, you're still lacking motive and any sort of evidence to back it up," said the judge.

"What exactly is your relationship with Mike Maguire?" asked Agent Kent.

"Junior or senior?" Liam asked.

"Senior."

"He was my dad's best friend, growing up, and he and his family took me in when my dad was away at the war."

"I see. Well, it was recently brought to my attention that Mr. Maguire was in debt to a local bookmaker for a little over four hundred thousand dollars. His debt was paid in full out of the blue. Now how does a recently released convict, who has been away for over ten years, come up with that kind of money? Is it a payment of sorts from a job? Did he sell anything valuable? Was he lucky at the ponies? What?"

"I paid off Mr. Maguire's debt in January of this year. That was three months prior to the robbery. This is a signed receipt by Mr. Evans that states as much."

"You just paid off his debt for no reason?"

"Mikey and I are brothers. The Maguires *are* family. There is an old Gaelic saying, Agent Kent; it's says, 'Teaghlaigh thar gach.' Do you know what that means?"

"No."

"It means 'family over all.' If I can help and put Mr. Maguire on the right path, then that's what I'll do. I also set aside five million dollars in a trust for my other brother, Ray Mahoney, so that he would never have to move out of his house and in the event of my untimely passing. Otherwise, he will live with me until he no longer wishes to do so. Does that make him a suspect as well, Agent Kent?"

"Liam, you didn't have to do that," said the judge as he turned to Liam.

"Yes, I did. It's the least that I can do for you both, Judge. You saved my life."

Turning back to Agent Kent, Liam said, "We'll talk later. Is there anything else, Agent Kent?"

Kent seemed resigned. "I'll follow up on everything I have here. If there is anything else, I will let you know."

"In the meantime, I'll have a chat with your supervisor," said the judge.

"I'm sure that you will, Judge."

As Liam walked out of the interrogation room, Agent Kent stopped him. "You know, kid, you have too many perfect answers. Something is up, and I'll get to the bottom of it."

"Give it your best shot, Agent Kent, but you are chasing your own shadow. Why don't you try the Triple O? I heard that Connor recently became very fond of art."

"Okay, Liam, thanks for the heads-up. I'll have to check into that."

Two weeks later, Big Mike was summoned to the Triple O by Connor. He greeted Eddie at the bar, "Eddie, how the hell are you!"

"Hey, Mikey! Good, thanks. How about you?"

"Good, thanks, Eddie. Say, is *he* around? I got summoned."

"Yeah, he's at his back table; go ahead over if he's expecting you."

"Thanks again, Eddie."

Mike sat down at Connor Quinn's table.

"Mike, thanks for coming in," Connor said, waving him in to sit down.

"Connor, Tony." Mike nodded to each of them. "Did I have a choice?"

"Mike, come on, everyone has choices. It's just how you decide to act on those choices that make the difference," said Connor.

"Okay, I'm here, so what's up?" asked Big Mike.

"A little birdie told me that you were interviewed again about that Gardner thing."

"Yeah, so? So were several other guys. I assumed that they were just making the rounds."

"The FBI thinks that you may have had something to do with that robbery."

"From what I heard, they thought that you, Tony, and Colin had something to do with it too. In fact, I heard that all three of you guys were brought in for questioning; so what's your point?"

"My point is that the FBI thinks you had something to do with it, along with the O'Hara kid," said Colin.

"Like I told the FBI, I had a broken arm at the time. I was in a cast two weeks before the robbery and six weeks after. When they asked about my son, Mikey, I told him that he was being held by Boston PD on a D-and-D charge stemming from a fight at the parade that night. I picked up Mikey at around eleven o'clock that night, and then we went home. All this is on the record. Why are you asking?"

"They still think that you and the O'Hara kid had something to do with it."

"What can I tell you? When the FBI asked me about Declan's son, Liam, I was told that he was at the parade with my son, but then he had to go back to school to study," said Big Mike.

"Hey, I also heard that you owed Frankie Evans four hundred grand, and you paid him off just a couple of months after you got out. How'd you do that?"

"It wasn't my debt. It was my son's debt that I took over for him. I borrowed the money from Liam."

"O'Hara? How does a kid that age have that kind of dough?"

"Not sure. Declan left him some money. Then there was his life-insurance policy and military benefits I guess."

"You sure it wasn't an advance on a job?"

"Nope! I made a promise to my wife that I wasn't going back inside. And what can a guy with a broken arm and a cast do anyway?" Big Mike paused. "Now, is that it?" Mike said in an annoyed manner.

"For now, Mike." Mike got up from the table. "You know, Mike, if you *did* have something to do with this, you owe taxes and then some."

"Connor, if I had something to do with this, my wife would have killed me already." Mike walked away with a smile, and everyone at the table laughed.

BOSTON BASEBALL BEANPOT

ONE MONTH LATER AS THE dust was settling from the FBI's inquiries, and after Connor's summons of Big Mike to the Triple O, everything was getting back to normal. Since Liam couldn't play football anymore, he decided to play baseball for Harvard.

Every year the Baseball Beanpot is played at Fenway Park. Basically, this tournament is comprised of Boston's four major Division I baseball teams (Harvard, UMASS-Amherst, Boston College, and Northeastern); they play each other in a two-day tournament. The judge, Ray, Cam, Mikey, June, and several players from the Harvard football team were in attendance to cheer Liam on. Before the Boston College game, Liam sneaked Mikey onto the field so that they could play catch and take pictures next to the Green Monste; where their boyhood heroes Yaz and Jim Rice had patrolled. They were in their glory! During batting practice, Liam was putting on a hitting show for those in attendance. Liam was simply acting out certain professional ballplayer mannerisms at the plate. He had Yaz, Fred Lynn, and Bernie Carbo down to a tee as he was launching balls over the Green Monster and around the Pesky Pole in short right field. (It's a lot easier to do so with an aluminum bat.) Liam was selected to pitch the first game against Boston College, and their ace, Cy (Cyrus) Decker, who was drafted by the mariners in the third round of the amateur draft, would pitch in the next game against either UMASS or Northeastern.

After the fifth inning, Harvard were winning 3–1 against one of the top teams in the Big East conference. Liam hit one solo home run at the plate and struck out seven batters on the mound. Unfortunately, he gave up a monstrous home run to their first-round draft pick, Peter Collins. That ball may still be orbiting the earth to this day; that's how far he hit that ball. As he was looking into the stands, he saw the nucleus of his friends nestled right behind the Harvard dugout (the Red Sox home dugout). All of a sudden, he saw Agent Kent arrive, and he started to talk to June. Liam realized that June didn't know anything about what happened, but just the fact that he was questioning her made him uncomfortable. He finished the sixth inning by striking out the last batter. After the inning he was pulled from the game because his coach wanted to save him just in case he needed to face a couple of batters in relief tomorrow afternoon.

As he was sitting in the dugout, he got a pen and a brand-new baseball and started to draw on it. He quickly drew a Picasso-inspired cubist face on one side of the ball and "Teaghlaigh thar gach" on the other side. Liam gave the ball to the ball boy, Roy Tanner, and told him it to give it to the man wearing a tie sitting next to the pretty girl behind our dugout. A couple of minutes later, Roy returned to the dugout with Agent Kent's FBI card, and on the back, it read, "Liam O'Hara, Walpole Prison Class of 2012." We eventually beat BC 3–2 and made it to the championship game.

"Hell of a game, son."

"Thanks, Judge."

"Yeah, Liam, I'm so proud of you," said June as she hugged him.

"Next time you jack one out of Fenway, I expect you to do a pimp walk around the bases. I mean, take your time, for goodness' sake," said Cam.

"Next time, Cam, I promise."

"Yeah, Liam, awesome game," said Ray.

"Thanks, Ray. They gave me that home-run ball. Do you want it?"

"Really? You're gonna give it to me, Liam?"

"It's all yours, buddy. Let's put it in your case at home." Ray hugged him.

"Nice game, young man," Agent Kent said as he walked up to him.

"Gee, thanks, Agent Kent. Are you a scout for the Sox now?" Liam asked.

Kent was grinning. "No, I'm just a fan of the game. And it was an opportunity to meet your extended family."

"I see. We can catch up later, unless you need to speak to me now."

"No, I'm just here as a fan, and I simply wanted to say nice game to you."

"Agent Kent, this is bordering on harassment. Do I need to get a restraining order?" said the judge.

"Judge, as I said, I'm just here as a fan."

"I'll keep that in mind at your disciplinary hearing."

"I get the message, Judge." Agent Kent nodded to the judge. "Liam, we'll catch up soon."

"I hope *not*, Agent Kent."

Agent Kent walked away.

"What is that all about, hun?" asked June. "That man was asking me a lot of questions about you. I thought that you two were close friends."

"Nothing, June, I'll tell you later. Come on, everyone—let's all go out for pizza. It's on the judge!"

CONNOR'S CALL

ABOUT A WEEK AFTER THE baseball season was over and Liam was just about finishing his junior year at Harvard, he received a call at his dorm that Connor would like to speak with him back in Boston. The following day Big Mike and he entered the Triple O to meet up with Connor.

"Hey, how's it going?" Liam asked the bartender.

"What can I get you, kid?"

"Nothing, thanks. I'm here to see Mr. Quinn."

"Your name Liam?"

"Yeah."

"He's in the back over there," he said, pointing to the seat next to the window. "He's expecting you, just one of you, though."

"You go ahead, Liam; I'll be right here," Mike said.

"What can I get you, pal?"

"I'm good. Where's Eddie?"

"Eddie works nights. I'm Chris, and I work the day shift. And if you want to sit on these stools, you need to order a drink or get the fuck out, pal."

"Listen, kid, I'll sit wherever the fuck I want, when I want. You open your fuckin' mouth again, and I'll put your head through that fucking wall."

"Easy, Mike, easy," said Patrick Sullivan Jr. "Relax, Chris; he's a friend of Connor's."

"Sorry, pal, I didn't know."

"Gee, thanks, Patrick, thanks for saving me from the likes of that piece of shit Chris over there. And I thought I told you to steer clear of this place and these guys?"

"You did. I'm just here to collect on the last thing I did for them, and then I'm out."

"Good for you, kid, because this ain't no life. I got twelve years inside away from my wife and kid that says it's not worth it. The one thing that you don't want, kid, is your father to be visiting you for the next few years between six inches of Plexiglas; that's for sure."

"I get it, Mike. My dad told me all about you and that you're a stand-up guy. My dad and I are gonna open a local hardware store in town here. That's what this last score's money is going toward."

"Good for you. I'll see you when it opens."

"Hey, Mike, one last thing. That kid you came in with."

"Yeah, what about him?"

"I overheard Connor say that the kid has something of Connor's, and he's either going to take him out, or he wants me to kidnap his girlfriend from Connecticut, so I'd stay close."

"Thanks, kid."

"I consider us even now, Mike."

"Fair enough, Pat. Give your dad my best, and I'll see you around."

"Yeah, see you around."

Meanwhile, at Connor's table, Connor was sitting with his bottle of whiskey to his left and two shot glasses to his right.

"Mr. Quinn."

"Liam, you've grown over the years. I've been reading all about you in the papers. You've made quite a name for yourself in Cambridge."

"Thanks, Mr. Quinn. Just lucky I guess."

"Luck has nothing to do with it. We make our own destiny."

"Okay, thanks," he said with an inquisitive look on his face.

"You know, I asked you here alone, and I see that you brought Big Mike."

"I wasn't sure of the address, so I asked Mr. Maguire to escort me," he said with a smirk.

"Funny, kid. Do you know why I called you here, Liam?"

"No, sir."

"Tony, Sammy, give us the table, would you?" Both men got up from the table. "A little birdie told me that you had something to do with the Gardner thing. Do you know anything about that, Liam?"

"Well, then, both you and the FBI are misinformed, Mr. Quinn. Like I told them, I was at the Saint Patty's parade all day, and then I went back to school."

"Well, they think otherwise. That agent Kent has a hard-on for you, boy," said Connor.

"That's funny. I'm not sure why you would say that they're looking at me, especially when he told me that friends of yours left DNA at the scene of the crime. Or at least that's what Agent Kent told me."

"No, it's more than just that. I heard that you paid off Big Mike's debt of four hundred grand in cash, and you bought the Shamrock Car Wash. The only way you're getting that kind of cash is if it's an advance on a job like the Gardner."

"Sorry to disappoint you, Mr. Quinn; you see, I bought the car wash last year. I paid off Mr. Maguire's debt with part of my dad's insurance money and a cosigned loan. I used my trust fund as collateral, which I get when I turn twenty-one," Liam said.

"I don't believe that bullshit, not for a second. Where's the artwork, kid?"

"Like I told the FBI, I don't know. The day of the robbery, I went to the Saint Patty's parade, and then I went back to school. All this is on record. Mikey was in jail with BPD, and Mr. Maguire was in a cast at the time of the robbery with a broken arm. I don't know what else to say, Mr. Quinn."

"You know, boy, taking a hit out on your best friend, Mikey, would just be a cost of doing business. Unfortunately, things would get real messy with his father involved. He's one tough son of a bitch! Then there is the judge; nobody in his right mind would hit a federal judge or his retarded kid—that's just plain stupid and bad business. So the question is, how do I get *your* attention, Liam?"

"I thought that we have a standing agreement? That thing my father worked out with you years ago?"

"And that agreement still stands. But that's just with you! I hear that you're dating some serious piece of ass in Connecticut. Is this her?" He handed Liam an eight-and-a-half-by-eleven manila envelope.

"It is." Liam's voice lapsed dead serious. "This sounds like a threat, Mr. Quinn. She has *nothing* to do with any of this, and I still didn't take the art!"

"Liam, if I even sniff that you had something more to do with that robbery, all bets are off. I'll cut her up like fish bait and feed her to my dogs. You think about that."

"What if I go public with my dad's information? Then it gets ugly for you and Agent Carey."

"Did you open the envelope?"

"I did. And I listened to the tapes too. Seems to me that you and Agent Carey have far more to lose than me. Remember your brother, nieces, and nephews too."

"I'm betting that you don't have it in you, Liam."

"I may not, but my dad's friends surely do."

"True, true, but I'm not going after you, just your girlfriend."

"That's a matter of semantics, Mr. Quinn. Purely semantics."

"I don't see it that way."

"Then with all due respect, sir, open your fuckin' eyes." One of his soldiers got up to defend the insult, and Connor waved him back. "And tell your puppy over there to sit down before I forget my manners and take him out."

"Now *that's* Declan O'Hara's son! I just wanted to make sure you knew where you came from, son."

"I remember, and you never seem to let me forget it. Is that all, Mr. Quinn?"

"Think about what I said. Liam, if I sniff that you had anything to do with that robbery, all bets are off, and we're gonna have issues, boy."

"Let me be perfectly clear, Mr. Quinn: you may think I'm not capable of a lot of things, but if you go near my girlfriend, I'll show you just how capable I can be. You forget, Mr. Quinn, I *am* from here, and any time you want to play King of the Hill, you just let me know." He got up from the table and left.

"You okay, Liam?" Mike asked as he saw Liam walking back toward him.

"Let's go for a walk, Mr. Maguire."

They left the tavern and continued talking.

"He knows nothing, but the FBI is feeding him information that I was involved in the robbery."

"What about Mikey and me?"

"Not a word. What could he say? Mikey was in the can the entire time, and you had a broken arm. Seriously, those were *great* covers." He smiled.

"So what about you?"

"I'm still solid with my alibis. The FBI requested tapes from Harvard security and a date stamp on when my backup ID was taken. They even subpoenaed my original dinner receipt from Visa to do a handwriting analysis from that night. I'm solid, but they *still* think I had something to do with it. Do you have any contacts with the Italian mob?"

"Why don't I just take out Connor, Sammy, and Tony myself, and we would be done with it. Not to mention, I'd be doing society a favor."

"Because one of his cronies would come after you and your family as some sort of retribution."

"Why do you want to get the Italians involved?"

"Because Connor just threatened June!"

"Seriously? That's out-of-bounds," said Big Mike.

"That's what I said! Nevertheless, Connor threw it out there."

"How high do you need to go?"

"Whoever is running Boston."

"That would be Tony Pesini."

Liam nodded. "Then that's whom we have to meet."

"I'll see what I can do. I did some favors for those guys in Walpole. I'll make it happen."

"Great! Tell him that we want to meet him at the Boston Public Library on the third floor in the reading room. And tell him not to be followed. He can bring three men to keep everyone away from us."

"Okay, I hope that you know what you are doing, Liam, because these are serious men," said Mike.

THE CHANGEUP

THE GOOD THING ABOUT THE Boston Public Library is the fact that you have four different entrances to the building via Dartmouth Street, Huntington Avenue, Exeter Street, and Boylston Street. This will allow you to sneak in and out of the library without anyone seeing you. The meeting was at three o'clock, so Mike entered through the Boylston Street gate. Liam came through the Huntington Avenue entrance around two o'clock. Mr. Pesini and his associates entered through the main gate on Dartmouth Street around quarter to three. As they made their way up to the third floor, they were very careful to make sure that they were not being followed.

"Mr. Pesini, I presume?"

"Yeah, and you must be Mike Maguire."

"I am."

"Who's the kid?"

"He's with me. That's why we're here."

"Normally, I don't do this cloak-and-dagger shit, but I'm taking this meeting as a favor to people whom I respect. Those people in Rhode Island say that you're a stand-up guy and that you did some favors for them inside. I've been instructed to give you whatever you need. So how can I help you?"

"No, Mr. Pesini, you misunderstood the intent of this meeting. It's not what you can do for me; it's what I can do for you."

"And what may that be, kid?"

"*Time*, Mr. Pesini, time."

"Kid, I don't have time for riddles. What is it that you want?"

"I'm serious, Mr. Pesini; I can give you time," he said.

"Okay, I'll play. How?"

"I'll need you to take care of a few people who would otherwise take time away from you."

"What the hell is he talking about, Mike?"

"What he's trying to say is that you have a problem that you don't even know about, and you need to take care of it, or you'll be locked up for the rest of your life. You both have mutual interest here in seeing this problem go away."

"So why didn't *you* take care of it, Mike?"

"Because if I took care of it, those people would just come after me and my family. However, if *you* do it, they'll think that it's just the cost of doing business," said Mike.

"Why do you want this person or people gone?" asked Mr. Pesini.

"They think that I was in on a job—the Gardner Museum robbery."

"Were you?"

"No!"

"I was in school."

"Mike, you?"

"No, at the time, I was in a cast with a broken arm. Then I was picking up my kid who was in jail on a D and D that night. What better alibi is there than the cops?"

"Okay, who is it?"

"First, I'll need your word that you and your people will owe me. No matter what I ask, when I ask, my request *has* to be granted. Keep in mind that I may never need anything."

"If your information is good, you can take this ring," he said, handing it to Liam, "and show it to any of my people in Boston or Rhode Island, and they'll know what to do. They'll bring you right to the head of the family." The ring was very simple in design; however, it had the crest of the Patriarca family on the top, with a shield emblem and a sword through the center of it. Around the crest were the words *lealta'*, *L'onore,* and *la famiglia*, which translate to "loyalty," "honor," and "the family," respectively.

"Thank you," Liam said.

"The only thing, kid, is that this info had better be rock solid, or you'll be in deep shit."

"It is, but there is one last thing."

"What's that?"

"Nobody can know our identities. The more people know what we're up to, the higher probability that something may get leaked or go wrong."

"Let's hear it. Who's the rat?"

"It's plural, Mr. Pesini, and you can take down the FBI too. It's Connor Quinn, Sammy, Tony Costin, and—get this—Joe Carey."

"Fuck you, kid! There is no way in hell those guys would be rats and working with that prick Carey."

"Here, look at these." Liam handed Mr. Pesini a large manila envelope with some pictures in them.

"Okay, so it's a bunch of pictures—big fuckin' deal. You could have the same type of pictures with me based on the amount of times those fucking feds talked to me."

"Really? How many times has Agent Carey invited you over to his house to sample his wife's apple pie?" Liam dropped another envelope on the table.

"No shit! Those motherfuckers!" Mr. Pesini reviewed the second set of pictures. "What else, kid?"

"Here are a few others where Colin is giving Agent Carey several envelopes of cash."

"They're all fucking dead! Dead! Dead! Dead!" Pesini yelled as he banged his fist on the table.

"And here is a tape of them talking about you and some guns that were seized in Gloucester a few years ago."

"I knew that fucking mick was in on that Gloucester thing! What a piece of shit! I knew it! Okay, kid, what's our play here?"

"Well, since an indictment is just around the corner for you, we have to act quickly. If Connor and his top guys disappear, the feds have nothing against you. Here's the plan: Mike and I will go meet with Connor and tell him that we want five hundred grand for the museum pieces. The pieces are worth over five hundred million, and the reward is up to a million and a half, so he can either cash in on that or sell the pieces on the black market."

"You know he'll kill you both after he gets that kind of loot."

"Well, that's where you come in. You'll be hiding in the weeds to take them all out. After that, I'll give the info I have to a friend at the FBI who can bring it to their Internal Affairs Division. About a week later the same info will go to a friend who is with the *Globe*, and he'll blow this thing wide open in the press."

"Beautiful, kid, just beautiful!"

"Mike will get in touch with you when we're ready to go."

"Okay, kid." Mr. Pesini nodded. "Mike, they were right about you; you're a solid guy. Thanks! And I want to hear from you soon," Mr. Pesini said as he shook Mike's hand.

"Yes, sir."

THE SETUP

THERE ARE VERY FEW ASSURANCES in life, but greedy gangsters are one such guarantee. Mike and Liam were counting on Connor's greed to do him in.

"Hey, Eddie," Mike said to the man behind the bar.

"Mike, how's it going?"

"We're here to see Connor."

"Is he expecting you?"

"No, we don't have an appointment. Is that an issue?"

"Let me see what I can do. Who is the kid?"

"Declan's son."

"Liam? My, he has grown up. I was friends with your father. I'm Eddie." Eddie extended his hand in friendship.

"Pleasure to meet you, Eddie."

"Same here, kid."

A couple of minutes later, Eddie returned and said, "Mike, he'll see you both after he wraps up his business with the Mason brothers. They're working out weekly receipts and who owes what."

"Thanks, Eddie."

"Sure, no problem, Mike. Hey, there he is waving you both down there now. Good luck."

"Thanks again, Eddie!"

When Liam sat down at Connor's table, Connor asked, "So what can I do for you guys?"

"Someone approached me about the Gardner Museum pieces," Liam said.

"Someone approached you?"

"Yeah, that's right; someone approached me."

"I thought that you said that you didn't have anything to do with it?"

"I didn't."

"Then how did they know to contact you?"

"They said that they heard that you were talking to me about that job."

"What do *they* want?"

"Well, the reward is up to a million and a half by the insurance company. They'll give you everything for five hundred grand cash and for you not to ask any more questions. They don't want you or your guys coming after them when this is over. So you can either make a quick million dealing with the insurance company or start selling pieces on the black market. That's your call."

"It's bad business if I let this pass. People will start to think that they can operate in my backyard without paying any type of tribute. I can't let this precedent be set, or I'll look weak. If I look weak, those guineas will try and take over. Do you want fucking Italians to run Southie?" said Connor.

"Well, the way I see it, you're getting at least one million as tribute, so nobody is getting anything over on you," Liam said.

"Okay, that's another way to look at it."

"Wait—does that mean that we are in agreement on his exchange?" he asked.

"Yes," said Connor.

"So how do you want to do this? And when can you get the cash?"

"I can have it by the end of the week.

"When can you get all the paintings together?"

"I've been advised by the people who have them that they're all set to go. We just need a place for the meet."

"How about my garage?" said Connor.

"Think again. How about the parking lot of Copley Plaza?" Liam said.

"No, too public, boy."

"Then we need a neutral place."

"Okay, how about Frankie's junkyard on Friday at nine p.m.," said Connor.

"Frankie's, nine p.m., it is. Don't be late. One minute past nine, and the deal is off. Understood?" he said.

"Got it, kid. Just be there with the swag, and come alone."

"I'll be with Mr. Maguire, and that's it."

"Big Mike is fine. See you at nine o'clock."

Liam got up from the table to leave, and Mike walked outside and joined him.

"How'd it go?" asked Big Mike.

"Fine. We're on for this Friday at Frankie's garage at nine p.m. You know he's gonna try and kill us and keep everything, don't you," Liam said.

"Yeah, I know—that backstabbing lying piece of shit!" Big Mike said with a scowl.

"Let's get in touch with Mr. Pesini right away," Liam said.

"I'll go see him tomorrow," said Big Mike.

Back in the Triple O, Connor plotted the exchange with his soldiers.

"Tony, Sammy—we're on for this Friday at nine p.m. at Frankie's garage. The kid and Big Mike want five hundred grand for the Gardner stuff," Connor said.

"You're not going to give it to them, are you?"

"Fuck no! Then people will think that they can walk all over me! We'll bury them in back of Frankie's. Tony, bring plenty of lye."

"Got it, Connor."

"Sammy, you bring the shovels."

"Gotcha."

"Just remember, nobody makes a move until we get all thirteen pieces. I'll tell you when to go."

LET'S MAKE A DEAL

PRIOR TO GOING TO AGENT Kent's house, Liam mailed the Quinn/Carey files along with copies of the tapes to his good old reporter friend at the *Globe*, Doug Chase. His instructions were to open the file if Liam did not contact him within a week. After a week, he would read all the material, call Agent Kent for comments, and then publish his findings. If Liam was still alive after the meeting with Connor, then Doug would wait to publish the story until Agent Kent arrested Agent Carey for corruption. At that point, Agent Kent would offer Doug an exclusive story.

Agent Kent and his family lived in the town of Wellesley, Massachusetts. Wellesley was an affluent suburb just twenty minutes outside of Boston, and the Kents lived in a nondescript house on the corner of Humphrey Street and Bay View Avenue.

There was a knock at the door.

"Hi, little man, is your father home?"

"Liam? How did you...what are you doing here?"

"Sorry for stopping by unannounced like this, but we need to chat."

"Can it wait until tomorrow in my office?"

"Unfortunately, no, there are too many holes in your ship, if you know what I mean."

"Okay, give me a minute. Hun, I have a work thing. Can I have a minute in my study?"

"Sure, but remember we have Robert's birthday party in an hour."

"Understood. We won't be that long."

"Mrs. Kent, my apologies for the intrusion, especially over the weekend," said Liam.

Agent Kent and Liam proceeded into his study. As Agent Kent closed the French doors to his study, he said to Liam, "Okay, Liam, how can I help you? How did you find me? And how do you know that you can trust *me*?"

"Agent Kent, are you familiar with a Sun Tzu saying in *The Art of War*, 'Know thy enemy.'"

"So we're enemies now, are we?"

"No, not in the literal sense. I just needed to know who you were, if I could trust you, and what I was up against."

"Why would you need to do that?"

"Because you work in a corrupt office."

"I've heard rumors of agents being too familiar with CIs, but an entire office being corrupt is hard to swallow."

"Well, you believe what you want, but they're not rumors."

"Says you, unless you have proof."

"I do, and so does my guy at the *Globe*."

"What's this all about, Liam?"

"I need to go off the record here before we proceed."

"Okay, we're off the record. Are you in some sort of trouble? Do you need help?"

"No, not exactly."

"Does the judge know that you are here?"

"No, and we need to keep it that way."

"Okay." There was a pause. "So how can I help you, Liam?"

"Nice place you have here, Agent Kent."

"Thanks. It's small, but we like it."

"Hey, I see that you still have the ball I gave you during the Boston College game. By the way, nice touch with the 'Walpole Prison Class of 2012' response."

"Thanks, I have my moments. So how can I help you? Are you here to confess?"

"No! But what if I were to deliver to you all the items that were stolen from the museum?"

"That's great! But that kinda sounds like a confession. And what do you want in return?"

"I would request a blanket, iron-clad, *sealed* immunity-from-prosecution agreement, both state and federal, for all the people involved in the theft. This agreement would need to include all crimes that led up to and were done in consequence of the robbery."

"Sealed?"

"Yes, sealed. Nobody can know who did these crimes."

"How many people are we talking about here?"

"Less than ten."

"That's really vague. I may need more information here."

"Okay, just five people."

"Anything else?"

"Yes, the million-dollar reward—it would need to be split evenly to the following nonprofits: South Boston Little League, Dana Farber Cancer Research Center, the ARC of Boston, the Cathedral Church Food Bank, and the South Boston Shelter for Homeless Vets. Oh, and I'll need all this in writing by the end of the week, or else the offer is off the table."

"That's quite a list. Why would I do all this without any proof that you either have or know the whereabouts of the Gardner pieces? As an outsider looking in, one would think that I'm getting closer to solving this case."

"Seriously, Agent Kent, you are so far off that you have a better chance of locating D. B. Cooper than solving this case."

"I'm not sure that I can get the agency to work that quickly."

"We're talking over five hundred million dollars in artwork here, Agent Kent. This is career making!"

"Again, I'm not sure that they can work this quickly."

"Okay, how about I throw a cherry on top?"

"That depends on how big the cherry is."

"I can give you Agent Carey as well."

"Bullshit!"

"I'll let you look and listen, but you cannot keep anything, agree?"

"Agreed."

"Take a look at these." Liam showed him one set of photos. "And these over here are at his house. And this last envelope is him taking cash. Didn't you guys ever wonder how an agent of his grade can own a house in Lynnfield, a vacation home in Key Largo, Florida, and a cottage on the Cape?"

"Holy cow! Where did you get all of these?"

"That doesn't matter. It gets better, though; listen to this."

Agent Kent put on his earphones.

"Holy shit, he's conspiring with these guys! Okay, you have a deal. I'll fly down to D.C. tomorrow morning and get in front of the director myself. You need your guy at the *Globe* to hold off until we speak, though. I don't want this in the press before we can contain it internally. He'll still get his exclusive story; tell him that. You have my word."

"No, I want the deal in writing, and nobody in your office is to know about it. There are too many leaks there."

"Understood. Give me twenty-four hours. I'll call you from D.C. tomorrow afternoon."

"Okay, I'll wait to hear from you." Liam turned to leave.

"Liam."

"Yes, Agent Kent."

"So how'd you do it?"

"I'll wait to hear from you, Agent Kent." Liam walked out.

Later that evening back at the Shamrock Car Wash, Liam went to visit Big Mike to give him an update on his conversation. "Mr. Maguire," he said, "let's go for a walk."

"Sure. So are we all set?"

"Well, I spoke with Agent Kent. He's going to D.C. tomorrow to try and get our deal."

"Let me get this straight: you're getting a deal of immunity on the Gardner heist, and then you're going to blame Connor for the robbery?"

"That's the plan."

"You've got balls Liam; I'll give you that."

"Where do we stand with Pesini?"

"He'll be at Frankie's with his guys in the weeds, waiting. This had better work, or we're all dead."

"I know. Does he know when to crash the party?"

"Yeah, when you say, 'Seamrog dubh.'"

"Okay, he had better. And where will Frankie be during all this? I mean it is his garage after all."

"Frankie will be on vacation in Rhode Island, visiting 'friends' of Mr. Pesini."

"Perfect, so now all we have to do is wait on the feds, bring the swag to the exchange, and make sure Connor falls for the bait," Liam replied.

"That's a lot of moving pieces here, Liam."

"I know, but we'll finally be done with Connor and his goons for good if this goes as planned."

The following day around three o'clock, as he was trying to study for his midterm exams, the phone rang.

"Hi, this is Liam."

"Liam?"

"Yeah."

"This is Agent Kent."

"Hey, Agent Kent, how's the capital?"

"Well, it took a lot of convincing, but against his better judgment, the director has agreed to your terms, providing of course that we get all the artwork back and we get all the original pictures and tapes. We're drafting an indictment now for Connor, Sammy, Tony, and

Agent Carey. We just need that evidence first before we file anything formally."

"And this will be a sealed agreement. Correct?"

"Yes."

"That's great, Agent Kent—thank you! When you land back in town this evening, please bring the agreement over to ADA Tom Demps's office in downtown Boston, and we can review everything there. In good faith, and should anything happen to me, I'll give you the *original* pictures and tapes after the paperwork is signed. I'll tell you where you can find the artwork the following day. At that time, you will 'stumble' upon these pictures and the tapes, okay?"

"Got it. But remember, Liam, if we don't get everything that we discussed at that time, the deal is off. It states as much in the agreement."

"Understood, Agent Kent, understood."

FRANKIE'S GARAGE

ENTERING FRANKIE'S PROPERTY, THERE WERE only a few dimly lit lights on in the main garage bay. In fact, most of the light that was in the shop was coming from the streetlamps outside of his garage. It was dark, and they could barely make out some figures off in the distance.

"Hello? Connor, you here?"

"Yeah. Big Mike, is that you?"

"Yeah, I'm here with Liam."

"Come on in; have a seat. You got the stuff?"

"Yes, do you have the cash?"

"Yeah, that was the agreement."

"I thought that you were coming alone."

"Tony and Sam go everywhere with me—you know that."

"Can we see the cash?"

"Sure. Where's the stuff?"

"It's in that bag we brought in."

"Tony, Sam, go over there and check it out. That's five hundred million dollars' worth of paintings and sketches, and you put them in a burlap sack?"

"It causes less suspicion."

"Okay, I can see that. Boys, how do we look with the swag?"

"It looks like all thirteen pieces are here, Connor."

"Now can we see the cash?"

"Here you go." Connor threw a briefcase in their direction.

"Thanks. Can we go now?"

"No, both you guys take a seat; don't you want to count your money?"

"Why would we have to do that?" Liam asked.

"Just do it." Connor, Tony, and Sam all pulled their guns.

"What the fuck, Connor? What's with the pieces?" asked Big Mike.

"Open the briefcase, Mike."

"Okay, okay," Big Mike said as he unlocked the sides of the brief-case. "It's just filled with cutout paper," Mike said, showing him the contents of the case. "What's with the double cross, Connor?"

"Mike, these paintings are worth over five hundred million! Did you really think that you were going to walk away from all this?"

"I kept my mouth shut for you for seven years inside! You gave us your word! I knew we should have given this shit to Tony Pesini and the Italians."

"Fuck the Italians and that fat fuck Pesini! They'll all be indicted in a few weeks anyway, and we'll run the entire city. Too bad the both of you will be dead, and you won't be able to enjoy the fruits of my labor," Connor said with a smirk.

"What? Now all of a sudden you don't have anything to say, kid?" Sammy slapped him across the face, making him bleed on the right of his lip. Connor and Tony laughed.

Mike immediately got up to defend him, his fists clenched.

"Easy, Mike," Connor said, aiming his gun at him, "I like you; yours can be a quick death, a shot to the head, or you can suffer like this one will. So sit down!"

"Yeah, I have something to say."

"I always enjoy hearing someone's last words. What is it, kid?" Tony and Sammy grinned.

"Seamrog dubh!"

"What?"

"I said, 'Seamrog dubh!' It means 'black shamrock.'" Just then the lights were turned on, and Connor, Sammy, and Tony were surrounded by a group of Tony Pesini's men, who were all aiming M-16 rifles at them.

"So I'm just a fat fuck, am I, Connor?"

Mike and Liam quickly got up from their seats.

"No, you didn't hear everything, Tony."

"Fuck you, Connor! Boys, tie them up, and get the pliers and the blowtorch."

"Wait, wait—there's over five hundred million in that bag over there. We can split it! No, you can have it!" said Connor.

"That's very generous of you, Connor, seeing as I have all the guns. Not to mention, the boy and I have an agreement. The difference between you and me is that I keep my word."

"Wait, wait...wait a minute. I have more money in my safe," said Connor.

"We know about your safe. In fact, that's where all the artwork is going, along with these guns."

He handed Mike a bag filled with three semiautomatic handguns, which would tie Connor back to the murders that he was going to pin on Tony and his crew.

"Guess who will be on the hook for those murders now? And guess what, Connor? The feds will find all those pictures of you getting cozy with Agent Carey and the audio tapes as well. Now he's fucked too! Everyone will think you're on the lam, but you'll really be at the bottom of the Boston fucking Harbor. Every time I look over the ocean, I'll smile, knowing that you're at the fucking bottom of it."

Mr. Pesini gave Liam a gun.

"It's your call, kid; do you want the honors?"

"Fuck you, kid!" Sammy said to Liam.

Liam turned to Sammy. "Does it hurt, Sammy?"

"Does what hurt? Fuck you, you don't have the balls, kid," Sammy said.

"This." Liam fired a shot into Sammy's left kneecap.

"Like I said kid, fuck you!" Sammy growled as he buckled to the ground in pain.

"Thanks, maybe this will make you feel better." He fired another shot into Sammy's right knee as he screamed in more pain.

"For the record, Mr. Quinn, all this could have been avoided if you didn't bring my girlfriend, June, into this."

"She's dead in twenty-four hours if my guy down there doesn't hear from me in the morning. He's got instructions to rape that bitch first and then cut her up into small pieces. She'll be fish bait in the Long Island Sound before morning, kid."

"You mean Patrick Sullivan Jr.? Who do you think told us about the double cross, you piece of shit! You forgot, Mr. Quinn: teaghlaigh thar gach."

"Thanks, Mr. Pesini, but the honor is yours. Are we good, sir?"

"We are, kid. And Mike?" Tony took the gun from Liam and looked over to Mike.

"Yeah, Mr. Pesini?"

"It looks like we owe you *again*."

"No, Mr. Pesini, you do not. I'm out of the game for good. I'll see you around."

As Mike and Liam walked out of Frankie's garage, they could hear the muffled screams of the men being tortured inside the garage.

"Liam?" Big Mike turned to him and said.

"Yeah?"

"What did you say to Connor?"

"I told him an old Gaelic saying that my dad taught me: teaghlaigh thar gach."

"What does that mean?"

"It means 'family over all.'"

"That's perfect!"

"Come on, we have to put all this stuff in Connor's floor safe and then call Agent Kent."

Where Are They Now

AFTER PUTTING ALL THE PAINTINGS and sketches from the Gardner Museum into Connor's floor safe, Mike deposited the guns that Mr. Pesini requested as well. They also took a few hundred thousand dollars that was in the safe, for all their troubles. As soon as they left Connor's office, Liam contacted Agent Kent and notified him of the paintings' whereabouts. A search warrant was issued immediately for Connor Quinn's residence and his office. In Connor's home, the FBI found a cache of guns, ammunition, money, and several fake passports and IDs behind newly placed drywall on the second floor. During the search of Connor's office, the FBI found all the Gardner Museum pieces, along with some incriminating photos and audiotapes that implicated Agent Carey in several crimes, including several murders. Agent Carey was immediately arrested and suspended. The theory was that Connor Quinn, Sammy Dobbs, and Tony Costin were all warned by Agent Carey that they were about to be picked up, so they went on the run. Connor remained on the FBI's most-wanted list. Agent Carey would later be found guilty on multiple charges of corruption, racketeering, and murder.

Agent Kent was promoted to a coveted position, the director of the Major Crimes Task Force, out of Washington, D.C. Liam saw him on the news from time to time. They even managed to keep in touch when Liam was in D.C. or he came up to Boston. It still drove him crazy that he couldn't figure out how Liam and his group pulled off this job!

The judge, Ray, and Liam still lived in the brownstone on Beacon Hill. The judge recently retired from the bench but taught part time at Harvard Law as an adjunct professor. Ray continued to work at the car wash, and he even had a small office next to Big Mike's.

The Maguire family continued to run a profitable car-wash-and-oil-change business in South Boston. Mikey and Sue were still dating and thinking about getting married as soon as Mikey finished college. Mikey was accepted to UMASS-Boston and was studying business. Sue was finishing up her sophomore year at the University of Connecticut, and she planned to work in the fashion industry.

Cam finished his football career at Harvard as their fourth-leading rusher in Harvard history. Even though Cam went undrafted in the NFL draft, he had several free-agent tryouts with the Patriots, Jets, Colts, and the Raiders. Cam eventually signed a nonbinding free-agent contract with the Patriots that summer, and he hoped to catch on as a special-teams player. If professional football didn't work, Cam had a standing job offer as a financial analyst from the First National Savings Bank of Boston.

Uncle Joey and Uncle Tommy were running their satellite Shamrock car-wash-and-oil-change business in Portsmouth, New Hampshire, while still working their construction jobs. They were no longer dependent on subcontracting jobs when things got tough.

Liam was recently drafted by the Boston Red Sox in the seventh round of the amateur baseball draft. He was also awarded a Rhodes Scholarship to study at Oxford University next year. While studying at Oxford, Liam plans to ask June to marry him.

Teaghlaigh thar gach!

About the Author

GREGORY ABBRUZZESE WAS BORN AND raised in the small town of Swampscott, Massachusetts. He attended high school at Phillips Exeter Academy. Abbruzzese went on to receive his bachelor's degree from Columbia University and his Master's degree from New York University.

Abbruzzese lives with his family in Teaneck, New Jersey. His wife, Professor Laurel Abbruzzese, PhD, and four children (Lydia, Emily, Chloe, and Grayson) all share his love of Columbia Lions football.

Abbruzzese is already hard at work on his next book. *The Black Shamrocks* is his debut novel.

As of March 17, 2018, the Gardner Museum is offering a $5 million reward for information that leads to the recovery of the stolen artwork. If you have any information please call the FBI at 1-800-CALLFBI (225-5324).

Made in the USA
Middletown, DE
04 April 2018